Published in the
United Kingdom by Fulmar Publishing

ISBN-10 1493651358
ISBN-13 978-1-49365-135-1

A CIP catalogue record
for this ebook is available
from the British Library.

Pre-press production
www.ebookversions.com

This book is dedicated to four remarkable women in my life – Christine, Nicola, Ellie and Isabel – and to Joe. Their combined encouragement and inspiration were essential in enabling me to write it.

I express my sincerest thanks also to Steve and to Zoe – without whose support, expertise and generosity this novel would be a pointless file cluttering up my hard drive. I wrote it – but without all the aforementioned, you would not be reading it now.

The Remains of the Living

Ian Church

FULMAR PUBLISHING

Prologue

In the darkened corner of the room, from the turntable drifted the closing bars of Erroll Garner's tranquillising interpretation of "Skylark". The vinyl disc was feeling its age, the sound having degraded noticeably, perhaps inevitably, in some slurred passages after thousands – or could it be millions? – of revolutions.

He had tried for another copy, but the only record shop now remaining – a relic with not much of a future, much like its ageing customers – offered no hope of success. Terry, the proprietor, unshaven as usual, was wearing a soup-stained T-shirt boasting of a rock concert he had attended 10 years before. The details were long forgotten in a haze of sweet smelling, musky smoke. He had shaken his head as he turned the sleeve back and forth. "You won't get that for love or money. Sorry."

He wasn't.

Then, as an afterthought: "Perhaps they've put it on CD."

His response to Terry was a look of disappointment tinged with disdain. A CD? He admired Garner, who had avoided the inconvenience of an academic education and instead pursued his musical genius. Paradoxically, having used his hands – fists to be precise – in the ring to beat his subject into submission, he had then laid them on a piano keyboard gently to coax and seduce it into producing those soothing and magical sounds.

When he handled the LP, he sensed a direct connection with Garner, felt the lifeblood of the music flow into his fingers. It was all there, captured on that glossy, black plastic disc. It was beyond science to commit the meaning and emotion it conveyed to the sterile and lifeless mechanics of a cold, metal, digital product with its flashing lights and gimmicks. Might as well print the Mona Lisa on a beer mat and expect to be just as entranced by that enigmatic smile while you poured a pint down your throat. The medium must respect the artists and their art, and, somehow, a circular piece of aluminium could not do that. At least, that was his view.

Anyway, what did Terry mean about love and money? Typical. Why did people rate them as the two big things in life? They all said it: "You couldn't get that for love or money." So, if you can't get something for love or money, you are not going to get it.

Most people would go for one or the other. Probably most of them thought that anything worth having could be bought, especially people. Wealth brought privilege and opportunity. Women would queue up to shower you with their favours. Fawning yes-men would flock around you hoping for a few crumbs. Yeah, if that was your thing, money was the answer. Money could get you

2

anything you wanted. You win millions on the lottery and your troubles are over. Sure, money's powerful. Money talks. But people forget that what can talk can lie.

What do you want? To be happy? Money says: "I can do that for you." That's a lie. To be free of worry? Money claims: "I can give you that." Another lie. Good health? The cemeteries had plenty of headstones for the millionaires who had learnt the bitter truth of that one.

Money was too slick, too plausible. It promised but it didn't deliver. So it talked and it promised. And it talked big and it promised lots. And just like people, it let you down. But it did a lot more besides. It perverted, it corrupted and it destroyed. That was obvious from what people were prepared to do to get it.

Perhaps love and money went together. His worst moves had come from ditching loyalty, dedication, commitment, principles and belief and doing something for love or money. They were similar in some ways. They both built you up and then left you to crash down. There was nothing half so sweet as love's young dream, the poet said. But when sweet turned bitter and you awoke from the dream to an emotional nightmare, you were left with a rage and a raft of regrets. Love, like money, perverted, corrupted and destroyed. At least, it did when it took control, pushed suckers to do things that, in their right minds, they would never contemplate. And it certainly did when it turned sour.

He sipped his drink, drew on the cigarette and blew smoke towards the ceiling, watching it evaporate into the darkness. The record player had lapsed into silence. He certainly knew all about love turning sour. He'd watched it cross that very thin dividing line on to the territory marked hate.

Amor vincit omnia. Yeah, love sure does conquer all, especially common sense. It certainly pushes rational thought into the back seat. When love is racing round your head like some demented dog chasing its tail, what chance do you have to think straight? Like money, it promised but it didn't deliver.

He hummed a tune and mentally ran through the words that claimed that love is the sweetest thing. People too often made the mistake of falling for that old tripe and it made them drop their guard. One day you are light-headed with excitement. Your heart can't seem to beat fast enough. Every time you think of her you get short of breath. The next thing you know, it's all gone wrong and you feel like your guts have been ripped out.

Love should come with a health warning. And if it's songs that get you through the day, how about the one that says you always hurt the one you love? And if you'd hurt the one you love, what would you do to them when, blinded by scalding tears, you stumbled over that line and your love turned to hate?

Anyway, a big part of love was possession – you are mine, you belong to me. That's when it started getting really nasty. Particularly when someone else came along and took what you reckoned was yours. That's when love started to corrupt and destroy. Far from being the route to happiness, it became a malevolent force driving you down the highway to hate.

So, without the power of love or money you can't get it? Oh yes you can. Try using something with real muscle. Try something he knew a great deal about. Try fear. Fear made people do things they would never do for love or money. Frighten someone enough and they would give you their money. Terrify them enough and watch them betray the ones they loved. "Not me," they would say. "I could never do that." He had news for them: yes, you could – in the grip of blind terror you would do it.

People betrayed their loved ones for a lot less. A quick fondle at the office party with that bimbo from accounts that your wife has always accused you of fancying – that's betrayal. And after a few more drinks, you'll want more than a fondle – a lot more. That's real betrayal. And what's happened to love in that distasteful little episode? It's been trampled in the rush, that's what. And if a bloke is so genetically weak that he would do that to satisfy a bit of lust, think what fear would make him do when someone was about to tear his dick off with a pair of rusty pliers or burn his eye out with a blowtorch.

There were always exceptions. There were those – very few – for whom no amount of money and not even the greatest fear would induce them to betray and desert. They would never sell out or bail out. Well, that was not him. He knew that not because he had ever been offered a bribe – well, nothing to merit serious consideration. But fear – yes, he had known fear and now he had to live with the thought of what it had made him do.

Never judge another bloke's courage until you've felt fear turn your guts to a bubbling soup and the shit has poured out of your bowels like water out of a drainpipe. He knew. For him, fear was a demon that sat watching him from the darkest corner of an anxious and sleepless night. Love, money, fear. The bottom line was people, and, as yet another song would tell you, people were no good.

"No faith, no trust no honesty in men." Yeah, and in spite of what women liked you to think, they were no better.

How long had he been gone – months, not even a year? And where was she when he got back? With someone else. Well, sod her. Love? Hate? Two sides of the same street, just don't get run down crossing it. Possession? OK, no one owned anyone, but with Susie it came as close as it could get. Susie was his kid, too.

The truth was that it was Susie who had pulled him through. In the darkness he could see her face, and every time he woke he could feel her tightly gripping his finger. He came to terms with the constant, shattering disappointment to find it was only a dream. But it was a dream that had provided life support. Without it, without Susie, he would never have made it.

Even now he awoke – not that he ever really slept – feeling her hand holding his. Again, it was a dream, because she was gone. His wife – ex-wife – despised and resented him for that. He had not been around in those days of shock and loss when she had needed him so badly. Love, soft, sweet and warm, had cooled and crystallised into cold and bitter hatred when he had not been there for the funeral. When he got back she had at first refused even tell him where Susie had been laid to rest. Fucking cow. OK, so it was all over for them by then, but it wasn't all his fault and they still had one thing in common – broken hearts.

Susie had been the most important thing in their lives. Perhaps they should have realised that she was the cement that held them together, stopped their relationship from crumbling. With her gone, that bond had been broken and the whole structure had collapsed so completely that there was nothing left to salvage. If his wife could have understood what he had been through, or if he had not been through it, everything would have been so different. What a disastrous bloody mess. Best to look to the future now. No point in looking back. Didn't want to look back. Didn't want to see what was there.

He tried to resist. But an overpowering and inexplicable compulsion drove him to snatch that quick glance over his shoulder. It was fatal. He became transfixed, sucked in by the irresistible power generated by what had happened and what it had done to him. And then he could not drag his gaze away. He stared, mesmerised, into the past, and what he saw was a black hole. A stinking pit. In a debriefing, some toffee-nosed colonel had asked whether he'd been held in an oubliette. Yeah, it was an oubliette all right, but to him it was the mouth of hell. And it had opened wide and swallowed him. And his life. And his future. And his daughter. And his marriage. When it finally spat him back out, all that was gone.

He realised much later that he had no idea what it was really like in there. He could touch it and smell it, but he couldn't see it. In the complete darkness he could see only the glimmer that seeped through the slot where what passed for food was shoved in. When they opened the door he was so blinded by fear and by the light that flooded in that he could see nothing anyway.

He knew so little of it, but it had become an organic part of him. He had known at the time that if he ever got out of it alive, and that was a belief he had clung to in desperation and with increasing difficulty, he would never prise it from the clenched grip of his memory. The smell of the place would always be in his nostrils. But then his concern had been not whether to remember it or how to forget it, but how to get out of it.

It was, after all, almost inevitable that the tortured occupants of these stinking dungeons would never again be free. To all intents they were buried alive. An oubliette – a graveyard for the living, a place for those who were interred therein to be thrown and forgotten. Except that every now and then their tormentors remembered them. And from the stygian darkness their wrecked bodies would be dragged to suffer unspeakable treatment at the hands of people who enjoyed their work and were good at it.

Afterwards, racked with agony, they would be hurled back into a world reserved for those who hovered in that uncertain void somewhere between life and death. Perversely, those sepulchral depths became a sanctuary.

Being cast back into them meant that the infliction of pain had ceased. It provided a release from the torment.

Some sanctuary. Some release.

But he did survive. And now he was free. But what sort of a freedom was it? He had progressed from captive to captor. He now oversaw his own personal oubliette. No stone bound hole beneath a prison full of tormented souls was this. It was far stronger, more durable, more impregnable, more indestructible than mere iron bars and stone. It was the most powerful confinement of all – it was his mind. And that was a place of pain and torture as fearsome as any with shackles, red hot irons and those innocent looking electrodes. It was a place he didn't want to go. But how could he not?

The inmates were now in his charge and they were the horrors that were locked in his brain. Now, he stood guard over his memories – memories that resurrected the despair and fear and, perhaps most important, the guilt. His constant task was to keep the nightmares that haunted his past under mental lock and key so that they never saw the light of day.

But, somehow, when his guard was down, when he retreated into a moment of weakness, the fiends and phantoms that were the past slipped out beneath the cell door like shadows. Having escaped, they were free to taunt and terrify him, their catcalls echoing provocatively through the cold corridors of his mind, until he confronted them, forced them into submission and wrestled them back into their confinement, into the darkness where they could be ignored and forgotten. But

9

they would always escape again, constantly seeking the light. There was always the next time. His body was free, but he knew that his mind would serve a sentence for life.

Some freedom. Some life.

He ground his cigarette into the ash tray, swallowed the last of his drink and looked at his watch. Midnight 20. He reached across to the bedside lamp and stared at it, steeling himself for the moment, just as he had on countless nights. He clicked the switch. Pitch black darkness. He was trembling. Get a grip, he told himself. He slid down under the covers and his head sank into the pillow. Perhaps tonight would be different. Tonight he might sleep. Tonight the terrors might not come.

Chapter 1

The Underground train clattered along at 30 miles an hour less than 20ft below the traffic jams and the foundations and basements of the offices, hotels, shops, and homes that constituted the skyline of that part of London. Paice sat staring at the hemline – with luck, beyond the hemline if he was honest – of the beautiful dark-skinned young woman opposite him.

His gaze ascended slowly, mentally caressing her perfect calves and the sheen of her thighs, lingering at strategic points, not least the swell of her breasts revealed by the neckline – slightly lower than was strictly proper – of her pristine white blouse. He lingered on her lips before he reached her eyes. They were large and brown and beautiful. They were also loaded with contempt and looking straight into his.

He knew what they were saying. It was a message that would be repeated later that evening when she was sipping a cocktail with a friend as she recounted the incident. "Pervert," and "dirty old fool" were expressions that would feature in her account of the moment.

He was not bothered. His visual ascent continued until he arrived at the advertisements ranged above her head. He hated travelling on the tube at this time of day. The City workers were heading back to fashionable Pimlico, Chelsea and Earls Court and their less than sumptuous and ridiculously overpriced apartments. Their sour breath, reeking from lunches with too much wine, probably cheap wine, in the bars of the famous Square Mile, hung in the still air of the carriage and almost made him retch. Desperate for distraction, his eyes returned to the girl's thighs. She uncrossed and crossed her legs — deliberately, he knew.

It would be good to allow his imagination to embrace the dark-skinned girl, but for the moment he had bigger issues on his mind.

He thought back more than a month to the last time he had met Burkins face to face. Paice had an unbreakable rule that he met all his contacts in a pub, with many of which he was familiar. The pub was, as for most Fleet Street journalists of his era, an extension of the office. Sometimes it became the office. That meeting had been in the Black Lion. Burkins had been late, and when he had arrived he had been agonisingly slow coming to the point, saying nothing until Paice had bought him a drink. When he finally spoke, the news was bad.

"What do you mean, you're moving?" Paice had demanded.

Burkins had shrugged and dropped the corners of his mouth before quickly restoring it to a shape better suited to the rim of the glass.

He took a gulp, swallowed and looked across the bar at nothing in particular. "They're cutting back, and it was this job or no job."

"So you're no longer working for the Home Office?"

Burkins made full use of a very mobile mouth. It assumed the shape of one of the spans of Blackfriars Bridge as the corners drooped once again. This time, though, his eyebrows also arched and he shrugged his shoulders, his whole body silently saying more eloquently than any words he could muster that there was nothing he could do about it, that it was all beyond his control.

"And what, precisely, is 'this job'?"

"It might be Overseas aid."

"Overseas aid? Did you say Overseas Aid? What bloody use is that? Well, mate, I have to tell you that your take-home emoluments are about to take a nose dive. You had better warn your bookmaker that his wife has just bought her last fur coat."

This time the drooping oral parabola recurred and froze on Burkins's face. His ferret-like eyes stared in alarm. "Why? I can still find you stuff. We can carry on just the same."

"Burkins, the simple fact is that nothing ever happens in Overseas Aid, and even if it did nobody would give a toss."

He downed the rest of the scotch and waved his glass at the barman. This had suddenly turned into a bad day. No, not bad – the worst. Burkins had given him the jumping off point for some of his best stories. As a low grade filing clerk Burkins had been surprisingly well placed surreptitiously to pick up high grade information on sensitive issues that the Government would rather did not see the light of day – certainly not on the front page of one of the nation's best regarded daily newspapers.

The only jumping off point Paice had now was probably Blackfriars Bridge. Sure, he had other contacts, but it was only the sheer quality of Burkins's tip-offs that kept him on the front page and ahead of the other hacks who haunted Westminster and Whitehall. He had status to maintain and it had been hard earned. Burkins had been a lifesaver. Before Burkins had dropped in his lap, Paice's career had been on the down escalator, heading for the front door. If the stories stopped coming, Williamson, the editor, might tell him to do the same.

"Look," Burkins stuttered, " I'll keep my ears open and my nose to the ground."

"Sorry, Jake. The clichés don't pay the rent. I – you – need good material. Good material makes good stories. Good stories get good money. And vice bloody versa."

"Look, Mr P, if there's anything ... anything interesting ..." He was now thinking of his bookmaker and starting to get panicky. He had been picking up the regular £50 and the odd £100. He may have been Paice's lifesaver, but they were in a two-way street. When his weekly take-home was only £400 after tax and deductions, watching the goose flap off into the distance and take its golden nest egg with it was the end of life as he had come to know and love it.

"Why the move? You don't think they suspect you?"

Burkins shook his head. "No way. I'm too careful. I am just one of several people who handle the material. Anyway, they think I'm too thick to understand it, so they are unlikely to make the connection. No, the explanation is departmental reorganisation and cuts."

"Well, all I can say, Jake, is keep in touch. If you do come across something juicy, give me a call. The money is always there if the goods are saleable." He sounded unconvincing and felt even less confident.

Burkins finished his pint, dejectedly gathered up his raincoat from the adjacent stool and slid his feet to the floor. "OK, Mr P. You'll see that I'm right. We'll be back in business in no time."

"Let's hope you're right." He had watched Burkins push his way through the early evening crush and head for the door and the drizzle of a chilly April in London. The weather did not help Nick Paice in his cheerless task of deciding where he went from here. The competition for space in the paper made life a daily struggle.

He looked back with affection to those far-off days when the job had been just to report what had happened, perhaps with slight enhancement. A bit of journalistic licence was often an essential lubricant that made the facts easier to swallow. Thirty years on that was not enough. The pressure to get the best front page, to take the story a stage further than the competition, to get that

15

special angle that gave your story the edge could now mean that you were required to write not just what had happened, but what you thought about what had happened. Your opinion might be based on complete ignorance, but it was guaranteed to yield better copy.

So what if you could not find someone to give you the quote you needed to get the story off the ground? No problem, you created someone to utter those opportune words. Conveniently, "a source close to..." or "a friend of the couple" would say exactly what you – and the readers – wanted to hear. Or there was always "An onlooker said....", the onlooker who was alleged to have made this fanciful observation being a mythical creature who was about as substantial as your average mermaid or unicorn.

Anyway, all that was reduced to insignificance by the constant regurgitation of unchecked and unsubstantiated rubbish fed to you by PR companies, agents or anybody else who hoped the paper would print it because it would put money in their pockets, get them more votes or just make them or their clients a bit more famous. In all this miasma of fiction masquerading as reality, any vestige of the true facts seemed to have disappeared without trace.

Against that dismal background he had to contend with the ambitions of a flush of young hotshots, male and female reporters, keen as mustard to make their names. He could not get on with them. They spoke a different language. They seemed to be obsessed with computers. No matter that every so often the IT system crashed and left them wondering whether the paper would ever appear.

And as they had entered the twenty-first century, they had all just congratulated themselves on having outwitted the so-called millennium bug, something Paice never understood and did not believe even existed. They had different values. One or two of them did not even drink and he could not believe it when that thin faced little ginger girl had berated him for swearing. Team spirit had taken a bit of a knock when he had told her to fuck off and grow up.

He shook his head in disgust and thought back to when he was their age. Five in the afternoon and the news room would empty as every reporter and half the sub editors suddenly disappeared on urgent missions elsewhere. And, lo and behold, they would all bump into each other in the saloon bar of the North Star pub across the road. Funny coincidence that. The landlord called it the rush hour, but that was stretching time.

Rush it may have been, but it was more like 10 minutes as the noisy gathering swiftly downed their pints and headed back to their desks, refreshed and ready for whatever the world of news was about to chuck at them. Most of them returned to the office, but for a fortunate few it was the end of the shift and, occasionally, one or two of them actually went home. But not often – at least, not before chucking out time.

Life seemed so much simpler then – in some ways more laid back, but in others more practical and down to earth. Good stories meant a good paper. And the stories were good, and so were the circulation figures. Newspapers were an organic living thing. The smell and

17

dirt of the composing room with hot metal typesetting and getting ink all over your shirt cuffs – your mother constantly fretting over how to shift it. None of those sterile and inanimate computers. No granite-faced, cold-blooded accountants always looking at the bottom line. Instead, there were bosses, admittedly hard driving and ruthless, but who had news and booze in their blood in equal measure but still with room for raw enthusiasm. And none of these arty-farty university types with their degrees in this or that which were now a prerequisite for a reporting job.

In those days, consumption of alcohol was part of the job description. It was akin to a qualification, a mark of attainment, that got you through the door of an exclusive club of kindred souls. If you didn't drink, you were not a member. You were something odd, not one of the boys – and "boys" included the girls back then. When you went out on a job, you knew that the first port of call was the nearest pub, and when you got there and found all your mates from the other papers, somehow you felt at ease. He had seen drink take its toll on some fine journalists, but he never knew whether it was the booze that made them as good as they were, or whether they were that good in spite of it. It killed some, but that was the price to be paid.

He'd left school at 15, taught himself to type and got a job as a messenger on a picture agency, delivering the prints to the various news rooms. One of them was the Chronicle. After months of studying the captions on the back of the prints he realised that writing them was a piece of cake. A vacancy came up and he went for it and doubled his pay. Now he was writing – after a fashion.

At the bar of The Crown and Anchor pub he had bumped into the Chronicle's news editor. Assisted by two pints of best bitter, he had screwed up the courage to make the approach. "Excuse me, Mr Lawson, I want to be a reporter. How do I do that?" It had been a good move. Angus Lawson ruled his newsroom like a tyrant, breathing fire at sloppy reporters and conducting a general reign of terror, but he was always ready to procreate, to do his bit to spawn fresh faced beings into the world of news.

First and foremost Lawson was a newspaperman whose life's mission was to get stories into print. And he did not care how many toes got trodden on, noses got put out, hearts got broken or reputations got ruined – in fact, the more the better. That was the doctrine he practised. His day was truly spoilt when one of the other titles beat the Chronicle on a good story. And when his day was spoilt, all those within swearing distance found that their days were spoilt, too. "Find me stories," he had told young Paice, "write them and if they're any good I'll use them and pay you for it. If they're no good, I'll spike them – but I'll tell you why. That way you'll learn."

And learn he had. In his spare time he had taught himself shorthand and haunted the streets and courts and cop shops of London looking for small items that the others overlooked or could not be bothered with. If he got a paragraph in the paper, that was a triumph and an improvement in his finances. He made a breakthrough when the paint factory near his home exploded in flames just as he was passing. Three men dead and a very tasty interview with a distraught wife at the factory gate calling out in vain for her toasted husband.

The Chronicle was the only paper to have the story, and he could see that Lawson was delighted with what he had done. OK, perhaps he had slightly embroidered the words of the shell-shocked, freshly widowed wife – but nothing more than was absolutely necessary to make the story run. And, OK, maybe she had complained, but Lawson had backed him up, told the boss upstairs – with some justification – that the woman was so shaken up she could not possibly reliably recall precisely what she had said and that "our man" should be given the benefit of the doubt.

"Our man." Lawson enrolled him on the company's internal training scheme and he said goodbye to the picture agency.

Over a pint in the North Star, Lawson told him that it was good to use one's imagination, exploit to the full the elasticity of the truth and the flexibility of the direct quote – "but don't let it get out of hand." Later, as the alcohol worked its magic, the news editor had become more thoughtful, even philosophical.

"We're different Nick. We're newsmen. Some people believe in Jesus and the Virgin Mary. Some immerse themselves in communism or capitalism. For some, only money matters. We might also be interested in some or any of those, but for us, first and foremost, it's news.

There are no facts, no truths, no friendships, only good stories.

"The page of a newspaper is two dimensional. It goes up and down and across. Your job when you write your stories is to surmount that limitation and add that third dimension so that what you are telling the readers isn't just flat and factual like a bloody encyclopaedia. You have to make the words jump off the page at them, bring that print to life, make it dance around them and grab their imagination.

"Just remember that you never allow anything to stand in the way of a good story – no sentimentality, sympathy, favouritism or fear.

"There will be times when you have to cut corners. When it comes to it there are only two rules. Rule one: don't land the proprietor or the editor in court. Rule two: apart from rule one, there are no rules. You do whatever the story demands. When all the ingredients are there, never be afraid to write the story."

Lawson finished his drink and ordered another. They sat in silence while the barman complied. He placed the glass on the bar and Lawson paid up and downed a large proportion of its contents.

"You think I'm a heartless bastard?" Paice shrugged an ambivalent non-reply. "Fair enough," he continued. "You're probably right. But always remember we are in a war and it's best not to take prisoners. The enemy come at you in a number of forms. That's your first enemy." He pointed at the clock on the wall. "That fucking thing there never stops. There is never enough time.

21

"The second enemy is the competition. You don't like my attitude? Well, if you don't go that extra mile, the other titles always will. And when they go that bit further, they get the stories. When they get the stories, they sell the papers, and when people buy their papers, they don't buy ours."

He paused, lit a cigarette and took another pull on his drink. "But the biggest enemy is all those people out there who want to stop us finding out what we want to know. They don't like us knowing the what, but they will do anything – whatever it takes – to stop us finding out the why."

Paice was quick to realise that Lawson reserved a special part of his venomous ability to despise for the nameless entities he encompassed within the word "they".

"Say a passenger jet crashes on to a school and kids are killed. That's a big story and we put it all over the front page. So we have the what – the crash and its consequences. But what we want to know is the why – why did the plane crash in the first place? It might be a design fault in the plane. It might be poor maintenance. It might be that the pilot was pissed and his co-pilot was shagging a stewardess at the critical time. That's what you call news.

"We're here to expose all that sort of stuff. They are out to stop us. That's what news is – it's the stuff that people have a right to know but that they" – he added rancorous emphasis to the word – "don't want them finding out. And it's only us who are in a position to tell them. Sometimes you have to be the heartless bastard you think I am, and if you can't handle that you're in the wrong business. Piss off to Calcutta and give Mother Theresa a hand instead."

Paice had sat silently listening. It seemed a good move to say something. "As long as we give readers the truth – "

He got no further. Lawson jabbed him in the chest. "But, young sprog, what is the truth? That's the big question. The answer to it is that it is what you've come up with, using all your digging and hunting but when they refuse to tell you what you want to know.

"You see, it's all right if you are sitting at home with your feet up watching the telly and someone comes on and feeds you a load of crap. You can mull it over, twist it this way and that and think that it may be the truth or it may not.

"But we don't have that luxury. We're here trying to write the story and that" – he pointed at the clock – "won't stop ticking while you think it over and sit on the fence. You've got to get it into the paper, so you have to go with what you've got. What else can you do? The truth is what you think it is, and if you get it wrong, better luck next time and hope that it's not such a massive cock-up that you lose your job."

Paice realised that he had just heard an exposition of Lawson's credo, the belief that got him out of bed in the morning and drove him to work and kept him fired up all the time he was there. And it was a theology that Paice would come to embrace with complete and undiluted commitment.

Those were the good times, when every day was better than the one before and he did not think about where he was going because, wherever it was, it was exciting and he wanted to be there. His star was in its ascendancy as he moved from one paper to the next, each offering money and better expenses. That was before the fucked-up marriage, the consequential financial hardship – and the drink. The bloody drink.

Turning up at the office mid morning too pissed to stand up at the age of 50 had not exactly worked wonders for his performance-related bonus. But after what he had seen in more than his fair share of wars abroad and heartbreak and tragedy at home, who could blame him?

He'd always thought that the coppers had the rough end of the deal, having to knock on someone's door at 3am to tell them that an untimely death was about to destroy their lives, to shatter a future of hope and promise and leave them to contemplate the emptiness and futility of grief while they tried to get answers to the endless questions that followed in its wake.

And who was hot on the heels of the cops? Yours sincerely, that's who. But at least the cops were doing a necessary job and not getting paid enough for it. Too often he had come to feel like a bloody vulture, wheeling overhead waiting for death and the chance to swoop down and gorge himself on the next story and not caring a damn about the feelings of the bereaved, the dispossessed, or the plain and simple depressed, just so long as the story stood up.

Somewhere along the line it had ceased to be fun. And as the fun evaporated, so, it seemed, had his magic touch. The stories stopped coming, and he had lost interest – or was it the other way round?

Then Burkins had happened along, the stories – good, solid stories – had fallen in Paice's lap. Life and his demeanour had begun to improve. He was back on top and enjoying doing what he had been best at. That was until a month ago when Burkins had dropped his bombshell. But whatever his shortcomings, Burkins was assiduous, especially when it came to financing his little weakness, which enriched his bookmaker in inverse proportion to his own impoverishment.

The train lurched as it slowed for the Westminster stop, and Paice was yanked back to the present. He took a last quick look at the beauty across the carriage. She sneered back at him. He rose and headed for the door as it slid open. That afternoon Burkins had made the call that Paice had thought he was unlikely to receive."I might have something for you, Mr P."

The fact that Paice had felt a slight surge of excitement was more a reflection of his desperation than the scale of his expectation. Nothing ever happened at Overseas Aid, but he was nonetheless pinning a lot of hope on what was about to ensue.The simple fact was that he had little choice.

Chapter 2

Whereas most London pubs got busier the later the hour, it was a quirk of the clientele that in this part of the city that trade was at its height during the day and at going home time and then began to tail off by 6 or 7pm when the customers could defer no longer their return to their loved ones.

It was shortly after 5pm, so the bar was getting busier as people finished work and began to leave their offices. He immediately spotted Burkins sitting at the bar, a spare stool beside him. He slid on to it.

"Good evening, Jake. How are things?"

"Not bad, Mr P. How about yourself?"

"I'm hoping I'll be feeling a lot better when I have heard what you've got to say, Jake. So, fire away." He caught the barman's eye and pointed at the beer pump nearest to him.

"Well, for starters, I told you I might be moved to Overseas Aid."

"Yes, Jake, you did, and a dark cloud of depression hovered over me for a week afterwards."

"Well, Mr P, for you the sun came out. I got shifted to the Foreign Office."

Paice looked Burkins in the eye, silently assessing the potential. "I don't want to rush to judgment, Jake, but I'm sensing that this might be good news." The FCO – the Foreign and Commonwealth Office was, along with the Treasury and the Home Office, one element of the triumvirate of great offices of state. Having a mole burrowing silently beneath the verdant turf of such an establishment might be an enormous asset.

"I think it might be good news, Mr P. Are you interested in Latin America?"

"Not as such, but if there's a story in it...."

"You're the expert, so you tell me. It looks as though a little situation is developing in the region. My guess, from the staff involved, is that it is Colombia, Venezuela or perhaps up into Panama. I think it's right up your street, Mr P, because they are desperate to keep a lid on it which we both know could mean a good story." He winked slowly and slyly.

Paice pulled out his wallet as the barman put the drink in front of him. "And one for my friend, please." Burkins nodded his thanks and ordered a pint from the same pump. "So what sort of 'little situation' might we be talking about here?"

"From what I have seen it is some sort of major event – mud slides, floods, volcanoes. That sort of thing is always going on down there. There was talk of getting Overseas Aid involved – perhaps they want money from the UK aid budget to help to try to sort it out, but the

Foreign Office doesn't seem to see it that way. Anyway, it can't be a straightforward natural disaster because everyone would know if there had been an earthquake. So why do they want to keep it quiet?"

Paice thought for a moment. "They only ever keep hush-hush if something is embarrassing or they have done something wrong and want to cover it up. But no Government would worry about being accused of starting up a volcano. Quite the opposite – they would want to claim the credit for stepping in and helping, so they would make a big thing of it. Any idea of the scale of it?"

Burkins drew closer and lowered his voice. "That's the thing, Mr P. I overheard the deputy director say something about casualties running into hundreds. I gather that the Foreign Office has been in talking to No 10, which makes it even more likely that it is more than just an aid or disaster issue."

"Hundreds of people killed and the Government is trying to cover it up? Something is very wrong, Jake. Someone has fucked up and they don't want us to know about it. Seen any papers?"

"Not yet. But that's the point – they are keeping everything within a tight circle, which is what aroused my suspicions in the first place. I've asked a few very discreet questions, but the only answers have been along the lines of 'Mind your own business'. Anyway, I'll keep my eyes open for anything that might be interesting. Is that likely to be of use to you, Mr P?"

Paice had no trouble interpreting the last sentence as "Will you be paying me for that information?" He reached into the jacket of his waterproof jacket to where, earlier, he had placed a £20 note. In a well-practised routine he slipped it to Burkins beneath the level of the bar.

"Thank you very much, Mr P. Pleasure to do business with you."

"It will be if you can come up with the goods, Jake. On the face of it, it looks promising, so keep plugging away and keep me informed."

Burkins downed his drink, slipped off his stool and headed for the door. Paice finished his beer and caught the barman's attention. "Scotch, please – large one." He racked his brains in an attempt to make something of the flimsy facts that Burkins had given him. He had been to south and central America a few times, and he knew that it was an area where money could buy just about anything and the price put upon life was a bit less than a bacon sandwich – if you could get one, which you couldn't.

A heavy hand on his shoulder brought him back to Tuesday night in the bar of the Black Lion. "Hello young man. Good to see you."

This was when his finely developed strategy of defence based on complete denial kicked in. An unexpected encounter with the wrong participant from some unfortunate past event could spell trouble, so as he cautiously looked round he prepared to deny who he was and certainly what he was about to be accused of. But not this time.

"Eric?" He looked in disbelief at the mountain of a man who now leaned over him and put his arm warmly around his shoulder. "What in god's name..." He struggled for words. "Christ, Eric, how long since..." Lost for words again. By now he was on his feet and working Eric Stilwell's arm like the village pump.

"Ten years, I reckon. How are you. You look knackered – in fact, I wasn't sure it was you until you turned round as your friend was leaving." He let rip with his own peculiar brand of unrestrained laughter.

Paice grinned. "Well you look great – you haven't changed a bit. What are you doing in these parts?"

"This used to be my local when I worked at the Ministry of Defence." Eric jerked his head in the general direction of the MoD.

Paice could barely believe his eyes. "What are you drinking, Eric? Pint? Blimey, it's good to see you." And he meant it. The list of people he was glad to see was remarkable both for its brevity and its exclusivity, and it worked the other way, too. But then the bond between these men was as strong as it was unspoken.

"It's good to see you, too, Nick. Just a tonic water. I've been off the hard stuff for years now." Paice raised his eyebrows, remembering nights when they would polish off a bottle of Scotch each before staggering out into the bright, hard painful edge of a new day.

Paice climbed back on his stool. Eric was about to occupy the one recently vacated by Burkins, when a hand reached for it. Eric put his hand on the stool. "It's taken," he said quietly.

"Yeah, by me, mate." The young bloke clearly fancied himself as he squared his shoulders to face Eric. His bald head was extensively tattooed. He wore a nose piercing and several ear rings. His sleeveless vest was worn to show off muscular shoulders and biceps.

Eric was unimpressed. He moved in very close, looked the youth straight in the eye. "You sure you want to go there, son?"

The upstart shifted uneasily, now not quite so sure of himself. There was something about this old geyser – a natural authority.

"You wanna watch yourself, mate," he said as he backed away.

Eric took a step forward to maintain the proximity, his gaze never shifting from the younger man's eyes. "No, son. I won't be watching myself – I'll be watching you. And that is something you really need to worry about."

He casually turned his back in a way that told his opponent that the threat had been relegated to negligible and settled on to the stool.

"Still the same old Biff," Paice said with a smile. Eric's enthusiasm for getting stuck in when the fists began to fly had earned him the nickname Biffo. And although he was in stature a bear of a man, anyone confusing him with a cuddly cartoon character of the same name soon became aware of their mistake – sometimes to their physical discomfort and disadvantage. Biffo was no joke, and when trouble blew up the abbreviation to Biff became more apposite.

Biff eyed the glass of Scotch in Paice's hand. "And still the same old Paice the Ace?" he inquired, with a knowing wink.

"There are times when we all need a bit of help – I just happen sometimes to find it in a glass."

"In that case let me do my bit to assist." Biff held up his hand to attract the barman's attention and, when secured, pointed down at Paice's glass with unnecessary exaggeration.

"So, how are things? I see you get some good stuff in the paper. I read the Mercury like my bible. I saw your story this morning about that property fiddle. You have obviously got a straight line to the inside. People wonder how you do it."

"It's not difficult – you just keep your ear to the ground and aim the right questions at the right quarters, and then sort the lies from the truth," Paice explained.

"And it's at that point that you decide which of them to print?" Biff's booming laughter drowned out the ambient noise of the pub.

"You expect me to say anything other than the truth, Biff? But the truth is an odd piece of work. One man's truth is another man's lie. And sometimes you have to pick the truth that suits your story. Anyway, which 'people'?"

"Which people?"

"You said that 'people' wondered how I did it. Which people?"

It was clear from Biff's impenetrable smile that the question would not be answered. Paice suppressed a brief

33

flicker of annoyance and changed the direction of the conversation. "How about you? What were you doing in the MoD – telling the deskbound generals about soldiering in the real world?"

"Nah. They wouldn't listen to me, and even if they did they wouldn't understand. After I'd served my time, I left the regiment and looked around for something different. Nothing much came along, so I put out feelers. I went back basically to doing the only thing I knew – the Army. I joined the MoD security branch, and, at first, it seemed a good move, but it didn't work out as I had hoped. After some of the capers I'd been up to, it was a bit quiet. But that was not why I chucked it in. I got fed up banging my head against a wall of bureaucracy, so I left and set up my own security business.

"With my background and experience, I reckoned I had something more to offer. And now I'm the boss running my own business, I get to choose when I work instead of being ordered here there and everywhere at a moment's notice and having to stay out all night. It's for the best. I've been trying to get back with Louise, and to get to know my kids – and now their kids – if it's not too late."

"You were never there when Louise and the children needed you Biff – always putting Queen and country first. Now they don't need you, you must be reduced to hoping that they'll want you." He was treading familiar territory. "At least you did it for Queen and country. I did it to get the front page lead. It's too late for me – that part of my life is a smoking ruin. I've tried raking through the ashes, but there's nothing recognisable left to salvage."

"Christ, you're a cheerful bastard. As I said, same old Paice the Ace."

"You know what it's like, Eric. If life teaches you anything, it is that we are our own worst enemies. We are always looking over our shoulder to see who's going to stab us in the back. All the time we should be looking in the mirror because that's where we will see the person who poses the most serious threat to our health and happiness."

By now Biff had his tonic water. He rattled the ice in the glass and fished out the slice of lemon before sucking it and wincing at the result. "I know who I would rather face out of myself and some of the murderous, evil bastards I've bumped into over the years, Nick."

"Oh, sure, Biff. Don't forget that I have been with you once or twice when you encountered them. But that was short term and once you'd put a bullet through their forehead or planted your knife through their ribs, that particular risk was disposed of. My point is that you knew they were the enemy and after five minutes you'd dealt with them and moved on.

"The real danger is long term – it's you because you are always there, and when your guard is down or your temper is up, or the booze is doing the thinking, that's when you'll do something stupid that will change your life forever, and not for the better.

"The way I see it, Biff, is that we are the product of our own actions. I am today what I did yesterday, so I

35

have learnt to try to make sure that I don't do anything today that will fuck me up for tomorrow."

Paice was not thinking of any particular selfish transgression or indiscretion, but he seemed always to carry with him these days a past strewn with a litany of wrong moves born of an inability to know when he was well off, when he had had within his grasp something valuable and worth cherishing. People had wanted him and to be a part of his life and he to be part of theirs. But he had put no value on their loyalties and affections – even their love – instead always looking beyond them for something else. The problem was, he did not know what.

He pushed the thought from his mind but he knew that the respite was only temporary because it would seep back like rising damp penetrating the foundations of a rotten edifice.

Eric spotted the onset of self-recrimination and decided to stem it. He gave Paice an avuncular slap on the back. "Never look back, mate," he advised. A less practised boozer would have succumbed to the friendly assault and spilt his drink, but the grip Paice kept on his Scotch would have survived an earthquake.

He smiled, emptied his glass and banged it down on the bar. "No, you're right, Biff. I must look forward – at least I must look forward 20 minutes, which is when I am due to meet Sir Oswald Bellamy in the House of Commons."

Biff made a face indicating distaste. "That crook. What's your interest in him?"

"The property fiddle you read about this morning – St George Consolidated Land."

"Is he involved in that?"

Paice nodded. "Only up to his neck. But, of course, he's the small investor's friend – like hell. I reckon he's made a packet. The poor sods who put in their life savings hoping to get rich quick but who ended up getting poor even quicker are left to carry the can."

St George Consolidated Land had been hitting the business page headlines as the "SGCL scandal". The City whiz kids had dubbed the company "Say Goodbye to your Cash, Losers." It had been a property and tourism investment company operating around the Black Sea. The aim was to take advantage of low tax, an improving economic climate and, with cheap air fares from western Europe, a blossoming tourist trade.

Backed by extensive advertising and lucrative commissions, the business had taken off like a skyrocket. Now the law of gravity had asserted itself and the rocket, along with the hopes of thousands, had crashed to earth. Regardless of the millions poured in by investors in the UK, the business was now worthless. What could be traced of the property portfolio had been snatched by the banks, and the principals had disappeared into thin air, along with the money. The administrators had been left counting small change.

Sir Oswald had been the respectable front man, pushed forward to inspire confidence in the viability of the scheme. Its failure had given him the opportunity to sidestep his involvement and champion the cause of the investors, asking questions in the House, tabling motions and tackling Ministers, but not a penny had been forthcoming. The Government was remaining at arm's length, apart from calling in the Crown Prosecution Service, the Serious Fraud Office and the Fraud Squad in the City of London.

Bellamy had been unrepentant. "I've done no wrong. I'm a victim, too," he had declared. "We are all in this together." Slippery as he was, he had managed to distance himself from the blame. But while the little old lady in Eastbourne was wondering how she was going to pay next winter's gas bill, Sir Oswald would doubtless be keeping warm. He was still planning his customary winter break at his 25-bedroom villa in the West Indies.

"I intend to discover his involvement in this scam, and the first port of call is Bellamy himself," Paice explained.

"You should watch yourself," Eric advised. "You are spending too much time with those politicians. You are much safer dealing with a man with a gun or a knife."

"Well, you meet all sorts. Remember the famous Yank who told his father that he couldn't lie to him? So he told the truth and his old man beat the crap out of him. After that he found out it was better to lie, and when he got really good at it he didn't know whether to go into politics or journalism."

Eric smiled. "Yeah, the world's a wicked place. The question is are you trying to make it less wicked."

"I hope that I am about to do just that, so I'd better be pushing off. I don't want to keep our eminent elder statesman waiting. You leaving now?"

"Yeah, but let's keep in touch."

"Well, you know where to contact me. What about you?"

Biff fished into his jacket pocket and produced a business card. "The numbers are there – try the mobile first."

Paice barely looked at the card before pocketing it. "OK Eric, I'll see you around."

At that point Biff's mobile phone began to broadcast the music that introduced the BBC programme The Archers, the ring tone cheerfully notifying him of an incoming call. He studied the telephone. "I'll just answer this and I'll be a few steps behind you," he said.

Paice stepped out of the pub and into the street. A cold wind was blowing, but the rain had stopped. The clocks were now on summer time, but even so it was almost dark. As he buttoned his waterproof jacket against the chill, he bumped into a familiar figure. It was the tattooed head and ear rings, blocking his path and out for trouble. Paice looked into the shadows where four others of a similar appearance were waiting.

"I want a word with your mate. Where is he?" baldy growled, trying to inflate the threat to invoke fear.

Before Paice could reply a quiet voice, but one with real menace, said, "You looking for me, turd?"

Biff had left by the other door and come up behind the intended ambush. Baldy wheeled round. "You're a dead man," he spat as he threw a punch at Biff's face. In a flash, Biff snatched the impending fist out of the air. With his left hand he held it momentarily, keeping it suspended in space. It seemed to hang there for an eternity as the thug stared, transfixed by his inability to move. "I told you I was watching you," said Biff. "Your trouble is that you don't listen," he growled.

The look on the man's face evolved from command to submission to fear as he realised that he had been outmanoeuvred. Biff's huge hand completely enveloped the assailant's and closed around it like a steel clamp. In a smooth and combined movement, his right fist now came from nowhere out of the darkness, landing on baldy's cheekbone with a squelching crunch, while the grip of steel flicked the now imprisoned fist. The sharp twist was accompanied by a sickening crack and a shriek of pain.

The blow to the face would have been enough to put him down, but Biff did not want that. Thrown off balance, his adversary was now a useful projectile. As Biff maintained his grip on the fist and now shattered wrist he used his right hand to grip the throat. Putting his full weight into the task, he hurled the writhing body into the shadows where the threat now resided.

The whole incident had taken no more than 20 seconds, during which baldy's four henchmen had been stunned into inertia, mesmerised by the speed of the action. As baldy crashed into their midst, one decided to run for it, one cowered in a heap, one whimpered an apology.

The fourth made a dreadful mistake. He pulled a knife. As it was raised, intended for Biff's vulnerable back, the polished steel flashed, reflecting in turn or in combination the orange of the street lamps and the red and white lights of the passing traffic. But that was where it stayed – momentarily. A dark and silent force now made its presence known. "Blimey, Biff, he's brought some cutlery to the party." The newcomer's black skin had rendered him almost invisible in the gathering dusk. Knifeman suddenly discovered that a knife is a double-edged weapon, physically as well as metaphorically.

Biff's unexpected ally had grabbed the knife hand with his right while thumping a balled fist solidly into the man's exposed rib cage, driving all wind and resistance from his body.

The knife was turned and used to slice into the man's cheek. The job was completed by the delivery into the defenceless crotch of a very expensive, hand-made shoe.

"Sorted, Biff," he stated as thug number four slumped into the heap.

"Thank you for that, Winston. Although I could have managed without your very kind assistance," Biff declared, straightening his tie and smoothing his hair.

"Of course you could, Biff, but I wasn't about to let you keep all the fun to yourself. You've got to learn to share."

Poised for the counter attack that would never come, they stood surveying the barely moving mass of bodies that moments before had thought itself an invincible force.

41

Paice had taken three steps back, away from the scene of the action, but he moved forward now. "Why am I not surprised to find Winston Jones on hand when Biff is in trouble," he said holding out his hand.

Gripping it, Jones flashed a brilliant white smile and nodded towards Biff. "Someone's got to keep an eye on him. How are you Ace?"

"What is this, a bloody reunion?" Paice asked. "Just what's going on?"

"Winston worked for me..."

"With," Jones interjected.

"Sorry, Winston – with me – in the MoD. I invited him here for a quiet drink to talk business. I am trying to get him to give up working for the Government and join my outfit. Winston's quite good at what he does. I might be able to find him a junior position." He grinned as he uttered the compliment wrapped in an insult.

"What Biff hasn't mentioned is that he wants me to become a partner in the business, so I would be after a bit more than a junior position," Winston explained.

"So, it would be an investment as well as a job?" Paice inquired.

Biff shifted uneasily. "I've told Winston that things are a bit quiet at the moment, but that's the best time to get involved. Business is due to pick up. We are really going places."

Paice guessed that he was voicing an ambition rather than a prediction. "I'm sure you are right, Biff, but this is a difficult time," Winston explained. "My wife wants me to put down a deposit on our own house, so I'm a bit short of the extra funds. It's a nice thought to be running our own business, but I've told Biff that at the moment the priority is a secure wage, not forgetting the pension. Not that that has stopped him pestering me. He obviously needs a good man to sort out the mess he's made of his business." Now it was Winston's turn to grin.

Biff did not smile in return. Paice sensed that the big man might be struggling to get the business off the ground. He probably desperately needed the injection of funds that Winston might provide.

The conversation was cut short as a police patrol car, blue lights flashing, skidded to a halt in the kerb. Three policemen piled out of the vehicle, their yellow high visibility vests dazzling as they picked up every stray beam of light. The sergeant pulled on his cap as he approached. "What's happening here?" He took a torch from his belt and flashed the beam across the sorry pile of humanity lying on the wet pavement. He concentrated on the blood pouring from knifeman's face. He turned to the constable closest to him. "Whistle up an ambulance," he barked. "You three, up against the wall."

"Let me explain, sergeant –" Paice began, but was cut short.

"I said up against the wall. Now, move." The third officer began grabbing arms and pushing.

"You 'eard the sergeant. Now back up."

They complied as the sergeant did a quick assessment of the fallen, assuring himself that emergency medical treatment was unnecessary. Satisfied that no one was about to die, he turned to Paice and his companions.

"Right," he declared. "I need some identification."

Winston pulled his wallet from the inside pocket of his coat. He flipped it open and the sergeant used his torch to illuminate the contents. He studied the MoD security identification card, shone his torch into Winston's face, then went back to the wallet.

"OK, mate. That's fine. What about you two?" He turned to Biff and Paice.

"This gentleman was just a bystander, officer. He is not involved," Winston explained.

"Very well. If you say so." He turned to Paice and gestured over his shoulder with his thumb. "Right, you can go, sir." He turned back to Winston. "How about you? You'd better fill me in. What have we got here?"

Winston winked furtively at Paice and jerked his head to indicate that Paice should get going before the sergeant changed his mind. Paice did not need telling twice. As he hurried away from the scene, Winston was explaining what had happened, and the ambulance arrived, its flashing blue lights complementing those of the police car.

As he headed for the House of Commons, his thoughts turned to the ease with which Winston had been able to use his MoD security status to smooth things over with the copper, not least in assuring him that Paice was an innocent passerby. The rain started to fall, pattering on his waterproof jacket and feeling fresh on his face. He sprinted for cover.

Chapter 3

The missing L had turned the English half of the bilingual sign from a greeting to a statement. "We come to General Rafael Cisneros International Airport."

Stepping from the chilled interior of the 747, the man in faded blue jeans and a check shirt walked out into the laundry-like atmosphere, down the aircraft steps and towards the sun-bleached blue and white terminal buildings.

He looked up at the incomplete sign. It was different from the last time. Then the airport had been named in celebration of the rule of Gomez Callo. But Callo was now gone. So, with him, was a fair proportion of the country's scant gold and convertible currency reserves. The new man was there to protect the people. The trouble was, as usual in this part of the world, only the name had changed. This was Tierra del Aguila – the name chosen by the conquistadores after the regal birds that then soared in its skies. But the country was no more regal than any of the other many impoverished and backward nations.

By the time he reached the sanctuary of the air conditioned arrivals building he was already feeling the effects of the overbearing humidity as the sweat began to patch darkly through his shirt. April marked the end of the hot dry weather; the rain was due any day, and the humidity offered a forecast to match any satellite prediction.

He headed straight for the hard currency shop. The shelves were lined with goods that the people could not buy. Here, their local currency was treated with a disdain that reflected its value on the international exchanges. He homed in on the rum, good quality unlike the paint stripper on sale on the streets. At the cash desk he peeled off just the right number of dollar bills. Minutes later he had passed through customs and immigration, scarcely giving the guards – mere kids fingering their AK47s – a glance, and was pushing his way through the black and brown faces of the anxious and the curious on the landward side of the arrivals gate.

Out front, the 20-year-old Chevrolet stood in battered anonymity among the parked cluster of Detroit-made cars of similar vintage. More youthful vehicles were rare, the privileged preserve of the ruling elite and foreign diplomats. He surveyed the accumulated years and the millions of miles ranged along the kerb. Most of them would probably still be providing transportation 10 years hence.

Opening the back door, metal grinding painfully against metal, he threw in his leather holdall then yanked open the front passenger door and slumped into the superheated tatty plastic upholstery next to the driver.

"Let's go, Ed," he said. Eduardo Barillas turned the key, provoking a throbbing V8 growl from beneath the bonnet. He was well above average size for Central America - several inches over 6ft, with the rest in perfect proportion. His smooth, flawless skin was taut over high cheekbones and muscular features. His glossy black hair was swept back and worn long.

For several miles the car's tyres thumped and slapped over the patchwork blacktop that passed as one of the best roads in the country. The Chevrolet waited for an oncoming lorry to pass before overtaking an ancient pick-up laden with watermelons. Half a mile later it slowed, then bounced and slewed to the right leaving the metalled surface and becoming consumed by a cloud of red dust on a side road lined with mango trees.

The big car plunged on, only rarely slowing to acknowledge the worst aspects of the deteriorating track, its bow wave elegantly building into a streaming plume, belying the inevitable degradation, within moments of its passing, into a choking fog.

The blue hills had seemed determined to remain obstinately out of reach, but eventually the car began to climb. The two men had said nothing throughout the journey, a mutual recognition of the fact that their purpose required cold professionalism, not warmth, not friendship, and certainly not polite conversation.

Only as they approached the decaying colonial house did the passenger speak. "Is everything ready?"

The driver half turned his head and nodded. "Sure, Bart. The Yank wants no delay. He keeps saying 'In and out. No messing'."

The man reached back and gathered the straps of his bag as the big car stopped in front of the building. "I'm all for that."

Half an hour later, Bart was settled in and had opened the bottle he had bought at the airport and poured three drinks. The third man, Harry Scrantz, rolled a half-smoked cigar between thumb and forefinger and swilled the last of the rum around his glass. Slumped in an old cane armchair, he exuded an air of lethargy, an impression that, from experience, the other two knew was light years from reality. He was in his late 40s, and older than the other two.

"I want to do this thing tomorrow night. The less time we spend here the less suspicion we'll arouse. In and out with no messing." Eduardo caught the Englishman's eye and smiled. "It's crucial that this operation is not discovered as an act of sabotage, so that means no killing, no shooting and no mayhem, just carefully arranged destruction. Is that understood?" He applied his lighter to the extinct cigar, puffed vigorously for a few seconds, and then peered at the two men through the ensuing curtain of blue smoke. "Any questions?"

The Englishman stood up, walked to the table and poured himself another large slug of rum. "I always think that economic warfare is so much more civilised than the other sort, don't you Harry? No blood, no shattered body parts, no screams of agony. Gives you a nice warm feeling inside – just like this stuff." He waved his glass in the air.

Harry shrugged. "I'm not paid to make those judgments, Bart, and nor are you. And before you get too smug, just remember that we are here to do our little bit to cripple the country's economy, and that will mean hard times with starvation for a lot of people." The American grinned and held out his glass for another helping of the spirit. "Sometimes you gotta be cruel to be kind. These people have to be helped to see the light."

"We should see the target in daylight so that we are all familiar with the layout," Eduardo pointed out.

"Don't worry Ed, my boy. Uncle Harry will give you a bird's eye view of the entire set-up. I want us all to know exactly what we have to do because I don't want any foul-ups. We'll be leaving at first light. Don't carry anything incriminating. We just might get stopped. The army does put the occasional patrol through these hills."

By 8am and before the thermometer had started its inevitable climb they had crossed the ridge of the hills and descended on the other side to a rocky outcrop. It was a natural balcony that gave out on to a breathtaking view of the country's largest lake - almost an inland sea. It was connected to the ocean by a broad highway of water that provided the overflow to discharge from the lake the product of the hundred rivers that laboured incessantly to fill it.

Directly beneath them lay a small town with a harbour. Just offshore a sprinkling of islands, lush with vegetation, marked the peaks of submerged volcanic stumps that rose from the depths of the lake bed. A few small fishing boats were plying between the islands, joining the green dots, their progress barely disturbing the mirror surface of the clear blue water.

But the three observers saw none of the beauty. The object of their attention was further around the sweep of the shore. The petrochemical complex that was ranged along the water's edge was a crucial component of the nation's economy. It processed all the crude oil that was pumped from the fields in the north. Until the change of regime and the arrival of the president's new best friends from the East, it had been owned and operated by one of the oil multi-nationals. Now, however, it had been liberated for the benefit of the people to whom it now belonged. In theory.

Its silver painted storage tanks and fractionating plant glinted in the sunlight. The sooty flare of waste gases left a sweet odour on the morning air, but showed that the plant was open for business. It had to be. It was the country's principal source both of refined petroleum and vital foreign earnings. It enabled the new regime to fend off the worst effects of the trade embargo imposed by their powerful, and erstwhile friendly, neighbour in the north. Without it, power generation, road transport and air links with the rest of the world would be virtually impossible. For the country's new rulers it represented the difference between success and failure in a hostile world that demanded scarce dollars for petroleum.Scrantz handed the Englishman a small pair of binoculars. "What do you think?" he asked after a few minutes.

"I think that it won't be easy, Harry," he replied as he studied the layout of the plant. "How do we get in and what exactly do we hit, always remembering that it has to look like an accident?"

Eduardo put a hand on the Englishman's shoulder and pointed to where the refinery adjoined the harbour. Harry nodded his agreement. "The tanks at the end there are no longer used. At one time one of the big American chemical firms ran a small operation based on petroleum byproducts and phosphates from a mine up in these hills. Because it's redundant they don't seem to guard it so well. That is where we go in."

"OK, so we get in. Then what? It has to be an accident - a natural man-made disaster. These places don't just blow up on their own."

"They do when they are being run by a bunch of ditch-digging farm boys," Scrantz growled. "That is the whole point. Sure, we hit them hard in the economy, but we also show them how they need us technically. We demonstrate the foolishness of them trying to go it alone. 'Look how disaster strikes when you mess with things you don't understand,' we'll say. If we pull this off properly, they'll welcome us back with open arms. Our respective countries' spheres of influence around here once more will be complete. And you, Eduardo, will be back in favour, my boy."

For an hour, as the sun climbed higher, in tandem with the temperature, they watched the security operation at the plant. The personnel numbers were impressive; their methods were not.

"Piece of cake," Scrantz snapped. "In and out with no messing."

They headed back over the hills retracing their steps of the morning along little used tracks. Travelling in silence and resting up occasionally, they reached their base by midday. The cool, dark interior of the old house provided a sanctuary from the unremitting heat and the chance to relax with a beer and discuss tactics.

Weapons were produced from a large rucksack. "Only for use in an emergency," said Scrantz stroking the blue-black body of a .44 calibre Colt automatic pistol.

"What have we got to go bump in the night?" the Englishman asked."What we got, buster, is the latest technology. It's a development of C4, but a bigger advance on that than C4 was over RDX."

Eduardo broke his silence for only about the fourth time that day. "I only ever used RDX. I always thought it was a product of the USA. What's C4?"

Scrantz's eyes glinted with enthusiasm. This was his subject. "Not so, Eddie. RDX, the big advance in plastic explosive, was provided courtesy of our friends the Brits." He turned and smiled at the Englishman. "It was just what people in our line of business had been crying out for and it made a significant contribution to operations in the second world war.

"But like all these things, the technology had to move on. RDX had certain drawbacks - for one thing you couldn't detonate a small amount. My stout-hearted countrymen came up with C4, which gives a bigger bang for your money. The Iron Curtain boys got their own version on the market. It's called Semtex. We sometimes use it when we don't want to leave a calling card - the eggheads can look at the remains and work out what explosive was used."

He reached into the rucksack with a mischievous grin, producing a small package with a flourish. "This, comrades, is the answer to our prayers. It's C4 with teeth and the gloves off."

"What does it do?" Eduardo asked.

"It packs one hell of a lot of punch, directed to and concentrated on one very small area. Tonight we put a small amount around one of those gas tank valves. They're cast metal and brittle. It will smash them like a piece of glass and, with the ensuing inferno, leave no detectable sign of an explosion. The gas ignites, the plant goes up in a ball of smoke and our Governments are back in business in this part of Central America." His enthusiasm for the venture mounted as he went into more detail about detonators and timers.

"The guards do four six hour shifts. The third shift comes off at 2am. We go in at 1 o'clock just as they are turning their attention away from the plant and towards their beds. Eduardo, have you any problems about the boat?"

The big man shook his head.

"And the plane?" the American persisted.

"That's OK, too, Harry."

He started to put the gear back in the rucksack and looked up at the Englishman. "We've done this sort of thing before. You know the form. You keep watch and

I'll fix the charge. By the time it goes up we'll be well away.

"Eddie, I'll have to go over the route with you again," he said, unfolding a large-scale map of the region, the lake a wide blue expanse on a background of green and brown. They spent 10 minutes pointing out features on the map and muttering to each other before Scrantz was satisfied that they would get to the target on time.

"We also have the old blueprints of the layout of the complex. Bart, I'll show you where we hit, but not where we go in. That will depend on the integrity of the perimeter wire, but I'm hoping we'll do it here at the point nearest to this big tank." He unwound a finger from his rum glass and waved it in the air over the largest of a series of squat, cylindrical storage tanks precisely arranged in the now-disused chemical plant area of the complex. Scrantz moved him through and out of it into the heart of the operation. "This is our little baby," he said finally, tilting his empty glass in the Englishman's direction. "Gas," he declared, beaming with satisfaction.

"Gas as in gas, or gas as in petrol?" Bart queried.

"Gas as in gasoline. Boy, are we going to light up the sky."

By now Eduardo had gone out into the kitchen to make coffee. The Englishman picked a gun from the rucksack and began to check it over. "Doesn't seem like four years since we last worked together," he said, releasing the magazine. "Did you and Eduardo have any problems getting here?"

"It wasn't easy. We had to come in by foot over the border. Boy, would they like to get their hands on Ed."

The Englishman looked puzzled. "Why him particularly?"

Scrantz roared with laughter. "Because he was the son of a bitch who bombed their victory parade, that's why."

"I heard about the bombing. I didn't know who did it."

"Well, now you do. After the rebel takeover, they captured Eduardo and a few of his buddies out at the Arevalo air base. You know Eduardo. Takes a real good man to hold him, and they didn't have one that good.

"Seems that with one bound good old Eddie was free. Found himself one of those old Starfighters that he used to fly. It was gassed up with a full bomb load. He just climbed aboard and went up and away. He came in over the capital as the General was marching victoriously up to the presidential palace. Eduardo showered him with love, affection and a stick of bombs, and then flew the plane to a friendly airfield on the other side of the border.

"If they knew Eduardo was here they'd clip more than his wings, and that's a fact."

Chapter 4

The pavement punch-up and the security checks as he entered the Palace of Westminster – the Westminster parliament building really was a royal palace – meant that Paice was over 15 minutes late for his appointment with Bellamy.

Once inside, he hurried up towards the Central Lobby past marble statues and murals depicting historic events. At the top of the three steps at the entrance to the Lobby, two policemen stood surveying the visitors. Paice was about to push through when one of the PCs gently put his hand on the newspaperman's chest and halted his progress.

"I take it that you are going to behave yourself today, Nick."

"Hallo, Pete. Yes, I promise to be a good boy. I'm here to see Bellamy for a story I'm putting together. And I am sober."

"Just be sure you keep it that way. Off you go."

Paice made his way through the clustered groups of people who were standing around waiting to be met or collected by the MPs and officials they had come to see. He walked up to the reception desk.

"Will you please call Sir Oswald Bellamy's office and tell them that Nick Paice is here for his appointment with Sir Oswald?"

The attendant, impeccable in a uniform that seemed more appropriate to the nineteenth century than the twenty-first, looked up the number and made the call. He nodded and thanked the person on the other end.

"I have been asked to tell you that you are late for your appointment. Sir Oswald waited well beyond the agreed time, but, being extremely busy, he felt compelled to move on to other, more urgent, business. They say that you will have to make a fresh appointment."

"Pompous old fool," Paice muttered only just under his breath.

The attendant smiled as he lied. "I did not quite catch what you said, sir." Paice had come to learn that the staff who worked in the House were intensely loyal to the Members, but even they had their likes and, as was evident in this case, their dislikes. "Why not visit one of the Committees while you are here?" The suggestion was loaded with a meaning that was not lost on Paice.

"That sounds a good idea. Any suggestions?"

"Ask Fergus up on the Committee Corridor. He might have a recommendation. I believe that, like my mum, his parents lost money with the St George scam – not that I have any opinion about that, you understand."

"Of course not. Why would you?" Paice gave him a knowing nod and thanked him before heading across the

Lobby to the Lower Waiting Hall, up the white marble staircase and into the Committee Corridor. This was an area that he, like the public, could enter without a security or press pass. Ahead of him, another reception desk. "Are you Fergus," he asked the young man who looked up from the sheet he will filling in.

"I am, sir. If I were you, I'd look in on the Trade Tariffs Bill – Committee Room 12."

"Thank you, Fergus. I might just do that." The necessary telephone call had been made, and now Paice knew exactly where to find Sir Oswald.

He made his way along the corridor – its length was more akin to the main runway at Heathrow – checking off the room numbers as he went. He came to Room 12, which, like all Committee Rooms had two entrances, one for the Members and one for the public.

He pushed open the massive oak door beneath the gothic inscription "Public Entrance" and walked in. The policeman just inside the door gave him a quick once-over and nodded to indicate that he should take a seat. He was spoilt for choice. The 30 or so public seats were occupied by only half a dozen people, so the Trade Tariffs Bill Committee was clearly not the hottest ticket in town.

The Committee brought the people surprisingly close to their elected representatives. The public shared the room with the Members, sitting only feet away from them, unlike in the Chamber of the House where they were segregated into a Gallery high above and separated by massive sheets of bullet-proof glass. Here, the only thing between the Members and the people they were there to serve was a wooden rail, and even that had a gap in it to enable the Members to come and go.

Paice looked along the Benches. There were about 15 or 20 MPs present. One was speaking at the far end of the room, talking about imports of Chinese machine tools. Paice was not here for that. He ran his eye across the remaining Members. Bellamy did not appear to be there. Then he saw him. He was skulking behind another MP. He had clearly seen Paice as he entered the room and was hoping to make himself invisible.

There was no way to attract Bellamy's attention. If he waved or called out, he would be out on his ear and, with his record, probably never allowed back in. But Paice had been around this place for a long time on and off and he knew how the system worked. He fished in the copious pocket inside his jacket and took out his notebook. Scribbling a note to Bellamy he went back out to the corridor to wait.

After about 10 minutes he saw what he was hoping for – the attendant whose job was constantly to circulate the areas frequented by Members, in her hand a sheaf of messages which she was required to deliver when she spotted the intended recipient. She was a pretty blonde. Even that antiquated uniform did little to hide the fact that beneath it was the sort of heavenly body that caused the male Members to have thoughts that would guarantee them a prominent place on the front page of one of the more disrespectful tabloids should thought evolve into action.

But Paice had other things on his mind. "Excuse me, Miss. Can you get an urgent message to Sir Oswald Bellamy for me, please?"

"I'm not supposed to deliver messages for the public. Sorry."

He took a long shot. "It's really urgent. I'm writing a story about the St George scam, and I need to talk to him."

She smiled, exposing a perfect row of beautiful white teeth. His resolve faltered as he looked into the blue-grey mist of her eyes, and as he peered through the mist hoping to see he knew not what, his attention began to wander from the task at hand. She shook her head and tutted, which brought him back to reality. "Fergus mentioned that someone was on to that. My auntie lost all her savings in that fiddle," she said. "Just this time, I'll make an exception. I'd do anything if it would help my poor auntie."

Paice's focus was starting to slip again as his imagination of just what she might do accelerated into fantasy, but she again dragged him back to the here and now. "Give it to me," she said. She took the message from his hand and disappeared into the Members-only door.

By the time he got back into the public seats, the message was being passed across the benches to Bellamy. He read it, looked across at Paice and signalled for him to meet outside the room. The old blackmail had worked yet again. The message had simply said that he was writing a story and he wanted to give Bellamy the chance to put his side of things. Without that input, the implication went, who could say what might be printed?

He was slightly surprised that Bellamy, a seasoned campaigner who bore many battle scars from the war with the media, had fallen for it. The worst possible response for Paice would have been "Well, go ahead and write your story. I'm saying nothing." But Bellamy did not know what Paice knew – which, in fact was nothing – and he probably wanted to talk just to confirm that. Paice knew it was time to bullshit.

Back in the corridor, Bellamy gestured to him to sit on one of the green leather benches that lined the corridor. He was in his 60s and his immaculate tailoring and rotund figure showed that life had been good to him. He was living and demonstrable proof, however, of the fact that life being good to one is not necessarily good for one.

He slumped onto the bench, relieved to get the excessive weight off his feet. His puffy features and florid complexion broadcast the unwelcome truth about the nocturnal consumption of pink gins in the Members' Bar at a time when most people were abed. Doubtless, if asked, he would plead that democracy did not come cheap, and that being kept from his bed was the price he was prepared to pay.

He pulled a red silk handkerchief from his top pocket and wiped perspiration from his forehead. His crinkled grey hair gleamed with what Paice guessed was 1950s brilliantine.

"Right, so what's the story?" He avoided looking at Paice, instead tilting his head back and studying the painting of Admiral Jellicoe that looked down from the wall opposite.

"That's what I'm hoping you'll tell me, Sir Oswald. You are the man at the eye of the storm. I was looking to you for the latest news on the position of Saint George."

"I read your story in the paper this morning. I would advise you to proceed with care – speculative libel can be very costly."

"There was certainly nothing libellous or actionable in what I wrote. I was simply setting out the facts as they currently stand. Those facts appear to be that thousands of small investors who were reassured by your participation in this – I hesitate to use the word 'scam', so I'll say highly speculative investment, have lost their money. What I want from you is an update on the situation and, even better, an assurance that my readers and many more like them stand a chance of getting their money back."

Bellamy shook his head. "I can't tell you any more at the moment than you probably already know. We are still awaiting the findings of the administrators. It is for them to determine what assets remain and how they should be distributed."

"Is that the best you can do? We are talking of – again, I won't use the word 'scam' so what can I call it? Let's say that it is a company failure that has cost investors over £100 million – we are talking about people sinking money into this venture, banks lending vast sums on assets that proved to be non-existent, respected financial institutions having been duped, and all you can say is 'Wait and see what the accountants turn up'?"

"Look, I cannot tell you what I don't know. Apart from consultancy fees – which were openly declared in the register of Members' interests in accordance with the rules of the House of Commons – I have not touched a penny of investors' or banks' money. I am a victim in all this, too, you know."

"I hope that you are not looking for sympathy, Sir Oswald. Have you lost your home or your life's savings? Are you worrying about how you will pay for your old age?" Paice did not wait for an answer. "I didn't think so.

"Well, if you won't give me answers, we have people out in the eastern Balkans and the Black Sea looking into this mess. Already they are telling us that there may be evidence that company property has been sold to major figures in the company at, shall we say, less than market prices."

Paice was lying through his teeth, but he was anxious to provoke Bellamy into a response.

"I have no knowledge of any such transactions, which would, of course, be highly illegal not only in the UK but in all of the countries in which we were operating. I do not need to tell you that, should what you say be true, which I do not accept for one moment, I would have no part of any such conduct. I also do not need to tell you that any suggestion in your newspaper to the contrary would be greeted with legal repercussions of the most severe kind."

Paice maintained the pressure. "I would be correct in writing, then, that you deny that you acquired any of the company's property at a knock-down price – or even for no price – in the period immediately preceding the failure of the company?" This time it was Paice who turned his face away to contemplate Lord Jellicoe's stern demeanour.

Bellamy turned to him with gritted teeth. He knew that "MP denies being a crook" would leave readers saying "Looks like that MP's a crook."

"Look, Paice, don't you try that old trick with me. I know all about you. You're an unreliable drunk who's well past his prime, if he ever got there. Just watch your step. I have powerful friends, and if you put one foot out of line you will find that life can become extremely difficult and unpleasant. I'm warning you. And if you come back here pestering me again, I'll have you thrown out just as you were the last time, and then you'll never get back in here. See what that does for whatever remains of your career."

Paice kept his nerve. "Do I interpret that as a denial, then?"

Bellamy leapt to his feet with an agility that owed more to his fury than to any scant residue of physical fitness. "Do not contact me again, Paice, damn you. Any questions should be referred to Cromwell Associates." He flicked a business card into Paice's lap.

Paice persisted. "Are you denying that you acquired property...."

The sentence was brutally cut short. "No fucking comment," Bellamy roared. The convivial buzz of conversation among the dozen or so bystanders in the corridor was cut as though someone had thrown a switch. The stunned gathering stared with a combination of disbelief and disapproval as he roughly pushed his way through them and disappeared.

"Haven't lost your winning way with politicians, then Nicky boy." George Lockhart, political correspondent and long term fixture at Westminster, plonked down beside him on the bench.

"Hello. George. It must have been something I said. We were getting on so well. How are you? How's life on The Globe?"

"Well, despite everyone's worst predictions, we're still in business – and keeping our fingers crossed. I'm surprised to see you back here. I heard they'd withdrawn your press pass. The word is that you had one too many and upset the wrong person."

"Not quite. Seamus McNally was celebrating in the terrace bar on his first day as an MP – he'd just won the Killingar by-election. I knew him – more to the point, knew all about him – from Northern Ireland, and he knew that I knew. I was having a quiet drink and he saw me and came over. He started getting nasty – shouting about the lies he said I had written and how I had been just a PR man and propagandist for the security forces."

"Were you?" Lockhart was blunt, as ever. "We both know that the security forces used us when it suited them.

They were no angels and it was a dirty business – the dirtiest."

Paice shook his head. "You're right, George. It was hell on earth back then, but my stuff was as straight as anything anyone was putting out – I exposed the villains whichever side they were on, and that included our own people, who, as you say, weren't exactly angels. Couldn't afford to be.

"Anyway, as one of the villains, he wants history to be the way he writes it. He can't stand the inconvenience of having someone around who knows what really went on. That's why he went for me. I said that I thought we were all friends now and all that was in the past. He said he would rather lick shit off the pavement than admit I was his friend.

"The trouble was that I know what he got up to during the troubles. I said that it was a pity that the electorate had been so gullible as to vote for a cowardly, murdering bastard to represent them. One word led to another and he warned me that I had upset the wrong people, and that those people had very long memories and weren't renowned for their forgiving nature."

Lockhart shrugged. "Well, he's right about that. There's too much history over there and the Irish never forget. They still get upset over what happened three centuries ago. Anything you did 10 years ago would be as fresh as this morning's milk. So how did it end?"

"He said that I should keep watching my back. He then made other, more specific threats. I told him that he was the expert on backs since that was where he usually shot people, which was when he took a swing at me."

"How pissed were you?"

"Not half as pissed as he was. Which was why his punch missed and mine didn't. Security were called, and after a brief chat they carted him off to the nurse and then took away my pass and walked me out of the building. It was a choice between me and that thug, and they backed him."

"He's an MP and this is Parliament, Nick. They are bound to side with him."

"If they knew him like I do, they wouldn't make that mistake."

Lockhart shook his head . "They're not the only ones making a mistake."

"What do you mean by that?"

"It seems that whatever you do, you end up making an enemy. It pays to have friends – people in the right place who can help you when you run into trouble. Your problem is that you have never understood the value of making friends with the right people. You are very good at making enemies, but when it comes to making friends you're a dead loss."

"No, George, my problem is that the people I write about are the sort that no decent individual would want as a friend, even under a flag of convenience. And if you are suggesting following your example and spending time with oily, shoulder squeezing Cabinet Ministers at their weekend retreats, I'd rather have a pizza and a pint and turn in for an early night."

Lockhart stood up to leave. "You are misunderstanding the word 'friend', Nick. In truth they are just contacts, and I am using them – which they understand, because they think that they are using me.

"Take my advice, start making friends, not enemies. And you can begin with making friends with the most important person – yourself. At the moment you are your own worst enemy."

The observation touched a raw nerve with Paice as he remembered the conversation with Biff in the Black Lion only a couple of hours previously. "I've had some good stories in the last year, and all without the so-called friends you are so keen on."

"Yes, Nick, it's true you've had some good stories, which we both know have pulled you back from the brink, but if you had cultivated the right contacts who could have eased you through the system, they could have been great stories. Instead, you have broken the stories, but others have picked them up and run with them. My point is that it could have been you."

Chapter 5

Easter was late, but even so it had been accompanied by a flurry of snow, a reminder that, although spring was imminent, winter was not yet done. As he made his way through the evening crowds, the cold wind compelled Paice to button his jacket and pull up the collar around his ears. He was warmed by the thought of the food he would soon be savouring at Kouzina tis Amalias – Amalia's Kitchen – the homely and hospitable Greek place around the corner from the house where he had a room.

It was a 20-minute walk, and, as he approached, he could see the light splashing out onto the wet pavement, a beacon to guide in the famished passer-by. Paice set a direct course for it. He pushed open the door and paused briefly as he looked around at the mostly empty tables. He preferred to sit at the back, which was where he headed. The warmth of the surroundings and the aromas of Amalia's cooking set him at ease. This was a place where he could push to one side the pressures and memories that dictated the pace of his life, a rare haven of relaxation. His visits here caused him to reflect on how infrequently he attained that happy state.

It may have been Amalia's kitchen and her name may have been over the door, but it was Philo, her husband who ran the place, a fact of which he was never reluctant to remind anyone who was disposed to listen. He continually complained about the burdens of command, but the impartial observer might conclude that running the place appeared to constitute a less demanding role than cooking and serving the food and attending to the requirements of the customers.

The scene that played out before Paice was a familiar one. Nikki, the couple's daughter, was busy wiping tables and tidying up the menus. She smiled at him as he walked through. He could see Amalia out at the back, wiping her brow as she clattered around in the heat of the kitchen. Philo, an improbable Zeus, wielded his Olympian authority from the table nearest the till. It was his customary station where he sat drinking coffee, reading the paper and sizing up the patrons as they entered. Occasionally, he would look over his shoulder and issue a thoroughly superfluous piece of advice to Amalia as she strove, unaided, to complete the outstanding orders.

And that was where he sat tonight. He waved to Paice with a casual flick of the wrist. "Good evening, young man. It is a great pleasure to see you again." He looked over his shoulder and shouted something in Greek to Amalia to announce Paice's arrival. She came through from the kitchen, threw up her arms and beamed at him.

"Lovely to see you, Nick." She kissed him on both cheeks and ushered him to his usual table.

She flicked her fingers at Nikki. "Get Mr Paice a glass of wine." In the background, Philo was shaking his head, certain that Amalia was making too much fuss, and muttering something in Greek to that effect. Amalia turned to him and snapped back an acerbic riposte. He shrugged his shoulders and held up his hands in a wounded gesture that implied an apology for daring to assume the authority to question her conduct. He smiled and nodded at Paice. Paice grinned back. He always enjoyed the verbal exchange of fire that constituted a significant part of the couple's relationship. He had also long since realised upon whose shoulders the fate of the restaurant rested, whatever Philo liked to believe.

"Tonight you will have tomato keftedes to start and then soutzoukakia and rice." Paice was not inclined to argue. As Nikki placed a dish of olives alongside the glass of wine, Amalia declared: "This you will enjoy." There was a finality about her statement that Paice knew was fully justified. He did not doubt for one moment that she was right.

An hour later, his meal finished and Amalia's prediction fulfilled, Paice felt satisfied and more relaxed than he had all day. The restaurant was now empty and Nikki had flipped over the sign hanging in the door telling late arrivals that the establishment was now closed. She switched off some of the lights. Paice ordered two large brandies and invited Philo to sit with him. He knew that Amalia would fuss around them, but she never touched alcohol and he knew that she would not join them. "Come, Nikki, leave them to their talk. It is what men do best," she declared with a hint of contempt. Philo waved his hand dismissively at her as he took the chair opposite Paice.

"I saw your story in the paper this morning, Nick, about the St George crash. It is a bad business for many people." The Greek took a cheroot from a packet and slid it between his lips. The gas hissed from his lighter as he carefully applied the flame to the tip, and the red and orange glow intensified as he pulled on it and drew the smoke into his mouth. The law prohibited smoking in restaurants but this was Philo's fiefdom, and here Philo's word was law, regardless of what was on the statute books.

Nick sipped his drink and nodded. "You know the area where they operate, Philo?"

"Yes, I know it. It has its share of thieves and gypsies, but this does not seem – how can I put it? – home grown. It is very sophisticated. It is possible that Russian gangsters are involved, but this politician who is mentioned ..." He paused. "Surely no British MP would be so corrupt, and even if he were he would not become involved with such people."

"You may be right. I would think that Sir Oswald would have been a little more selective than to associate with outright gangsters. No, I reckon that the people who pulled this one off were able to present a very solid and respectable outward appearance. That rather points the finger at dodgy financiers who are not satisfied with the pot of gold at the end of the rainbow – they want the rainbow as well."

Philo looked thoughtful as he rotated the cheroot between thumb and forefinger, gently abrading the accumulated ash on the lip of the now empty dish from which Nick had eaten his olives. "I may be able to assist you. Perhaps you should speak to my cousin. He is engaged in various businesses back home. He may have certain interests in this area. He will certainly have a view about what has been happening . Perhaps he is better informed than many."

"That might be very helpful, Philo. How do I contact him?"

"I shall speak to him to ascertain that he is willing to talk to you. Then perhaps he will get in touch. In return, Nick, I ask a small favour. After you make contact, I wish to hear no more of the matter. I do not wish to be involved. For the sake of your health, I would suggest that you also should not look too closely at this activity, but..." He hesitated and studied the hot tip of his cheroot. "Well, it is your job. I am sure that you can take care of yourself and require no advice from me. I make no promises, but I shall speak to my cousin. Leave it with me."

They talked further until they had finished their drinks. As Paice rose to leave, Amalia kissed him goodbye and handed him a paper package. "For Jessica," she said, squeezing his hand. He said his goodnights and left the comfort of the restaurant for the chilly walk home. The parcel of warm pastries gave up a delicious bouquet of spice and honey, and he looked forward to the smile that would greet the gift.

It was a 10-minute walk back to his lodgings. As he entered the front door, Mrs Evans, his landlady, popped her head out of her room at the foot of the stairs. "Good evening, Mr Paice. I hope you have had a good day." It was her standard greeting whenever he arrived home, and although he occupied only one room upstairs and had exclusive use of the adjacent bathroom, to him it was home. He had lived here for two years, and the arrangement suited him very well.

"Is Jessica still up," he asked, hoping that, even at 9pm, the answer would be yes. However, no answer was needed. The smiling face of a small child appeared from behind her mother. "Hallo, Mr Nick," she said with a giggle. But the smile was not quite right.

Paice knelt and held out the sweet-smelling parcel. "I have something for you." She left the security of her mother's skirt and approached him shyly. And the gait was not quite right, either. She looked up at her mother who nodded her approval that she should take it.

"What do you say to Mr Paice, Jessie?"

"Thank you, Mr Nick." She took the parcel and limped back into her mother's room.

Paice smiled and headed for the stairs. He looked through into Mrs Evans's room and could see Jessica staring with delight at the exposed contents of the parcel, Only her indecision over which pastry to choose was causing her to pause before realising the ecstasy of sinking her teeth into the honey and nut titbit.

He shook his head in sadness. It had been two years previously when he had been passing the house that the child had run into the road and been hit by a speeding car. When he first got to her, she had stopped breathing. Using his basic skills in resuscitation, he had blown life-giving air into her lungs. With a cough she had gasped her way back from the abyss. He had then cradled the broken little body in his arms as Mrs Evans had collapsed in distress. The journey to the hospital in the ambulance and the hours spent comforting the heartbroken mother had seemed the right thing to do. He had left only when Jessica was out of immediate danger, but he was back at the house the next evening to ask how she was.

Over a cup of tea he told Mrs Evans that he had been in the street the previous evening to view an apartment in the area. She had suggested that he might like the room upstairs in a house that was too large for her and her daughter. He moved in within a week and had been there since. The arrangement was mutually ideal. He had exactly what he needed – modest accommodation in a hospitable atmosphere – and Mrs Evans, a single mother, received a much-needed weekly income from the rent.

The weeks and months after the accident had been difficult, at times had verged on the impossible for Mrs Evans. The consequences of the accident would probably be with the child for the remainder of her life – her leg seemed unlikely to mend completely and it was feared that the damaged facial nerve might for ever affect her smile. Paice was always ready to console and support. It was rare for him to find an interest that was unrelated to his ambitions and to the callous demands of the career he had chosen to pursue.

The blokes at the office guessed that his principal aim was to get Mrs Evans into bed – she was a middle-aged woman and was not unattractive. But – and he, too, was surprised by it – they were wrong. Such a motive had never entered his head. They could not accept that Paice, the hard-bitten newsman for whom the story always came first and human emotions and entanglements followed so far behind that they were out of sight, could exhibit the altruism of caring for two strangers. But it was so. The man who had knelt beside a helpless child that evening was a stranger, both to the child and to himself.

Paice had been troubled at first by the emotional attachment. But, as time passed, he had given up analysing the process and settled into the role. It had evolved into a unexceptional part of his life and he allowed its presence to occupy no more than the occasional passing thought. And it was only a passing thought. He was instinctively reluctant to dwell for too long on the fact that while these two people were held in his affection, he was held in theirs. It was as though the stranger was constantly with him these days. It was a stranger he made no effort to acknowledge, but one whose presence he was prepared to tolerate.

In his room, he hit the key on his mobile phone and called the news desk. "Hi, Bryce. How's life putting the boot in to you tonight?"

Bob Bryce was the night news editor. He leaned back in his chair and swung it 180 degrees. "With about the usual vicious intensity, mate. How about yerself?" He blew smoke at the fluorescent strip light that hung suspended above his head.

"I decided not to file on the Bellamy story. I winkled him out of a Commons Committee, but he would not comment – in fact, he said, and I quote, 'No fucking comment.'"

Bryce tut-tutted. "Such language, Nick. What's your instinct on this one?"

"He is definitely rattled, which means he's worried, which means he's hiding something. We need to do a bit more digging." He thought back to Philo's promise at the restaurant. "I have got a line of inquiry under way. I've got a couple of other irons in the fire" – more of an exaggeration than a lie, but it would keep Bryce off his back – "so I'll be back on to it tomorrow."

"OK, but tread cautiously. Bellamy's a mate of the proprietor and Williamson was in here earlier reminding me of the fact." Jack Williamson was the Editor, and when the proprietor, Sir Gavin Hartington, wanted something to happen, Williamson made sure it did. It was the way he kept his job, a technique that two previous and fairly short-term predecessors in office had failed to grasp.

"Listen, mate. I only write the stories. If I write them, they stand up. If they stand up, and they are good, we should run them. But that's not my decision. But if I give you a good story and you don't print it, I shall be seriously pissed off, particularly if I then see it on the front page of the Chronicle."

There was silence as Bryce contemplated whether to try to placate Paice with an assurance that would be spotted instantly as another lie. He thought better of it. Anyway, he took pride in being a straight talking Aussie and while he had spent a lot of time in the bush, he was genetically incapable of beating around it.

"I know, Nick." He dropped his voice. "Just remember, mate – you think you are out there in the real world. You're not. The real world as far as you and I are concerned is back here, and I have to live in it. Just write the stories and I will do my best. If it's good enough, they might just print it, even if it puts Hartington off his breakfast."

"OK, Bob. I know you'll do your best. Anyway, what else is happening in the world?"

"We're leading the front page with the Government's U-turn on cutting unemployment benefit. Police in Manchester have broken up a big drug dealing network. The Hackney couple have gone down for life at the Bailey for kicking the life out of their two-year-old – the bastards. Hope they have a good time in prison when their new room mates find out what they've been up to. And there was a pile up on the M6 in the fog – two dead. All the usual. Oh, and I have saved the best till last. Someone has nicked a dunny cart."

Paice waited for Bryce's laughter to subside. "A dunny cart? What do you mean?"

"A shit wagon – the lorry they use to pump out the cesspits. And this one was full to the brim. I know the world is going completely nuts, but for Christ's sake, who would want to nick a lorry loaded with shit?"

"I don't know, Bob, but I reckon you've found your front page lead. But seriously, what happened?"

"Seems the driver had just finished up at his last customer of the day and was headed back to the depot. He walked round to the back of the lorry to check his pipes were stowed right. Next thing it's disappearing down the road at what passes for a high speed for one of those rigs. Took the driver 20 minutes and three phone calls to convince the cops that it wasn't a joke."

"Life is never short of surprises, Bob. See you tomorrow." He hung up, smiling and shaking his head.

Chapter 6

Paice was standing naked in the news room of the Mercury. Everyone was watching him. For some unfathomable reason, he was powerless, in spite of a desperate wish to do so, to turn and leave. He was trapped, glued to the spot. He struggled to cover his nakedness. Then he heard his phone ringing. He knew he had to answer it, but his plight had reduced him to paralysis. Gradually, he emerged into consciousness as the dream left him. He cast around in the darkness trying to make sense of where he was. The phone persisted. Suddenly, he was awake and reaching for it as it rang, hummed and vibrated on the bedside table.

He fumbled as he hit the key to answer the call. "Yeah?" His voice did not make it through the mouthful of cotton wool that sleep had contrived to place there. He swallowed and tried again. "Hello?"

"Hi Nick. Sorry to wake you." It was Bob Bryce.

Paice knew instantly that it would have to be something significant. "That's OK, Bob. I was only dozing. What's up?"

"They've found the dunny cart. You had better get down there." He gave Paice the location. "I've sent a cab for you. It'll be outside by the time you get your strides on."

A little over half an hour later, Paice was standing outside the magnificent home of Sir Oswald Bellamy. Or it would have been magnificent had it not been for the nauseating stench of sewage. The huge bulk of the cesspit tanker loomed alarmingly close to the front of the house. It's progress across what had undoubtedly previously been the green velvet of a meticulously tended lawn could be traced by the trail of tyre tracks, flattened shrubs and ploughed flower beds.

The police were there in some strength. As were the fire and rescue squad. It was they who faced the distasteful job of pulling the tanker clear of the property. Paice found the most senior copper he could spot and identified himself.

"It seems that someone had it in for the occupant..."

"Sir Oswald Bellamy," Paice interjected.

"I could not possibly confirm ..."

"Look, I know him and I know this is where he lives, so you are not giving away any state secrets."

The Inspector nodded. "Well, off the record, it looks as though Sir Oswald has upset someone and they've driven the tanker close enough to his house to knock out his front lounge window, push that bloody great hose through the hole and then empty the contents of the tanker into his home."

"Very nice," Paice observed.

"Yes, not very," the officer said, holding a handkerchief to his face to counter the stink. "He must really have upset someone."

"Oh, he has, officer. He certainly has. Do you know where he is – he surely cannot still be inside?"

"They've got a quite substantial summer house in the grounds of the property. One of my men escorted Sir Oswald and his family to it. They are in a state of shock at the moment, so I cannot let you go in."

"Look, I'm a family friend," Paice lied. "I'd like to see if there is anything I can do for them."

"Wait here and I'll see if I can get in touch to ask them whether they will see you." The radio on his lapel crackled and another patrol car arrived on the scene. Preoccupied with deploying the occupants, he promptly forgot about Paice. With the copper's back turned, Paice dropped into the shadows of a shrubbery and made for the side of the house.

He unlatched the gate that opened on to the grounds at the rear. A small fountain spurted and spluttered in a pond sunk into an extensive patio area running out from French windows in the rear of the house. The doors were open, swinging lazily in the breeze. That same breeze carried the overpowering reek of effluent from within. Paice approached to look inside. The lights were on. The scene that greeted him made him draw back, and not only because of the stench. He looked in disgust at the ankle-deep lake of human waste that shimmered as it spread over Bellamy's best quality Wilton.

Holding a handkerchief to his mouth, he swung round and almost stumbled over a sun lounger that was hidden in the shadows. Thirty yards away, he could see the lights in the windows of the summer house. Inside, someone was moving around.

He crossed the lawn and stepped up onto the boarded verandah. It creaked underfoot as he walked softly to the door. He tapped on the glazed panel. A grotesque image, stretched and distorted by the swirls and flourishes of the patterned glass, appeared. Paice could just make out the outline of Oswald Bellamy.

The door opened. It took Bellamy several seconds to recognise Paice, and several more to conquer his disbelief at his sudden presence. He stared at Paice, his lips quivering in anger.

"You bastard. You absolute fucking bastard." He lunged forward, but Paice stepped deftly to one side, deflecting the onslaught. Bellamy carried on under the momentum of his charge, tripped and landed heavily in the grass. Paice bent down, grabbed Bellamy by the arm and pulled him upright. Bellamy shook him off. "Are you behind this disgusting act? Did you set this up? Is there nothing you won't stoop to just to get a story?" He was shaking with rage and anguish in equal measure. Paice again took his arm and helped him to his feet.

"You can rest assured that neither I nor any other journalist was involved," Paice said. "I would not wish this on anyone." He summoned up as much sincerity as he was capable of. It wasn't enough. Bellamy snorted in disbelief.

"I don't think there can be much doubt, Sir Oswald, that this is the work of one or more of the people who were fleeced by your land company."

Bellamy's ire surged again. "It is not my company, and I did not fleece them," he bellowed angrily.

"What on earth is happening out here?" The slim figure of Lady Bellamy stood silhouetted in the doorway. "Ossie, what are you doing? And who is this?" She stepped out on to the verandah. Paice stepped forward, holding out his hand. The light was poor, but there was something familiar about her. She was quite a bit younger than her husband – 15 years at a guess, Paice reckoned.

"I'm Nick Paice. I'm with the Mercury. How do you do, Lady Bellamy?" She hesitantly took his hand in response.

"Don't shake that bastard's hand. He was probably the one who got us into this," Sir Oswald growled through clenched teeth.

"I think we know who got us into this mess, Ossie. Calm down and come inside. Please come in Mr Paice."

The summer house was comfortably furnished. In the far corner, two teenagers – Paice guessed they were the son and daughter – were hunched over a handheld computer game, teasing each other over their respective scores. They did not seem particularly stressed. Typical kids, thought Paice. It was not cool to appear to be bothered by events, no matter how earth shattering. Bellamy slumped into a cane armchair and reached for his drink. "You know the situation, Maria. You know it is not down to me."

The light was much better in the room. Paice looked at her again, more closely. He had a good memory for faces. It annoyed him that he could not place her.

"Can you tell me what happened?" Paice asked, looking at his watch. He had missed the last edition of that day's paper. That meant that the story would be done to death on the television news before the Mercury hit the streets again. He might yet be lucky, though. In the cold light of day the Bellamys would almost certainly decide against giving interviews. This could be the last opportunity anyone would get to speak to them. He knew that he was fortunate to have got this far and to have beaten the opposition.

Bellamy shook his head. He looked just about all in. Lady Bellamy, however, did not. Paice studied her body language. He guessed that, although Oswald was the big shot politician, this lady was the stronger half of the partnership. Paice felt a growing respect for her. He had met her only a few minutes before, but he knew that a woman who could remain composed after all that had happened was pretty special. Some people exuded strength and resilience, and, with her calm authority, Maria Bellamy seemed to be one of them.

"It happened just after 2am." She instinctively looked at her watch. "Our bedroom is at the back of the house. I was awoken by a noise. The police asked me, but I could not say what it was. Then I heard the glass being smashed. It took me a while to wake Ossie. I ran to the children's rooms and woke them."

"You did not go down to see what the noise was?"

"No, Mr Paice, I did not. And nor did Ossie. We all got back into our bedroom and locked the door. Friends of ours had a similar experience when a gang broke in and terrorised them – did unspeakable things. And we have had our own frightening experience, which is why our bedroom door is reinforced. It would take an army to break it down. The important thing was that we were safe. All the rest can be replaced."

She looked across at the children. Bellamy put down his drink and took his wife's hand, squeezing it in a gesture meant to offer comfort and support. She forced a smile at him.

"There was silence, and then we heard a car drive away. We waited for what seemed like an age, and still there was silence. Then we realised that the alarm had not been tripped. We guessed – hoped – that that meant there was no one actually in the house."

"You must have been terrified." Paice wanted to put the word in her mouth. He knew it would be the headline.

"Terrified, Mr Paice? Yes, we were terrified. It is one's worst nightmare – waking up and knowing someone is in your house."

Paice nodded, more in satisfaction that she had used the word "nightmare" – more good headline material – than in agreement with what she had said.

"I decided we should risk opening the door." Bellamy had regained his composure. He stared hard at Paice. It was not a look that conveyed affection. "That was when the stench hit us. We did not know what to make of it. I told Maria and the kids to stay put and started to go down the stairs. There's a switch at the top of the stairs to turn on the downstairs lights. That was when I saw that....." He shook his head, lost for words. "Anyway, I called the police and we got out of the house by the outside stairs from our bedroom balcony."

Paice stared back at Bellamy. "Well, Sir Oswald, I knew that you had made a lot of people very angry – very poor, as well and therefore perhaps understandably angry. They hold you responsible for the biggest fraud in years. But it takes a particular type of anger to inflict this upon your family."

"I think that you should tell Mr Paice the truth, Oswald. It is not fair that you should be subjected to such hatred."

"We keep these matters to ourselves, Maria. Tell Mr Paice and by the morning the world will know. Then what?"

"At least the world will know the truth and we will not be subjected to this appalling treatment. Anyway, as I have told you, the more people who know the truth, the safer we shall be." She turned and crossed the room to the children.

Paice sensed that the story was about to take an interesting twist. "Anything you tell me will be off the record, Sir Oswald."

"Off the record, Paice? What does that mean? You know and I know that nothing is ever off the record."

"All I can say is that whatever you tell me, I shall tell only Sir Gavin. He will decide what shall be done. I would not trust me if I were you, I admit, but Sir Gavin is a friend of yours, I believe. I am sure that you would trust him."

Bellamy stared at Paice. Then he nodded. "I have known Gavin Hartington since we were at school together. Come outside," he said, his voice lowered. "This is not something I want the children to hear."

A chill April breeze was blowing from the north east. Paice buttoned his coat, but Bellamy did not seem to feel the cold. Paice guessed that the traumatic events of the preceding hours had probably left the man feeling insensitive to the physical discomfort of a mere cold wind.

Chairs and a table occupied one end of the verandah. Bellamy nodded at them and Paice sat down.

"I must ask you to believe that I did not know what I was getting into. I can promise you that I was certain that St George Land was bona fide."

"But at some point you must have realised that you were involved with something crooked, Sir Oswald."

"Yes, but not at first."

"Then why, when you did find out, didn't you tell the authorities – the Trade and Industry Secretary. He must be a pal of yours and it is his territory. At the very least you should have got out."

"That is the problem. I cannot get out. Believe me, I would have done so had that been possible."

"You said 'not at first', so when did you realise that you were involved in something dodgy?"

"A constituent came to see me at my weekly surgery – you know what I mean by 'surgery'?"

"Of course. I know you're no doctor. It's the session you hold in the locality where constituents bring you their problems and you tell them what you can do to help them."

Bellamy nodded. "Yes. This chap had sunk his retirement nest egg into St George's, and when he needed the cash they told him he couldn't have it. The poor fellow was beside himself with worry."

"So what did you do?"

"I phoned the investment manager – at least, the man who was alleged to hold that position. I was told that he had left the company. I asked for his deputy. I was told he had no deputy. I asked to speak to anyone who was dealing with the investors' funds. I was told that no one was available.

"Later that day, several other MPs contacted me saying that their constituents could not get access to their money. That was when I started to get really worried.

"I had been dealing primarily with the person I thought was the managing director and, occasionally, the finance director. The names of other directors were on the headed notepaper. I did not know any of them, but I had heard of the MD, a man by the name of Giles Beaufort. I invited him to the House of Commons. We had tea on the Terrace. I told him of my suspicions and said that in the absence of proof that everything was above board, I would be expressing my concerns to the appropriate authorities. After all, as I said to him, it was my reputation that was at stake if anything was fishy."

"And?"

"He said that he, too, was a bit worried about how things were going, but he assured me that there was nothing illegal about the venture. He made a phone call. When he had finished, he said that he had called a meeting of the directors for the following day at the office in the City. It was essential that I should attend so that I could express my concerns and be reassured."

"You attended the meeting?"

"Yes, I went along. But the place was almost deserted. The reception area was empty – none of the fancy furniture that had been there on my previous visits. There were no staff about. Beaufort came out to meet me. His explanation was that they were moving office but were not ready at the new place."

"You believed him?"

"No, I did not, but I did not say so at that point. We took the lift to the third floor to the board room. It was empty. When I asked where the other directors were, he said that they had been delayed and would be arriving soon.

"That was when I blew my top. I told him that he was telling me a pack of lies and that I would be reporting everything to the City of London fraud squad. By this time I was very worried. I could see that I had been sucked into something very serious. I got up to leave and he put a hand on my shoulder. 'There are a couple of people you should meet, first,' he said."

The dawn was beginning to seep into the eastern sky. Just recounting the events was clearly taking a toll on Bellamy, and the pale light of the breaking morning did nothing to improve his complexion.

He fidgeted nervously. "I need a drink," he said. "Can I get you one?" Paice nodded. "Scotch, please."

Bellamy went back into the summer house. Paice fished into his breast pocket. He took out the tiny digital recorder that was his constant and very unobtrusive companion. It was running OK. The display assured him that he still had plenty of recording time left. This would be the best story he had uncovered in a long time. It was dynamite. He felt a sense of relief that at last something had come good for him. And that he was no longer wholly dependent upon Burkins.

Bellamy emerged from the summer house and put Paice's drink on the table. "Sorry, no ice." Paice smiled to himself. Across the lawns the police and fire service were trying to sort out the mess that had been Bellamy's home. The stink of sewage hung in the early morning air. And Bellamy was up to his neck in something that could see him in prison. Yet here he was concerned that there was no ice for his "guest".

"So who were these people?"

"Uh?" Bellamy looked puzzled.

"You said that this bloke Beaufort said he wanted you to meet someone."

"Oh, yes. He told me to wait and left the room. A few minutes later, two other characters came in. One was very smartly dressed – expensive suit, silk tie and crisp white shirt.

The other was completely the opposite – T shirt, zip-up padded jacket, jeans, and those sports-type shoes – "

"Trainers," Paice prompted.

"If you say so. The one in the suit did the talking. He did not look English, and when he spoke his accent confirmed it."

"What did he say?"

"He said 'I understand from Mr Beaufort that you are unhappy about our little arrangement?' I asked him who he was. He said his name was 'unimportant', but he was an associate of Mr Beaufort's. 'I take care of any problems. Mr Beaufort thinks that you might be a problem. Are you a problem?'

"I told him as plainly as I could that I thought the whole endeavour was crooked and that I was getting out of it. Furthermore, I would take everything I knew to the authorities. I said that I was a Member of Parliament and a personal friend of the Prime Minister.

"At that point, he turned to the other man and said something in a language I did not understand. The other man smiled and unzipped his jacket. He held it open. Under one armpit he had a holster in which was a handgun of some sort. Under the other was a sheath carrying a large knife.

"Up to that point I had been worried about my reputation. Now, I was frightened for my life. Then he said: 'You say that you are a Member of Parliament, Sir Bellamy. Where we come from we use them as target practice.' He translated his words to the other man and they both burst out laughing.

"I asked if they were planning to kill me. 'Of course not, Sir Bellamy. At least, not at the moment and provided you continue to cooperate. You are far too valuable to us. You are the respectable face of our business – it is a face that will keep the enforcement authorities at bay.' He made no bones of the fact that this was my job, why I had been brought in – ensnared – in the first place.

"Then, in a calm but sinister tone, he said that not everyone was indispensible. He warned me that I would be ill advised to say anything to anyone. 'After all, Sir Bellamy, you have a wife and two children. You would not want to put their lives at risk.'

"I asked him what he meant about putting my family at risk. He said that if I were to breach what he called 'the confidentiality of our commercial arrangements' certain people might be greatly displeased. 'They could make their displeasure apparent in the most forthright way, Sir Bellamy. It might put the safety of your family at unnecessary risk.' I realised that he was making it absolutely clear that if I blew the whistle on him and his fellow gangsters, Maria and the children would be hurt, perhaps even killed."

"And you took the threat seriously?"

"Look, Paice, they were deadly serious. They knew where I lived. They went on to tell me the schools the children attended, the hairdresser Maria used and where she shopped. And to prove it they had photographs of them at all those locations. I am realistic enough to know that it is impossible permanently to protect someone from that sort of evil. Believe me, Paice, it was no empty threat.

"He said that the other thug was very good with a gun. 'But his preference is to use the knife. He feels it is so much more personal. He is very keen on job satisfaction.' I was absolutely bloody terrified. And they knew it. I got out of there as fast as I could to ring Maria to make sure that she was OK, although I could not bring myself to tell her what had happened. As I left I could hear them laughing and joking."

"Did you speak to Beaufort again?"

"Not on that day and not since that day. In fact, he disappeared. A subsequent examination of the company accounts showed that he had been systematically syphoning off cash into offshore accounts. He was very clever. The money has disappeared and it will be impossible to trace it, or, in other words, to recover it."

"So did he take the lot?"

"No. He pocketed about £20 million."

"But that's only about 20 per cent. of what's gone missing – stolen – so where is the rest?"

"I have no idea. If I had, I would be telling the authorities so that the money could be recovered. Do you really think that Beaufort would have turned those two thugs on me if I had had any part in all this? He only did that because I wanted to bring the authorities in to investigate."

"Have they contacted you since?"

"Oh yes, indeed. That evening, I got home to find a stranger waiting for me. He had told Maria that we had arranged to meet at my house. He pretended to be slightly annoyed that I was not there to receive him as had been planned. She gave him a drink and kept him company until I arrived.

"In Maria's presence I apologised for what I thought must have been a misunderstanding, but I knew immediately, of course, that this man's presence was related to my earlier ordeal. When we were alone he said he had a message for me. He was polite and even charming. His manner was relaxed and polite but laced with menace and, because of that, all the more chilling. He spoke with an accent that I placed as central European. The message was that I should confirm that I knew what I had to do and was prepared to do it. The implication was all too clear. They knew where I lived and this was a demonstration of just how easily they could get to my family.

"I tried to appeal to him – begged him – not to threaten my family. But he said that he was merely a messenger. Had I received the message? Did I understand what was required of me – to comply with their demand that I carry on fronting up this criminal scam?

"I told him that he should leave. I just wanted him out of my house. And I threatened to call the police if he did not go. He said that I was making a serious mistake and that I would be hearing from them."

"And he left?"

"Yes, he left. Maria could see that I was upset, but I did not tell her the purpose of the visit. We went to bed. I was asleep when I felt Maria shaking me. I opened my eyes to see a torch shining a light on the blade of a knife being held at her throat. Somehow, the man had got into the house, but this time he was not alone. I turned on the bedside light. The man holding the knife was the one who had been in the office earlier in the day.

"The other one – the one who had been waiting for me when I had returned home – sat on the bed beside me. He spoke with that same polite manner. 'You see, Sir Oswald, our employers are very serious about this matter. They have asked me to impress upon you the need for you to do as they tell you. Keep your mouth shut until they want you to speak, and then say only what they will tell you to say.'

"I looked at Maria. She was terrified – and so, Mr Paice, was I. The thug had his hand over her mouth and the knife at her throat. 'You have to agree,' said the messenger. 'You have no choice. Do you want your children to wake in the morning to find their mother dead in – what shall we say? – unpleasant circumstances. And discover their father swinging by his neck over the staircase?'

"'They would grow up believing that you had killed their mother and committed suicide. That would not give them the best start in life. It would be a burden for them to carry for the rest of their lives. They would grow old cursing your memory. That is not what a father wishes of his children. That is, of course, assuming that your children are alive in the morning. You might go down in the public eye as the man who slaughtered his entire family. And all that would be so unnecessary.'

"You can see how desperate I am, Paice. I have told you all this in confidence so that you will understand that

I am as much of a victim as all those poor people who have lost their money at the hands of these gangsters. It's the stories you have been writing about me that have provoked whoever did this vile act." He waved his hand towards the house. "I have told you so that you will ease up in what you write about me."

Paice did his best to appear sympathetic. True he felt some sympathy for Bellamy, or, more precisely for his wife and kids. But his mind was preoccupied with how good the story would look on the front page. Hartington was the owner and Bellamy was his friend. The question was whether the owner would cut his friend loose and run one of the best stories of the year. And fuck Bellamy and his tale of hard luck.

Bellamy looked broken up. He was terrified for the safety of his wife and children. They might even be murdered by the thugs who had Bellamy by the throat. But that was Bellamy's problem. He had all the contacts, the money, the influence. Paice had seen children slaughtered in other parts of the world. Where was Bellamy when they needed help, when some drug-crazed savage with a blood lust and a sharp machete was hacking into their defenceless, terrified and innocent bodies? Where was he when some so-called freedom fighter nonchalantly emptied the magazine of his AK47 into a huddled group of villagers?

He was probably poncing around the corridors of power in an expensive suit pushing the case of the oil companies or the arms manufacturers who stood to lose if the Government backed the wrong side. Paice had written enough stories from bloodstained locations to let people know what was going on. Bellamy did not heed then what Paice was putting in front of his eyes, did nothing to get the people with the power to act to step in and stop the madness. But now he was in trouble and he wanted Paice's help.

"So how did it end?" Paice asked.

"How did it end?"

"Yeah, how'd you get rid of them?"

"Well, the bastard had one thing right. I did not have a choice. I said that I would go along with it. I am convinced that the man with the knife looked disappointed that he was being deprived of the chance to use it. The one who did the talking simply got up, said 'Good. You have made the right decision. Do not change your mind, or....' He left the sentence unfinished and they left."

The door of the summer house opened and Maria Bellamy stepped on to the verandah. She had Bellamy's mobile telephone in her hand. "It's the Prime Minister, Ossie. They woke him to tell him what had happened. He wants to speak to you. He is sending a car for us and says we can stay at his London flat."

Bellamy took the phone and moved out of Paice's earshot.

If Bellamy could pull down that sort of support, Paice felt even less inclined to help him.

Chapter 7

It was light enough by now to see across the garden. Lady Bellamy walked Paice back the way he had come. He remained impressed with her strength of character in dealing with the traumatic event that had turned her and her family's life upside down. She remained cool and very much in control. He felt what was for him a rare pang of sympathy for the misfortunes of someone who inhabited the privileged stratosphere of the social order.

"It must have been very frightening for you," he said, not sure quite what other consolation to offer.

"You mean all this?" She waved a hand towards the house. The stench had not diminished.

"I was thinking more of the intruders who broke in to threaten your husband. They clearly meant business. There's nothing worse than physical violence when it involves intruders in your own home, the place where you think you're safe."

"I have faced worse." There was no emotion or feeling in the words, just a plain statement of fact. She stopped and held out her hand to shake his. "I have to get back to the children," she said. "Good bye, Mr Paice. I hope that you will not make life more difficult for us than it already is."

Paice was not about to make any promises or give any guarantees. He wanted to get the story on the front page, but he knew that he had to get it past Gavin Hartington first.

He nodded without giving any commitment and shook her hand. He watched her walk away. "Do I know you from somewhere, Lady Bellamy?"

She paused and looked back. "I am sure that, with your powers of observation, if you did you would remember."

Paice made his way out of the property. Outside, the police had established a cordon, and the TV crews and a crowd of newspaper reporters were being kept firmly on the other side of it. He felt a surge of satisfaction that he had got there first. Twenty minutes later he was in a taxi and heading home. A bath, some breakfast and an early meeting with Hartington and Jack Williamson, the editor, were his priorities. But as the cab bumped its way back to London, Paice was still searching the past for some reference to Maria Bellamy. He was more certain than ever that he knew her. She was probably right. If the memory was there, it would work its way to the surface in due course.

He rang Williamson at home, outlined what had happened and asked for the meeting. Williamson rang him back within five minutes to tell him to be in Hartington's office at 10am. That was good. The first editorial conference – where all the major players examined the options for the next day's paper – was at 11. If Hartington agreed to run the story, it would give Paice plenty of time to write it – not that it needed much writing. A story this good would write itself.

At 10 o'clock on the dot, Williamson and Paice were waiting outside Hartington's office pacing around his secretary's desk. Her phone rang to tell her that she should send them in. Sir Gavin was sitting behind a desk that to Paice possessed all the daunting presence of the west front of St Paul's cathedral. Its carved, confrontational classicism cried command and comply. As soon as you saw it, you knew that the man behind it was giving the orders. And that you were taking them. It brooked no argument or contradiction.

"Come in. Take a seat. I'll get some coffee." He picked up his phone and told his secretary to get it organised. "OK, tell me what we are dealing with here."

Williamson began to speak. "We believe that..."

Hartington cut him off. "Sorry, Jack. I think it's best if I hear it from the horse's mouth." He looked straight at Paice. "Shoot."

Paice desperately wanted to get his story on the front page, but he knew better than to pull any stunts where Hartington was concerned. He set out all the facts. He played a short excerpt from his digital recorder where Bellamy had recounted the terror of being woken by his midnight visitors. "The story is there, Sir Gavin, and it is one hell of a story. The decision to be taken is how we write it."

"Give me the options."

Williamson took over. He was the editor, and the paper's content was under his day-to-day overall control. But he knew that what the proprietor wanted, the proprietor normally got. And on a story that involved a personal friend, the proprietor might want something different from what the news instincts of the two professionals sitting in front of him told them was the best story.

"My preference, Sir Gavin, would be to come clean. We write the story with no punches pulled, tell the world how Sir Oswald has had a gun put to his head, and expose the crooks behind the scam." He shot a sideways glance at Paice and was unsurprised to see him nodding in agreement. They had coordinated their approach over cups of tea in the staff canteen half an hour earlier.

Hartington massaged his right temple and looked out of the window at the serried landscape of the roofs and chimneys of the city. "And what happens to Oswald and his family?"

Paice shrugged his shoulders. "They will have to take their chance. This is a great story, we have got it all to ourselves, and it will sell papers."

"And are we condemning the Bellamy family to death? Oswald has been warned that if he opens his mouth, retribution will follow."

Paice shook his head. "I don't think so, Sir Gavin. Once it is all out in the open, my guess is that the rats will scurry for their holes and Sir Oswald will hear nothing more from them."

"But there are no guarantees, are there?"

Paice paused before answering. "There are no guarantees."

Williamson leaned forward. "Would we be having this conversation about anyone else, Sir Gavin, or would we just run the story?"

For a fraction of a second Hartington looked uncomfortable and then annoyed. He rarely interfered in editorial policy, but – and this was unsaid but was a consideration of pachydermal proportions – it was his newspaper, and everything flowed from that simple fact.

"I asked for options. So what else is there?"

Paice remained silent. He wanted no part in watering down the best story that the Mercury would carry this year just because Hartington and Bellamy had once shared their tuck box in the dorm half a century ago.

Williamson had a well-deserved reputation for backing his reporters in tight situations, especially good reporters like Paice. But he also knew that, as the editor, he had a loyalty to the proprietor. Choosing between them was the part of the job he disliked most. He was glad it occurred only rarely.

"The only other story is the one that is already running on the TV news and that will be in the evening newspapers 12 hours before we hit the news stands."

"Except that we still have an exclusive."

"Which is?" Williamson's tone was unable to hide his growing frustration.

"Which is the exclusive interview that Paice has secured with Sir Oswald and Lady Bellamy telling of their distress and how they hope that the police will soon find the culprits. I am sure that you can get some good quotes out of what he told you – without, of course, writing anything that will jeopardise the family's safety. They've gone to ground and are giving no interviews. We have that to ourselves, and that will give us a nice fresh angle. Unless you can persuade me otherwise, Jack, that is the way we should handle this one. Thank you, gentlemen."

The meeting was over. Williamson and Paice got up to go. "Jack, please hold back for a moment, will you. And, Paice..."

"Yes." Paice stopped by the door to look back.

"Well done. It is a good story. Not for the first time the Mercury has reason to be grateful to you. And if you can find out anything about the scum behind all this, that would make for a very good exposé. Jack will give you any resources you need." Williamson nodded, acknowledging what he recognised was an instruction.

Ten minutes later, Paice was standing in front of Williamson's desk. The editor was leaning back in his chair. "That's a bit of a bugger, Jack. The story was a knockout. And we never did get the coffee."

"I know, Nick, but we've had our instructions." He looked up at the clock on the wall. Ten minutes to the 11 o'clock conference. "I'll tell the news editor and the chief sub that this is our front page lead."

"OK, Jack. I'll get it knocked out. What did Hartington keep you back for?"

"To tell me three things. First, the full story goes no further than we three, so you have to keep your mouth shut in the news room and anywhere else. Second, the Prime Minister rang him to say he would prefer that we handled the story 'sensitively'. Third, Lady Hartington's sister is married to Oswald Bellamy's nephew."

"He should have told us that at the outset. We never could have won that one, Jack."

The next morning, over coffee and a cake in the corner cafe, Paice surveyed his work. The sub had done a good job on the layout. "Nightmare" made the headline a tight fit in 60 point type, but it delivered the impact the story merited.

Chapter 8

Paice was sitting on the edge of his desk staring into Olivia Hankinson's eyes. They were brown, cold and hard. Like glinting shards of a broken beer bottle. Olivia was half his age, wrote a regular comment piece, and was probably earning more than he did. He did not like her. She did not like him.

"I read your piece today, Olivia."

"Congratulations, Paice. I knew you'd manage it one day. I must have used lots of single syllable words. Let me guess – you are about to tell me what you thought of it."

"Let's just say that by the time I had waded through to the end, I was wishing I hadn't bothered. By the way, don't call me Paice. It creates the ludicrous and false impression that you are somehow superior to me. My friends call me Nick. You, however, may address me as Mr Paice."

"I am sorry, Paice. If I start calling you Mr, people will gain the ludicrous and false impression that I have some vestige of respect for you." Her hostile and contemptuous gaze did not flicker.

Bob Bryce chose that moment to intervene. "Nick, am I right in thinking you were in Kamina Bassu?" It was one of those West African states that had been racked with and wrecked by a very bloody post-colonial civil war.

"Yes, Bob. That was 15 years ago. That was when Olivia was probably reading about it in her geography class. They exported a lot of cocoa. Oh, and wiped out the Kebama tribe, although your teachers would probably not have told you about that, Olivia. Wouldn't want to upset the little diddums in that posh school."

"I went to a comprehensive in Rotherham, Paice, so don't give me any of that posh school crap. And one of my classmates was a refugee from Kamina Bassu. Most of her family died in the fighting. Anyway, what were you doing there? Taking an exotic holiday?"

Paice could not suppress a smile. He did not like her, but he had a reluctant respect for her. She was as tough as nails. He had overheard her lamenting the closure of a steelworks where her father had worked. The Rotherham upbringing came in handy when dealing with the likes of Paice.

"Is it true that the rebels engaged in cannibalism, Paice? That was what my friend told me but I did not know whether she was exaggerating."

"She was not exaggerating, Olivia. The rebels were known as the Path to Paradise. They committed some pretty appalling acts. Dining on their vanquished foes was one of their less attractive habits, although they had quite a few others."

"Well they are all rehabilitated now," said Bryce. "Since last month's elections, a new president has been installed, and a coalition government is now in office, healing old wounds. You've not been back to the place?"

"Only in my worst nightmares – and I had quite a few of those when I came home. As for a holiday destination, I would not want even you to go there, Olivia, my sweet."

"You see, Paice, you can be nice. It's good to know you care about me."

"No Olivia, I would not want you to go there. Those poor bastards have suffered enough without having to put up with you."

She nodded thoughtfully. "When I've got the time, you and I must have a chat about what you want to be when you grow up." With that, she gave Paice a V sign and walked off, smiling.

Bryce laughed loudly, "Talking of holidays, I need a break, Nick."

"I know just what you need, Bob. I can recommend a nice little B&B in Clacton. The landlady is Mrs Clapp. View of the gasworks and spam fritters every night."

"Sounds wonderful. I'll drop her a line."

"Two Ps."

"What, to go with the spam fritters? Only two peas?"

"No, she spells her name with two Ps."

"Not spelt like that nasty rash you get from an ill-judged one-off assignation after too many drinks on a Saturday night, then?"

"No, Bob. Anyway, what's your interest in the Democratic Republic of Kamina Bassu?"

"In the wake of the elections the incoming government has sent a new ambassador to London. He's having a reception at the embassy. Thought you might like to look in on it on your way home. There'll be a few free drinks in it." He handed Paice an expensively embossed gilt-edged card. Paice examined it for a few seconds. How many mouths could be fed in Kamina Bassu for what it cost to print a couple of hundred of these, he thought.

Paice hailed a taxi outside the office and told the cabbie to head for the Belgravia address printed on the invitation. He did not know who was in and who was out in KB, but if the wrong people had made it to the top, it was pretty certain that, invitation or not, he would be given short shrift. He would be lucky to get past the security on the front door. His reports from the country during the civil war had made him extremely unpopular in certain Kaminan circles. As Paice saw it, he was simply telling the very unpleasant truth and, as can often be the case, the truth had the capacity to hurt.

The cab got in line behind the queue of limousines and taxis dropping the guests off for the event. Eventually, it was Paice's turn to get out. He thrust a £20 note through the cab window and asked for a receipt. The cabbie, familiar with most clients' preference, gave him a blank receipt and a wink. "You put in the amount, guv." Paice thanked him, but cursed him under his breath. The accounts department at the Mercury had a database of taxi fares. He'd had a few rejected, and, once rejected, they stayed rejected. And all subsequent expenses claims were examined in minute and forensic detail and at great length. This was one of those rare occasions when crime did not pay.

He flashed the invitation at security and found himself in the embassy's entrance foyer. So far, so good. The Kamina Bassu flag dominated the staircase that wound up to the floor above, where the chatter and hum indicated the setting for the ambassador's reception.

A short queue had formed at the door as the ambassador greeted each guest individually. Finally, it was Paice's turn. The flunkey looked at his invitation and in an unnecessarily loud voice, tinged with disdain, announced: "The representative of the Daily Mercury." He was ushered in. The ambassador held out his hand. He was a big man. Although not long out of his forties, he had greying hair and a face creased with lines that told of a life of deprivation, stress and anxiety.

"Hello, Moses," Paice said with a grin. "It's good to see you again."

Moses Mkoko's face lit up with a broad smile. "Nick! Is it really you, Nick? I can't tell you how good it is to see you." He put his arms around Paice and hugged him. The ambassador's minders were thrown into consternation. This sort of physical contact was not how things were done in the world of diplomacy. "It is really good to see you, Nick. We must talk later. There is so much to say."

"I'd like that, Mr Ambassador. We have many shared memories, not all of them good."

"What is in the past must remain there, Nick. My country is now looking to the future. For the sake of our people, we must all take our lead from that. I will speak to you later. I am sure that you will see some familiar faces here this evening – old friends and perhaps old enemies, too. Help us to celebrate our emergence from the darkness."

Paice smiled. "That sounds good to me, Moses," he said as he moved into the room. Other embassy officials were strategically located to smile at and greet the guests. Paice shook hands with people he did not know, but some of whose faces looked vaguely familiar. A waiter offered Paice a drink from the silver tray he was wafting around the room.

"Good evening, Mr Paice." His heart seemed to skip a beat. He paused before turning round, but he knew that voice and he knew that he was about to come face to face with a small, wiry man with a wispy beard and eyes that instantly put one on one's guard.

He turned slowly. Stanley Mwamba had barely changed. Time had not softened his rodent-like features, and he still projected an aura of evil. "Hello, Mwamba." He ignored the proffered hand. Moses might want the past to remain in the past, but, for Paice, where this man was concerned the past was always present.

"You look well, Mr Paice. It is good to see you again."

Paice struggled to summon a response and when it came it was the bare minimum. "Is it?" He could scarcely believe that, after a decade and a half, he was once more in the presence of the man who was responsible for the deaths of literally thousands of innocent men, women and children. Mwamba had been the military commander of the rebels, who, on his orders, had cut a merciless swathe through the heart of Kamina Bassu.

"Eat anyone interesting lately?" Paice looked him straight in his ferret-like eyes.

"The allegations of cannibalism have been shown to be nonsense. I am surprised that you still repeat them."

"That doesn't wash with me Mwamba. Remember, I was there and I saw the results. Anyway, just what are you doing here?"

Mwamba smiled – smirked was a better description. "I am the military attaché. Who'd have thought it, eh? After the terrible times we all endured, we have at last, after a process of truth and reconciliation, come together in the interests of all our people. We are acting in the national interest."

Paice could contain himself no longer. Mwamba had endured nothing. For him, the truth was an alien concept. And Paice could only guess at how much cash he had salted away in an anonymous, offshore, no-questions-asked bank account.

"Who'd have thought it, indeed." He clenched his teeth, determined to maintain control over his words. "Here you are in the very heart of civilisation." He paused, looked Mwamba straight in the eye and swallowed. "And I suspect you don't feel in the slightest discomforted or out of place."

"No, why should I?" The veneer of diplomacy was starting to wear thin. Now it was Mwamba's voice that assumed a harder edge.

"Why should you? Let me put it like this: I would find it difficult to put the words 'Mwamba' and 'civilised' in the same sentence. As I recall, the last time we met you were encouraging a bunch of your killers to hack the breasts off a pregnant woman. It was only the clatter of the motor drive on my photographer's Nikon that stopped you. And as I further recall, you told me to get out of KB or the next time we met I'd be dead."

Mwamba's eyes narrowed. "My advice to you Mr Paice is to leave all that in the past. Unless, of course, you want to risk incurring my anger yet again. And the next time you might not be quite so lucky."

"Just get something straight, Mwamba. You are in London now. We are not in the jungle where you could enjoy yourself slaughtering people with no questions asked."

The cocktail party chatter had subsided around them as Paice's voice took on an angrier tone and the other guests began to take an interest. Mwamba looked around him in discomfort. Paice was not about to call it a day.

"And as for leaving everything in the past, I can promise you that if I can stir up your shitcan and make a stink, I'll take pleasure in doing it. Just think yourself lucky that you've got diplomatic immunity."

Mwamba looked to the edge of the room and flicked his finger. Two men were instantly by his side. He said something in their language. Paice picked up only one word that he understood – enemy.

"What's this, Mwamba, your personal bodyguard? "

"As a matter of fact, Paice, yes. Two of my best men from the old days." He lowered his voice and drew close. "I have just told them that you are my enemy. That means that I am yours. They know exactly what that means. Perhaps you should watch your step. This may not be the jungle we are used to, but a city like London is a jungle just the same. And in the jungle, danger resides."

"Well, welcome to the club, Mwamba. I've got almost as many enemies as you would have deaths on your conscience if you had a conscience. I can handle another enemy, especially if it's you. You don't scare me here any more than you scared me back then. And you may have diplomatic immunity, but I doubt that it extends to your thugs. Let them put one foot out of line, and I'll make so much trouble for them that it will bounce right back on you. And just think how that will look back home where everyone has – I'll bet reluctantly – turned a blind eye to your little indiscretions with the machete and the bullet.

"You may want to leave everything in the past and forget it, but there are too many crippled and mutilated kids, with missing limbs, hanging around the street corners as a reminder of your handiwork. You might be able to forget, but they won't – not any time soon."

Paice turned away and slapped his unfinished drink back on the silver tray. He needed air, and the nightmares of 15 years before were, he knew, awaiting him the moment his head hit the pillow that night.

The guests were arriving in ones and twos and the ambassador was starting to circulate. Paice went up to him to say farewell. The news of the confrontation had got there first.

"Sorry to hear you bumped into Mwamba. I understand how you feel, Nick, but, hard as it is, we have to push all the terrible memories, well, if not out of our minds, then to the farthest recesses of them. We must concentrate all our energies on the task of rebuilding."

"I know, Moses. I know that you have to do that, but I don't. I'll say goodnight, but we must get together when you are less preoccupied. We can have a drink and a chat. It's been too long – and there were times when neither of us thought tonight would have been possible."

The ambassador took Paice's hand with a firm grip. "Let's do that, Nick."

Paice left the room and headed down the stairs. An intangible instinct prompted him to pause and look back. Watching him from above was one half of Mwamba's protection squad. Standing with arms folded, the man held one hand to his face as if to stroke his chin. In spite of the shadows, Paice could clearly see the extended index finger and the next digit moving as if to pull the trigger of the make-believe gun. The man nodded slowly to ensure that Paice had got the message. Paice knew better than to doubt that, while the gesture was play acting, the gun would be considerably more substantial. And the intent could be lethal.

Chapter 9

Outside in the cool London air, Paice paused and took deep breaths. He was surprised at the extent to which he had been overcome by the evening's events. But they had taken him back to a terrible time, a time he had largely managed to put behind him. Until he came face to face again with that rat-faced psychopath.

He made his way up the street, not sure whether to stop to search the traffic for a cab or to jog on and quickly put distance between himself and the Kaminan embassy. He turned corners and brushed past people without seeing them. Eventually, breathless, he managed to suppress the panic. A bus shelter offered a convenient sanctuary. It was empty. He sat awkwardly on one of the uncomfortable folding seats and stared at the passing traffic. But the cars and the vans and the buses did not register. He could see only burning villages, terrified women, clutching their children to them or dragging them in futility and panic to non-existent safety.

One image remained tattooed on his memory. The nuns lay scattered around the courtyard of their medical station. Mwamba's men had been through earlier in the day. The black of their habits emphasised the starkness of their white flesh while their blood, red on their skin stained the dusty ground black. They lay lifeless, indecently exposed. And around them, in a state of trauma and shock, were those to whom they had brought help and compassion. Injured or violated themselves, they were sitting in the dirt, wailing and crying. One child – no more than four or five years old – was staring, as he was staring now, seeing nothing but with a fixed and somehow horrific grin on her tear and mud-stained face, completely unable to believe – refusing to believe – the full horror and reality of what was laid out in gruesome clarity before her.

And the man who was responsible for this appalling and violent obscenity was even now sipping champagne and making polite chit-chat in a building in one of the most expensive areas of London, not five minutes from where he was sitting. Truth and reconciliation? Mwamba could tell the truth until the cows came home, but Paice could never come to terms with what he had witnessed, what that monster had perpetrated, even for the distant golden horizon of a hope filled future.

He began searching his pockets. Then his wallet. He found what he was seeking. He turned towards the orange sodium glare of a street light. With difficulty, he made out the number on the card that Eric Stilwell had given him. He called it on his phone. The number rang several times before Eric answered.

"Hello, Biff. It's Nick Paice."

"Hello, Nick. How are things. Good to hear from you."

Paice felt slightly breathless. "He's here, Eric."

Stilwell picked up the tension in Paice's voice. "Steady, Nick. Who are we talking about?"

"Mwamba."

There was a long silence. "Mwamba? What do you mean when you say he's here? Not in London." The final three words were a statement, not a question, uttered in that tone that implied "You must have got that wrong."

"Yuh, he's here all right. I have just been speaking to him."

"Are you sure, Nick. I thought that bastard was rotting in a black hole in some prison in Kamina Bassu."

"Well, he's not. It's all forgive and forget and let's get on with each other in KB now. Don't laugh when I tell you he's the military attaché at the Kaminan embassy here in London."

Eric sighed down the phone. "Don't life impress you with its unfailing ability, when you think you've just about seen it all, to come up with another nasty surprise? What did you say to him?"

"I told him not to get too comfortable because if I could cause him trouble, I'd be keen to do that."

"He won't have liked that."

"No, he threatened to let his boys loose on me."

"Bloody cheek. He's brought his heavies with him, then. Anyone we know?"

"No, they were young blokes, probably just kids when we were there."

"His boy soldiers, I guess. Catch 'em young was his style. Seasoned killers before their balls dropped."

"The question is, Eric, what can we do?"

"Off the top of my head, Nick, short of going round there and putting a bullet in his vicious little brain, I can't think of much. Can't you do an exposé in your paper?"

"What's there to expose? There's nothing new about Mwamba's antics. I've written enough about him. And back home, they've forgiven him. Anyway, it's not that simple. Moses Mkoko is his boss. He's the new ambassador."

"Moses? Moses is here in London? I'd like to meet him again."

"Yes, we should do that, but he's not out to settle old scores. The trouble is, he is committed to this truth and reconciliation idea. He says it's the only way forward for his country. Forgiving Mwamba must be difficult for him to swallow, but he's giving it a go. Personally, though, where Mwamba is concerned, that would be too big a mouthful for me. I take it rather personally that he tried to kill me – and you..."

"And Moses."

"Quite. Moses needs to watch his back. I wouldn't trust that little turd an inch. Moses would be safer tied up in a sack with a rattlesnake."

"I'll give it some thought, Nick. Give me your mobile number and I'll call you tomorrow if I come up with something. In the meantime, watch your back. A threat by Mwamba isn't something you can just brush off. And if he thinks you can damage him, he might just make good on that threat."

Paice hung up and looked for a cab. His conversation with Stilwell had calmed him. The taxi pulled into the kerb and he told the driver to head for Kouzina tis Amalias.

Philo was at his usual station, slowly turning the pages of his newspaper and shaking his head in mute disapproval of what he was reading. He threw his hands up in a welcoming embrace as Paice entered the restaurant. He did not bother to get up.

"Nick, my boy. Good to see you. Take a seat." He gestured at the empty chair opposite him. He looked over his shoulder and shouted something in Greek. It was evidently to inform Amalia that Nick had arrived. She emerged from the kitchen, came over to where Paice was standing and gave him a hug. Paice kissed her on the cheek. Most of the tables were occupied. Amalia pulled back the chair and told him to sit with her husband.

"Manolis, a glass of wine for Mr Paice." She had directed the command to the young man who was the other half of the waiting staff. Nikki was busy attending to a family group at the front of the restaurant.

Manolis swiftly jumped into action, bringing a clean wine glass and placing it in front of Paice.

Paice held up his hand. "I'd rather have a beer, please Manolis."

"No problem, Mr Nick." A glass and a cold bottle of Mythos were almost instantly set out before him. Manolis removed the cap and poured the drink. Paice took a long pull. "I needed that, Philo. It has not been an easy end to the day."

"Well, you are here now, so just relax. Have something to eat." He had removed the newspaper from the table and was folding it. He waved it at Paice. "Why you newspaper boys don't write something to cheer us up for a change, Nick? Every page I turn, I get more depressed. No wonder the suicide statistics are on the rise."

"Are they?" Paice raised his eyebrows in surprise.

"Probably. If not, it would be a miracle."

"Our job is to tell you what's going on, Philo. And to persuade you to pay for it. Good news doesn't sell newspapers."

"Your story on this Bellamy person was terrible."

"I thought it read rather well."

"It was written, Nick, with your customary literary skill. I meant that it was a terrible story. The world is going mad."

"I can't argue with that, Philo. The fallout from the St George Land scam is bringing misery and grief to everyone it touches, and that includes Oswald Bellamy."

"It brings unhappiness to everyone but those who now have the money."

"I'd give anything to know who they are, Philo."

The Greek lowered his voice and leaned closer to Paice. "Perhaps it may be possible that someone will help you in your quest?"

Paice sipped his beer and looked at Philo over the top of his glass. "Perhaps you know something, Philo."

"I know nothing, Nick. It is not a matter of concern or interest to me. I certainly would not wish to involve myself in the affairs of people who are best kept at a great distance." He watched the condensation drip from Paice's beer glass on to the table cloth. "You need a beer mat, Nick. Let me get it for you. And I will check on your meal."

He got to his feet and disappeared into the kitchen. When he returned to the table he was able to report that Amalia would serve the food within a few minutes. He placed a beer mat in front of Paice. Putting his glass upon it, Paice realised that the printed side advertising Mythos beer was face down. The blank white underside was uppermost.

"How's your brother these days, Philo? Seen much of him lately?"

"He is well, Nick, thank you. Yes, I was speaking to him only today." Paice finished his beer as Nikki brought him his meal. The conversation revolved around the Greek economy, the situation in Cyprus, what Philo thought of the Turks, what Paice thought of the European Union.

Paice excused himself and headed down the basement stairs for the toilet. Locked in a cubicle, he took the beer mat from his pocket. On it, Philo's spidery handwriting was barely legible.

"The canny old bugger should be in MI5," Paice muttered to himself. Philo had promised to ask his brother for information, and he had provided it, but in a way that did not leave a trail back to the source.

He angled the mat towards the ceiling light. The handwriting was poor and the light was dim, but he could read what was written.

" 'Titus Refik', whoever he is."

Chapter 10

"You know Paice, then Eric?"

"Know him and owe him."

Sheila Burke looked across her desk and studied Stilwell's face, hoping to discern a meaning beyond the mere words. His face wrinkled into a smile.

"When is he due?"

She looked up at the clock above the door and checked her diary. "We've got 10 minutes. You asked me to see him. I hope I'm not wasting my time. It's not the sort of thing I usually do. It's probably contrary to the Civil Service code, and it is almost certainly against Foreign Office regulations. This is a favour to you, Eric."

"I know, and I appreciate it."

"So how about telling me why you owe him?" She tapped her pencil on the pile of paper in front of her, feigning impatience.

"What I owe him is more important than why."

"OK, so what do you owe him?"

"Let's just say that if it hadn't been for Nick Paice, I would not be sitting here today."

"Sounds like you owe him a lot, Eric."

"It's not unrelated to what we will be talking about."

"You mean Kamina Bassu? I know you were there for the worst of it."

"That's right, Sheila. We were sent when the killing started in earnest. It's where I met Paice. He was covering the war for his paper. I'd always been suspicious of reporters. In my experience they'd sell you out for a story. I learnt never to trust them and never to believe them."

"But Paice was different?"

"He was. He stuck with us through some very dodgy situations that I did not particularly want to be in – but, of course I had no choice. He did. While most of his counterparts seemed to spend their time sipping gin and tonic in the bar of the Intercontinental and phoning their 'I was there' stories from bar by the pool, Paice was determined to find out what was really going on. He exposed himself to serious risk and gave himself some scary moments, but he was determined to get the real story.

"His big problem was getting his stuff back to London, but somehow he always got through and his copy blew the lid off just what was happening and how bad it was. In fact, it was his stories that led to us being sent out there. The Prime Minister had said that we could not stand by and watch the wholesale killing of innocent people, so, as usual, while the United Nations discussed it over lunch and at champagne parties, Britain decided to get stuck in.

"Those Path of Paradise thugs had been hacking their way through the Kebama tribe – they were going for the full genocide thing and making good progress. Our rules of engagement said that we were there to protect, which meant that we could fire only in self defence. That was a bit difficult for our blokes to swallow when they saw the results of the wholesale slaughter of defenceless women and children.

"We had been there a few weeks and were feeling frustrated and powerless. Then we received orders to patrol along the foothills of the mountains that cross the north of the country. The rebels were active in the area, but we always seemed to be one step behind them. Then, one morning, we heard gunfire. We got to a village where huts were ablaze and people were scattering in terror. Boy, were those poor sods glad to see us. We had at last caught the PP in the act. But they were not getting it completely their own way. A few government soldiers were trying to hold them back. That was when we met Moses Mkoko. He was doing his best to keep together a diminishing band of loyal troops. We arrived in the nick of time.

"We started putting down fire as best we could, but it was a confusing picture with people running all over the place and the rebels difficult to identify and pin down. When the PP realised they were up against real troops they made a run for it, but not before we had taken a few scalps. By the time we had driven them off, Moses was down to just three of his own men. We really went to town that day. It felt great at last to be doing something.

"I did not appreciate at that point just how significant Moses was. Nick Paice did, however. He knew that Moses was one of the key figures in holding the administration together. It turned out that the attack by the rebels was not directed at killing the villagers and burning the place down. It was Moses that they were after. They had been on his tail for days, and they had finally got him in their sights – literally – in the village that morning.

"It was clear that we had to get him out. We did what we could to help the villagers. We calculated that the rebels would lose interest now that they knew they were up against us. The trouble was that we were only at section strength – there were eight men including the corporal who was in command – an old mate of mine, Winston Jones. I was the platoon sergeant. The lieutenant who commanded the platoon had sent me along 'for the ride', as he put it.

"By the time we had done what we could to sort out the village it was mid afternoon and we decided to continue the patrol as ordered. We were all for pursuing the rebels, but the rules of engagement said that we were there only to defend civilians – or ourselves if attacked. We took Moses and his three men with us. As night fell we came across three deserted huts – a large one and two smaller – and decided to stop there for the night. We took the big hut – the other two were in pretty poor shape. The blokes were quite exhausted and Moses insisted on his men taking their turn at keeping guard."

Sheila looked over the top of her spectacles. "Was that wise, Eric?"

"It seemed a safe bet. After all, those lads knew the terrain and, to be honest, we were not expecting trouble. There had been no sign that the rebels had been following us, and we felt secure enough to let his boys take their turn.

"It was late – getting towards midnight – and Nick said he was going outside for a breath of air before turning in. One of Winston's golden rules was that everyone kept their personal radios with them, and Nick was included in that. Of course, he did not carry a weapon, but he was regarded as one of the squad in most other respects.

"He'd been gone for no more than five minutes when he radioed in telling us to get out of the hut – 'and don't hang around.' Of Moses's three men, Nick had found two of them dead and the third nowhere to be seen. The urgency in his voice left us in no doubt that we had to get out of there.

"Fortunately, another of Winston's golden rules was that he never went in without having at least two ways out. He had recce'd the scene when we arrived and he had a clear idea about the exit route. We had just cut out through the back of the hut and reached the cover of the surrounding bush when all hell broke loose.

"The rebels had moved up and opened fire on the hut, raking it with machine gun fire and lobbing in a few RPGs. Within minutes it was a blazing inferno, but we were not in it. If Nick had not warned us to get out, we would not have survived. We all owed our lives to him."

"He got you out, but what happened to him?"

"He managed to lie low during the action, but he was able to maintain contact over the radio, and later, when the situation had calmed down, Winston sent a couple of his men to find him. There wasn't a man there who did not believe that Nick's quick thinking had saved his life. Afterwards, Winston told everyone that Mwamba had not counted on us having an ace up our sleeve. That was how Nick came to be called Paice the Ace."

The phone on Sheila's desk rang. She picked it up. "Will you send Chris down to pick him up, please?" She hung up. "Mr Paice is at the front reception. Once he has cleared security, they will bring him up."

Ten minutes later Paice was seated opposite Sheila Burke. "I am very grateful to you for agreeing to see me," he said. She smiled and nodded. "Eric will have told you what I am hoping for."

"He says that it concerns an accredited diplomat at the Kamina Bassu embassy."

Paice nodded. "Well, I am assuming that he has that rank. He is the military attaché, so I guess he operates under the protection of the embassy's diplomatic status."

She looked Paice in the eye. "I have a problem, Mr Paice."

"Please call me Nick."

"OK, Nick. My problem is that I am not here to give you material for your next story. I suspect that it will not worry you, but it will cause me embarrassment and career potential if what I say to you today appears in the columns of your newspaper tomorrow morning."

Paice held up his hands and began to shake his head. He opened his mouth to speak, but she cut him short.

"Let me finish because I want us both to be in absolutely no doubt about the status of this conversation. As you know, we have a press section and nothing is said to the media that is not cleared by those people. And when they want confirmation about what should or should not be said, they go right to the top, by which I mean the permanent secretary and Ministers. It means that people like me who occupy a much lower position in the food chain don't blab to people like you.

"You are here only because Eric trusts you and has promised me that you will not cause me problems. If you betray that trust, you will be sticking the knife in him and me. You see, Nick, I know of your reputation. You are a good journalist, but that means you are probably not a nice person that I can trust. Without Eric's assurance, you would not have got within a mile of my office door."

Paice was silent for a few moments. "Fair enough. Let's be clear about what we are doing here. But let me also tell you that I always – always – protect my sources, Sheila."

"That is the point, Nick. I am not one of your sources, and if that is how you see this conversation, it ends now."

"Agreed. Look, Sheila, I spent some very painful and traumatic times in Kamina Bassu. That poor bloody benighted country has suffered more than any nation has a right to. And the one man who did more than any other to inflict and increase that suffering is in London right now. I am not here for a story, but I will be honest with you. I want to get that bastard, and if that means having to write a story to expose him, that is what I will do."

"So why, if you know all the facts, don't you just do that?"

Paice shook his head. "Because that won't do it. That is basically why you have nothing to fear. What is the story? He was sent here by a Government that is struggling to get its country back on its feet, to bring back together people who are sick of the bloodshed and killing that tore them apart. Everyone in Kamina Bassu knows what Mwamba got up to. There is nothing I can write that they don't already know. They are prepared to turn a blind eye to it in the desperate hope that everything will turn out fine."

"Then why can't you move on?"

"Because I know him. Eric knows him. Everything is not going to turn out fine. Leopards can't change their spots. Another thing they can't do is resist using their claws and their teeth. That is what he will do. During the war he was running an extermination campaign, not only because in his twisted mind he believed it was right but because he was enjoying it. Sooner or later, he will be back to his old tricks. I want him out of this country for two reasons. First, it pains me to think that he is parading about in an expensive suit and a chauffeur driven Mercedes and is breathing the same air as me.

"Second and more important, I don't like to think of him being within touching distance of Moses Mkoko – "

"Their new ambassador."

"Yes. Moses is a good bloke. Mwamba did his best to kill Moses because of what he stood for and his significance in the Kaminan administration. But for Eric here he would have succeeded."

"That was also down to you, Nick." Eric jabbed his finger at Paice.

"Be that as it may, Eric. You know as well as I do, that Moses will have to be constantly looking over his shoulder, especially now that we know that Mwamba has a couple of thugs here to do his dirty work.

"Let me make you this promise, Sheila. If I do end up writing a story about him, I will run it past you first so that you can be confident that I have not breached a trust. That is not something I would ever do for anyone else."

"Very well, Nick. But I am not sure quite what you want of me. You seem to know more about this man than most, so what can I tell you?"

"First, does he have diplomatic immunity? I have assumed that he does, but I don't know for certain. I've looked up the Diplomatic List, but he has only just got here and the list is not bang up to date. Second, what's the view in the FCO about him being here? Do they know what sort things he got up to during the civil war? I know that your lot are keen for peace to persist in KB, but I cannot believe that your Ministers would want to be seen to be too close to someone like that. Third, is anyone keeping an eye on him? He cannot be trusted, and if no one is watching him, they should be."

She studied him for a few minutes before responding. "I'll see what I can find out and what the department's view of him is. I'm making no promises, but I will do what I think is acceptable within the rules."

Paice nodded in appreciation. "I can't ask for more than that."

Getting up to leave, he asked whether Stilwell had plans for lunch. "Fancy a pint and a sandwich?"

"Sounds good to me, Nick."

"Is this private or can anyone come?" Sheila smiled at them.

It was early lunchtime in the Black Lion, which meant they could get a table. Paice bought the drinks as they ordered their food.

"Do you mind me asking what you actually do in the department, Sheila?"

"I am deputy head of the Balkan section."

"Which means?"

"Which means that I am answerable to my boss for my team. My boss is answerable to his boss and his boss is directly answerable to the Minister of State. Our job is to keep tabs on the political and economic developments as they affect, or might at some time affect, the UK's interests in those areas of activity. We have to keep ourselves up to date on what is happening so that we can make an educated guess about what will happen in the future. Such information is crucial in the formulation of policy."

"And how do you know this bloke?" He jerked his thumb towards Eric. The big man chuckled and then burst out with his trademark booming laughter.

"Now that's a real story – but definitely not for publication, Nick," he said. By now Sheila was laughing, too.

"In those days I had applied for foreign posting," she explained. "I was working in one of our embassies in south-east Asia. Eric was serving there as diplomatic security. One evening the ambassador threw a party for the local dignitaries, so the entire embassy staff was on duty to host the event."

Eric chipped in: "Sheila won't mind me saying that she looked particularly good on that evening, and that view was obviously shared by a government minister who had been invited along as one of the guests of honour."

"What Eric means is that, after a few glasses of wine, he couldn't keep his hands to himself. He got a little over-excited, no doubt encouraged by my plunging neckline, because that is precisely what he did – he plunged into it.

"I'd had just about enough of him. I was drinking a large glass of fruit juice – we were on duty and we were advised to keep off the alcohol. He was wearing a very nice cream embroidered dress shirt. I threw my drink all over him – made a terrible mess of his shirt. That is when all hell broke loose."

"And that is where I came in," Eric said. "The minister started getting violent. The ambassador was furious with Sheila and was terrified that the incident would lead to a breakdown in political relations.

"He told Sheila to make herself scarce and asked me to escort the minister to his car. Unfortunately, he had had far too much to drink and as he came out of the front door of the embassy he stumbled and fell down the half dozen steps that led down to the road."

"Tell the truth, Eric. You threw him down them."

"It wasn't like that Sheila. I was supporting him to his car and I dropped him – down the steps." Eric grinned mischievously and winked at Paice. "It was nothing less than he deserved."

"How did it work out?" Paice asked.

"Not well for me," Sheila said. "The ambassador was not in the slightest sympathetic. He said my dress had been provocative and I should have been nimbler on my feet to keep out of the minister's reach. He said I had failed to exhibit a fundamental requirement of a diplomat – the ability to handle people in a way that did not upset them.

"The next day, word came from the President's office that the minister had learnt his lesson and they were prepared to overlook the incident provided I was required to leave the embassy. My continued presence would be embarrassing and not conducive to the maintenance of good relations with their administration."

"Yeah, and it was made clear that I, too, was no longer welcome," Eric added. "Within a week we found ourselves both on the same flight home. I was returned to my unit – "

"And I was given a week's leave while they decided what to do with me. I was taken off the foreign service rota for six months. Things have never really improved much after that."

Paice took a long pull on his pint. "That was hardly justice for you, Sheila."

"No, but in the world of diplomacy justice doesn't count for much. It is much more a matter of not saying what you mean and bending over backwards to accommodate your adversary while maintaining sufficient balance to put the knife in while smiling sweetly."

An hour later they were shaking hands and bidding their farewells outside the pub.

"I'll wait to hear from you, Sheila," Paice said. Almost as an afterthought, he added: "Can I ask you about something else?"

"Try me," she replied.

"Have you heard of a Mr Titus Refik?"

"Perhaps. What's your interest?"

"I have to see him on a private matter. He's a bit of a mystery and I cannot discover much about him. I think he is from your part of the world – the part you cover, that is. It would be helpful to have a bit of background about him. Forewarned and all that."

"I'll give it some thought."

"Thanks."

They parted, Eric Stilwell disappearing into the crowds, Sheila Burke weaving through the traffic on

Whitehall, and Nick Paice heading for the Underground station.

Chapter 11

Paice had finished the story he had been working on and seen it in the first edition of the paper as it came off the press. After consultation with the chief sub, Bob Bryce suggested a few changes, which Paice had incorporated before leaving for the night.

The weather was warming up and, in spite of a day of showers, it was now dry. By the time he got back to his digs it would be too late to eat at Philo and Amalia's, so he dropped into a pub on his way home and had a couple of pints of beer and a pork pie that, while it did not look particularly appetising, at least seemed not to be lethal. He made a rueful comparison between the sorry offering before him and the delights of Greek cuisine that he could have been eating if he had finished earlier.

The taxi dropped him outside his place and he entered carefully lest Mrs Evans had retired for the night. Not so. Attentive as ever, she came out of her room as he headed for the stairs.

"Good night, Mr Paice. I hope you had a good day."

"As good as one can expect, thank you Mrs Evans. I hope your day went well." It was past 11pm so he knew that Jessica would be sound asleep long since. "How's the little one, Mrs Evans? Good, I hope."

A cloud of sadness passed across the woman's face. Paice could see immediately that the news was not good. "Jessica saw a maxillofacial specialist today. He said that she has facial nerve damage, Mr Paice. It's unlikely to heal itself, which means that she will never be able to smile properly."

Paice felt an overwhelming sense of wretchedness. "A young woman has a god-given right to smile, Mrs Evans. She has a right to enjoy life, and to show that she is enjoying it. It is contrary to nature to deprive a beautiful woman – and that is what she will be – of a lovely smile. In spite of what young men may think, they fall in love with a smile. It tells a young man that she is happy to be with him."

"Everything you say is true, Mr Paice. But I think that life has other plans for Jessica."

"Is there nothing the surgeons can do for her?"

"They could try, but they warn that surgery carries a huge risk of further damage and possibly causing complete facial paralysis."

Paice ran his fingers through his greying hair. "Medical science progresses so fast these days, Mrs Evans. Surely one day there will be the hope of a cure."

"There is. The consultant told me that a surgeon in the United States has perfected a procedure that offers a very high success rate in cases such as Jessica's. It seems that he has been working with a university in

Massachusetts and they have developed micro-surgical equipment specifically for the repair of nerve damage."

"Then what's stopping them sending her there?"

"The national health service won't fund it, and it will cost more than £100,000, plus the expense of getting and staying there."

"Then we will have to find a way round that little obstacle, won't we? Good night, Mrs Evans."

"Good night, Mr Paice."

"I have just made a pot of tea, Mr Paice. Would you like a cup to take up with you?"

Up in his room, Paice sipped the tea while preparing for bed. A subsequent bath and a glass of cognac helped him fall asleep without the problems he usually endured, problems that left him turning restlessly, the green digits on his alarm clock almost mocking him with the information that he had been doing so for three hours. Not so tonight.

That did not mean untroubled slumber. In deep sleep, he returned to his personal hell. Children were screaming and gunfire thumped and crackled. He looked on in horror and terror, but he was powerless to act. His body would not respond. He wanted to do something, anything. His mind and his body were detached, the former screaming the orders, the latter refusing to obey.

The sense of frustration and helplessness generated a rage within him. It was as intense as anything he had ever experienced. There was blood – on the ground, on the people and, worst of all, on him. But however hard he rubbed and scrubbed, he could not remove it. He looked at the ground. Rivulets of blood were running towards his bare feet, forming viscous streams, and then trickling between his toes. Hypnotised by a spasm of horror, in helpless panic, he was incapable of moving to avoid them.

Now it was raining. Thank heaven for the rain and its cleansing power. But it wasn't rain. My god, it was raining blood. He was standing, drenched, in the clammy crimson downpour. All around, men, women and children were writhing and jerking in their death throes. And walking through the deluge, avoiding every drop, in crisp green battle fatigues, a machete in one hand and a gun in the other, was a man he recognised. It was Mwamba.

Paice wanted to snatch a weapon from him and use it to end the carnage. He knew that if he killed this man, the horror would stop, the rain would cease and the people on the ground in that sticky morass of mud and blood, would rise and thank him.

But his leaden limbs would not respond. Paice screamed at Mwamba to halt the bloodshed. His mouth opened, but sound came there none. Mwamba laughed, waved his machete at the slaughter around him, at the hospital courtyard where so many had died, and swaggered past unscathed and undeterred. The killing would continue. One face watched him from the window of a burning house. It was a face that pleaded for help. It was a face he recognised.

The knocking, a frantic hammering, finally roused him. He woke to hear Mrs Evans at his door.

"Mr Paice. Mr Paice. Are you all right?"

Half asleep he sat up and swung his legs off the side of the bed. "Yes, Mrs Evans. I'm OK."

"Are you having one of those dreams again?" she asked through the closed door.

"I'm sorry. Did I wake you?"

"That's all right, Mr Paice."

He heard her footsteps cross the landing and descend the stairs.

In the darkness, he sat, cradling his head in his hands. They were shaking. Perspiration had soaked his nightclothes. But he now knew. Tomorrow, he had a phone call to make.

It was 2am, and although he was fearful of going back to sleep, he lay down and closed his eyes. After what might have been half an hour, or could have been two hours, he finally drifted into an untroubled slumber, waking only when he heard the traffic outside as the rest of the world got itself into gear and began the grind to work.

Half an hour later he was ready to go. On the way out he looked into Mrs Evans's room. The door was open and she was putting the finishing touches to Jessica's hair as they both prepared for the journey to school. Jessica waved to him and gave him a shy misshapen smile. He waved back.

"I apologise for disturbing you last night, Mrs Evans. I hope that I did not wake the little one."

"You did not, Mr Paice. Don't worry about it. It's none of my business, but I really think you should see someone about those dreams. Look at you, for god's sake. You look absolutely drained. It cannot be doing you any good."

"Curiously, Mrs Evans, last night's dream did me a great deal of good. It answered a question that has been troubling me for some time. And today I shall be doing something about it."

He looked down at Jessica. "You have a good day at school." He winked and waved farewell.

She nodded vigorously and smiled again, vainly attempting to return the wink. Paice made a mental note to teach her how.

Paice strolled into the office. Harry Draper, the florid faced and neurotic day news editor, looked up in surprise. "I thought you were on later today, Nick."

"Yes, Harry, but something has come up." Paice was convinced that Harry was heading for an early cardiac arrest. He thought, but did not say, "It's not worth dying for, Harry."

He looked through his contacts book and made a telephone call. Then a second. Allowing plenty of time for the journey, he took a cab from outside the office to Waterloo station.

Eric Stillwell was waiting on the station concourse as agreed. "Good morning, Biff. I'm glad you could make it."

"When you invite me to lunch and tell me you're paying, I drop everything, Nick. Are you going to tell me what this is all about?"

"All in good time, mate. You just sit back and enjoy the ride."

The train journey took them to a station deep into the Surrey countryside. Outside of the rush hour, the place was almost deserted, with just the occasional traveller making a leisure trip to London. They were fortunate. As they emerged, a taxi was dropping off one such traveller. The two men waited until he had paid the driver. Paice stooped down to speak to her. They got in the back and, after a bit of polite chat about the weather, the ride was completed in silence. The cab pulled up in front of the Seven Stars pub. Garden furniture was arranged outside and white and green striped parasols flapped in the breeze. It was May and the weather was warming nicely.

"Let's sit outside, Eric. I'll get us a couple of beers."

They sipped their pints of London Pride ale. "This is very nice, Nick. Is the food here good?"

"So I am reliably informed, but it's the company, not the food that is important today, Eric."

They were halfway down the glass when a silver Jaguar slowed on approaching the pub and pulled silently into the car park located at the rear, the crunching of the gravel under its tyres the only sound to indicate its presence.

"I'll go and greet our guest." Eric nodded in agreement. Paice disappeared round the corner of the pub. Minutes later he reappeared. Walking beside him was Maria Bellamy.

Eric stood to greet her. "Hallo, Biff," she said with a smile. "You haven't changed a bit."

Stilwell was speechless and caught between recognition and puzzlement. It was a face he knew, but

151

his expression was a clear indication that he knew not from where. Before he could utter a word, Paice broke the silence. "Mr Stilwell, may I introduce you to Lady Maria Bellamy – better known to you as 'Maria the Machine Gun Medic'?"

The big man threw out his arms and embraced her. "My god, this is a surprise. Paice, you are a magician. How did you find this lady." She kissed Stilwell on the cheek.

"We met in, shall we say, unusual circumstances. I did not recognise her. In different surroundings, different circumstances and from the distance of more than a decade and a half, I failed to make the connection. But I had a dream last night, and that face came to me. Then I knew." He turned to Maria. "Did you recognise me?"

"Nick, I did not have to recognise you, although I did. I knew your name. Above all, I knew that I could trust you. Why do you think I was happy for Oswald to tell you the full story?"

The bond between the three had been forged at a small hospital in the jungle of Kamina Bassu. The rebels had descended on it, intent on slaughter. The frantic nuns who ran it knelt to pray in the face of the attack. Maria Falco, a volunteer helper, took a more positive line. As the rebel troops began rampaging through the hospital buildings, she chose her moment. She allowed one of them to see her disappearing into a store room doorway.

With a roar of triumph, and fired up by lust, he leapt through it in pursuit. It was the last roar he was to utter. Out of the bright sunlight he was temporarily blinded by the sudden darkness of the room. It was to prove fatal. Among the tools kept there was an axe. Maria swung it with all the force she could summon. It came at him out of the gloom and sliced his face in half, the blade penetrating the bridge of his nose and lodging itself in his brain. It stopped him dead – very dead – in his tracks.

The initial shock at what she had done had momentarily transfixed her as she stared at the result. But the screams from the courtyard jerked her back into action. She took a deep breath and steadied herself, picked up his AK47 and, calmly and with great presence of mind, collected up his spare magazine.

Out in the courtyard, the other soldiers were too busy tearing the clothes off the nuns to notice her. That, too, was a fatal mistake. Her father, a post-colonial army officer serving in East Africa, had taught her to shoot. Moreover, she was familiar with the most widely available assault rifle in the world that she now clasped to her chest. She looked it over quickly and checked that the selector was in fully automatic mode.

With a discipline drummed into her from an early age, she took deliberate aim and, with short bursts, shot four of the rebels dead. The others, armed mostly with machetes, now blood-stained from hacking the life out of their defenceless victims, panicked. They ran for it.

Maria quickly gathered up the distraught nuns and the women and children and ushered them into the hospital building. With all the occupants lying flat on the floor, she took up position at the door. It commanded a good view of the courtyard, a square of about 20 metres bounded on four sides by low buildings. There was only one entrance, a gap in the buildings in one corner. It was not long before the insurgents had regrouped and steeled themselves for a counter attack.

A small exploratory group came at a crouching run through the gap and into the courtyard, keeping close to the walls. Maria remained hidden and held her fire. Emboldened by the absence of a reaction and calling encouragement to each other, they stood and cautiously walked forward. The closer they came, the more they came into the open and the further they moved from the protection of cover.

Their leader stood brazenly taunting her and shouting a challenge as his comrades laughed at his antics. She shot him with a short burst from a distance of 20ft. Two 7.62mm rounds hit him in the chest. A third went through his throat, almost decapitating him. The fourth, on an upward trajectory, entered just below his right eye and blasted a path into the back of his brain. It was a messy death but a quick one.

She ducked quickly out of the doorway as the others opened fire, but she was the one with the cover. And she was a much better shot. A series of controlled bursts were sufficient to finish off or scare away the others. Two were shot down as they fled, the bursts of fire hitting them in the back and adding to their momentum, paradoxically propelling them towards the shelter that would have saved their lives but that they were destined never quite to reach.

She quickly reloaded in time to see a youth wearing a bandanna and bright red T-shirt step into the gap from behind the building opposite, poising himself to throw a grenade. He paused momentarily to locate his target. Mistake. She opened fire and dropped him where he stood. The grenade fell from his grasp and exploded, putting down the two men closest to him.

She was contemplating what she would do when the ammunition ran out, which would be soon, when she heard firing of a different sort. After a short but intense engagement, all went quiet. Then the hulking figure of Biff Stilwell had ventured cautiously into the courtyard. Like the Seventh Cavalry, the section from the second battalion had arrived in the nick of time. The battle was over. The rebels had been put to flight, and Maria Falco had saved from a horrific fate the patients and those who cared for them. In the process she earned herself the rare accolade of hero of the second battalion.

Nick Paice was immediately on the scene. His story of "Maria the Machine Gun Medic" hit the front page in London and within days it was syndicated to newspapers around the world. It mattered not – certainly not to Paice – that neither had she used a machine gun and nor was she a medic. The alliterative appeal and the dramatic effect of his words made them irresistible both to him and to the sub editor who was looking for a headline.

As is the way of such things, the British troops having moved on and other atrocities having snatched the attention of the media, Maria Falco was soon absorbed back into the anonymity from which she had been plucked and to which she was happy to return.

Over the pub lunch, accompanied by two more pints and a glass of wine, they brought Maria up to date with their personal circumstances.

"So, does that mean you are now a home loving boy, Nick. No more romantic foreign travel?" she asked. "And you, Biff? You've given up the soldiering?"

He nodded. "Yes, I'm running my own business now. I've done my bit for Queen and country, Maria. Now it's time to do it for wife and family."

"And how is business?"

"I had a slow start. It's picking up. We are certainly going places. And it is important because, for the first time, I am there when my wife needs me and it is enabling me to build a real family life."

Paice concentrated on his food. "You are lucky still to have that, Biff. There's nothing like that left for me.

"Anyway, Maria, what about you? How did you become Lady Bellamy?"

"It all happened because I became a patient in my own hospital," she explained. "I was suffering from a severe intestinal infection. I was in a pretty bad way, lapsing into and out of unconsciousness. I had our one and only doctor puzzled. He was getting increasingly anxious about my condition – in fact he thought that I was going to die. Our hospital was fairly primitive and he had neither the expertise nor the drugs I needed.

"That was when Oswald walked into my life. He was part of a delegation of MPs from the UK. They were there to assess how best to direct British Government aid to Kamina Bassu. It was purely by chance that they came to our hospital, but it was lucky for me.

"The doctor asked them for help. He suggested that the only way to be sure I survived was to get me to a hospital with the necessary resources and facilities. Oswald took over. I was flown to London the next day. Nature took its course. I recovered and Oswald and I fell in love. I loved Africa, but I never returned, and now England is my home and I have a family here."

Paice wiped his mouth, sipped his beer, and looked at her intently. "You may love Africa, Maria, but Kamina Bassu has not been a nice place to be. The fighting went on for years until the Government just about got the upper hand. The problem was that while it restored legitimate government, it simply did not have the power decisively to defeat the rebels. They carried on the fight from their stronghold in the north east of the country, attempting to destabilise the elected administration with assassinations and car bombs."

"Yes, I know. But it has all come right in the end. Reconciliation and forgiveness by both sides has finally brought democracy and peace, has it not? Common sense has prevailed, although I have to confess that I would find it very difficult to forgive some of the appalling atrocities that went on under the banner of that Path of Paradise gang of thugs. I see that the UK Government has formally recognised the new administration. I read that they have even sent an ambassador to open an embassy in London."

Stilwell nodded. "You're right. Nick met the ambassador – Moses Mkoko. Do you remember him?"

She nodded. "I read his name in the paper, and I remember that he was a prominent figure on the government side during the fighting, but I never met him. To be frank, it is a time in my life that I prefer now to forget. It was like living through one of those horror films that my children insist on watching. To them all that blood and cruelty is fascinating and frightening, but somehow they find it entertaining. I suppose we can all do that when we are protected from the reality by a sheet of glass and a silver screen. We are safely removed from it. But you and I know the horror and the terror of being the participants, not just detached spectators."

A silence descended on the three. They sipped their drinks. The events that they had witnessed and experienced had suddenly returned to them, a grotesque intrusion into a sunny day in a Surrey pub garden with its backdrop of flowers and birdsong.

"I still get dreams – well, nightmares, I suppose." Paice felt that he could make to his two companions a confession that he would not dare to talk about to anyone else.

"It's a form of post-traumatic shock, Nick. Talk to any of the lads who have been in heavy combat and most of them will admit to something similar." Biff laid his hand on Paice's shoulder: "You should talk to someone about it. Surely your newspaper would have access to a therapist who could help."

Paice gave a slight nod. "Yes, I suppose so." He could not go so far as to admit that it was not something he could talk about to anyone else. It came as an unexpected relief that he was able to talk about it to two people who had shared what he had seen.

"I had similar nightmares for years, but it is much better now." Maria spoke quietly, a slight break in her voice betraying an emotion that still endured, defying the passage of time. "It is much better now, but I expect that our reunion will do nothing to guarantee me a good night's sleep tonight."

Paice was curious. "Did you dream of people you had known, or was it events or places? I remembered who you were, Maria, because I saw your face in a dream."

"Hang on a minute," Stilwell interjected. "Are you sure we should be raking all this up? If we are all trying to forget it after all these years, shouldn't we be putting it out of our minds?"

"I wish I could, Biff," Maria said. "The trouble is that none of us will ever forget it, and I reckon that sitting here talking about it is probably a therapy in itself. You two are the only ones I can talk to about it because you were there and you understand. Don't you feel the same?"

Paice knew she was right. He was feeling more at ease with himself in their presence than he had for as long as he could remember.

"I guess that I understand what you are saying, Maria," Stilwell conceded. "After your little encounter at the hospital, it would be impossible to wipe all that from your mind. But surely the best thing is to leave those memories buried along with the dead 3,000 miles away in Africa."

A sad smile crossed her face. "How can one forget? Curiously, Biff, the hospital was not the most persistent memory. After we parted and you organised our evacuation to a safer position behind the government lines, we came across a burning village. The rebels had not long departed. The one substantial building there was the village school."

She paused, visibly preparing herself to go on. "The rebels had gathered all the children in the school. You remember how those savages hated education. They had told the children that it was time for all children to go to school. Every child in the village did so with their teacher. Once everyone was inside they had raked it with machine gun fire and grenades before burning it down. No child escaped. That is my worst memory from the most horrific time of my life."

She was palpably upset, but holding her emotions in check. Biff reached across and took her hand.

"How could any man do that?" she asked. "To this day, I still do not understand. The mothers who had not been slaughtered were gathered by the burning ruin wailing and calling out their children's names. The smoke and the flames combined with the acrid, nauseating smell of burning flesh. It was truly one of the worst moments of my life. Some of those women actually ran into the flames to be with their kids.

"And, in a sense, I feel even greater sadness and greater anger now than I did then. No civilised person could fail to feel distress, fury and frustration at the sight of those poor mothers. But now I have children of my own. Only when one experiences the maternal bond does one come to understand the full weight of their grief. I suppose that, as a mother, I can put myself in their position on that dreadful day. I know that my love for my kids would probably cause me to run into the flames, which was something I did not understand then."

She paused, but neither Paice nor Stilwell felt able to attempt to fill the silent void.

"It seems that the village had been specifically targeted because it was a Kebama village that supported the government. Most of the men had joined the government army, which was why it was left largely unprotected. I spoke to a number of the survivors. They told me that the atrocity had been committed by a rebel leader who called himself the Black Lion."

"The Black Lion?" Paice queried. "I never came across that name."

"Nor had I at that point," she continued. "But I found out afterwards. It was a man named Stanley Mwamba."

Paice was about to take a mouthful of his beer. When she uttered the name, he froze, the glass suspended in mid air. Then, quietly, he put it down on the table, pushed his chair back and walked across the grass to the shade of a chestnut tree, shaking his head as he went.

Maria followed him. "I'm sorry, Nick, I have upset you." Stilwell joined them.

161

He looked at Stilwell. "Shall I tell her?"

"I think you will have to now, mate." At that moment his mobile phone began playing the theme tune from The Archers. The jaunty melody that he had chosen as a ring tone was entirely appropriate to their rural surroundings, but it was an intergalactic journey away from what Maria was about to hear. He walked away to take the call and left them alone.

"Tell me what, Nick?"

Paice stared at the ground, gently shaking his head. "Mwamba is in London."

"What? Now, do you mean?"

"Yup. He is the military attaché at the new embassy."

Tears were welling up in her eyes. "Surely not, Nick. How can that be? You must be mistaken."

He told her of the process of forgiveness and conciliation that was intended to set Kamina Bassu on the road to what was hoped would be a better future.

"Forgiveness? How could anyone possibly seek or be given forgiveness for what that man did?"

"It is something that the United Nations, including Britain, has agreed to. He has been welcomed here with open arms. There is no question or prospect of pursuing him to get him to face justice for his merciless campaign of mass murder."

She turned away, wiping her eyes. "Then there is no justice, not for those dead children, those raped and mutilated women, not even for you and me for what we endured, although we are the least important."

"That man is pure evil, Maria. He may make a big thing about forgiveness, but he's not interested in that. He is not in the slightest bit bothered about what he did. I have nightmares about what happened, but I'll bet he doesn't, and he's the one who did it. For him, the conciliation process is a get-out-of-jail-free card.

"It's one thing for him to get away scot free, but where does he go from here? If he is the military attaché this year, who is to say that he won't go home and head up the armed forces next year or the year after? And once he gets his hands on that sort of power, we should really worry about what he might do next."

Their unfinished meals remained just that. Paice and Stilwell had to get back to their respective offices and Maria had the children to collect from school. She drove the two men to the station. She pulled into the pickup area. They all got out of the car to say their farewells. Stilwell went ahead to check on the time of the train. Maria kept Paice back with a gentle tug on his sleeve.

"Thanks for coming to see me, Nick. And thank you for bringing Biff."

"No problem," he smiled. "It was a reunion that was long overdue. How is Sir Oswald?"

"He is still playing ball with those crooks, but, as things stand, he has little choice. We were very pleased with the story you wrote. Have you uncovered anything else about them?"

"A little, Maria." He was keeping to himself – at least for the time being – the identity of the man behind the fraud. "I am making inquiries but I cannot promise that I will have any answers any time soon. I'll certainly do my best, though."

"Will you make me a promise, please?"

"Sure, what is it?"

"Don't do anything that will let Mwamba know anything about me. I don't think he would know who I was, but, thanks to you, my name appeared in newspapers everywhere after the hospital business, and he might just remember. He probably forgot about me long ago and I want it to stay that way. So that especially means not writing a story about me in the Mercury."

"I promise. But it is a story that is begging to be written. One day I'll have to break the promise – but not yet." He kissed her cheek and joined Stilwell on the platform.

The journey back to London passed mostly in silence between the two men. Each was entertaining his own private thoughts. Stilwell was reminiscing about the Kamina Bassu operation and the comrades who had served there with him. They had all returned safely – in no small part thanks to Nick Paice. Some had then gone on to serve in other campaigns where Britain had felt compelled to stick its oar in. And from those not all of them had returned.

Life was a contract, with rewards and obligations. But it came with more small print than the London phone book. And how much of the phone book did you ever actually read? The small print told you about the sorrows and the heartbreaks, the sadness and the inevitable regrets. Like losing mates and loved ones. Read the small print. That way there are fewer nasty surprises.

Paice's musings were dominated by Maria. Her reaction to his news about Mwamba had hit him hard. He had not known of the school massacre. In that country at that time atrocities were commonplace.

She was a remarkable woman. She had proved that in the hellish conditions in Kamina Bassu. He had seen the same spirit and courage the night that the sewage truck had dumped its cargo in her front room. And she had been made a hero of the second battalion, a rare accolade.

He resolved there and then that he would do whatever it took to help the Bellamys with their problem with Titus Refik's crooks.

Chapter 12

The taxi stopped opposite the symmetrical perfection of Victorian engineering. "You gonna be OK round here, guv?" Paice thanked the cabbie for his solicitude, assured him that all was well, and paid him the fare plus a good tip.

The mundane and soot-stained ribbons of brick railway viaducts that carry commuters from the south of the capital into central London attract barely a second glance today. But when Britain led the world in such endeavours 150 years before, their construction was a minor architectural miracle.

Elevated above the common man, nineteenth century travellers sped to their destinations 40ft up, oblivious of the dirt and commotion, and the people who generated them, in some of the poorest districts of working class London that spread out beneath them.

Had they been aware of it, they might have stared in awe at the seemingly endless continuum of arches that supported their progress. But then a different century brought different values. Yesterday's admiring gasp became today's stifled yawn. Sparkling symmetry became grubby repetition. Brick artistry was now used to enclose utilitarian space. Within the spans, beneath the 100 million bricks that vaulted over their occupants' heads, design studios, motor repair shops, warehousing, vehicle storage and even fancy restaurants carried on business.

The cabbie's concern was not misplaced. This was a part of London where the unwary and those unfamiliar with the underclass activities of the city rarely ventured. Paice did not fit either of those descriptions. He looked along the range of arches, which disappeared round a far bend in the road, and headed for one of them.

The extraction fan that rattled and roared a few feet above head height pumped the smell of greasy cooking into the street. Paice peered through the condensation that streamed down the windows. This wasn't fancy. It wasn't even a restaurant. This was a prime example of Britain's contribution to the culinary lexicon. It was the cafe. Pronounced caff, English, not cafay, French. To be precise it was Mick's Cafe, as the painted sign confirmed.

The constant rumble of trains overhead reminded those beneath that the establishment helped bear the weight of one of the busiest lines into the city. Not that they even noticed the noise. Constant aural assault meant that immunity was quickly, if forcibly, acquired.

Through the fog of the window, Paice could distinguish the plump figure of Mick Gentle moving around behind the counter. He could not see, but he knew that Mick would have a half smoked cigarette between his lips. The menu did not vary much. Fried eggs, fried bacon, fried sausages, fried chips, fried bread. If your arteries could survive such a diet, a few flakes of cigarette ash in your meal weren't about to kill you.

He pushed open the door and went in. Mick looked down the length of the establishment through the blue haze. He nodded a greeting and returned his attention to the huge frying pan that was sizzling and crackling on the stove.

Half a dozen customers were happily attacking the meals that Mick had prepared. Some sat studying the racing pages, lingering over their mugs of tea. An elderly woman in a white overall was fussing over the tables, wiping up and clearing away dirty plates. She smiled at Paice.

Mick occasionally looked up at the visitor as he progressed towards the counter. What might have been a smile, or perhaps a scowl, contorted his lips. "Hallo, son. 'Ow yer doin'?" Paice responded with a non-committal nod and a grunt. "That bad, eh? I see you was 'angin' about outside." He directed a raised eyebrow to the TV monitor above his head. The closed circuit cameras located above the sign outside gave a perfect view of anyone approaching the cafe door.

"How are you, Mick?"

"Times are 'ard. You know what they say, Nick. Crime doesn't pay. They must be right otherwise everyone would be at it." He smiled another scowl.

Paice smiled back. "I thought they were, Mick."

"I 'adn't noticed that, Nick. Still, as we are always being told, competition keeps us on our toes."

Paice knew that competition was one aspect of business about which Mick was vigilant but fairly relaxed. Competition tended to be short-lived. That was because competitors tended to be short-lived. Not that the local competing cafe owners needed to worry about their life expectancy – apart from having eaten too much of their own cooking.

Competing against Mick did not mean frying more eggs or plating up more chips. It meant selling cocaine in Mick's territory. Or opening a new gambling establishment without obtaining a licence. And Mick had stopped issuing licences. Or dating one of Mick's girls – without paying Mick.

Mick was also in import/export. His transactions, however, failed to find their way into the official trade statistics. Mick preferred not to allow the complexities and bureaucracy of Her Majesty's Customs and Excise to impede the smooth flow of business. Cigarettes and booze were sold from the backs of vans and the boots of cars. Cigarettes could seriously harm your health. It said so on the packet. In Mick's fiefdom, that was especially true if the fags you sold were not supplied by Mick.

In short, Mick was what Paice would describe in print as a crime lord. Not that it was a story Paice would ever write. And not that anyone would guess the truth about Mick from seeing him in his greasy apron behind the cafe counter. That was all part of the game. It was perfect cover. And, to prove it, the cops from the local nick were among his best customers – for egg and chips.

They even came to Mick for takeaway food for those unfortunates who were banged up overnight in the cells.

The only man who did not fear Mick was Tom. He was Mick's twin brother. They were not identical – in looks or outlook. Paice had never established the same relationship with Tom. He ran the supply side of the brothers' legitimate business – meat. He was good with a knife. And a cleaver. He knew just where to slice and chop to get the desired result. That was why they called him The Butcher. Well, that was what was on the sign outside his shop – half a dozen arches away. But that was the retail side of his business. The other side was wholesale – usually wholesale violence.

Without asking, Mick poured a mug of tea and placed it on the counter. "On the 'ouse, young man. And it's better for you than all that booze. I 'ope you're keepin' off the sauce."

"Yeah, I've eased up. But I'll give up the drink when you stop smoking those bloody cigarettes."

Mick laughed. "My lungs will outlast your liver, mate. Anyway, what can I do for you?"

The two men went back a long way. They had been at school together. Had shared the mischief of youth. Their fathers had drunk beer at the same pub. They had grown up in the same community – council flats where feuding and fighting were not unknown but where everyone stuck together and kept their mouths shut when the police came knocking.

And when Mick and Tom went away for a five year stretch for removing cash from an armoured security van in Essex without asking permission, Paice was the first to step in and help their ageing mother with her rent and the food bills. Mick had never forgotten the kindness. Where they came from, you remembered little things like that. You also remembered if people stabbed you in the back – figuratively and literally.

Paice lowered his voice. "I need a discreet word, Mick – a bit of info if you have it."

Mick was not in the habit of talking about any aspect of his business to just anyone. He might, however, talk about other people's. After being grassed up over the security van job, he had learnt the hard way to be careful about what he said and to whom. Years before, he and Paice had arrived at an unspoken agreement. Paice would be diplomatic about what he asked and Mick would be careful about what he told. Mick knew that Paice would not ask for something that was "out of order." The arrangement had given Paice leads that generated good stories that had helped him build a reputation.

Mick looked over Paice's shoulder towards the door. A woman in her late 40s had come in, nervously looking around her. "This way, luv," Mick called out. Then to Paice: "I've got a little problem to sort out and then we can talk." He looked towards the door where the woman was still hovering uncertainly. "Come on in, luv. I don't bite." He gave her one of his smiles in an attempt to reassure her. Paice was unsurprised that it did not work. Mick's smile would never get his face on the toothpaste adverts.

The woman finally summoned up the courage to approach the counter. "Come on through, Mrs Brooks." He looked around for the old lady who was tending the tables. "Aunt Tilly!" He had to shout, because Aunt Tilly was a bit hard of hearing. Eventually, after another failed attempt at catching her attention, he walked over and yelled in her ear to tell her to take over while he attended to business in the office.

He told Paice to take a seat and finish his tea. "I shan't be long," he added as he shepherded Mrs Brooks towards a connecting door which led through to the next arch where he had his office. Paice had been there before, but, to Mrs Brooks, passing through the door was to experience a miraculous transition.

She caught her breath as she entered a glossy black and chrome palace, with sumptuous white leather upholstery and thick pile rugs. Having divested himself of his apron and rinsed his hands at a basin set in a glittering black granite counter top, Mick eased himself into a high backed white leather executive chair behind his desk. To Mrs Brooks the glossy expanse seemed to be the size of a tennis court. Not that she played much tennis. He signalled to her to take a seat facing him.

"We have a small problem, Mrs Brooks – can I call you Sheila?" He smiled that smile. She flinched, then nodded. "Lee has been a naughty boy, Sheila, and we need to work out what we do about it."

"Yes, Mr Gentle." Her voice barely rose above a whisper.

"I have to say, Sheila, that I am disappointed that Lee did not have the courtesy to come here to talk to me in person. Instead he has sent his mum. That does not look good."

"He's scared, Mr Gentle. He knows that he's made you angry. Anyway, he went out yesterday and he hasn't come back."

"So he has done a runner. He has made himself scarce until the dust settles and then he will be back hoping that all will be forgiven. Let's be clear about what he has done to make me angry, Sheila. He has been buying his CDs, DVDs and cigarettes from the Nashes and selling them in my territory." The mark-up on pirated music, computer games and movies made them almost as profitable as the cigarettes. Mick had a copying suite that could turn out hundreds a day, and there was no shortage of customers.

Mick knew just how much Geoff Nash would love to move into his area. Using little creeps like Lee Brooks to ship in his merchandise was one way of getting his foot in the door.

"What am I supposed to do, Sheila?"

"Can't you give him another chance, Mr Gentle? I know he's learnt his lesson."

"But Sheila, this is the fourth time he has been caught. He's trying to make me look stupid. I don't take kindly to that sort of behaviour. It shows a lack of respect. I let him get away with it and, before I know it, every little squirt is out there taking the piss. Then I'm finished. Do you think that your Lee is a big enough man for me just to stand aside and let him take over?"

She shook her head and stared at the floor. "Please don't hurt him, Mr Gentle. Please don't tell Mr Tom." Tom was well known for being permanently fresh out of forgiveness.

Mick looked across the desk at the pathetic figure hunched before him. He got up and walked round to where she was sitting. He helped her to her feet and put his arm around her shoulder. "Leave it with me, Sheila. I'll see what I can do. You go home, and when he gets back tell him to come and see me so that we can sort this business out, man to man."

"Thank you, Mr Gentle. I knew you would understand." She sniffled and held a tissue to her face.

He escorted her to the door and watched her leave. He looked across to where Paice was sitting.

"I'll be two minutes, Nick. I've just got a call to make." Paice waved an acknowledgment. Mick returned to his desk and stabbed out a number on the phone. It rang only twice before it was answered.

"Yes, boss?"

"How's our guest, Dave?"

"He's a bit tied up at the moment, boss." They both chuckled.

"His mother's been round 'ere in tears. The little bastard deserves a good hiding just for upsetting her. What is wrong with these kids today? They've got no thought for their parents."

"What do you want us to do with him?"

175

"Against my better judgment, Dave, don't do anything terminal."

"It's not really my place to say, boss, but Tom won't like that."

"I know, Dave. Perhaps I'm getting soft, but I can't break that poor cow's heart. I'll talk to Tom. Just break the kid's legs and make his face look a little bit less beautiful. Cut off a bit of his ear, just so he remembers every time he looks in the mirror not to fuck with me ever again."

"OK, boss. Will do."

"Oh, and Dave."

"Yes, boss."

"When you clip his ear, don't give him the bit you cut off. He'll only take it with him to the 'ospital and ask them to sew it back on."

"OK, boss."

Mick hung up, went to the door and beckoned to Paice to join him. Paice came into the office. He was always impressed with what he saw. The decor was top notch. Even the trains running overhead seemed somehow more subdued. He sank back into the comfort of soft leather. Mick joined him, bringing two glasses and a bottle of single malt Scotch. He unsparingly poured two drinks, handing one to Paice.

"I'm not encouraging you, but I haven't seen you for some time, Nick. Mates have to share a drink. So, what you doing these days? Been anywhere interesting?"

Paice sipped his drink, savouring the quality and holding the glass up to the light to study its rich golden amber hue. "No, Mick. My travelling days are over. I've had enough of all that."

Mick gestured with his glass. "Good 'ealth, Nick," and took a gulp. "Our mum used to follow all your moves, you know. She bought your paper every day. She used to say to Tom and me, 'Have you seen where Nick is now? Why don't you boys get a good job like him?' She was really proud of you. After what you did for her, she thought you were a bit special."

Paice fidgeted self-consciously and smiled. He took another sip.

"So, if you've done with travelling, does that mean you're settling down at last?"

"It does. Eventually, you realise that there is no limit to the appalling things people are capable of and you get sick of writing about it."

Mick slowly shook his head and sighed. "I know, Nick. People do some terrible things. You wonder what's in their 'eads."

Paice continued. "I have spent too much of my life seeing young men with guns destroying the lives of innocent people just because they think they've got some religious or political dream. Or because they want to get rich.

"It's good to live in a civilised country. People here never stop complaining about this and that, but they haven't got a clue how bloody well off they are."

Mick looked at him in mock disbelief. "Civilised? You're out of touch, mate. You should come back a bit more often and see what life's like round here." He concluded the sentence with a grin that exposed tobacco stained teeth. "Anyway, what can I do for you?"

"It's a bit of a long shot, Mick, but I'm exploring every avenue. Ever heard of a character called Titus Refik?"

"Tight as what? I've heard of tight as a duck's arse – and that's watertight, as in a good alibi." He laughed out loud at his own joke, then realised Paice was not joining in. "Sorry, Nick. This is serious for you."

"It is, Mick. I need all the help I can get on this one."

He sat back, thinking, as he ran the name through his memory. "It doesn't ring any bells, I'm afraid, Nick. What's he done?"

"I've been following a fiddle that this bloke is running – we're talking about potentially millions – and he's pinched the life savings of thousands of ordinary people. The paper ran my story as the front page lead the other day."

"Sorry, Nick. No offence, but I didn't see it. Why don't the cops just nick him, then?"

"Because, Mick, like you, this bloke is too smart for them. He's made sure that the trail doesn't lead back to his door. His hands are clean. The trouble is that the truth is that they are anything but clean. To make matters worse, his thugs are threatening someone I care a great deal about, someone who needs help and who I intend to ensure gets it."

"All I can do is make inquiries for you. What exactly do you want to know?"

"Anything at all. What I really want is to find out where he is, if he is in the UK. The man is a bit of a mystery. He's got eastern European connections or origins, if that will help."

"Is he a Russian?"

"I don't think so, Mick. Perhaps Turkish or Bulgarian – somewhere like that. If he is into this sort of activity, he could be into other things, too."

"OK, I'll see if I can find out anything for you. You had better write the name down for me."

Paice took a notebook from his jacket pocket and carefully printed Refik's name before tearing the page out and handing it over.

Mick stood and walked across and dropped the paper on to his desk. "While you are here, I want you to have a look at something for me." He pulled open a drawer and took out a plain blue cardboard box about twice the size of a matchbox.

"I have had a business proposal from an anonymous party who has approached me through one of my contacts. Hold out your hand."

Paice did as he was instructed. Mick tipped the contents of the box into his outstretched palm. "What do you make of them?"

Paice examined what appeared to be two misshapen pieces of translucent glass. One was colourless. The other had a yellow hue. Each was smaller than a cube of sugar.

"Do you know where these came from?"

Mick shook his head. "Not at this stage. This is a first introduction. They were given to me as an act of good faith. If I am interested, more can follow. What do you think they are, Nick?"

"Well, I'm no expert. They could be pieces of glass, or stone, but they could be raw, uncut diamonds. What are they being offered as?"

"They are being offered as diamonds. The problem is, how would I know what they are?"

"Your problem is finding someone straight who you can trust to tell you what they are and what they're worth, and all without then telling the cops."

"That's less of a problem. I have the contacts, which I will need if this is a runner."

"Are they stolen or smuggled?"

"I have been guaranteed a regular supply, so I guess they are not nicked. And I know that if they are diamonds, they weren't dug up on Clapham Common."

"Why you, Mick? This is a bit outside your usual, isn't it?"

"It seems that they are being brought into the UK. Whoever is bringing them in is new to the game and needs a means of moving them on to buyers in this country, or on into Europe – probably Amsterdam – or even back across to India. without the authorities having to be bothered with all that nasty paperwork."

"And leaving no trail back to them? They think that because you can get stuff into the country, you would be able to use the same methods in the opposite direction?"

"Yeah, I guess so. The trouble is they want me to buy them upfront – admittedly at what they say will be a knockdown price – and then give them 10 per cent. of the profits less my expenses when I offload them to the next buyer. They reckon I will double my money or better."

"So you end up taking all the risk and they get a nice wad of cash for doing bugger all. Have you decided what you are going to do?"

"I'm still thinking about it. The problem is, I don't know anything about diamonds – I've nicked a few from jewellers' shops, but they were in gold rings and were something I could flog. But I don't even know if these are diamonds, and I certainly don't know anything about their value. I know it all depends on colour and clarity – "

"And size, and what sort of a stone they end up with after cutting and polishing. Christ, Mick, you'd need to be a bloody expert to find your way through that minefield. And you are not talking chickenfeed. You could come badly unstuck."

"On the other hand, Nick, the profit potential is good – really good. It's worth thinking about at the very least."

Paice rose to leave. Mick shook his hand. "It was good to see you Nick. I'll see what I can find out about your bloke..." He hesitated as he looked at what Paice had written then struggled with the pronunciation – "Titus Refik."

Chapter 13

At the busy times the Central Lobby of the Houses of Parliament is the parliamentary equivalent of Heathrow airport. Crowds of people come and go, look for friends or associates, or wait to be met. Some of them mill around expectantly, listening over the babble for their names to be announced over the public address system, confirmation of the arrival of the person they are there to meet. Some lounge about on the green leather sofas, tired of waiting, or perhaps just watching, fascinated by the sideshow of politics and democracy as it is performed before them. The doorkeepers, impeccably turned out in white ties and tail coats, their gold badge, a depiction of Mercury the messenger, as befits their role, glittering across their midriffs, move briskly through the mêlée in search of their quarry to deliver that urgent summons or communication.

Paice was no stranger to the place and he barely noticed the crowd. His mind was above the hubbub and deafening chatter. He cut straight across the Lobby and into the corridor opposite, his heels rapping out on the tiled floor a rhythmic beat that bounced back at him from the stone walls and columns as he passed.

He nodded to the policeman who stood watch, turned on to the familiar stone staircase leading to the Committee corridor, and took the stairs two at a time past statues and stained glass windows. The event he was due to cover had already started. Not unusually, he was behind time. He always underestimated how long it would take to clear the security checks. He quickly located the room. Outside, a small chalked board mounted on an oak stand announced that it had been reserved by Mr Seamus McNally MP for a meeting.

Harry Draper, the day news editor, had smirked when he had handed Paice the press release announcing the meeting. "I believe Mr McNally is a particular friend of yours, Nick." Everyone in the office was familiar with the history of his relationship with the former terrorist. Paice's response to Harry included words that would never find their way into the columns of any family newspaper.

He reached into the oversized pocket of his waterproof jacket, fished out his notebook, pushed through the heavy swing doors and entered the room. His arrival temporarily interrupted the proceedings as everyone turned to see who had entered. McNally was on his feet and speaking. He looked at Paice with a sour demeanour that projected hostility. Paice returned the compliment.

"As I was saying before that untimely interruption, ladies and gentlemen, our purpose in inviting you here today is to launch our campaign for the creation of a compensation fund for the victims of our struggle against British imperialist rule."

There were about a dozen news and TV reporters in the room. Paice took a seat next to George Lockhart. "Hi, George. Have I missed anything?"

"No, Nick. He's just getting to the point. We've had a load of old flannel about his desire for peace and reconciliation, so you've missed nothing."

McNally was flanked by a team of his cronies. Paice surveyed the faces. The last time he'd seen a line-up like that they were wearing ski masks and sporting Armalite high velocity rifles, courtesy of a lunatic middle eastern dictator whose principal aim in life was to foment revolution and support the struggle for freedom. The pursuit of freedom did not extend to his own country where anyone contradicting the brother leader would be beaten to death in front of their family. Paice guessed that the cast was unchanged from those previous performances. Now that peace had come, they felt secure in revealing their identities so they had dispensed with the masks.

McNally continued: "As you know, a number of our people were killed, injured and imprisoned as a result of their participation in the struggle. Now that we have a British Government that we can talk to, and now that our people have sent me here to represent them, we think it is possible to open a dialogue that will lead to those wrongs being put right.

"Our followers suffered grievously and we are now urging the British Government to fund a compensation scheme to give them reparations for the injustice they had to endure."

He went on to outline the sort of scheme he had in mind, the levels of compensation that the victims should receive, and the timescale of payments.

Paice sat silently as the other reporters asked questions and McNally provided what appeared to be well reasoned and plausible replies.

Paice raised his hand. McNally ignored him and took a question from the political correspondent of one of the TV channels. It was all done on first name terms. "Can I ask you Seamus ..." and "Thank you for that question, John ..." Paice could feel his temper building.

He raised his hand again. McNally looked the other way."No more questions, then, ladies and gentlemen?"

Paice stood up. "Yes, Mr McNally. I've got a couple of questions." McNally glanced uncertainly at his henchmen, first on one side and then the other, his face showing impatience and annoyance. "It seems, ladies and gentlemen, that now that Mr Paice has decided, belatedly, to grace us with his presence, he intends to prolong the proceedings unnecessarily."

Paice looked around at the assembled press corps with a disarming smile. "Well, Mr McNally, correct me if I'm wrong, but you sent my newspaper an invitation to..." he took exaggerated care to read the sheet of paper that he held up for all to see ... "a press conference. I may be less experienced in these matters than some, but my understanding is that a press conference is an opportunity for the press to ask questions." His gaze hardened as he stared at McNally. "And I've got some questions."

McNally shook his head. "I don't think it's any secret that I don't like you, Paice. You've always caused trouble and, quite frankly, since we are aiming for a constructive dialogue, it would have been better for our campaign if you had not come."

Paice cocked his head to one side and adopted a puzzled expression. "But I have it on good authority that before I arrived you were preaching peace and reconciliation, Mr McNally. You could demonstrate your sincerity in pursuing those admirable objectives by sending some in my direction."

Now it was McNally's turn to get irate. "Why don't you admit, Paice, that all you ever want to do is cause trouble for the people of Ireland. You've no time for the Irish. Admit it."

"You want the truth, McNally? I'll give you the truth. The people of Northern Ireland are good and courageous people. On both sides, they have shown that they've got guts and the sense to try to sort out their problems by talking, not fighting. The simple fact is that they deserve better than you and your hoodlums.

"Is it true that you won the election only because those people your boys did not buy were warned that they had better put their cross in the right place or else? Is it the case that they voted for you not because they love you but because they're scared of you."

McNally's voice moved an octave higher as emotion began to take over from reason. "You are talking rubbish, Paice. I won that election fair and square. I'll sue you for that lie."

"I was asking a question, Mr McNally. You can't sue someone for asking a question. And while we're at it, I've got another one for you. You want the Government to shell out taxpayers' money to line the pockets of you and your thugs. Is it true that your outfit was behind the raid on the Commercial and Industrial Bank where the thieves helped themselves to £10 million and killed three guards in the process?

"If that were so, wouldn't you have enough money already to finance this so-called compensation scheme yourself? Is the truth that you and your self-styled freedom fighters are just a bunch of gangsters and killers who have used the violence and strife as a cover for profitable pursuits such as protection rackets and money lending?"

McNally's eyes blazed with anger and he lunged forward towards Paice. He was restrained by the huge man who stood to his left side. He grabbed McNally's arm and muttered something into his ear. McNally pulled himself free. "Right. Let's get out of here." He turned to Paice. "You've just made a big mistake, Paice," he snarled, then he pushed roughly past his associates and left the room.

The big man sidled up to Paice. His soft Irish accent belied his rough hewn appearance and massive, muscular build. "Congratulations, Mr Paice. Quite a performance.

Pity you arrived late. Still, it will be all the more appropriate for when your headstone bears the words 'The late Mr Paice.' That might be sooner rather than later. You never know what's round the corner."

Paice turned away from him and bumped into George Lockhart. "Still making friends, Nick? I bet McNally's personal protection wasn't inviting you for tea and cakes."

"No, George. It sounded more like a warning bordering on a threat."

"I told you to watch your step with those people, Nick. They are dangerous."

"All the more important to show them up for what they are, George. When you ask the right questions and don't get the right answers you know you're on to something."

Back at the office, his first port of call was the lawyer to clarify what he was allowed to write without running the risk of legal action against the paper. He always remembered Angus Lawson's advice: never land the editor or the proprietor in court. The lawyer told him that some of the potential beneficiaries of the proposed compensation scheme were convicted murderers, however much McNally might want to dress them up as freedom fighters.

The next morning Paice's story was second lead on page 3 under the headline "Killers demand taxpayer handout". It contained only the broadest hint of the theme of his questions to McNally.

Chapter 14

Bob Bryce sauntered across the news room to where Paice was sitting. He leaned on the partition behind which Paice's desk was located – "like a bloody battery hen" as Paice described it – ducked his head and peered over the top of the half-eye glasses that clung precariously to the end of his nose.

"In your work on St George Consolidated Land what have you discovered about Giles Beaufort, Nick?" he asked.

Paice flicked a lever under the seat of his chair and gently rocked back and forth, clasping his hands behind his head. "Not as much as I would like, Bob. He was the managing director and he has done a disappearing act. He's got a lot of questions to answer. I am just amazed that the cops are not after him. I expect that they will get round to it. He is someone I would very much like to meet."

"Well, it's just possible that you could get your chance, mate. He is being chucked out of Singapore. You know how squeaky clean they are out there. It seems that with all that's happened over SGCL they've decided they don't want Beaufort littering the place."

He dropped a sheet of paper on the desk in front of Paice. "That's an email I have just received from a mate of mine in Singapore. He works for an English language paper there."

Paice quickly read through the message. "So that's where the bastard went to ground," he muttered. It seemed that the Singaporean authorities had been politely asking Beaufort to get out of their country, but he had shown no signs of complying. "Your pal says that their patience ran out, Bob, and they've just virtually dragged him to the airport and put him on the first plane out. He cannot get official confirmation of the airline or the flight, but he has it from one of his contacts that the first available seat was with Far East Air Services to Geneva. It's not definite but that seems to be where he is headed."

Paice reread the email. "There's no word of his onward travel plans. One thing is certain. If he is heading for Geneva, he won't want to hang around there. He'll be keen to get back to the UK where he has friends and somewhere discreet to stay. With what he's been up to, he will want to keep his head down and avoid people like us. The question is how's he going to get back from Switzerland."

"You're the hotshot reporter, Paice. I'm sure you can find that out." Bryce made no attempt to suppress the sarcastic tone. "I'd hazard a guess that it's worth a phone call to the airline, but what would I know? I'm just a burnt out, deskbound has been."

"All that is very true, Bob, but you left out the bit

about also being an unreformed piss artist. And when you describe yourself as a has been, can you remind me just what you have been?"

Bryce smiled. He and Paice enjoyed the banter that characterised their frequent encounters. Each seriously respected the other, but in their verbal battles no quarter was given and none was sought. Honours were usually about even, so there was intense competition to get the upper hand.

" I am surprised you've forgotten what I have been, Mr Paice." He accentuated "have been."

"I have been putting up with your crappy reporting. I have been signing off your fictitious expense claims. I have been propping you up. And I have been keeping your cock-ups from the attention of our beloved leaders. But do I get thanks, or even a kindly word for attempting to keep you on the straight and narrow? Not on your life."

Paice slowly shook his head in mock sadness. "Straight? The only time you can walk straight is before the pubs open at 11am. And since you don't get out of bed until midday...."

Bryce roared with laughter and began to walk away. He paused and looked back. "It is true that I have been known to consume a restorative draught or two, but that would be only to enable me to recover from a day of coping with you or to reinforce me in preparing for the challenges of contending with you in the day ahead. Unless, of course, you have a day off, in which case I stick to tea and coffee."

Paice allowed his adversary to take a few more paces. "Tell me, Bob, is it true that the only two man-made structures visible from the moon are the Great Wall of China and the pile of empties outside your back door?"

Bryce turned on his heel and dispatched one final, Parthian, shot. "No, Nick, it's not true. It's a myth that you can see the Great Wall of China from the moon."

It was Paice's turn to laugh. He took the phone book down from a shelf, found the number for Far East Air Services and dialled it. He listened impatiently to the recorded music and the message that lied about "all" their operators dealing with other customers at what was a very busy period. He guessed that it meant that there were two people manning the phones and three people ringing in. Finally, he got through.

"This is Far East Air Services reservations. My name is Agustina. How may I help you?"

Paice suppressed his annoyance at having been kept waiting while listening to that damned music. He wanted help so he needed to come over as charming.

"Hallo, Agustina. I have a problem and I hope that you can help me with it."

"I'll certainly do my best for you, sir."

"I know you will, Agustina. The problem is that my brother is on one of your flights from Singapore and I don't know which he is on. Can you give me that information?"

"I cannot give you the details relating to any of our passengers, I'm afraid, sir. We never divulge personal information of that nature."

"And I am very pleased to hear that, Agustina. However, I am in a real difficulty. I really need to know when my brother will arrive."

"I'm really sorry, sir, but I don't think I can help you."

"I can see it is a problem for you, but this is a family emergency. We think that my brother is flying in to Geneva. Can you at least confirm that he is on a flight from Singapore to Geneva, please? His name is Giles Beaufort." He spelt the name for her.

She paused and sighed. "I'll see what I can do." He could hear her tapping the keys on her computer. After about half a minute, she came back. "I am probably saying more than I should, but I can tell you that he is on one of our flights."

"I need to know what time the flight will land at Geneva, Agustina."

"I really cannot say any more than I already have."

"Look, Agustina, I understand your difficulty. But, as I said, this is a family emergency. Our mother has been taken seriously ill and Giles doesn't know. When it happened last night we were unable to contact him. We knew that he was planning to fly home but we did not know which airline or precisely when. I need to meet him at the airport to tell him about mother and get him to the hospital as quickly as possible.

"If he is flying into Geneva, I shall have to book him a connecting flight to London. But I need to know what time his aircraft will land."

"I can see that these are special circumstances, Mr Beaufort. In this sort of situation we try to be as helpful as possible. I can't tell you about Mr Beaufort's movements, but I can say that flight FE006 lands in Geneva tomorrow afternoon at 17.00 local time."

"Agustina, you are wonderful. Can I book a connecting flight for him with you?"

Agustina hesitated. "I would not think that was necessary, Mr Beaufort."

"Not necessary? What do you mean?"

"Look, Mr Beaufort. I am not permitted to divulge personal information but may I make a suggestion? Why don't you have a word with Harrier Aviation. It is a private charter company. They may be able to help you." She had given Paice all the information he needed without actually saying very much at all.

So, before he had been put on board in Singapore, or perhaps by using his mobile phone before takeoff, Beaufort had organised a private flight to get him back to England. Crafty sod. It meant he could slip into some quiet little airfield tucked away in the rural backwoods with no one to spot him coming into the country. Well, Paice intended to be there to welcome him home. It would be nice to organise a brass band, but that would probably be going too far.

"Thank you, Agustina. You have been most helpful at a difficult time for our family."

The next call was to Harrier Aviation. They were based at Redcorn aerodrome. The former RAF world war two fighter base was tucked away on the border of Kent and Sussex. By now they would have filed a flight plan with an arrival time back in the UK.

The phone rang only four times. No music this time. Instead a perky voice announcing that Paice was through to Harrier Aviation and asking how she could help. He made a mental note that if he ever came into sufficient funds, this was how he would fly. "Dream on, sunshine," he muttered to himself.

"Hallo, I am hoping you can help me. You are flying my brother from Geneva tomorrow afternoon back to the UK. He's arriving on Far East flight 006 at 17.00 tomorrow. I need to know what time he will arrive back at your base, please?"

"Just a moment, sir." The line went silent. Then a bloke's voice, not perky, sounding slightly officious and not particularly helpful.

"Hallo, sir. You are asking for information about one of our charters. We don't give out that information, I'm afraid."

Time to bullshit. "I appreciate that – I'm sorry, who am I speaking to?"

"My name's Peter Andrews. I'm the flight controller."

"Well, the situation, Mr Andrews, is that you are flying my brother back to the UK tomorrow and I need to know what time he will get back so that I can meet him. While he has been airborne we have had a family emergency – our mother has been taken ill. When Giles arrives I shall need to get him to the hospital with all speed.

"I'm not asking for anything too confidential. I know that you are picking him up in Geneva and I just need to know what your timings are so that I can be at Redcorn to tell him face to face what has happened – it's not something I want to tell him over the phone. I'm sure you understand that. I assume you know the times of the flight. I guess you will have filed a flight plan by now."

"What is your name, please?"

"I'm Giles's brother Antony."

Andrews was silent as he considered what Paice had said. "We wouldn't normally give any information, Mr Beaufort, but you clearly know your brother's movements and, from what you tell me, these are exceptional circumstances.

"We have been cleared for takeoff from Geneva at 19.00. Our aircraft is scheduled to return to base at 20.05. The times are all local. The immigration and customs authorities are aware of your brother's arrival and they will have someone here to deal with him, but please bear in mind that clearance will take a little time. However, it is the only flight due from abroad tomorrow so the formalities should be completed quite quickly."

"Thanks, Mr Andrews. That's very helpful of you. Oh, by the way, I don't want my brother getting wind of my having made these inquiries. He'll start to worry. I'll tell him everything when I see him."

"That's quite understandable, Mr Beaufort. We won't mention that you've been in touch."

Paice hung up and told Bryce the good news. "I know where he's coming in and at what time, Bob."

"I'm surprised they gave you that information, mate. They won't usually tell you a thing."

Paice smiled. "It depends how you approach them, Bob. In my experience, if you are straight with people, they will be straight with you."

"Next you'll be telling me that honesty is the best policy, Nick."

"Every time, Bob. Every time."

They discussed the logistics of the next night's operation. "You'll need a photographer. I reckon it would be good for you to take Olivia with you. You might need to cover more than one exit at the airport. You don't want the bloke to slip out of the side door while you're waiting at the front, do you?"

"I reckon I can manage, Bob. Taking Olivia will be a bit of overkill." Paice did not want to share the story with anyone, least of all Olivia.

"Perhaps, but we don't want to take any chances. Olivia is going with you, Nick."

Before going home, Paice liaised with the picture desk. "Yeah, Nick, we've had a call from Brycey. We're sending Steve Maine. We've got all the details – Redcorn at some time before 8pm. Steve says he'll see you there."

Paice was pleased. He was generally impressed with the snappers. They usually got one chance at the right shot, and it was all credit to them how often they did it. But then they were a pretty ruthless bunch. And Steve Maine was among the best – and the most ruthless.

Chapter 15

The next afternoon was sunny and warm. Just as well. He had been reluctant to take Olivia with him in the first place. If he'd known that they would be travelling in her car with her driving he would have put his foot down. The trouble was that was precisely what Olivia was now doing.

Paice found that the best approach to bends was to close his eyes. Olivia drove what he thought was impossibly fast. He was hesitant to be so generous as to describe the machine as a car. It had no roof, its utilitarian, two-seater interior was functional to the point of starkness, and his buttocks were alarmingly close to the tarmac. It was a mercurial and highly strung creature that delighted in responding to the slightest movement of her wrist and jab of her right foot. After 10 minutes on the open road he had put aside all his preconceptions and misconceptions about women drivers.

He clung to the dashboard with his left hand, crossed himself with his right and screamed "Jesus Christ!" through clenched teeth. Olivia laughed loud enough to be heard over the rush of the wind that tore at his ears, made his eyes water, and made a mockery of the suggestion that the shield part of the word windshield implied even the most minimal form of protection. Even in July, he needed warm clothing to travel like this. He had only his faithful waterproof jacket. It was buttoned up to his neck.

She accelerated down into a dip in the road that was followed by a gentle right hand bend quickly succeeded by a sharp left. Her left hand flicked the gearstick and the car responded with a howl from the exhaust that was poised just over Paice's right shoulder and roared in his ear. Her right hand had complete mastery of the steering wheel and they swept smoothly through the twists in the tarmac at speeds that caused Paice to question the principle that the shortest distance between two points is a straight line.

They stopped at a crossroads to study the signpost. Paice realised he was slightly short of breath. "Just what is this bloody thing, Ollie?"

"It's a Caterham 7, Nick. Too much for you is it? I heard you resort to religion. That's got to be a first."

"Let's just say I think I left my intestines at that last corner and I'd very much like to go back and collect them."

She laughed again and he felt an unseen force press him back into his seat as the engine howled and they catapulted across the junction, accelerating hard in the direction of Redcorn.

Steve Maine was waiting for them in the road beyond, and out of sight of, the entrance to the aerodrome. He was sitting astride a large and self-evidently powerful motorcycle. Paice groaned. Another speed addict. A crash helmet dangled by its strap from the handlebar. Maine caressed his back pack containing his precious cameras and lenses as it rested on the petrol tank.

Paice struggled up and out of the low-slung car, thinking that it was how one might climb out of one's grave, and walked over to him. They exchanged greetings and Olivia joined them.

He walked up to the chain link perimeter fence and looked through. This was no Heathrow or JFK. A collection of low buildings and Nissen huts ran off at a right angle from where he stood. Across a wide expanse of grass he could see the end of the single runway with the old wartime control tower located to one side of it. A dozen small private aircraft stood neatly parked in front of a hangar large enough to accommodate a couple of executive jets. He looked at his watch. It was 7.40. At this time of year it would remain light until well after the aircraft was scheduled to arrive. That was good. They would see it land.

He returned to where the others were standing chatting. Steve was flicking the ash off his cigarette. "I don't want to go in too soon. If we are seen to be hanging around too much they might start asking us questions. It will be a dead giveaway if they see your camera, Steve. It might be better for you to stay outside. Olivia and I will go in to meet him when he comes through from sorting out the customs formalities. Olivia, when we've made contact, you get outside and warn Steve that we are on our way. Beaufort will have organised some sort of transport to take him out of here. You'll get your pictures as he goes to his car, Steve. Meantime, we'll wait until the plane actually touches down before we make a move."

Olivia looked across to the entrance. "I take it you've seen the security bloke on the gate, Nick. Hadn't we better just be sure he's not going to give us trouble about getting in? I might be able to persuade him that we are kosher visitors."

"And just how are you planning to do that?" Steve's many dealings with security people had taught him that persuading them was often neither straightforward nor successful.

Olivia unbuttoned her jacket and slipped it off, revealing a tight woollen sweater that filled out in what Steve silently acknowledged were the right places. He glanced down at the designer jeans. They hugged her hips in a way that he could only fantasise about emulating.

She grinned. "In war, you always bring out your big guns. He's a bloke, isn't he? I know exactly where he keeps his brains – somewhere south of his belly button." The two men laughed. "Rather like you two," she said with a raised eyebrow and a sigh.

She set off for the entrance. They watched the undulating denim as she walked away. Steve slowly shook his head. "In the face of that firepower, the poor sod is dead in the water."

Paice followed her at a distance, ensuring that he kept out of sight behind the roadside vegetation. He stood behind a bush and pulled down a branch to watch her approach the man. They exchanged a few words that Paice could not hear, and it was soon evident that the encounter was going well. There was laughter and then Olivia was on her way back, glancing over her shoulder and waving flirtatiously to the guard. He grinned and returned the wave.

As he watched her walk towards him, Paice knew precisely what was going through the man's mind. That was because he was thinking much the same. But perhaps with a more realistic appreciation of the chances of success. Olivia was pretty impressive in a whole variety of ways. It was slightly disconcerting to realise that she was only too well aware of all that. And of what he and the guard were thinking.

She rejoined him and as they strolled together back to where Steve was waiting Paice observed, "It seemed to go well."

"Better than well, Nick. I told him my boyfriend was coming in on the plane and that I and his brother had come to meet him off the flight. He said that he wished I'd come to meet him – all the usual crap – but I played along and he agreed that we could take the car into the car park.

"Well done, Ollie. That's good."

"Yeah, but what's not good is that his other brother is already in there waiting."

Paice stopped dead in his tracks and looked at her. "His what? His other brother?"

"Yes, he told me that this was the only flight and that only one passenger was expected tonight, so he assumed that we were all there to meet the same man. He said that Beaufort's brother and a friend are already in the terminal building waiting."

Paice rubbed his chin. "There's just one problem, Olivia. I have checked this bloke out. Beaufort hasn't got any brothers."

"So who are the two men who are in there waiting for him?"

"It's unlikely to be anyone from the opposition." Paice was confident that none of the other media had picked up that Beaufort was on his way back, and, even if they had, that he was coming in to Redcorn. "There's only one way to find out. Let's get in there and have a look."

He looked at his watch to check how long they had to wait, but Olivia held up a hand for silence. "Listen," she commanded. The whining buzz of a twin engine light aircraft carried on the evening air, growing in volume. Then, suddenly, The red and white craft streaked directly over their heads and touched down on the runway.

He turned to the car. "Right, let's move. We've probably got 10 minutes before our man emerges. Olivia has got the OK to drive in and park. We'll go on ahead, Steve. Give us a few minutes and then see whether you can follow us. If the guard won't let you in, chuck some money at him and see whether that works."

"And if it doesn't?"

Paice grinned. "Try flashing your tits at him. It worked for Olivia." Steve laughed and put two fingers up. "See you in there, Nick."

Olivia stopped as they were about to get into her car. "One curious thing the guard did say, Nick. He asked whether my boyfriend was a foreigner."

"What prompted that question?"

"Precisely what I asked. He said that the brother had a foreign accent." Paice stood and thought for no more than a few seconds. A couple of foreign sounding men? Could it be that Titus Refik had sent Giles Beaufort a welcoming committee? But how would he have known that Beaufort was coming back to Britain? Silly question. He probably had contacts everywhere, and he would certainly have put the word out to discover where Beaufort had disappeared to. Bellamy had told Paice that Beaufort had gone AWOL with £20 million of the company's money. Now Refik wanted it back.

Paice had a pretty good idea who was awaiting the unfortunate Mr Beaufort in the terminal.

"We'll have to keep on our toes, Olivia. If these people are who I think they are, they can be very unpleasant."

They got into the car. Olivia fired up the engine and headed for the entrance. The guard was still smiling at her. He barely noticed Paice sitting beside her as he waved them through. They followed the sign to the car park.

It was almost empty. Half a dozen cars were randomly parked in spaces marked out with white lines.

Olivia neatly followed suit, picking a bay closest to the terminal building. They got out and walked the short distance across the car park heading for the front entrance. A small blue van had pulled up by a large double door in the side of the building in an area designated for deliveries. Paice noticed that the driver had left the sliding side door open.

Inside, the lounge served both arrivals and departures. It was little more than a large room with two rows of less than comfortable seats and a desk with a receptionist. Paice looked around anxiously. The place was empty. No sign of the so-called brother and the friend. He walked up to the reception desk and called out for attention. An attractive young woman in a dark blue uniform and hat with a nondescript but official looking gold embroidered badge that could have been for anything from the Stasi to the Girl Guides emerged from an adjacent room. "Yes, sir, can I help you?"

"Yes, I've come to meet Mr Beaufort off his flight from Geneva. Will he be coming through soon?"

She smiled a smile that said "Hang on a minute," leaned back and looked through the door from which she had just come. "I think..." She continued to look through the door. "Yes, sir, I'm afraid you've missed him."

Paice felt a surge of panic. "Missed him? How can that be? He hasn't come through here."

"No, sir. He was met by his brother. We were told that his brother was coming to meet him. Customs failed to show – we did warn them that he was coming – so we allowed the gentleman to go through and meet Mr

Beaufort off the plane. I think they went directly to the car park."

Paice spun round to tell Olivia to get after them. She was ahead of him, disappearing through the door. As she got outside, the blue van sped past. She ran to the car park to see whether Beaufort was there. There was no one to be seen and the only vehicle missing was the blue van. Beaufort had to be in it. She sprinted for her car, leapt in without opening the door, the engine burst into life and she headed off in pursuit.

She had had a head start over Paice who was now well behind her. As he turned the corner into the car park he was just in time to hear the tyres of the Caterham squealing at the tarmac, trying to maintain grip as she accelerated hard to follow the fast disappearing van. Paice could only stand helplessly, almost deafened by the howl of her engine, and watch her rocket out of the main entrance, into the road and out of sight.

The ensuing silence was broken by the rumbling bass of Steve Maine's Kawasaki. He suddenly saw Paice standing in the road and braked to a halt beside him. "Jesus Christ, Nick. Just what the fuck is going on? Olivia went past me like a whippet with its balls on fire."

"She must have seen Beaufort leave and she's decided to follow him."

"She seemed to be chasing a blue van. Perhaps she thought he was in that."

"Yeah, that makes sense. I've had a look and it's the only vehicle missing from the car park. My guess is that the two blokes who were here to meet Beaufort were the muscle who've been hired to handle any trouble. The side door of the van was open. I reckon they must have bundled Beaufort in and taken him somewhere for a bit of meaningful conversation."

"You mean he's been snatched? Why didn't he holler out? There are plenty of people about."

"It's amazing how having a 9 mil Makarov poking in your kidneys can restrict your power of speech, Steve."

"Are you saying they were armed, Nick?" The disbelief was evident in his voice.

"Almost certainly. From what I have been able to find out, these people are not well versed in the art of negotiation, and it is a very brief and one-sided process. They don't take many prisoners. All we can do now is wait and hope that we hear from Olivia. I'm stranded anyway." He nodded at the bike. "You're OK. You've got transport. I'm got to find my own way back to civilisation."

"There's always the pillion, mate."

"That's very kind, but I used up my nine lives on the way here with that crazy woman."

At that moment, Paice's phone rang. He looked at the tiny screen. "Talk of the devil...." He flipped it open. "Hallo Olivia. What's happening? I can't hear you very well." Olivia was speaking as she was driving. The blast of the wind and the noise of the car left Paice having to ask her to repeat herself several times. Finally, he said, "OK, Ollie. And by the way. Well done. Without you I'd have been well and truly stuffed." Steve looked at Paice in disbelief. Had he really heard him say that to Olivia?

Paice came off the phone. "What did she say, Nick?"

"She's following the van west along the A257. She'll call us when she finds their destination."

"Well, you make your mind up. You are welcome to come with me, but, with or without you, I'm heading for the A257," Steve declared. "At least I'll be that much closer. I've got Olivia's phone number so I'll ring her when I get there to find out what's happening."

"Do you know where you are going? You'll need a map."

The photographer cast a scornful glance at him. "Do you really think I'd set out on this sort of job without the essentials?"

Paice looked dubiously at the bike. He hadn't been on anything with two wheels since his boyhood. But he realised that he had little choice. "OK, I'm coming with you."

Steve took off his backpack. "You'll have to take this, Nick. Sorry, mate, but I don't have a spare crash helmet for you."

"Isn't that against the law?"

"Yeah, but so is going at twice the speed limit, and we'll be doing that, too."

It was the last thing Paice wanted to hear. With a show of extreme reluctance and much shaking of his head, he shouldered the bag of photographic equipment. He reached into one of the pockets of his waterproof jacket and took out a headset. Plugging one end in the phone he pushed the other end in his ear. "If Olivia rings while we are travelling, this is the only way I'll hear her," he explained. "You may have to stop so that I can understand what she says."

Steve climbed astride the bike, kicked back the stand and pressed his thumb on the starter button. The four cylinder motor coughed into life and purred smoothly on tickover. He settled into the seat and nodded to Paice to indicate that he had the bike steadied and that it was time to get up behind him.

In minutes they were speeding along the country roads. Paice huddled into Steve's back and clung to him, convinced that his life depended upon it. Men and machine became as one, banking and weaving with fluidity along the black ribbon of the road. Paice was surprised that he felt more at ease than in Olivia's car. With his head buried into Steve's back and his eyes shut he had succeeded in detaching himself from the blur of passing hedgerows, oncoming traffic and the expectation of his imminent demise.

They stopped at a junction and Steve pulled the map from a flap in his jacket. The light was beginning to fade, but he could make out enough without having to use the torch that he kept in another pocket. He flicked the bike into gear and was about to move off when Paice's phone rang and vibrated in the breast pocket of his shirt.

"Hang on Steve," he shouted. "This may be Olivia." It was. She had followed the van to the remoteness of the open country a couple of miles outside the tiny village of Croham. The headset incorporated a microphone, which enabled him both to converse and to take out his notebook and pen and write down the details as she recited them. "OK, Olivia, we'll be with you as soon as we can." He hung up.

He tapped Steve on the shoulder to tell him he planned to dismount. "She's followed them to a village called Croham, Steve. Can you find that on the map? She says she'll wait for us there."

Steve put the bike on its stand and got off. Reaching into one of the panniers, he found a road atlas that provided a gazetteer. Pulling off his gloves, he flicked through the pages, ran his finger down the list of names and came up with a map reference. After studying the map for a few moments, he found Croham and pointed it out to Paice. "We can be there in no time," he declared.

"No time" turned out to be 15 minutes at the sort of speed that Paice reckoned would be sufficient to get airborne.

Chapter 16

As they entered the village, they spotted Olivia leaning on her car in the forecourt of the local pub. She waved them down.

"It's no more than a few minutes from here, Nick," she explained. He got into her car and they headed off, with Steve Maine in tow. They left the village behind and were soon into open country, following a twisting lane with overhanging trees alternating with open fields as the landscape varied its offering to the passing traveller.

It was certainly isolated. Paice did not see another dwelling after they had left the village. Olivia slowed and pointed out a gap in the hedge where an entrance opened on to a muddy track. It descended gently into the darkness. Paice peered into the blackness but could discern no sign of life nor even a light to betray the presence of habitation or any human activity.

"That's where they went, Nick. At the end of the track are a couple of sheds and a barn. You can't see them now that it's dark, but I think the van pulled up by the barn."

She cut the engine and the lights and silently rolled slowly down the track. Steve freewheeled his bike behind her, holding his legs astride to steady his progress. Suddenly, the farm buildings loomed up out of the darkness. Paice could see the van parked by the entrance to the barn. He jumped out of the car and went forward to investigate.

Voices could be heard inside the barn. Along one side of it, between it and a shed, were windows from where the glow of electric light was shining. Careful not to trip or fall in the gloom and betray his presence, he gingerly walked to the first of the windows and looked in. Through the filthy glass he could just make out the two men standing over a recumbent figure on what appeared to be a bench or large table. Paice could not pick up what was being said, but the tone was hardly that of a brother welcoming his sibling home.

He carefully picked his way back to Olivia and Steve. In a subdued voice, he told them what he had seen. "It didn't look too friendly. They've got Beaufort laid out. I don't know whether he is conscious. I don't think their intentions are altogether benevolent."

"Well, there are three of us, so let's get in there and find out what they're up to." Olivia could not keep the enthusiasm out of her voice.

"It would help if we could get in without being heard," Paice suggested. "Steve, is your gear ready for action?"

The photographer nodded and held up his camera, complete with flash. "Before we do this, I want you both to understand what we are getting into and to give you the chance to back out. These two men are hired thugs. My information is that they will resort to any means to get what they want, so when we get in there we have to be ready to make a run for it if things get nasty. Are you both still up for this?"

"You bet your boots," Olivia said, her eagerness undiminished.

Steve grunted. "I've had to do worse, mate. So have you."

"Right. Steve, you will be our insurance. I want you to get the pictures and get out of there and on that bike, and no hanging around."

"No problem, Nick. Let's get moving."

Paice nodded and surveyed the front of the barn. "Let's see if we can find a way in without having to open that bloody great door."

They felt their way along the front of the barn. Paice was in the lead. He stopped abruptly and gesticulated to indicate that he had found what they were looking for. A wicket gate was let into the barn door. Even better, the abductors, no doubt confident that they would not be disturbed, had left it slightly open. Paice gave it a gentle push and it swung back noiselessly.

For the first time he could hear clearly what was being said.

"It is very simple, Mr Beaufort. We want the answer to just one question. Give us that and you can leave. I am assured that your stupid disloyalty will be forgotten." It was a foreign accent – Paice guessed Russian or Eastern European.

He beckoned to the others to follow him in. Just inside the door, bales of straw were stacked in a block. It provided perfect cover. Hidden behind them, they could listen to what was being said.

"Just tell me what I want to know, Mr Beaufort. If I have to, I shall squeeze the information out of you, as I would squeeze juice from an orange. And we know what is left of the orange, don't we?"

"I can't tell you what I don't know. You can ask as many times as you like, but I cannot help you." Beaufort was attempting to sound convincing and keep the desperation out of his voice, but he was not persuading Paice, and Paice guessed that his interrogator wasn't buying it either.

"Very well, Mr Beaufort, it seems that we shall have to resort to unpleasantness."

There was a metallic clatter as equipment was moved. Beaufort's protests became muffled and took on a note of panic.

"Sometimes, the application of heat allows the juices to flow like the blood seeping from a piece of rare steak, Mr Beaufort," the foreign voice declared. The second man laughed, with menace rather than humour. "I would like to avoid you getting hot under the collar, but that may not be possible, I'm afraid." This time they both laughed. With humour.

Olivia looked at Paice and crinkled her brow, the expression clearly asking what the hell was going on.

"So, do we need simmer or something a bit fiercer? Let's have a look and see what else we have. Personally, I like my steak done under a very hot grill."

Paice gritted his teeth. "Right, let's go." He walked out into the full glare of the electric lights. "Can I quote you on that? It would go nicely on our cookery page."

The two men were stunned into silence. But so was Paice. He looked in horror as he saw what they were about to do.

Beaufort was strapped to the bench. His head was jammed inside what Paice recognised immediately as a microwave oven. The bastards were going to microwave Beaufort's head. His mind flashed back to the last time Mrs Evans had cooked a fish in a microwave and he had seen its eyes pop as the waves from the magnetron had boiled the aqueous humour, the jelly inside the eyeball. Then his imagination moved on to the effect they would have on the cerebral fluid that surrounded the brain. His skull and its contents would be left, steaming, like boil-in-a-bag rice. He stood transfixed as he watched Beaufort's futile attempts to get free from his bindings, his stifled cries emitting from the tight confines of the oven.

He was jerked from his trance by a series of vivid flashes. Unlike Paice, Steve, fired up by years of experience of having only one chance to get the shot, had leapt into action. The shutter on his camera was chattering like a machine gun.

The two men had started towards them, but Steve was gone and Olivia had slammed the gate behind him and now barred the way. Paice saw an amalgam of cold rage and fierce determination on the face of the two men. For a heart-stopping moment, he was certain that the incident would end badly, and violently, for him and for Olivia.

He held up both his hands. "Hang on, fellas, let's talk about this. We are from the Daily Mercury. We're running an investigation on you." Now it was his turn to sound convincing and to keep the nervousness out of his voice. The first of the men to reach him grabbed him by the lapel with one hand. When the other hand appeared it was holding a gun. He pushed the muzzle up under Paice's chin, forcing his head back.

"You will now die," he said. Paice heard the hammer click as the man cocked the weapon. His throat went dry just at the moment he most needed the power of speech. The sound of Steve's bike bursting into life and accelerating away up the track could clearly be heard. It stopped the gunman in his tracks.

"Kill me and the police will be here in five minutes," Paice said. "And what you just heard is your pictures on their way to every television screen in the country. They'll have you before you have gone five miles."

A fellow journalist whom Paice admired had once written that "desperate men do desperate things and stupid men do stupid things." He wasn't sure which half of that sentence covered the bullshit he had just spouted. But it seemed to work.

"What are you doing here? You are sticking your nose into matters that are none of your business." The man moved the gun so that the muzzle bit into Paice's face just below his cheekbone. They were not out of the woods yet. Speaking of "they", where was Olivia? The answer was instantly provided. From behind the stack of straw bales the second man emerged, Olivia firmly in his grip and struggling unsuccessfully to free herself.

"Let me go, you bloody ape," she snarled.

The "ape" ignored her. "What you want I should do with her? I kill her?" He looked to the man with the gun for an instruction. The questions were cold and unemotional. It was chillingly apparent that he would terminate Olivia's life with no more feeling that flicking a light switch. Paice realised just how great was the danger they faced.

"Take your hands off her," he snapped. "If I don't make a call to my photographer within the next five minutes, he will call the police. And don't forget, he has your pictures. He didn't take them just to put in his scrap book. We know everything about you and your boss. We've got a file six inches thick on you and your operation."

Olivia chipped in. "You don't think we breezed in here without thinking it all through, without covering ourselves, do you? Anyway, we're not interested in you. It's him we want." She jerked her thumb at the writhing figure of Beaufort. "Just exactly what did you have in mind for him? That looks like something the cops would be only too keen to hear about." With that, she shook herself free, pushed her way past the gunman and walked over to where Beaufort lay. She began pulling the

221

microwave off his head and freeing him from the ropes that bound him to the bench.

Paice reckoned that he might have the upper hand. "We were asked to meet Mr Beaufort off his plane this evening. When he disappeared from the airport, we told the police we feared he had been kidnapped and they have put out an alert for him. The owner of our newspaper is very friendly with the Chief Constable. We have been getting excellent cooperation." Paice gambled that the thugs now realised that they would have to kill all three or let them go. And the former was not an option with those photographs floating around. Nevertheless, he was far from certain which way they would jump.

Beaufort sat up, rubbing his head. He looked at Olivia and then at Paice. A nasty swelling was ballooning around his left cheek and a dribble of blood ran down his chin from a cut lip. He reached into his jacket to rub his ribs but winced at the touch and left that area well alone.

"I need to make that phone call," Paice declared, trying to summon a tone of authority that brooked no argument. The two men looked uncertainly at each other. "If you are not sure what to do, why don't you call your boss?" The expressions on their faces told Paice that calling Titus Refik was the last thing they wanted to do. And if they did so, it might actually be one of the last things they did. He flipped open his phone and called Steve. It barely rang.

"Nick?"

"Hi, Steve. Just to let you know all is well. No need to involve the police at the moment."

At the other end of the line, Steve Maine breathed a sigh of relief. "Jesus Christ, Nick. I've been looking at the pix on my camera. Those are two nasty looking motherfuckers. I was beginning to wonder whether I would ever see you two alive again."

Paice continued with a one-sided conversation. "No, everything is OK. Will you tell the boss to let the Chief Constable know that we will be leaving here very shortly." A pause. "No, Mr Beaufort is fine. Yes, I'll call you back in 10 minutes to let you know we are on our way." He hung up.

He helped Beaufort to his feet and indicated to Olivia to start getting him out of the barn. He had to offer the two thugs a titbit. He took the gunman to one side and lowered his voice. "We are not interested in what has happened here tonight." He waved his hand around the paraphernalia on the bench. "Our only concern is to get Mr Beaufort to a place of safety. We don't want to involve the police unless that proves to be absolutely necessary. No doubt he will be happy to talk to your boss after we have concluded our business."

Now let's see if we can actually get out of here alive, he thought. He looked at the two men. The one who appeared to be in charge nodded and waved his hand as if to dismiss them.

The slow walk across the barn to the wicket gate, with Olivia supporting Beaufort, seemed to Paice to be the longest walk of his life. They made it to the outside and speeded up, heading for Olivia's car. "Come on, Beaufort, get your arse in gear. We've just saved your bacon and now you are going to show us how grateful you are."

Beaufort spoke for the first time. "Well, I am grateful to you, whoever you are. I cannot imagine what those ruffians were after. I was absolutely terrified."

"What they were after, Beaufort, was the £20 million you nicked from their boss." Beaufort made as if to protest, but Paice cut him short. "I know all about it, so don't even begin to think about bullshitting me. Let's get out of here and go somewhere we can talk."

He half pushed, half carried Beaufort across the yard and shoved him into the passenger seat. Olivia got behind the wheel of the two seater. "Where will you sit, Nick?"

"With my new best friend." With that, he clambered in on top of Beaufort, steadying himself by holding the roll bar behind Beaufort's head with one hand and the top of the windshield with the other. "Let's get out of here, Ollie." She started the engine and swung the car round in the yard before accelerating gently up the track to the road. Once back on the highway, she drove as fast as she could, bearing in mind Paice's precarious position.

Within a few minutes, a light appeared behind them in the distance and rapidly caught up. Propped up as he was over Beaufort, Paice looked back and could see that it was a single headlight. He guessed that it was Steve Maine's motorcycle. He shouted to Olivia over the noise of the wind, to which, in his elevated position, he was completely exposed, to tell her to stop at the next convenient location.

Maine stopped his bike behind them, put it up on its stand and came round the side of the car to confer. Paice rubbed his hands together to try to restore circulation. Even at this, the warmest time of the year, exposure to the wind in the way that he had been at that time of night took a toll on body temperature.

"We need to find somewhere to stay the night, get something to eat and get a drink. Any ideas?" He looked at the other two, hoping for a constructive answer. It was Steve who provided it.

"We are very close to the A257. I know where there's a motel that we could use."

"Fine, Steve. Let's go. I'm riding with you. It's not much of a choice, but I reckon it's the least dangerous option."

After about 15 minutes, they pulled up into the forecourt of the R'n'R Motel. The illuminated sign explained that the name meant rest and refresh. Paice was in desperate need of both. Olivia went ahead and booked a room for the three of them, as Paice had proposed. She had stipulated twin beds.

"Don't fret, Olivia. There are three of us."

"Yeah, that's what worries me," she quipped. "I don't want to see any 'three in a bed romp' headlines involving me, thank you."

He and Olivia would take turns sleeping. The other would keep an eye on Beaufort and make sure he did not try disappearing for a second time. Steve would be heading back to the office.

As they settled into their room, Steve reappeared carrying hamburgers and bottles of beer, and a carrier bag with toiletries provided by the motel reception. The food was quickly consumed. Beaufort had little to say, but Paice made it clear to him that the next day they would have a substantial discussion on matters of interest. Beaufort was left wondering precisely what that meant.

Steve left for London, but not before taking a series of pictures of Beaufort in the motel room. After ringing Bryce to keep him abreast of developments, Paice crashed out on one of the beds. Even the sight of Olivia freshening up in the bathroom with her top off could not keep him from tumbling into a deep and merciful sleep. He hoped that the next day would bring him within touching distance of the mysterious, elusive and thoroughly crooked Mr Titus Refik.

Chapter 17

Paice woke with a start. Olivia was sitting at the small table applying her mascara. She looked across at him.

"What time is it?" He sat up too quickly and the room spun. Olivia was alone. "And where's Beaufort?"

"Calm down, Nick. It's 7 o'clock and Beaufort is in the bathroom shaving." He looked at his watch. "I must have slept all night. You were going to wake me to keep watch so that you could get your head down."

"You call what you did sleeping? You tossed and turned for most of the time. I didn't have the heart to wake you. Anyway, who's Maria? You called out for her several times. Maria, Maria – I thought I was in for a performance of West Side Story."

He rubbed his eyes. "It's a long story, Ollie. But thanks for what you did. Christ, I need a decent cup of coffee. Did Beaufort give you any trouble?"

"He slept like a baby."

"In my experience, that means he kept waking up screaming."

"Not this baby, Nick. If there's truth in the saying no rest for the wicked, he must be as pure as a mountain stream."

"Well, let's hope that he pours forth like one when we start plying him with questions."

"Yes, let's hope so. What actually are we after?"

Paice had to think fast. There were two sides to the story – and only one of them was for publication. He had said nothing to anyone, apart from his contacts, about Titus Refik. It was a name that had not been associated with the fraud and was therefore not in the public consciousness. And, apart from Mick Gentle, those he had told had no idea of the true reason for his interest in Refik—clearing Bellamy's name and taking the pressure off Maria. The most important information that Beaufort could provide was Refik's whereabouts, and what Paice wanted with Refik was nothing to do with the story.

He walked across to the window and watched the stop-start of the commuter traffic on the road outside as it waited to negotiate just one of many hold-ups that would frustrate the progress of the drivers on their way to work.

"The fact is, Olivia, that it has been almost impossible to get anything definite on the St George land scam. Anyone who knows anything has either disappeared into thin air or is too terrified to speak. Beaufort was the company's managing director. I reckon that we saved his skin last night, so he owes us.

"What we want from him is the inside line on the whole stinking fiddle. It's great stuff. He and the other crooks who ran that swindle have robbed hundreds of thousands of people of their life savings. I want him to tell us what really went on. It's a story that will sell newspapers. And we have him all to ourselves." He refrained from mentioning Titus Refik.

"The problem is that Beaufort is hardly likely to say anything to incriminate himself, so he may be reluctant to tell you what you want to know," she pointed out.

"Yes, but when he realises that we are the only friends he's got, he may decide to give us enough to make the story stand up." He heard the bathroom door being unlocked. "We'll find out soon enough."

Beaufort came out of the bathroom carrying a handful of toiletry items. "Good morning, Mr Beaufort, how are you today?"

"I'm fine, thank you – and thanks to you." He struggled to summon a weak smile. It was Paice's first opportunity to look at him in daylight. He was of slim build, closer to 5ft 6in than to 6ft. His hair was thinning. Paice put him in his early 50s. He held out his hand to Paice. "Perhaps, since circumstances last night militated against it, we should do the introductions properly now. I'm Giles Beaufort and I am very pleased to meet you. I hope we can be less than formal. Please call me Giles."

Paice shook his hand. "I'm Nick Paice – call me Nick – reporter with the Daily Mercury. I have been reporting on the St George fraud case, hence my interest in you. I take it that you and Olivia have already taken the opportunity to say hallo."

Beaufort nodded. "I'd be fascinated to know how you found me last night."

"We have our methods, Giles. But, first things first. Shall we have breakfast? I suggest that we eat in the room. It was touch and go getting you out of there last night. I reckon that your friends will have recovered their composure by now. Our photos saved the day, but this morning we are in another time and another place and they won't carry much weight now. I suspect that those gentlemen are still quite keen to talk to you, so it is advisable for you to keep out of sight."

"I'll go to the fast food outlet and get us coffee and something to eat," Olivia suggested. "Any preferences?"

"Bacon sandwich and the largest black coffee you can carry, please," said Paice.

Olivia looked at Beaufort. "Just the coffee, please, Olivia. With cream."

When she had gone, Paice told Beaufort to sit down on the sofa. He pulled a chair from the table where Olivia had been putting on her makeup and sat directly opposite him.

"Here's the full picture, Giles. I want to write the best informed story yet to appear about the SGLC crash, and I want you to help me. I have a sketchy idea of what went on, but I need you to join up some of the dots. Do you understand me?"

"Yes, I understand you, but I'm not sure how much I should tell you. The financial authorities and the City of London fraud squad are looking into what happened and although you may have saved my life last night, I have to be very careful about what I say."

"I would not expect you to incriminate yourself, but you are probably one of the very few people who can tell the story of SGLC and that's what I'm after. If you help me, I can help you. I can persuade my newspaper to put you up in a hotel and keep you out of sight until you can organise your next move."

Beaufort paused before answering. "Let me think about it."

"OK, but while you are thinking I want you to think about something else. What I am going to say to you is a matter strictly between you and me. No one else – not Olivia and not my newspaper – is to be involved."

Beaufort furrowed his brow. He looked at Paice through narrowed eyes, attempting to fathom what was coming. "Go on," he said.

"I need to know the whereabouts of Titus Refik." Paice calculated that if he had hit Beaufort between the eyes with a sledge hammer he would have engendered much the same reaction.

Beaufort's mouth opened and closed a couple of times, but no sound emitted. Finally, he regained the power of speech. "How do you know... Who told you about....him?"

"As I said before, Giles, we have our methods."

"I know no one of that name. I can't tell you anything."

"I think you can. I think you know Titus Refik very well. I bet he even calls you Giles. Do you call him Titus? All I want to know is where to find him."

"I've told you, I don't know anything about him."

"Look, Giles. Let's stop fucking about, shall we? Let's just examine the facts. You are scared stiff to say anything about Refik because you fear he might kill you.

I remind you that last night two of his thugs were about to fricassée your brains in an attempt to get you to tell them where you had stashed Refik's £20 million. Until I turned up you had two choices: give him back the money or prepare to meet your maker with a bloody awful headache. My guess is that you would not have got out of that barn alive, whatever you had told them.

"My suspicion is that T. Refik Esq is not blessed with a forgiving nature. Your only hope now of staying alive is to give him back his money and then disappear. At least that way he might just lose interest in trying to find you. So, whatever you tell me will make not the slightest bit of difference to what he thinks of you and what he's got planned for you.

"However, if you help me with the story and the little bit of information I am seeking my newspaper will put you somewhere he can't find you. At the moment, you may have £20 million hidden away, but what you really need is friends. And as I see it, I am just about the only friend you have. If you don't respect my friendship, I'll just turn you lose and you'll be on your own. I give you two days before those gorillas track you down and turn you into the main course on their menu.

"One thing I can promise you is that I don't want to get to Refik for a story – at least, not unless I really have to. I just need to talk to him."

At that moment, there was bang at the door and Olivia's muffled voice appealing for someone to open it.

Paice bent down, got very close and looked hard into Beaufort's eyes. "Remember, Giles, my interest in Refik is strictly between you and me. Not a word to Olivia or anyone else. Take a chance and do the right thing. Tell me what I need to know."

He opened the door and Olivia tottered in with an overloaded tray and a paper bag gripped between her teeth. She put the food on the table and began handing out the coffees. Paice took a bite from his sandwich and sipped the coffee. "I need to make a phone call," he said to no one in particular and took his breakfast outside.

He called Jack Williamson, the editor, on his direct line, explained in some detail that he had Beaufort and how he had saved him, that he needed transport and accommodation for the man that would keep him safe. He added that he was certain that the story that would result would be worth the expense. "And, by the way, I think it will provide a way of getting Oswald Bellamy out of trouble and restoring his battered reputation."

He had saved the best bit till last, knowing that Williamson would agree to his requests because Sir Gavin Hartington would back any move that offered a chance to provide help for his old school chum, Bellamy.

The system swung into action and Paice and Beaufort were soon reclining in the back seat of the directors' Jaguar while Olivia followed behind. They were promptly established in a comfortable but unostentatious family-run hotel in Pimlico. It was one that was regularly used by the Mercury. It knew that to retain the custom meant being discreet and respecting the client's requirement for absolute confidentiality.

"The room is very nice, Nick, but how long do you

plan to keep me here?"

Paice shrugged his shoulders. "Let's be clear about one thing, Charles. We are not 'keeping' you here. We could not do that even if we wanted to. You can leave at any time. But if you leave, you will be on your own. That must be a risk, and, given the sort of reception you received from Refik's thugs, it is a risk I would urge you to think very carefully about incurring. If, on the other hand, you stay and if you agree to help, we will look after you. And the sooner you tell me where I can find Refik, the sooner I reckon I can sort all this out and get those goons off your back.

"If you are planning to stick around, give me a list of things you require and our people will see that you get them. They will need your size for shirts and so on. I take it that the Singapore cops gave you no time to pack your bags before they deported you. We'll have a word with our people out there to see whether we can get your stuff collected and sent on."

Beaufort nodded. "You are right about not having had time to pack. One moment there was a knock on the door. The next I was on my way to the airport in a police convoy.

"I need a number of things, but first and foremost I could do with a drink."

"Feel free to use the room service. I have to get back to the office, so I shall leave you now but here's my card with the contact numbers. Ring me if you need anything. We shall have to sit down very soon and agree on what you are prepared to tell me so that I can reassure my editor that he will be getting a story out of all this expense."

Chapter 18

Back at the office, Paice had two phone calls to make.

The first was to Mick Gentle. To those who knew Mick, the voice was unmistakeable, the sound of gravel being churned in a concrete mixer. The phone rang three times. "Yeah, can I 'elp you?" That was how he answered. No number. No name. If the caller asked to speak to Mr Gentle, it would be someone who did not know Mick, which meant it was someone Mick did not want to speak to. "You got the wrong number, mate," he would say, and hang up.

"Hallo, Mick. It's Nick here. How are you?"

"Nick. Good to hear from you. Yeah, I'm struggling on, know what I mean?"

"Fight the good fight, Mick. Got a minute to talk?"

"Sure, Nick. What can I do for you?"

"I wondered whether you had found anything out about that friend of mine I was telling you about."

Mick was always cautious when speaking on the telephone. Convinced that his line was being tapped, he spoke in a code that employed ambiguity and offered deniability.

"Not a lot, Nick. I've asked about him, but while he is known, no one knows much about him or where to find him. I've tried to track down people he's done business with. The ones we know about seem to have disappeared. It's possible that they may have upset him. He takes a grave view of that, I'm told. Word is that they've gone to ground. I'm sure if you dig deep enough you'll find them. I think it's a friendship you don't need, mate."

With that sort of terminology, Paice needed no pictures to be drawn. Face to face, Mick would have said that they had had "their 15 minutes of flame" or "retired early to a dirt bed", but, however the information had been conveyed, the warning was clear.

"Thanks, Mick. What did you decide to do about that new supplier?"

"I'm not interested, Nick. It's all a question of price and quality. I'm seeing him today to tell him I won't be placing an order."

So, Mick had opted not to get involved with the diamond smuggling. "OK. You know best. Take care." He hung up and dialled the second number on his "to do" list.

Sheila Burke was, Paice thought when he met her, the archetypal civil servant. Hair pulled tightly back, thick-rimmed spectacles, a complete absence of make-up, and a two-piece tweed suit substantial enough to wear on an elephant shoot. Her voice conveyed every aspect of her appearance – sharp and no nonsense.

"Hallo, Sheila. It's Nick Paice. I wondered whether you had come up with anything."

"Hallo, Nick. I'm having lunch in an hour. Join me. Black Lion." By the time he arrived, she had finished her sandwich and was halfway through her glass of wine. He bought her another and a pint for himself, jostled through the lunchtime crowd and managed to join her at her table without spilling a drop.

They exchanged greetings and engaged in small talk before getting to the point.

"Do you miss the foreign service, Sheila?"

"In many ways, yes, I do, but mainly because I enjoyed the work. When you live in some of those exotic locations, the glamour and excitement soon start to fade and you miss what you take for granted in the UK. Having said that, working at the Foreign Office in London has its share of tedium."

"You never told me where your next posting was after... well, you know."

"After the fruit juice incident? My next tour was more punishment than posting. The island of Nagua in the Pacific is just about as far from anywhere else as it is possible to be on this planet. But it is strategically important because we have a defence radar tracking facility there – one of the very few we still maintain – and the island, being a vital source of nitrates and phosphates, is a significant commercial location."

"Nitrates and phosphates?"

"Yes, guano. Bird shit to you and me. My punishment was to be sent to what amounts to a speck of bird shit on the map of the Pacific. We don't have a full embassy there, but we maintain a presence, and I was a part of that."

"Sounds wonderful."

"Yes, not very. But I learnt my lesson. I've adopted a much more cautious approach to how I dress at an official function."

Paice considered her rather staid appearance and thought she had overreacted. She was an attractive woman. She was simply trying not to look like it. "You did not get what you deserved, Sheila."

"I did not, Nick. But that's life. The only consolation is that the Minister who could not keep his hands to himself got precisely what he deserved. Six months after I left, an extremist from an anti-government group walked up to his official car as he sat in a traffic jam, pulled out a gun and shot him twice in the head."

Paice raised his eyebrows. "Nasty."

"I didn't shed any tears for him."

"Shall we get down to business, Sheila?"

"Sure. First, Nick, I remind you that you promised not to write anything as a result of what I tell you without first confirming with me that I am happy about it."

Paice nodded. "I give my word."

"Fine. You asked me about two people. First, Stanley Mwamba is, as far as HMG is concerned, a bona fide diplomat, accredited to the Kamina Bassu embassy. We afford him the same status and privileges as attach to any other diplomat. Unofficially, we don't like him much. To be fair, one could probably say that about a good percentage of the people sent here by their governments.

But, of course, we keep an eye on him, as we do on many of the others, and we think he is ... shall we say, not very nice."

"I can confirm your assessment from my own personal knowledge, Sheila. He is an evil bastard. However, are you saying that although her Majesty would be unlikely to invite him round for tea, he's not actually up to anything illegal?"

"I'd go no further than saying that we don't have any evidence to suggest that. Much as this will disappoint you, we have no reason to consider chucking him out."

"My advice is to keep an eye on him. He is a wrong'un. And talking of wrong'uns, have you found anything on Titus Refik?"

"You've got yourself an odd one there, Nick."

"So I'm finding out. What have you discovered?"

She sipped her drink and dabbed her mouth with a paper napkin. "Do you want to tell me why you are interested in this man?"

"To be honest, Sheila, I reckon I'm doing you a favour not telling you. But I can definitely promise you the same thing I did with Mwamba. I won't print anything without asking."

"Well, as they say in court just before deciding on the sentence, there's nothing known, meaning that he has no record of previous misbehaviour. So we cannot say that he's ever done anything wrong. But there's nothing known in the proper sense of the expression, either. He is a bit of a mystery. He comes from a part of the world where the past is something people either choose not to remember or refuse to forget. If he has got a past, it's well hidden. He has managed to cover his tracks very effectively until he first came to Britain 10 years ago. He applied for asylum saying that his life was at risk back home, and we allowed him to stay.

"It is a bit frustrating because we would like to know more."

"Why?" Paice put down his beer to concentrate.

"Because Mr Refik is applying for naturalisation as a UK citizen."

"What grounds does he have for thinking we'd have him as a British citizen?"

"He is entitled to apply because he is married to a Brit."

"That's all very convenient, Sheila. Does he remember her name or what she looks like? Or how much she cost?"

"The simple fact is that his application seems to be in order. It's going through the system. You know how long that takes."

"I very much want to have a word with Mr Refik. So, where does he live?"

Sheila reached down for her handbag, took out a folded piece of paper and slid it across the table. "That is the address he has given."

Paice studied it. "He says he lives in Hackney? I doubt it somehow."

"Why?"

"Because he is almost certainly very wealthy, and I can't see someone with money slumming it with the poor and dispossessed in Hackney. Anyway, where would he park his Rolls-Royce? It would stand out a bit if he left it in the kerb outside a block of council flats off Shoreditch High Street."

"Well, in his application that's where he says he lives."

"Thanks for your help, Sheila. I have to get back to the office. I'll check out the address tomorrow morning."

Paice phoned the office and checked with Bob Bryce. "Nothing much doing at the moment, Nick, but I'll need you around in an hour or two."

He cleared it for Paice to call in and see how Beaufort was getting on. Paice was less than confident that his fugitive informant would still be where he had left him. He was. He had established himself at the small hotel bar and was working his way through a bottle of Scotch whisky, at the Mercury's expense.

Paice joined him. After all, the Mercury was picking up the bill. "Make it a double, please, barman." It wasn't often he got to drink Scotch courtesy of Sir Gavin Hartington. And after the past 48 hours, Paice reckoned that Hartington owed him a decent drink at the very least.

Beaufort was in good humour, especially given that less than 24 hours previously two thugs had been preparing to cook his brains. Paice collected his belongings and turned to leave. "Eat in the hotel, at least until we can sort out what we do with you next," he advised Beaufort. "We – and that includes you – can't afford to run the risk of someone seeing you. The sooner I can speak to Refik, the sooner you might be able to get out of this game of cat and mouse. But, of course, in order to speak to him, I need to know where I can find him. I've got a lead, but you are the only person who knows his whereabouts with any degree of certainty. I need you to tell me."

"I'll have to think about it," Beaufort replied. "You're only interested in getting a story, then for you it's all over. It's my head that's on the block."

"In the microwave, would be a more accurate description of your plight, Giles."

Chapter 19

In the soft pink and magenta afterglow that embraced the dying of a perfect Mediterranean day, he had been driven along the Promenade des Anglais in an open-top Bentley. Not his. He had watched, from across a yawning social and financial chasm, the rich and famous doing their shopping on Rodeo Drive. And he had strolled along the black and white mosaic paved walkway of Avenida Atlantica, following its fringe along the golden sweep of Copacabana beach.

But this wasn't Rio or Beverly Hills. It was a main street in Hackney, and it was hardly the haunt of the rich and famous. Paice was looking for a millionaire and he knew that something was wrong. To be fair it was neither more nor less attractive than a busy street in one of the poorer districts of any big city. Mundane and anonymous, it was an architectural misfit.

People were there not for the pleasure of it. They were there because they had no choice – perhaps because they lived there and could afford nothing better, or because they worked there and could not get a job in Bond Street or Belgravia. The gloom of a wet Wednesday morning did nothing to improve its atmosphere or appearance. Paice used his sleeve to wipe away the condensation that misted up the taxi window and blurred his view of the street and the passing traffic.

The cabbie had done his best to engage him in conversation. He had failed. He began by asking Paice his opinion on the latest immigration figures. Then, without pausing for a reply, he had launched into a monologue explaining how he would solve the nation's financial and social problems. Paice stopped listening. Instead, he became engrossed in his own thoughts. Finally, the driver capitulated and lapsed into silence. The only noise was the distant hum of the engine punctuated by the occasional crackling message from the dispatcher on the taxi radio.

They turned left and right through a series of back streets and pulled into the kerb. The rain had stopped. "The address you want is along here somewhere, guv. I saw number 60 back there a bit. That'll be £14."

Paice got out and, reaching through the open window, handed over £15 and asked for a receipt. "Keep the change." The cabbie was subdued in his thanks. He was clearly unimpressed at the scale of Paice's munificence, which did nothing to acknowledge the fact that he now faced a three-mile drive through heavy traffic to get out of a barren landscape where fares were as rare as flowers in the desert and back to the lush pastures of the City.

As the taxi did a U-turn and drove off, its tyres swishing on the wet tarmac, Paice looked along the street searching for the property numbers to compare with the address Sheila had scribbled on the slip of paper. So this was where a man who had robbed thousands of people of their savings had chosen to live and enjoy those millions. "I don't think so," Paice muttered to himself.

A shoe shop, a bookie's, a Chinese restaurant and one of those Asian-run shops that never seemed to close, ranged along the pavement. The premises had seen better days, probably at about the time Queen Victoria went off to join her beloved Albert in that big Balmoral in the sky.

As he walked, looking up at the shop signs hoping to see number 78, the proprietor of the general store, typical in appearance of a thousand and one shopkeepers whose origins lay in the Indian sub-continent, came out holding a broom. Paice approached him. "Hallo there. Can you help me, please? I am looking for number 78."

"Yes, Sir, I certainly can help you. This is number 78." He pointed into the doorway of his shop.

"Then I must have been given the wrong address. I'm looking for Mr Refik who is supposed to live at 78."

"That is correct, Sir. He does live at number 78." He smiled and pointed his finger to the sky. "He lives in the flat above."

Paice smiled in return. "Thank you." He could see no obvious front door. "How do I get to it?"

"The entrance is round the back. You must ascend the outside staircase. But there is no point in you going round there. He is not in."

"Do you know when he will be back?"

"I do not think that he will be. He never comes."

"You mean he doesn't live there?"

"That is his business, Sir. But he pays me his rent very well and I am very happy to have him as a tenant."

So the crafty sod had fixed himself an accommodation address, probably just for the naturalisation application, although it also clearly had other uses. "Do you collect his post for him?"

"Yes, and he is most grateful to me for that." Another income stream for the shopkeeper, Paice reckoned.

"Do you have a forwarding address for the mail? I need to speak to Mr Refik."

"I am very sorry, Sir. I cannot help you."

"Did he tell you not to divulge it?"

"No, Sir, nothing like that. But it is a post office box, which I do not think will be of any help to you. When mail arrives, I simply put it in the envelope that Mr Refik has provided and put it in the post. I am very sorry."

A dead end. He might have guessed that Refik would have some devious trick to protect his anonymity. He cursed under his breath that he had let the taxi go. Nothing more to do here. Now he had to get back to civilisation. That meant a long walk. And it was starting to rain.

He pulled up the collar of his waterproof jacket and headed back to the frenetic cacophony of the main street. Within minutes, a bus came into view. He ran to the nearest stop, just getting his foot on the step as the hydraulic hiss signalled that the driver had hit the button to close the door. He flashed his pre-paid pass and took a seat at the back.

As they bounced and swayed through the traffic, he felt, rather than heard over the vehicular din, a call coming into his phone. He took it from his breast pocket. It vibrated in his hand, and the ringing confirmed that someone wanted him.

He flipped it open. "Hallo. Nick Paice."

"Hallo, Nick. This is Giles Beaufort. I hope this is not a bad time to call."

"No, Giles. I'm on a bus heading back to the office. What can I do for you?"

"You wanted to know where you could find Titus Refik. I've thought about what you said. I will tell you where he lives. I am uneasy about this because he will know that I told you. I am the only person, other than those close to him, who knows of his hideaway. He won't forgive me for breaking the confidence."

"As I recall the circumstances when we first met, forgiveness was not the foremost sentiment motivating Mr Refik's plans for you. I don't reckon you've got a lot to lose. Your prospects might improve if you give him back his £20 million."

Beaufort ignored Paice's last observation. "You're right, Nick. I don't appear to have much to lose. I'm more interested, however, in what I might have to gain. If I tell you where you can find Refik, I want you to promise to try to smooth things out for me with him."

"I would be happy to do that, Giles, but I keep coming back to the £20 million. I fear that he may do the same."

"Except that I know more about the St George Land operation than even he does. In fact, I am probably the only person who knows everything. It would be greatly to his advantage for it to remain that way."

"He could secure that objective by putting a bullet in your brain. But you know him, and if you think he might go along with the suggestion – I'm struggling not to call it blackmail – I'll happily put it to him. But I have one question for you. What was Oswald Bellamy's involvement in SGCL? How deep was he in?"

"Poor old Bellamy. How deep was he in? He wasn't. He only ever knew what I told him, and that was only the crap that we wanted him to put out. He was perfect. He was well-regarded, respectable – "

"Yeah, was," Paice interjected.

"Yes, was. He was just another casualty. But, let's face it, he was also bloody gullible. He was the perfect front man and, as it turns out, the perfect fall guy."

Paice suddenly realised that he did not much like Beaufort. The bottom line was that he was just a crook, a thief, and, like most thieves, he was callous and completely unrepentant. And while Beaufort was unprepared to extend any sympathy to Bellamy, he was only too keen for Paice to pull his chestnuts out of the fire with Refik so that he could keep the money he had stolen and walk away without so much as a backward glance.

"OK, Giles, so where is he?"

"He owns a place in Hampshire – Hounds Chase Manor. It's the other side of Basingstoke, tucked well away in a little spot called Golden Nab. You won't knock on his door by chance. It's a good mile off the public highway. It's five miles from the nearest village. He lives there in complete anonymity."

Beaufort gave him the detailed instructions on how to get there. "There are two entrances. If you take the main way in you will be seen arriving and Refik will simply not show himself. Instead, leave the road that would take you to the main entrance and turn instead into Four Mile Lane. If you are approaching from the direction of the motorway, it's on the left. About half a mile along there you will see a simple five-bar gate on the right hand side. The other side of it is a rough track.

"You wouldn't think it was the entrance to a house, but it is. It's Refik's escape route if he needs to get out in a hurry when he sees the cops coming up the main drive. That's your way in, but don't open the gate – it is fitted with an alarm that goes off in his kitchen. Avoid that and you can get close to the house without being spotted."

Chapter 20

It was a beautiful morning. The warmth of the sun was beginning to dispel the faint wisps of mist that hung in the still air within the sheltered nether reaches of the Hampshire countryside. Those wisps offered a portent of a wonderful day ahead. It was days like this that made Titus Refik realise that on a beautiful English country morning he wanted to be nowhere else in the world.

He leaned out of the open bedroom window, inhaled deeply and held it in. The fragrance filled his nostrils and almost caused his head to spin from the intoxication of it. Across a valley painted with the foliage and silhouettes of oak, beech and ash, a tractor worked its way across an emerald square sewn precisely into the quilt of fields – brown, green and yellow.

He studied his hands, front and back, then massaged his cheeks. He needed a shave. There's a thing: he was concerned about his appearance. It was never like that in the old days. Now, he cared about things that would never have occurred to his father. But so much had changed. He still marvelled at how a boy who had been born into deprivation, poverty and even starvation, who had seen death and violence as a routine of daily life in a country ruled by tyrants and despots, could find himself safe and secure in this paradox of such peace and beauty. He would rather die than leave. And he had the power to ensure that neither was about to happen.

He took the phone off its cradle and pressed the button for an intercom call. Down in the kitchen, Mrs Blackholly picked up the handset. "Mrs B, I'll have my breakfast on the patio this morning. I'll be down in 15 minutes."

"Yes, Mr Refik." Shirley Blackholly knew that 15 minutes meant 15, not 14 or 16. She was keen to keep her employer happy. He was strict and never smiled or joked with her. There was not a single word of redundant conversation. And he applied a rigid rule about her never speaking to anyone about him or his affairs. She was not even permitted to reveal his name to anyone in the village. But it was worth it.

He paid her twice what she would earn anywhere else, and the house had all the latest gadgets and equipment. That made the cleaning and cooking so much easier. Then there was the job he had given her husband of keeping the gardens in shape. Ernie was supplied with all the latest labour-saving kit. He, too, did precisely what the boss told him. Not that Mr Refik had ever spoken to her spouse. Or met him. Anyway, if there was any heavy work that Ernie could not manage, there were those two blokes usually hanging around who would give him a hand. They never spoke, either. She didn't like them much. Something not right there. Mr Refik had sent them

254

up to London to sort something out, so it was just her and him in the house this morning.

She set the table on the patio under the striped awning. She was always extremely careful with the china and glassware. It was the best that money could buy. Laid out on the crisp, white damask tablecloth, it presented a beautiful sight. Mr Refik might not be very talkative, but he had impeccable taste. And he insisted on perfection.

She put the dishes of food on the heated tray on the side table and went back for the coffee. A hurried look at the clock. He would be down in two minutes. She took the coffee pot outside, had a last quick glance at the table, and went back into the kitchen. Everything was just right, the way he insisted. That meant that she could leave him to his breakfast and make a start on the laundry. Her last task was to leave the Financial Times in its usual place by the door.

With his head buried in the stock market prices, Refik did not see, as he walked out on to the patio, that he was not about to eat breakfast alone. Until he lowered the newspaper. The shock of seeing Nick Paice sitting at his breakfast table, drinking his coffee, caused him to gasp. "Who the hell are you? What are you doing here?"

"Good morning, Mr Refik. You're a difficult man to track down."

Refik quickly recovered. He dropped the newspaper, and Paice found himself looking into the barrel of a small revolver. It must have been retrieved from somewhere in Refik's dressing gown and he quickly calculated that it was aimed at the space between his eyes. Refik pulled back the hammer to cock the weapon. "You've got 30 seconds to convince me that putting a bullet in your head is not a good idea."

With a degree of self-control that he was uncertain he could maintain, Paice held up his hands in mock surrender. "My name is Nick Paice. I am a reporter from the Daily Mercury. And I am holding up my hands like this so that my photographer, who is well hidden, can get a perfect shot of you holding a gun on a man who is offering you no resistance."

Now it was Refik's turn to struggle to maintain his composure. He succeeded, but he could not keep the anxiety out of his eyes as he scanned the hedges and bushes around the garden looking for the concealed photographer.

Paice continued: "And if you shoot me, he will get a good shot of that as well. He has an 800mm lens that he tells me cost our newspaper £15,000. He assures me that it will pick up the colour of your eyes from 500yds. So, why don't you put the gun away and sit down and talk, Mr Refik?"

The man was not of impressive stature or build. He was not much over 5ft tall, he had a good head of jet black hair and he was immaculately turned out – the dressing gown probably cost more than Paice had paid for his suit. There was a whiff of aftershave that was probably equally expensive. Paice made a mental note not to put it on his Christmas list. It tainted the aroma of his coffee.

Refik sized up the reporter. Cheap suit, scruffy shoes. The man needed a haircut. He began to relax. He had talked his way out of situations much more tricky, and infinitely more dangerous, than this. He slipped the gun back in his pocket. "I'll get another cup. Will you join me in something to eat?"

"I'll make do with just the coffee, thank you."

Refik disappeared into the kitchen and was back almost immediately with another cup and saucer. "You are the man – with that bloody photographer of yours – who has caused me so much trouble over that thieving little rat, Beaufort, Mr Paice."

"Thieving rat? Have you ever heard the English expression that revolves around pots, kettles and the colour black, Mr Refik?"

Refik smiled, pulled up another chair and sat down opposite Paice. "Well the fact that he is a rat is not up for argument. It was undoubtedly he who told you where to find me.

"I have been looking for you for a long time, Mr Refik. I knew who you were, but not where. Beaufort simply gave me the last piece of the puzzle."

Refik nodded. "So now you plan to write an exposé about me, I suppose."

"That is certainly an option." Paice sipped his coffee.

"An option, Mr Paice? That tells me that there may be another choice, or perhaps choices."

"Yes, let's consider them. First, let's consider Mr Beaufort. In return for telling me where to find you, he made me promise to try to make things up between you – the expression he used was to 'smooth things over'."

"Before we go any further, Mr Paice, I assume that you are tape recording this conversation." He held out his hand. "Hand it over, please, or this conversation ends here."

Paice hesitated, then he took the tiny machine from the top pocket of his jacket and gave it to Refik who dropped it on the floor and smashed it with his heel.

"Now that it is just the two of us, we can speak frankly, Mr Paice. So you are here to plead for the life of the little rat?"

"Frankly, Mr Refik, I don't like him and I have no more interest in protecting him than you have. As far as I am concerned, you can blow his brains out – after I have got a story out of him, of course."

"You say that you don't care about him, but you went to enough trouble to save his skin."

"Yes, but that was only because I knew he would lead me to you. It's you I wanted to talk to."

"But how did you get my name in the first place?"

"I have my sources."

"Ah, you journalists and your sources. I don't know who your source was, but it is one you should nurture. My identity is – was – a closely guarded secret, Mr Paice."

"Secret? Something ceases to be secret the moment more than one person knows it. You know as well as I that there is a better chance of two men keeping a secret if one of them is dead."

"That is an interesting postulation, Mr Paice. In my country, we have a similar concept. It is that if you must share your closest secret you reveal it not to your dearest friend but to your deadliest enemy."

"And why is that?"

"Because, Mr Paice, the next morning you will wake up realising that you should have kept it to yourself, and now you have to kill the person you confided in. It would be a pity if that were to be your best friend. But the other way you can make a virtue of a mistake. You get to protect your secret and you rid yourself of an enemy."

"I've heard that dead men tell no tales, Mr Refik. I have never felt compelled to consider the practical implications of such a proposition. You clearly have."

Refik poured his coffee and reached behind him for a croissant. By now he had completely recovered from the surprise of seeing Paice sitting there. His life had been full of surprises, some of them good, many of them very unpleasant. But he had developed the ability to absorb them without allowing them to frustrate his ability to think. Perhaps that was one of the qualities that had got him the success he now enjoyed – and kept him alive.

"I think it is time you came to the point, Mr Paice." He had spoken softly so far, but now his voice took on a hard edge. "What do you want?"

"My usual response would be 'a story', but I have probably already got that. I am interested in something else. I want you to let Oswald Bellamy off the hook."

"And what hook would that be?"

"Let's not mince words. He is the front man, the public face of your swindle, and you are forcing him to keep up the pretence, probably while you salt away the proceeds. If he doesn't comply, if he tries to defend himself, your hit men will go to work on his wife and children. If you are prepared to resort to such thuggery, you are, for all your expensive aftershave and fine china, just a cheap, callous crook, Mr Refik."

Whatever the outcome of this confrontation, Paice felt as though something had lifted him internally. He now realised that he had wanted to say that to Refik from the moment he had first heard the man's name and, having said it, he felt a sense of achievement.

Refik was unmoved by the verbal onslaught. His piercing black eyes held Paice's gaze. "In my line of work, such things are sometimes necessary. What's your interest in Bellamy? He is just another politician who was out for what he could get. Why do you feel you have to stick your neck out for him?"

"That's my business." There was no way he would explain his feelings for Maria and her children.

"So, what's in it for me?" Refik demanded.

"Possibly quite a lot. For starters, you are applying for naturalisation as a UK citizen. One of the qualifying conditions is that you must be of good character. If a story appears on the front page of the Mercury implicating you in one of the biggest swindles to hit the City in a decade, the authorities might conclude that you are not the sort of person we want in this country. And as a fully paid up, home produced Brit, it would give me enormous pleasure to deny you the chance of becoming one of us."

"Who told you that I was applying for citizenship?"

"As I said before, I have my sources. But think about it. Bellamy knows nothing about you and could not implicate you if he wanted. Beaufort is the man you should worry about. You call off your hyenas, and Bellamy's family return to leading an ordinary, happy life, I don't write the story, and you become British and enjoy all the benefits that come with that, including continuing to live in this palace.

"But there is more. If I don't write the story, the police and the financial authorities don't turn up here at 6.30 one morning to kick your door down. Most important for you, you get to keep all the money."

Refik sneered at him. "So speaks the champion of the dispossessed, of all the poor little people who were robbed by the beautiful and elegant St George Land swindle and who the knight in shining armour was riding out to save."

Paice ignored his mocking, sarcastic tone. "If I thought there was the slightest chance of recovering a penny of that money, Refik, your name would be on the front page of this morning's paper, and I wouldn't be sitting here talking to you as though you were a civilised human being, which you are not. The simple fact is that you have laundered the loot to somewhere where it cannot be found. Or do you deny that? Perhaps I have overestimated you. Perhaps you are just a cog in the machine. Perhaps you just take the orders and do as you are told."

Paice was taking a gamble. Even the strongest had a weak spot, and he hoped that Refik was no exception. He guessed that Refik's weakness was his vanity. A man who had achieved what Refik had would believe in his own superiority and invincibility. His ego was probably the size of the manor house in which he swaggered about in his expensive dressing gown.

"What do you know, Paice? You are just one of those little people who get used and walked on by those of us with the real power. Of course I have got the money safely away. And you in your cheap suit and dirty shoes, you would not know where to begin to look for it. And I don't take orders from anyone." His voice began to rise and he stood, leaning over the table and glaring at Paice.

"There is no one else who could have organised something as complex and as successful as the St George operation. I am untouchable and you can prove nothing. Print your photographs and write your speculation, I will deny it and then I will sue your newspaper into bankruptcy." Flecks of saliva had gathered at the corners of his mouth, and he was breathing heavily. "And one other thing. Watch your step. I can have you killed and give it no more thought than I would to swatting a fly with a newspaper."

Paice could not believe his luck. He really had touched a raw nerve in suggesting that Refik wasn't the top man. This was one top-notch, 24 carat control freak, a megalomaniac of the first order. Now it was Paice's turn to be unimpressed. He calmly poured himself another cup of coffee.

"Why don't you calm down and sit down and listen to what I have to say?"

Refik realised he had lost control. He was annoyed with himself. Paice was a nobody. He should have just thrown him out to begin with. If only he hadn't sent his personal protection to London this morning.

"So what do you have to say?"

"I've got a proposition for you. It goes like this. First, you let Bellamy and his family go. Why would you want to harm an innocent woman and her children? Second, you let Beaufort keep the money. In return, he goes to the authorities and admits responsibility for the whole scam, conveniently failing to mention your involvement, or even your existence."

"Why would he go for that?"

"Simple. What's he going to get? First offence, he'll get sentenced to seven years and do half that, probably in an open prison. And when he comes out, he'll have the £20 million to look forward to."

"I still don't see what's in it for you."

"Well, to finish with Bellamy, Beaufort tells the world Bellamy was an innocent dupe who acted in good faith all along, so Sir Oswald gets his reputation and respectability restored." He omitted the fact that securing that would please Sir Gavin. "But the best bit is that I get my story. The Mercury has Beaufort's version of events all to itself. And we get to run Bellamy's side of the story. We have an exclusive, and that's what I am paid to do."

Refik looked out across the gardens and thought through what Paice had said. "I don't like to think that that lying little rat is getting away with £20 million of my money."

Paice forced a laugh. "Whoever's money it is, it's certainly not yours, Refik. Anyway, if we are talking about not liking something, it causes me severe pain to think that you are getting away with swindling thousands of innocent people, but we are all having to make compromises here. Anyway, I'm a newsman, not a policeman. My job is to write stories, not to hunt down criminals like you. One day you will come unstuck, and I'll be there to write about it when you do.

"And as for Beaufort, I have no doubt that you will be holding a coming out party for him when he eventually gets out of jail. What sort of surprise you have in mind for him is entirely a matter for you. He's no better than you, and I hope the pair of you rot in hell."

Refik smiled. He paced silently to and fro under the awning thinking out the implications of Paice's proposal. "OK, you have a deal. What guarantee do I have that you will stick to it?"

"You have to trust me just as I have to trust you, Refik. Anyway, I wouldn't like to think of accidentally running into your playmates on a dark night."

"OK. We'll do it."

"There's just one more thing that you have to do."

Refik looked at him suspiciously. "What?"

"There's a little girl who needs an operation to enable her to walk and another to enable her to smile."

"So what does that have to do with me?"

"It will cost £200,000 that her mother doesn't have. You're paying for it. And that's non-negotiable."

"OK. I'll do it. At least it shows that my heart is in the right place."

"No, Refik. If your heart was in the right place it would be floating in a jar on the desk of the Commissioner of the Metropolitan Police. And if you rat on this deal, I'll do my damndest to see that that is where it ends up. Give me a contact number and I'll be in touch about the money."

Refik went into the house and came back with a gilt-edged business card, which he handed to Paice. "That's my personal number. It's not something I give out much, so keep the details to yourself."

Paice glanced at it and tucked it into his breast pocket. "Good. I think that's all I have to say." He stood up, finished his coffee and left.

On the way back to the car, Steve Maine was flicking through the images on his camera. "Got some good shots, Nick. I even got one of him smashing the tape recorder. Pity about that."

"No, Steve. You got a shot of him smashing a tape recorder." He pulled an identical machine from one of his many pockets. "He did not smash the tape recorder. I've got that bastard bang to rights admitting that he ran the scam and even threatening to have me killed.

"I'll get the IT blokes to run off a copy and send it to him on a disc to add to his record collection. And he can put your pictures in the family album. That's my insurance. It will guarantee that I have a good chance of living into old age. He won't dare to put a foot out of line while I can hold that over him."

Chapter 21

The pieces fell into place. Beaufort realised that he had no choice and came clean about how the scam was all his idea, Refik received his disc in the post, Bellamy jumped at the chance to clear his name, and the story almost wrote itself. It was plastered all over the front page. The TV news channels replicated the story, giving full credit to the Mercury, and Paice agreed to be interviewed by some ungracious presenter – the sort who thought that the programme was all about him and that the interviewee guests were merely extras – on a late-night current affairs slot.

Paice had insisted on sharing the by-line with Olivia, which had prompted her to observe that he was "not quite the arsehole everyone thought". He reckoned that was as close as he could get to a compliment from her. His opinion of her continued to rise.

Sir Gavin had invited him to the top floor. As he headed for the lift, he grabbed Olivia by the arm. "Come on Hankinson, get moving. We're going to collect our medals."

Sir Gavin was all charm and bonhomie. "That's one hell of a story, Nick. Exclusives like that sell newspapers." When he used Christian names, you knew he was pleased. Customarily, he stuck to surnames when dealing with the lower orders. A habit he had picked up at public school.

"It was very much a joint effort, Sir Gavin. Without Olivia, we would not have got it. And if you are handing out plaudits, don't forget Steve Maine."

"Well, thank you, Nick and thank you, Olivia. And I'll send a personal note to Steve. Well done all round." He waved his hand. Paice could not work out whether it was a gesture expressing the inclusive tone of the compliment or a sign that the meeting was over and they should leave. When Hartington swung round in his huge leather chair and put his back to them to look out of the window, Paice realised that it was the latter. They left.

In the lift, Olivia broke the silence. "All joking aside, Nick, I appreciate the way you have handled this. There are some backstabbing egomaniacs in that newsroom who would have kept it all for themselves. I'll buy you a drink later."

Paice nodded in agreement. He could have admitted to her that, at one time, he would have been the backstabbing egomaniacs' team leader. These days, that approach seemed less important, inappropriate, somehow.

Back at his desk, Paice rang Mick Gentle. He wanted to tell him to buy the paper so that he could see that he had cracked the story. The phone rang a dozen times without being answered. He gave up and hung up. Then he called Maria Bellamy to ask how the family was feeling.

"Huge relief, thanks. We owe you a great debt of gratitude, Nick. Do you think that the threats by those awful people have really gone away? Is Beaufort really going to admit that he masterminded the whole thing?"

"Yes, I'm confident about that, Maria. The next time we meet I will give you the full facts – there's even more to it than appeared in my story – but I can promise you that the person who was really behind the threats to you has given his word and he has a great deal to lose if he breaks it."

"It feels as though a huge weight has been lifted from us. Oswald said he would call you today. It's odd, he says, how his exoneration has prompted all his friends at Westminster to tell him that they knew all along that he was blameless. Until that story appeared, he was dining alone in the Members' Dining Room. Now he is never short of company for dinner."

"Well, that's politics for you. They are all terrified of being tainted by association. I suppose it is the parliamentary equivalent of having the plague."

Paice rang Mick Gentle several times during the afternoon, again without success. Eventually, before packing it in for the night, he called his home number. This time, there was an answer. It was Mick's wife, Tracey.

"Hallo, Tracey, can I have a word with Mick, please?"

"You can't, Nick. He ain't here."

"Well, it's not urgent. I'll call back a bit later."

"I'm not sure he'll be back later, Nick."

Paice sensed that all was not well. "Is everything OK, Tracey?" There was silence at the other end. "Tracey?"

"To be honest, Nick, I'm really worried. He's not been home for days. I just haven't heard anything from him. It's not like him. He sometimes goes off for a day or two, but he always keeps in touch. His mobile is switched off, or is out of range, and he hasn't called."

"Have you spoken to Tom?"

"Yes, he says not to worry about him. Says he's probably off shagging some tart and he'll be home when he sobers up."

Tom was demonstrating his usual degree of tact and sensitivity, thought Paice. "Tom and his sense of humour," he said.

"Yeah, I know he's only joking really." She did not sound convinced. "But I am still worried about him."

"Well, if you haven't heard anything by tomorrow, I'll make some inquiries and see what I can find out. Try not to fret too much. He will surface in due course, and all will be well."

But Paice, too, was worried. He did not realise then that his prediction would turn out to be only half right. Mick was engaged in an unpredictable line of business. Enemies were easily made, and they would settle disputes with a gun or a knife when a good kicking failed to do the trick.

When they had both finished their shifts, Olivia made good on her offer of a drink. Paice was feeling in good form later as he sauntered into Kouzina tis Amalias. Philo was on station as usual. Amalia gave him the customary hug and kiss, and Nikki was on hand with a glass of wine the moment he sat down.

"I read your story, Nick." Philo had the Mercury spread out on the table between them. "I see that you finally got to the bottom of it. Maybe you decided not to include everything in the piece you wrote for your paper, eh?" He shot a sly glance across the table.

Philo was no fool. And he knew a great deal more than he would ever talk about. There was no deceiving him. "Well, Philo, some things are best left unsaid – or unwritten."

"Of course, of course. Perhaps some day you will give me the uncensored version, eh?"

"When the time is right, Philo. If a man gives his word, he is expected to keep it." Paice knew that Philo would understand. He did. He nodded knowingly. Paice also knew that he had to show Philo that he was a man who kept his word. That way, Philo would be reassured that he could trust Paice in confidential matters.

After yet another delicious meal, Paice made his way home. Mrs Evans was waiting up for him. The customary pleasantries ensued.

"Good evening, Mr Paice."

"Good evening, Mrs Evans. How are you tonight?"

"Very well, thank you. I have a parcel for you." She turned into her room and reappeared carrying a cardboard box, securely sealed with parcel tape.

"It was delivered by hand. The man – I think he was a foreigner, but he did not say much – was a bit reluctant to leave it with me. In the end I persuaded him."

Paice laid it on the hall table and asked her for a knife. He carefully slit the tape and opened the box to expose a briefcase. Taking it out, he clicked the catches and lifted the lid. Refik had kept his word. Inside were neat bundles of £50 and £20 notes. Paice knew he did not have to count it to confirm that it amounted to £200,000. He pushed it across the table to the speechless Mrs Evans, who had never seen so much money.

"It seems that you and Jessica will be going to America." He snapped the case shut and handed it to her.

That night, he had the best eight hours' sleep he could remember.

Chapter 22

Paice rang Tracey the next morning and again in the afternoon. There was still no word from Mick. The following day he rang again and got the same result before setting off for a press conference on an initiative by an engineering industry group. They were launching a campaign to lobby the Government to put more support, by which they meant money, into stimulating the training of young people in the skills so desperately needed by their member companies.

The event was being staged at a posh new conference complex that had been built on the north bank of the Thames in a place where, generations before, dock workers had sweated and sworn as they humped and handled the trade of a dying empire. The trade was dying, too, although none of those engaged in it had had the foresight to realise that their working practices were hastening its inevitable demise. Paice reflected on the irony of a business that was desperately working to prevent its own untimely end gathering in the graveyard of one that had long before succumbed to commercial pressures, with which it was now contending.

He had picked up the press pack, a sheaf of papers full of words and numbers, asked what he thought were intelligent questions at the press briefing, and finally struggled out on to the extensive balcony that gave out on to the river.

It was fresh and beautiful. A warm breeze progressed, unimpeded, all the way from the estuary, just as the ocean going freighters, bearing the world's trade, had done decades before. It carried to the heart of the city the scents of the sea and that unmistakable smell of the river. Occasionally, the sun slid out from behind the clouds and bathed the buildings on the opposite bank in a brilliance that exposed them in all their detail.

He had been given a glass of wine when he really wanted a Scotch on the rocks. He put it down, leaned on the rail and looked out on to the swirling brown water. Further along, a short distance downstream, people were gathering to watch a police launch negotiating the shallows. It was keeping as close to the bank as it could, but was frustrated by the ebbing tide which was exposing the mud, shingle and jetsam that had been deposited by the current. Just beyond its reach, something rolled and heaved in the water as it lapped against the shore. Twenty feet above, people who had been enjoying the riverside walk were leaning on the wall of the embankment, looking down, pointing and speculating.

Paice smelt something more than the river. He smelt a possible story. Stuffing the papers into his jacket pocket, he left the press conference by a side entrance. He walked briskly along the narrow, cobbled street that was separated from the river by the waterside buildings. Once they had been warehouses stuffed with cargoes from the four corners of the earth – perhaps exotic spices from the East or wheat and maize from the Americas.

Now they had been converted into apartments, the abodes of what the estate agents loved to refer to as "young professionals", people who had got themselves up to their necks in debt in order to live in an area that was now fashionable but which their parents in their youth would have regarded as the grimy haunts of the lower classes. There still remained a small arched entrance set in one of the walls that provided access to a dark and damp passageway. Paice knew it would open out on to the river.

Fifty years before, it had provided access to the water for boatmen. It had long since been shut off by an iron gate, but the local kids, fascinated by the water and oblivious to the danger that had claimed a number of them over the years, had dispensed with the lock, and the gate now swung uselessly on its rusty hinges.

This was familiar territory to Paice. He had been one of the kids who had explored and larked about on just this sort of muddy foreshore. When he got to the end of the passage he was unsurprised to find a set of steps leading down to the water.

He went down and picked his way carefully, avoiding the mud. The police launch was about 20 yards further along. He made his way towards it. The group of spectators that had gathered on the embankment wall above were making animated gestures to the uniforms on the boat.Paice ventured as close as he could to the water's edge. He could clearly see now that it was a body.A passing tourist boat provoked a swell that broke on the shore in a series of waves. The last of them washed the corpse closer towards him. The face looked battered and swollen, but Paice would know those features anywhere. He said a final farewell to Mick Gentle. He did not believe in such nonsense, but for a moment he wondered whether Mick had fetched up at just this place and time to say farewell to him.

Suddenly the metallic shriek of a loud hailer cut through the air. "Keep back, please, Sir. Keep back. Do not touch anything." He looked up to see the copper on the launch waving at him to indicate that he should retreat from the edge of the water. He did not move. How could he leave his lifelong friend alone at a time like this?

Later at the hospital where Mick was taken, Paice stood at the entrance waiting for Tracey to arrive. When she came, it was in Tom's six year old Ford – none of Mick's flamboyance with the flash motor car. Paice waved to them as they drove past him and into the car park where began the hunt for an empty space. Ten minutes later, they reappeared on foot and he took them into the hospital.

It was a silent, grim gathering. Tracey dabbed her nose and her eyes with a damp tissue. Tom, awkward in the presence of grief and embarrassed at his inability to articulate his feelings at the loss of his brother, nodded, muttered and looked anywhere but at the other two.

The policewoman who had been instructed to liaise with the family expressed her condolences and guided them to the hospital mortuary. There the attendant pulled back the sheet that covered Mick's body. Tracey uttered a gasp. Tom stared at his brother almost in disbelief then shook his head and turned away. It required no pathologist to tell them that it had been a violent end.

Paice nudged Tom's arm and directed his eyes towards the door to indicate that they should leave Tracey alone with her husband. Outside, they sat uncomfortably together on adjacent plastic seats. He looked Tom in the eye, but the attempt at communication was not reciprocated. He had never established with Tom the easy relationship he had developed with Mick.

"Any idea who might have done it, Tom?"

Tom shook his head slowly then, for the first time looked Paice directly in the eye. "No, but I will find them. And when I do ... I'll deal with it."

"The police will want to talk to you. What will you tell them?"

Tom looked at Paice again. "Nothing. Not a thing. We don't need them. We can sort out our own problems. We don't want them nosing around in our business."

Paice knew only too well that the last thing Tom wanted – the last thing Mick would have wanted – was to have the police sniffing around, asking questions. The cops would have jumped at the opportunity to get access to the inner workings of the Gentle business empire.

"When did you last speak to him, Tom?"

He paused and thought. "That would have been Tuesday morning. He told me he had a meet with someone who wanted to do business with us. I never spoke to him again."

Paice guessed that the business was diamonds and he calculated that he may have been the last person Mick had spoken to before his meeting with the smuggler. He said nothing. He doubted that Tom would have favoured Mick sharing the information about the deal with an outsider such as himself. Better to keep quiet.

Nothing more passed between them until Tracey emerged from the mortuary. Paice put his arm around her. "Can you give me a lift, please, Tom? If you take me to Mick's place I'll stay with Tracey. Got anyone to be with you, Tracey?"

"My sister said she'll come round."

"OK, I'll stick around until she arrives."

"Thanks, Nick. Mick would have appreciated that."

Tom dropped them both off. They went up to the flat – a third floor council flat that the Gentle family had occupied since the war. As they climbed the stairs and walked along the open landing, Paice felt a sadness. He had been here before, but a long time before, when he and Mick had been children. Mick's mother always gave him a warm welcome. They were difficult times, but the memories were good. Once inside, he tried to think of words that might bring some comfort to Tracey, but not much came to him.

"Tom told me he last spoke to Mick last Tuesday morning. Did you hear from him after that, Tracey?"

"No. Before he left for the cafe that morning, he told me he was having a meeting with someone later in the day, but he didn't say who that was. Nothing unusual about that. Mick always felt that the less I knew the better for me. When he didn't come home I went round and asked Aunt Tilly if she knew where he was. She thought he'd gone off with some bloke. She couldn't tell me any more than that."

"Did she say what this bloke looked like?"

"She couldn't remember, Nick. She is in her eighties."

Tracey went into the kitchen to make a pot of tea, which gave Paice time to think. She came back with a tray bearing sugar, milk and a plate of biscuits.

"Have you got keys to the cafe? Would you mind if I went round there and had a quick look around?"

"No, help yourself." She went back to the kitchen and came back clutching a bunch of keys.

Her sister duly arrived and Paice took his leave. The cafe was shut up and the interior was in darkness. He went in and locked the door behind him. The stale odours of cold food hung in the air. Paice was confirmed in his view that he only wanted to smell food when it was cooking and when it was on the plate in front of him.

He stood and surveyed the place. The gloom was relieved only by an eerie glow up by the counter. The closed circuit television screens, which were suspended from brackets above his head, were all switched on. Mick had left the system running, and Aunt Tilly would not have known how to switch it off when she closed up for the day.

He studied the images being carried by the three TV sets – two of them fed by cameras covering the street in either direction, and the third showing the door. Mick was a cautious man. He wanted to see who was approaching and precisely what was happening on his doorstep.

The question Paice was asking was where the cables from the televisions went. In the darkness it was difficult to see, but he did not want to turn on the lights. He jumped up on the counter to get a better look and was able to follow them as they snaked across the wall and into Mick's office.

He went through the doorway into the leather and chromium plated luxury that Mick had created for himself. The cables led to a large drawer in the oak storage unit behind Mick's desk. Paice pulled it open. Inside was a video recorder. The tape had reached the end of the spool and had ejected itself. He guessed that Mick would normally have replaced it with an empty one. But on this occasion, he had not been around to do so.

Paice looked around. On a low table on the other side of the room sat a large television set with a video tape player on a shelf below. He fed the tape into the letterbox sized opening and set the control to rewind. It was a three hour tape so it took a few minutes to spin back to the beginning. Then he pressed play.

The time code showed the date for the day Mick had last been seen and the time at 9 am. That made sense. If

Mick put the first tape of the day into the machine when he opened up at 6 am, this would have been the second tape taking over after three hours. The images flipped from one camera to the next on a preset duration. After about 10 minutes, he realised the he would be sitting here for three hours watching the traffic and the clientele coming and going. He pressed the fast forward button. As the time in the bottom corner flickered towards 11.30, the arrival of a black Mercedes caused Paice to hit the play button.

The images resumed their normal speed. Someone was getting out of the passenger side of the Merc. Then, infuriatingly, that image was gone, replaced by the signal from camera two covering the front door. Then camera three looking in the other direction down the street. Then camera one again. The man walking towards the cafe was someone he recognised. Someone he had hoped not to see again. By now, he had been joined by the driver. Paice did not know him, but he had a pretty good idea who he was.

He froze the tape at that point and ejected it from the machine. He knew precisely what he had to do. He walked across to Mick's desk, turned the telephone to such light as penetrated the room and ran his finger down the speed dial list. He picked up the receiver and pressed the button.

The phone rang several times before it was answered. "Hello, Tom. It's Nick Paice. I'm in the cafe. I think you had better get here quick. I think I know what happened to Mick."

Tom took only five minutes to walk up the street from his shop. Paice let him in. He was dressed in his butcher's apron, and he was wiping his hands on a cloth. Paice led him through to Mick's office. He explained how Mick had told him about the diamonds and how he had decided not to get into that business.

"That's right. We talked about it over Sunday lunch and decided it wasn't for us. I don't know what Mick was doing talking to you about it, though."

Paice nodded. "Maybe, Tom, but what's done is done. Now, however, you need to see this." He pushed the tape into the machine and pressed play. The tape picked up from where the two men were walking towards the cafe. Then it skipped on to the next camera covering the door. It showed a clear shot of the man's head and shoulders. His accomplice was just out of the picture. He paused the tape and pointed at the face on the screen.

"I know him. He works as a bodyguard for one of the most evil men I ever met. The last time I saw him, he was standing at the top of the stairs in the Kamina Bassu embassy, staring at me and using his hand to mimic a gun. The implication was that he would shoot me. From what I know of these people, that would be no empty threat.

"His boss is a big shot diplomat at the embassy by the name of Mwamba. It makes sense. KB has plenty of people working in illicit diamond mining. Mwamba would be sure to be involved in that. Using the cover of diplomatic mail, he can get the diamonds into this country without the worry of being discovered.

"I reckon that when Mick told him he wasn't interested in doing business, Mwamba decided that he could not run the risk of being exposed by someone who now knew what he was up to. He is a ruthless killer. He would not have thought twice about getting rid of Mick."

Tom stared at the image on the screen. "You're sure about this?"

"Absolutely positive."

Paice turned back to the screen and pressed play. At this point, all the action moved inside the cafe where there was no camera. He fast forwarded for 10 minutes until three men were seen leaving the cafe. They stared at the screen, watching as Mick was led to the car. It was chilling to realise that he was going to his death.

"I don't understand why he would have gone with them. He should have kicked their arses and thrown them out," Tom said angrily.

"I doubt that he had a choice, Tom. They were almost certainly carrying guns, and there were two of them."

"So what are you planning to do – write a story? Put it all over the front page of your paper?"

"Look, Tom, I know that we never got on, but Mick was a good friend of mine and I cared about him. I'm here for him, not for me, not for my story and not for my paper. I don't like what you think of me, but this is not the time or the place to air our differences. I've done my bit. I've found out who killed Mick. You saw Mick's body. Those animals gave him a bad time before they killed him. Now it's up to you.

"I know you won't go to the police, but even if you did it would do no good. Under his diplomatic cover, Mwamba would be spirited out of the country before the cops even had a chance to ask his name and address. It's now for you to handle it the way you think right. Just do it for Mick."

Chapter 23

Out of the blue and after weeks of silence, Burkins finally called. "Hallo, Mr P. It's Jake."

"Jake! I thought you were dead. Long time, no hear." Paice could hear the noise of traffic in the background. Burkins was calling from a public phone box.

"No chance of that, Mr P. I'm still alive and kicking. I've nipped out for my lunch, so I took the opportunity to give you a call. You remember that business I was telling you about – in Nicaragua, I think I said?"

"Yeah, Jake. Anything materialised on that?"

"There certainly has. I take it that it will be worth my while telling you about it."

"I always take care of you, Jake. Nothing has changed."

"Good for you, Mr P. Shall we meet?"

That evening, the bar of the Black Lion was busy as usual for that time of day. Paice spotted Burkins sitting at the bar – without a drink. Paice dropped beside him on the adjacent stool.

"Hallo, Mr P. I could do with a pint." Burkins looked slightly dejected."Why didn't you buy one, Jake?"

"'Cos I'm completely skint, Mr Paice."

Paice caught the barman's attention and ordered two drinks. "Backed another one of your dead certs, did you?"

"I was so sure it was going to romp home at 10 to 1"

Paice smiled. "You didn't realise it meant 10 to 1 tomorrow afternoon, Jake."

Burkins managed a smile back. "The old jokes are the best jokes, Mr P."

"So, what have you got for me."

"Ever heard of Tierra del Aguila?"

"I've heard of it, Jake, but I don't know much about it. I seem to recall it is the only country between Venezuela and Mexico that has any significant oil reserves."

"Ah, that makes sense. They were talking about oil."

"Who were?"

"The officers in the Central American section. They are all working themselves up into a bit of a state, so I reckon whatever is going on is coming to a head. The thing is, Mr P, the Yanks are here for talks."

"Are they? Is that unusual? Do you know which Americans?"

"Oh, yeah, it's unusual. And, yes, I know who they are. There are three from the State Department in Washington plus a couple of top dogs from the embassy. But I don't have any names."

"Do you know what they've been discussing?"

"Will be discussing. They arrive tomorrow. It must be important because the boss is chairing the meeting."

286

"The boss?"

"The permanent secretary, of course, Mr P."

"Sir Stuart Strange?"

"The very one."

"Any Ministers involved?"

"No, that's the thing. I heard one of the secretaries saying that Sir Stuart says he definitely don't want the politicians involved at this stage – you've heard the word 'deniability', Mr P?"

"Yeah, Jake, but only when something fishy is on the go."

"Well, I heard one of them actually say it."

"So, the politicians are being kept out of the loop?"

"That's the thing, Mr P. No they're not. Sir Stuart's secretary, Marcia – got great tits, Mr P –"

"Yeah, OK Jake, spare me your fantasies."

"Sorry. Well, Marcia was creating merry hell this afternoon. She's being chucked out of her office while the meeting goes on. I bet you can't guess why."

"I give you money, Jake, so that I don't have to guess."

"I know, Mr P. I'm only pulling your leg. She's being moved out so that the Minister of State can listen in to the meeting. They've bugged Sir Stuart's office and run a wire into Marcia's room next door so that the Minister can hear everything that's said."

Paice took a mouthful of beer as he thought through the implications of what Burkins had just told him. The Minister of State was second only to the Foreign Secretary in the department. Why could he not just read the minutes of the meeting? He answered his own question with a question: because there won't be any minutes? He wondered what the Cabinet Secretary would say about that.

Why were the Americans involved? Obvious. It's in their back yard. Then why was Britain involved? Our only sphere of influence in that region was Belize, and, from what Paice could remember of the geography, that was nowhere near Tierra del Aguila.

"So, when are they meeting?"

"It's timed for 2pm tomorrow, and it's got to finish by 4."

"How do you know?"

"Because Sir Stuart is seeing the Cabinet Secretary at 4.15. And since it happens to be Marcia's birthday, he's taking her to his club for a drink some time after 5."

"You did say she had great tits, Jake."

"Now you're the one who's having fantasies, Mr P. He's also taking a couple of the others with them. He wouldn't dare do what you are thinking of."

"No, Jake, but when she comes into his office in a tight jumper, I'll bet his blood pressure rockets up into beta blocker territory."

"Mine certainly does, Mr P. Anyway, is that information of use to you?"

"Yes, Jake. You've done well." Paice discreetly slipped him three £20 notes.

"You're a life saver, Mr P."

"Try not putting it on a horse, Jake. The way you are going, you might as well flush it down the toilet."

"Horses are more fun," Burkins said with a grin.

"Well, at least give your mother some of it so that she can pay something off the gas bill."

"Yes, definitely. Good idea. Mum will be pleased."

But Paice knew that Jake had already identified the recipient of his little bonus. And it had four legs, not two.

Burkins got down off the bar stool. He downed the dregs of his pint. "Thanks for the nice dinner, Mr P," he said, tipping his glass towards Paice in acknowledgment before putting it down on the bar. "I must get on home."

Paice ordered himself another drink. There were logistical problems to be identified and solved if he was to learn more about what was so important as to bring State Department officials all the way across the Atlantic, pre-empt the time of one of the country's most senior civil servants, and get the second most important Minister in one of the three highest ranking departments in the Cabinet to hide in an ante room and eavesdrop on what was being said.

He knew that he would get nowhere by going through the Department's press office. He certainly was not about to ask the paper's political editor to sniff around for him. He knew better than to put a nice juicy story on someone else's plate and then watch them gobble it up. He finished his drink and went out into the evening traffic on Whitehall.

Across the road stood the Foreign and Commonwealth Office. George Gilbert Scott's magnificent classical creation was born more than a century before in the Victorian age of empire. Its majestic facade was designed to remind foreign visitors that Britain was the first super power and they had better not forget it. Paice knew exactly where the Americans would arrive and depart. He took out his phone and placed a call. It rang three times and was answered by a cheery cockney voice.

"This is Mel's Angels. We ride like the devil. How can I help you?"

"Hallo, Mel. It's Nick Paice here. How are you my darling."

"Don't you give me any of that 'my darling' stuff, you old sod. How are you?"

"I'm very well, thank you Mel. I've got a job for you. If you can spare Spike, that would be just great." Paice knew what he needed, and he knew who was best able to deliver it. Spike the Bike was probably the best cycle courier in London. The average speed of motor traffic in the afternoon peak was 10.3mph. Spike could easily average 25mph and had actually been stopped by the police for exceeding the 30mph speed limit. Pedal cyclists were notorious for flouting the traffic laws, and Spike was an arch offender. The cops had taken delight in telling him that he was nicked for speeding – what a laugh they would have back at the station.

But Paice had written such a delightfully sarcastic and tongue-in-cheek piece in the Mercury that the police were humbled into dropping the charge. And the Mercury had bought Spike a new bike and printed a picture of him riding it.

In less than 30 minutes Paice was relaxing in the warm comfort of Kouzina tis Amalias with Amalia fussing over him, Philo giving him the benefit of the wisdom he had accumulated over so many hours sitting at his favourite table, and Nikki pouring him a glass of wine.

Chapter 24

The next day at shortly before 2pm, Paice was hanging around at a discreet distance from the entrance to the Foreign Office. Dead on time, a black General Motors sport utility with dark tinted windows pulled up at the kerb. It had diplomatic number plates. It waited several minutes until a silver chauffeur driven Mercedes stopped behind it.

He watched as two men got out of the SUV. Paice recognised it as an embassy car. Two men and a woman got out of the Mercedes. Two of them carried briefcases. They exchanged greetings before heading for the entrance. Paice studied their faces, committing them to memory.

"That's them, Steve."

The Mercury's photographer stood behind Paice shielding himself from view. He propped his long lens over Paice's shoulder. The shutter clattered in a series of short bursts, the camera following the visitors until they had disappeared inside. He surveyed the results on the small screen on the back of the camera. "Got 'em, Nick."

"That's great, Steve. Tell the picture editor to hang on to them for the time being. I'm not sure yet how the story will work out." Then the photographer was gone. Paice kept watch in case the meeting ended early.

At 3.30 a slimly built young man wheeled his bicycle across the pavement and leaned it against the railings where Paice was standing. His normal work attire would be skin tight Lycra in Day-Glo yellow with "Mel's Angels" emblazoned across his back in fluorescent orange. It was designed to be highly visible. Discreet it was not. It was most definitely not the garb for a low profile tailing job. So for this occasion he was dressed in a more subdued ensemble of anonymous dark grey top and jeans.

"Good to see you, Spike," Paice said. They shook hands.

"Hallo, mate, How you doing?"

"Fine thanks. Let me fill you in. There'll be two cars. One is an American embassy car, and I am guessing that that is where it will return. I'm not interested in that. The other one is a silver Merc. That's the one I want you to follow. I'm banking on it taking three people back to their hotel. I just need to know which hotel it is. When you get there, give me a ring and I'll join you."

"What happens if they both go to the embassy?"

"Then we've got a problem. You'll just have to keep tabs on them the best you can. But I reckon that if they were all based at the embassy they would all be in the same vehicle."

Shortly before 4pm, the two cars returned and parked outside the entrance.

Paice nodded towards them. "On your marks, Spike. Just don't lose that Mercedes."

Spike grinned. "They'd need a helicopter to get away from me, Nick." Ten minutes after the cars had arrived, the five visitors emerged from the Foreign Office. They conferred briefly before shaking hands and getting into their respective vehicles. A gap in the traffic enabled the embassy driver to nose out into passing stream. The Mercedes followed closely, preventing other drivers from slipping between them. An insignificant figure on a bicycle rode after them. Within a quarter of a mile those fine examples of automotive technology, capable of carrying a man at speed and in cosseted comfort across a continent, had ground to a humiliating halt in the London traffic.

The insignificant man on the bike could have sailed past them and reached any destination well before they had extricated themselves from the congestion, but he hung back. He was confident he would have no trouble keeping them within sight.

Half an hour later, Paice's phone bleeped and vibrated in his breast pocket.

"Hi, Nick. They were delivered to the Glengarry hotel, spent a few minutes discussing their plans for the evening, and then went to their rooms. They are meeting in the bar for a drink at 6."

Spike would have had no problem keeping tabs on his quarry. He probably knew all the doormen and porters in the smarter London hotels. Paice guessed that he would have to reimburse him for the tenner that he would have slipped one of them for the information.

A taxi dropped Paice at the hotel entrance. The doorman opened the door for him. It was someone Paice did not know, so he discreetly dropped a clutch of pound coins into his covertly outstretched palm. Paice knew the value of the commercial friendship of such people. They were vital components in the information machine that he and everyone else in his business relied upon. And they remembered who paid and who did not.

Spike was a few yards away, leaning against his bike. It was propped in the kerb. He was drinking from a water bottle.

"If you are thirsty, Spike, let me take you into the hotel bar and buy you a drink."

"That's very generous of you, Nick, but it will have to be non-alcoholic. I don't want to get breathalysed by the cops on the way home. After all that has happened, they'd just love to get me for being drunk in charge of a bike."

"After all that has happened, Spike, I don't think they'd dare. But you are right to be careful. Anyway, it's not all down to generosity. There's something more I need you to do." He explained what he wanted.

"That sounds like fun, Nick. Are you sure?"

Paice nodded. While he waited, Spike secured his precious pair of wheels in the hotel's underground car park, carefully chaining the cycle to a substantial set of handrails. Then they headed for the sparkling brass and glass splendour of the hotel's main entrance.

The doorman grinned at Spike and nodded a greeting to Paice. They walked through the reception area to the bar. The place was almost empty. It meant that Paice could choose a strategic position at the far end of the semi circular bar from where he could see who came and went. He ordered a beer and an orange juice.

The clock showed that it was 5.45. "If all this works out, Spike, we don't have long to wait."

Spike took a sip of his drink. "I don't mind how long it takes. This is better than riding that bike through the traffic and trying to dodge being knocked off it by some loony van driver."

They were still discussing the pleasures and pitfalls of being a cycle courier in London when Paice spotted one of the Americans entering the bar. "That's our man, Spike. Just don't look at him. I don't want you catching his eye or he will get suspicious. We'll have to play this one by ear, but you understand what I basically need you to do, don't you?" Spike nodded.

The American walked to a table and placed his briefcase on a chair. He went to the bar and ordered a beer which he carried back the table and sat down. Paice lowered his voice: "OK, Spike, you're on."

He slid off his stool and made a show of saying goodbye to Paice. The next couple of minutes worked out better than Paice could have hoped. It was as if Spike had been practising the manoeuvre all his life. As he walked past the American's table, he stumbled. The victim had just lifted the glass to his mouth. The beer never reached its destination. Instead, a well directed nudge resulted in the contents of the glass showering over the table and the American leaping to his feet in a panic to avoid getting soaked. His chair was catapulted backwards, crashing to the floor. He knocked over the adjacent chair and sent the briefcase flying.

"Jesus Christ, buddy," he shouted. "What the hell do you think you're doing? Are you drunk?"

Spike mumbled an apology and made a half hearted gesture to indicate a desire to help but an absence of any idea of how to realise it.

Paice was instantly on the scene. "You are completely useless, Jenkins. Just get out of here and keep out of my sight." He turned to the American. "I am very sorry, Sir. I feel some responsibility. He works for me. I can only apologise." He righted the two chairs and picked up the briefcase, checking it carefully to make sure it was not damaged.

By now the barman had arrived with a cloth and began fussing around, trying to wipe up the worst of the spill. "You must permit me to get you another drink," Paice said, adopting his most solicitous manner while managing to exclude any trace of insincerity from his voice.

He looked round to see Spike still standing there, happily transfixed by the result of his duplicity, barely able to suppress a look of satisfaction. Paice glared at him. "Are you still here, Jenkins? I thought I told you to scram. Get out of here."

The angry tirade yanked Spike's attention back to the subterfuge. "Sorry guv'nor. I'm on my way." He hurried out of the bar.

Paice took the American by the arm, collected up his briefcase and guided him to another table. "Bring us two beers, please, barman."

The American tried to refuse the offer, but Paice was adamant. As they sat, he held out his hand. "Hallo. I'm Nick. I'm sorry about all this. Jenkins is just a clumsy fool."

The American looked uncomfortable. The barman placed beer mats on the table and carefully centred the glasses upon them. Paice paid for the drinks and included a generous tip. "Sorry about all the trouble," he muttered. The barman held up his palm, shook his head and smiled as if to say that for him it was all in a day's work. The £10 note clutched in his other hand provided a considerable inducement to be understanding.

For the first time, Paice looked the American full in the face as he raised his glass. He stopped halfway and stared in disbelief. "Don't I know you?"

"I don't think so. We've never met before."

"But aren't you... Wilson...Wilson..." He stopped and thought. "It will come back to me. We met at a conference. I know. Wilson? Wilson...."

The American looked at him in bemused disbelief.

"Wilson...Wilson Hardy – no, Wilson Harding. You are Wilson Harding. Yes?"

Harding nodded. "Yeah, you're right, but I'm damned if I remember you."

"We met at a conference. Was it Guatemala? As I recall your interest is the Caribbean and Central America. That right?" Paice was making it up as he went along. If Harding was here to talk about Tierra del Aguila, that area would have to be his speciality. "Are you still working for the US Government? What are you doing in London? Anyway, how are you? It must be years since we last met."

Paice's technique was to swamp the man with so many questions that he would be too preoccupied with finding the answers to ask any of his own. It did not work.

"Hang on...er...Nick, was it? I have never been to a conference in Guatemala, so we can't have met there. Who did you say you were?"

Paice went with a wild guess. "Surely, Wilson, you haven't forgotten the team at Global Food Programme? The guys and girls haven't forgotten you." He guessed that Harding would have had close contact with what was one of the major United Nations relief organisations.

"GFP? Of course I know the GFP people. So, who were you with – Juan? Andrea? Francoise?"

"I didn't know Andrea, but Juan and Francoise were certainly at the Guatemala conference." Paice felt that he was reaching out into the dark with his eyes closed.

Harding was beginning to relax. "I last saw Juan in Washington. I haven't seen Francoise since she went off to have a baby. I'm sorry I don't remember you. Are you based in London?"

"I am. So, what are you doing here? Are you still with the State Department?"

"Yes. I had a stint at USAID overseas assistance office, but I'm still handling the Caribbean and Latin America."

Enough pussyfooting. "It's looking very worrying over Tierra del Aguila, Wilson."

Harding looked as though he had been plugged into a high tension power supply. "Tierra del...How do you know...?"

"Is that why you are in London?"

Before Harding could reply, a female voice cut in. "Who's your new friend, Wilson?" It was the woman whom Paice had seen going into the Foreign Office with Harding. Standing with her was the other American. Paice had made the mistake of sitting with his back to the door. He hadn't seen them enter.

"Oh, hi Tricia...." Harding's voice trailed off into nothing.

"And you are?" It was the other American and he was seeking an introduction that did not include a handshake and a smile. And he was looking straight at Paice. His build, his manner, his interrogatory tone of voice and his US Marines-style haircut – especially his haircut – left Paice in no doubt. This was the two officials' personal protection. He was here to deal with any trouble. And to him Paice was trouble.

"He's been asking about Tierra del Aguila, Al," Harding said, almost apologetically.

Al shot him a look that said a thousand words, the first four of which were "Keep your trap shut." Harding realised he had said too much. "Do you know this man, Mr Harding?" His drawl reminded Paice of John Wayne.

"Well, he knows me, Al, but I don't remember him. He says he's with Global Food Programme in London."

It was Tricia's turn to chip in. "Wilson, GFP does not have an office in London. It is based in Geneva."

Al was determined to take charge of the situation. "I'm going to have to ask you to answer a few questions, Sir." Paice's experience in America told him that the word "Sir" was either a term of respect and an augury of good service, or it was a precursor to imminent arrest, detention and liberal dose of police brutality. He was pretty certain that respect and good service were not what Al had in mind. He did not much relish the prospect of what was left.

Tricia was annoyed and anxious. "What I want to know –" Al cut her off in mid sentence.

"Please leave this to me, Miss Daley. Wilson here has been suckered by this joker. I'll soon find out what he is up to."

"But he knows my name, Al," Harding whined.

Al reached across and flicked the name tag on the briefcase. "Sure he does, Mr Harding. He's a smart son of a bitch – he can even read." He turned to Paice. "OK, pal. Start talking. Just who are you and what are you up to?"

Paice had had enough. "Hang on a minute. Just who do you think you are? Wyatt Earp? Well let me tell you

Wyatt, if you want to be the sheriff around here, you have to wear a badge." He had adopted his most sarcastic tone.

"That's no problem, buddy." Al reached into the inside pocket of his jacket and pulled out a wallet. He flipped it open and held it under Paice's nose. There was a nice shiny badge, and Paice had no trouble reading "Federal Bureau of Investigation", which he knew was the organisation responsible for the safety of US citizens anywhere in the world.

He looked at the badge. If he was honest, he had to admit he was impressed. But he wasn't about to admit a damned thing. "Very pretty, Wyatt. Unfortunately for you, that doesn't mean a damn thing in this country. The simple fact is that you're just another fucking tourist, so back off."

It was obvious that the game was up. It was time to come clean. "OK, so I'm not with the GFP, but, Wilson, if you had listened more carefully you would have noticed that I never said I was. My name is Nick Paice and I'm a reporter with the Daily Mercury."

Harding recoiled in horror, Tricia Daley did a sharp intake of breath and Al was coming close to losing it. "Jesus Christ, I'll break your goddam neck you little piece of shit." He started towards Paice.

"Steady on, Wyatt. Just remember where you are." Paice hoped that he would. He was big, the way they tended to build them way out West. "You lay one of your paws on me and that barman will get the police here faster than you can count the tails on a rattlesnake. You'll be listening to your spurs jingle-jangle all the way to Bow

Street magistrates court. I'd be fascinated to know how your embassy people would react to that." Al gritted his teeth and took a step back.

It was time for Paice to get out of there. He had seen enough to know that the story would be massive – if he could unearth all the facts. These people had been terrified at what they hoped he did not know. He left them a parting gift. "Tierra del Aguila is a big story. When I've got to the bottom of it you'll be able to read all about it on the front page of the Mercury."

He walked out, winking at the barman and looking back to see three stunned and very unhappy people wondering about their next move and not having a clue.

Chapter 25

Unusually, Paice was early. Williamson, the editor, had summoned the meeting to consider the story Paice had floated before him the previous night. The question was how to write it. And whether to print it.

Paice sat at one end of the table in the conference room. Also present were Williamson, who was chairing the meeting, Harry Draper, Ed Hardie, the foreign editor, and Roland Hughes, the diplomatic correspondent.

"Let's begin by hearing from Nick just what the story is and what it's worth," Williamson stated, swinging round to look at Paice.

"Thanks, Jack. My source assures me that everyone involved – both here and in Washington – is working overtime to cover up what amounts to a major disaster or cock-up that the authorities have hushed up in Tierra del Aguila, Central America. It has to be something big, given the fact that the Yanks have come over to talk about keeping the lid on it. My information is that Ministers have been deliberately kept at arm's length to enable them to maintain deniability if anything goes wrong, but that officials are under orders to keep them fully informed."

Hardie had been the foreign editor for so long, it was suggested that he could remember covering Chamberlain's meeting with Hitler. What was true, however, was that he had an encyclopaedic memory, and he always demanded hard facts. This meeting was no exception. "Before we go any further, what is this – disaster or cock-up?" He directed the question straight at Paice.

It was just one of the questions to which Paice had hoped to avoid having to provide a precise answer. The simple fact was that he did not know. "I'm still working on that, Ed," was the best response he could muster. And he knew that was not good enough. "I was hoping you might have an idea of what had been happening out there."

"When?" Hardie held his unyielding stare at Paice.

"I don't know that either, Ed."

Hardie looked around at Williamson. "Jack, I have the greatest respect for Nick. He's a good man. If he sniffs a story, there's a good chance it's there somewhere. But until we get hard facts – what's happened, when and to whom – I'm not clear what we are supposed to be writing about."

Williamson turned to Hughes, the diplomatic correspondent. "You've got your ear to the ground, Roland. Have you come across anything from the Foreign Office that might give us a clue to what's going on?"

"Nothing at all, Jack. I think Nick is heading up a dead end on this one. If anything was on the go, I would have heard about it. I am, after all, closer to the FO – and the Foreign Secretary – than Nick as a general reporter can hope to be."

Paice could feel his temper building. Hughes's resentment at Paice trespassing on his territory was evident, but Paice wasn't about to let some prima donna Whitehall hack stop him writing a red hot story."Nothing?" Paice snapped. "You've got your ear to the ground? Perhaps you should get your head out of your arse and put your eye to the keyhole. You reckon you're best mates with the Foreign Secretary and you are close to his officials? Maybe you are a bit too close. Are you using them, or are they using you? You need to remember that you work for the Mercury, not the Government."

Now it was Hughes's turn to lose it. "Don't put the boot into me, Paice, just because you've fallen in love with a story that won't stand up. You reckon you can lecture me. Let me remind you that the basic requirement of a story is a fact, and you don't have one of those. You've got nothing, just some airy fairy theory based on keeping your fingers crossed. When you get your job sorted out, you can start to tell me how to do mine."

"You want facts," Paice snapped. How about this? Did you know that two State Department officials are in London, complete with an FBI agent riding shotgun, to discuss this issue with Foreign Office mandarins?

Doesn't that ring any alarm bells with anyone around this table?"

Williamson knew Paice well and he didn't need a weather forecast to work out that a storm was about to break. "Calm down, Nick. And you, Roland. Let's not get emotional about this. Let's find out if there's a story here."

Paice turned to the foreign editor. "Don't you have anyone in Tierra del Aguila, Ed?"

Hardie scoffed. "On my budget, Nick? You have to be joking. My nearest staff reporter is 3,000 miles away in Washington."

Williamson decided to wind up the meeting. "You are going to have to get something harder for us to do anything with this, Nick. Do some more digging and see what you can find, then we'll have another look at it. In the meantime, there will be a complete firewall around it. I want not a word said about this outside of this group. Is that understood? If there is a story here, we don't want the Government or the competition getting to it first."

They all nodded and grunted their confirmations. He looked across the table at Roland Hughes, tapping the table in front of him. "Not a word to your contacts at the Foreign Office, Roland. Understand? I don't want them closing the story down before we've even worked out what it is." Hughes muttered his agreement. He knew better than to contravene a direct instruction from the editor. Williamson picked up his papers and walked out. The meeting was over.

Back at his desk, Paice flicked quickly through the telephone directory. He soon found the number for the Tierra del Aguila embassy and rang it. "Press section, please," he told the embassy switchboard.

The extension rang several times. "Press office," said the voice at the other end.

"Hallo, my name's Nick Paice. I'm a reporter with the Daily Mercury. I am writing a story about Tierra del Aguila. Would it be possible for me to come along and have an interview with the ambassador, please?"

"Yes, Mr Paice, that might be possible, but I need to know what story you are writing, and we would require in advance a list of the questions that you would be putting to our ambassador."

"We don't submit questions in advance. Can I speak to the ambassador?"

"That is impossible. He is not in the embassy at the moment. And if you are not prepared to submit questions, we would not be able to facilitate an interview. I am sorry. Unless you can tell me what you want to write about, we can take this no further."

"I want to ask the ambassador about the major problem that you have been facing."

There was a pause. "Mr Paice, in my country we have many problems. Unless you can narrow your request, the ambassador would have to commit an entire day to talk to you about our problems. Much as he would like to speak to you, that is asking too much of his busy schedule."

Paice was desperately attempting to prompt the man into giving him a clue. Nothing was forthcoming. He thought back to what Burkins had told him. "You may have many problems, but they do not all involve such a heavy loss of life. You must regard it as serious if the Americans have come to London to discuss it. It would be helpful if his Excellency would just give me your country's side of the story."

There was another perceptible pause at the other end of the line. Then: "Just one moment, please Mr Paice." He was put on hold. After no more than a minute the voice returned. "I'm very sorry, Mr Paice. I have consulted my colleagues and none of us can identify a problem that matches your description. I have no further comment to make." He hung up, leaving Paice uttering four letter words into his phone, imprecations that were destined to progress no further than the mouthpiece.

It was a cover-up. Paice was sure that the man knew precisely what he was talking about. If he had genuinely known nothing, he would at least have asked a couple of questions, if only out of curiosity, to try to work out what Paice was driving at. Instead, he had slammed the door shut on any further discussion. Paice was even more certain that Burkins had given him good information. The problem was how to exploit it.

Chapter 26

Paice had exposed and enraged so many people in his career that, to the dispassionate observer, it would be surprising that no one had ever tried to kill him before. However, he, somewhat naively, perhaps arrogantly, subconsciously assumed that, being a reporter, he was isolated from the consequences of his writing, protected by an invisible shield that said "This ain't personal, I'm only doing my job." Anyway, surely no one ever did actually shoot the messenger.

He knew, of course, that he was not immortal, but he felt detached from the threat of any form of physical retribution. The only occasion when the job had brought him even remotely close to personal violence, apart from his time in war zones where the threat was never particularly personal, had been years before. He had been reporting the trial of a couple of South London gangsters. The prosecution had put one of the gang's victims on the stand and his testimony had been fatal to the defence case. It had also proved, subsequently, to be fatal for the witness, but that was another story.

The guts of the story were in his notebook. The intro was in his head. He was headed out of the court, leafing through his notes and not looking where he was going, when he bumped into someone coming the other way. A mumbled apology and a quick sidestep simply led him into another obstruction. Looking up, he was confronted with two men. One had the size and solidity of a small bungalow.

Before Paice could comprehend what was happening, the notebook was snatched from his grasp and a voice halfway between a growl and a whisper, told Paice: "You won't be needing that, son. You don't want to go writing all those nasty things about two innocent men, do you? Now run along and be a good boy." He knew better than to argue with the henchmen of the accused. He wrote the story, but it was sparse in detail, and completely lacking in direct quotation, limited only to what he could remember.

But that was a long time ago and, these days, the suggestion that he might be at risk never crossed his mind.

He had noticed the black car out of the corner of his eye as he crossed the road. He had noticed it – but not paid it particular attention – because it was neither stationary nor moving with any pace or purpose. It had not occurred to him that it was stalking him.

He had turned into a quiet street that provided a shortcut through to his digs. The rubbish bins were lined along the pavement, ready for the next morning's collection. The car mounted the pavement and accelerated hard towards him, a dark shape in the evening gloom, showing no lights. He heard the engine revving hard, but it was only when it hit the trash bin that he looked round and saw it bearing down on him and about to run him down. He threw himself into the gateway of the house he was passing and the car tore past, barely missing him. If he had stayed on the pavement, he would have booked himself both some space in the obituaries and a well attended memorial service at St Bride's, the journalists' church in Fleet Street.

By the time he had recovered and got to his feet, the car had disappeared. He could not even say what make it was, let alone provide the registration number. But it was black or perhaps dark blue. It was difficult to tell in the dusk. The orange street lights distorted one's perception of colour in the diminishing light levels.

He picked himself up, but then sank back on to the steps that led up to the front door of the house. His heart was pounding and he looked at his hands. They were shaking. He needed to pull himself together. As he did so he realised that he had come close to death. But was it a deliberate attempt on his life? Or was it some lunatic, drunk or idiot who had simply lost control?

The front door opened and a woman holding a baby looked out. "What's going on?" she demanded. Then she saw the contents of the dustbin scattered along the pavement and the smashed bin lying upside down in her neighbour's front area. "My god, whatever have you been doing? I'm calling the police."

Paice got unsteadily to his feet. "Calm down, missus. A car just mounted the pavement. It hit the dustbin – and it almost hit me." He straightened his waterproof jacket and patted his pockets.

The woman struggled to understand what he had told her. Then gave up. "Well... well..." Her voice rose a couple of octaves. "Well, what are you going to do about all this mess?"

Paice turned his back on her and walked away. Her shrill voice carried down the street but he ignored her and instead looked cautiously in all directions to see whether the black car – if it was black – had returned. It was nowhere to be seen. He resumed his journey home, still shaken from the incident.

In his room, his pulse rate returning to normal, he poured himself a large glass of scotch and sat on the side of his bed. Was it an attempt to kill him, and, if so, who would have wanted him dead? Titus Refik? Paice had seriously upset him. He wasn't the forgiving kind, and he came from a culture in which blood feuds, usually ending in plenty of blood, were the common currency.

Then there was Mwamba. He had seen Mwamba's hoodlum driving the black embassy car at Mick Gentle's place on the CCTV footage. Mwamba might have learnt that it was Paice who had made the connection over the diamonds. And if Paice knew about the diamond fiddle, that presented a major threat to Mwamba that he would certainly want to deal with.

Or was that crazy Irishman, Seamus McNally, making good on his implied threats. He, like the other two, had left a bloodstained trail throughout his career. And with what Paice knew about him, and with all that Paice had written in the past, making one more bloody footprint along that trail – traced out in Paice's blood – would present him with neither logistical nor moral problems.

Or it might be none of these. They were not the only people for whom he had been a thorn in the side. He had to start somewhere, so he rooted through his wallet, found the card Refik had given him and tapped out the number on his phone. Refik answered promptly. "Who is this?" he demanded.

"Hello, Refik. It's Nick Paice."

"Ah, Mr Paice. I'd hoped never to hear from you again. Courtesy requires me to ask how you are."

"I'm alive, which is fortunate for you because if the attempt that has just been made on my life had been successful, the photographs and recordings from our meeting at your place would be in the hands of the cops."

Refik's voice took on a more serious tone. "Someone tried to kill you?"

"Yes, about an hour ago. I seriously hope for your sake that it was nothing to do with you."

"I can promise you that it was not, Mr Paice. I am most anxious that you should die of natural causes – to be frank, the sooner the better, but not by my hand.

"But why should you think it was me? Surely, the number of people who would like to see your early departure from the earth would form a disorderly queue round the block."

Paice smiled to himself. He took satisfaction from having lost count of the number of villains, conmen and other lowlife undesirables whose activities he had exposed in the columns of the daily press. "That's true enough, Refik, but you are the latest on the list and I thought you might be first in line."

"Well, it wasn't me, Mr Paice, and I am concerned that you might be exposing yourself to such danger. We made a deal, and I want you to live long enough to stick to it. You must take more care – for both our sakes."

Paice hung up. He was reluctant to believe anything that Refik told him, but he knew the strength of his hold over the man and he knew that whatever else he was, Refik was no fool. So if it wasn't Refik, that left Mwamba and McNally as the most likely to try to kill him.

It transpired subsequently that it was not Mwamba.

Chapter 27

The next afternoon in the news room, Paice was sitting, nursing his bruises and the graze on his cheek. By now the whole office knew what had happened to him. Bob Bryce came across from his desk to ask how he felt.

"Did you tell the cops?" he asked.

"Tell them what precisely, Bob? That a car I barely noticed, whose make I did not get, whose colour I could not be certain of and whose registration number I did not see ran into a dustbin and nearly knocked me out of this world into the next? The police would say it was a drunk driver or young hooligans out for a joyride."

"Well, then, did you go to hospital?"

"Look, mate, I was knocked about, not injured. Anyway, I don't like hospitals – people die in hospitals, or hadn't you noticed? When did you last venture into a hospital?"

"As a matter of fact, Nick, just last week. I had to go for a check-up."

"Really? Did they find anything right with you?"

"If you must know, they said I had the body of a man half my age."

"Oh yeah? And then they said could they have it back, and, by the way would you stop nosing around the hospital mortuary – right?"

The phone on Bryce's desk jangled before he could retaliate. He trotted across to answer it. He was back by Paice's side almost immediately. "You've got contacts in the Kamina Bassu embassy, Nick. There's been a shooting there. Fatalities reported. Get down there pronto."

Fortunately for Paice, an empty taxi was cruising by as he ran out of the office. He was at the embassy in not much more than 10 minutes. Already the police had cordoned off the area and weren't letting anyone get close. The shooting had happened just outside the entrance. A black car was parked driver's side into the kerb. Paice recognised it from the TV pictures outside Mick Gentle's cafe. The driver's and passenger's doors were both open. One figure lay in the road. A second was sprawled on the pavement. Both were under makeshift covers – blankets or sheets borrowed from someone nearby. A third was being picked up and transferred to a stretcher by the crew of an ambulance.

Paice pulled a battered notebook from one of the pockets of his waterproof jacket. He found the number he wanted and stabbed it out on the keypad of his phone. He could tell instantly both from the tone of voice of the operator and from the background noise that chaos reigned inside the embassy.

"Put me through to the ambassador," he ordered.

"I'm sorry, Sir, the ambassador is not taking calls."

"Just tell him it's Nick Paice. He'll take the call." He did. Within five minutes Paice was inside the embassy by a side door reserved for trade deliveries and entering the ambassador's office. Moses Mkoko was pacing the floor, a worried man who was verging on panic.

"What's going on, Moses?"

Mkoko shook his head in despair. "It's Stanley Mwamba, Nick. Someone shot him as he arrived back at the embassy. They hit his bodyguards, too. They are both dead. I have just heard that Stanley is alive, but only just. He is being taken to hospital. I don't know anything about his condition, but it must be a cause for great concern."

Paice thought it would be bad timing to say that his only concern for Mwamba was that he might get to the hospital alive.

"Stanley and his boys arrived back from Kamina Bassu only this morning. They had come straight from the airport. He made so many enemies during the war. Did someone finally get to him, Nick? Has the past finally caught up with him?"

Paice quickly arrived at two conclusions. The first was that it was unlikely that Mwamba had been behind the attempt to run him down the previous evening. He and his thugs had been in Africa, or at least on the plane to England, at the time it all happened.

The second was that Tom Gentle had secured his revenge for the killing of his brother.

"Did anyone see what happened? Any witnesses?"

319

"I don't know, Nick. The police have told me only that Stanley is being taken to hospital, but beyond that I know nothing. They will want to talk to me. I'm not sure what I can say to them."

"Just be careful what you say, Moses. I don't think you should offer them your thoughts on this being an echo from the war. That won't look good for Kamina Bassu just when everyone is trying to put all that behind them."

"Can I speak to you in confidence, Nick?"

"You know that goes without saying, Moses."

"It's about Mwamba. The gossip around the embassy is that he has been smuggling contraband from Kamina Bassu in the diplomatic luggage – as you know it is not subject to the usual customs controls and examination."

"So, you're the ambassador, Moses, what have you done about it?"

"That's easier said than done, Nick. Kamina Bassu is a wonderful country and I would give my life for it – almost did more than once, as you know. But it is blessed and cursed by God."

"What's God got to do with it, Moses?"

"GOD the acronym, Nick, not God the holy father – G-O-D, gold, oil and diamonds, the natural bounty that could hold the prospect of a wonderful future for my country. That is the blessing. But it is also a curse because the riches that are there for the taking bring out the worst in man and attract the worst of men.

"Mwamba was just such a man. This may have been the work of his criminal associates – such activities bring one into contact with very dangerous people. What have I done about it? He has friends and allies back home. To do anything would have meant confronting those people and that would have meant putting not just myself and my family at personal risk but perhaps crushing the life out of the fragile democracy that is struggling to survive in Kamina Bassu. So, what have I done? I have done nothing. But now it seems that someone else has done something about him."

Paice looked out of the office window into the street below. "Were you here in this office when it happened?"

"I was."

"So you will have heard the gunshots."

"No, I heard nothing."

"But it happened right under your window. You could not have avoided hearing a series of gunshots from this distance."

Mkoko insisted that he had heard nothing. Paice was beginning to wonder whether Moses was being selectively deaf, perhaps having organised the shooting himself in order to get rid of Mwamba and put the blame on another or others who had fallen out with Mwamba over one of his shady deals.

"So you heard and saw nothing?"

"I heard nothing, but I saw it all," Moses replied.

"You saw it all?" Paice could not keep the astonishment out of his voice. "How could you see it but not hear it for Christ's sake?"

Mkoko walked across to his desk. "You realise, Nick, that I am talking to you in confidence. I am placing my trust in you telling you all this. And I do not expect to see the story plastered all over the front page of the Mercury tomorrow morning." As he turned he held up a glittering silver disc. "Our CCTV camera, which covers the front entrance, caught the whole episode, including the killer."

"Then why didn't you say so? Let's have a look at it. It will be vital evidence for the police."

"I do not intend to say anything to your police, and I do not want them to know of the existence of this disc. If Stanley was up to no good and was shot by one of his criminal associates, then that episode is closed. Stanley is dead –"

"If he is dead." Paice put particular emphasis on the "if"

"Indeed, if he is dead, but, with a number of bullets in him, he must be close to it. If he dies, that will be one criminal fewer to plague my country and for me that closes the matter, whatever your police might say. I have no interest is seeing the perpetrators brought before a court."

Paice was relieved to know that if Tom Gentle had been behind the shooting, Moses would be doing nothing to encourage the cops to uncover his involvement.

"But let us assume that it is the work not of criminals but of his political enemies. You are right in saying that this is not something that we want broadcast at a time when we are desperate to show the rest of the world that the war is over and that we have returned to peace and normality. I honestly know nothing definite that I can tell the police. And it is not in the interest of my country to speculate. The less I say, the better."

Paice could see the sense in what Moses was saying. Anyway, the world was certainly a better place without Mwamba. In fact, he would happily stand the man who pulled the trigger several very large drinks. He strolled across to the window and looked down at the activity below.

The forensics team had turned up and were on their hands and knees searching for clues. Screens had been erected around the car to shield the two deceased from the gaze of onlookers. When the crime scene had been swept for clues, photographs taken and the bodies examined where they fell, the body bags would be produced, filled and zipped up before being driven off in an anonymous black van to the mortuary.

"You may not want to speculate, Moses, but plenty of others will – not least the press and television. My editor will be expecting a well-informed piece from me, and I am afraid that I am going to have to write it. But I will only speculate – just like everyone else. You know you can trust me not to breach any confidence between us."

Moses waggled the disc in Paice's direction. Its pristine surface glittered as it caught the light, hues of green and blue reflecting from the encoded data fired by laser into the metal substrate. He took it over to the television that was set up in the corner of the room. "At least let us look at the pictures to see what they can tell us," he said, bending down to load it into the player.

The screen stuttered and flickered before stabilising into a surprisingly high quality moving picture.

"What time did it happen?" Paice inquired, checking the time code in the bottom right hand corner of the screen.

"About 2.45."

Paice picked up the remote control, studied the buttons and, finding what he needed, spun the scene forward, the numbers on the digital clock tumbling towards the target.

"Hold it there, Nick." Moses had spotted the arrival of Mwamba's car. Paice pressed the pause button and they surveyed the street scene. Both men had seen so much casual violence and death that they had become emotionally inured to them. Even so, there was a shared, but unspoken, understanding that they were about to witness the end of life for two men, three if Mwamba did not survive.

Events had moved so quickly that it was only now that the realisation seeped into Paice's mind that the death of a man he had wished dead so many times, after so many atrocities perpetrated by this monstrous killer and those under his command, might actually happen. He smiled at the irony of fate. Mwamba had walked unscathed through the savagery of a civil war in jungles nearly 3,000 miles away, but he had finally been shot down in the sophisticated surroundings of one of the most expensive neighbourhoods in London. Maybe in a more lawless environment he would have taken greater care.

Paice pressed play, and the dramatic events began to unfold. They watched as the car remained stationary in the kerb for a few minutes. The front passenger door opened and one half of the personal protection team stepped out. He looked along the street in both directions, tapped his hand on the roof of the car and the second bodyguard, the driver, climbed out and opened the rear door for Mwamba.

Up to this point, no one else had appeared. But as Mwamba stepped on to the pavement a figure appeared from the corner of the screen. "Watch that man, Moses." Paice leaned forward expectantly as the figure moved to the centre of the picture, then relaxed as he realised that it was a woman. She sidestepped the two men to avoid a collision and walked past. She was dressed in a dark two-piece suit with a fashionably short skirt.

Paice's eyes darted around the screen. The shooting must be about to happen. It would have taken Mwamba no more than a minute to leave his car and reach the safety of the embassy's main entrance, but it was something he had failed to do. The woman would have seen it all.

"There, Nick!" Moses's cry startled Paice.

"Where?" He scanned the screen for a sign of action, then saw that the woman had stopped. She turned and pulled something from her large shoulder bag. Paice could see that it was a gun, its size enhanced by the addition of a silencer. That explained why Moses had not heard the shooting.

The woman knew exactly what she was doing. She had walked past in order to get a clear line of fire around the car to the first bodyguard who was still standing in the road. The kick of the gun was only just perceptible as she fired at him. The force of the bullet knocked him back and he fell. Paice reckoned it may have been a head shot and that he was dead before he hit the ground.

In a smooth, sweeping manoeuvre, she swung round and, without pausing to take aim, took out the second bodyguard. He was fumbling to retrieve his weapon from inside his jacket. He was hampered by the fact that it was tightly buttoned. Small errors like that could prove very costly. He was personal protection. He should have known better. In life, one could learn from one's mistakes. In death, all learning stopped. There were no second chances. He slumped to the pavement, jerking involuntarily in his death throes.

Now it was Mwamba's turn. But she was taking her time. She held the gun out as she walked back towards him. He was scared. He was clearly begging. He had dropped to his knees, clasping his hands as if in prayer. Paice felt a hot surge of anger and revulsion. Here was a man who had mercilessly overseen, encouraged, orchestrated, the deaths and torture of hundreds, perhaps thousands, of innocent men, women and children, laughing as he did so. But when his turn came, he screamed and blubbered like a gibbering coward.

What happened next rendered both men speechless. Instead of shooting him, she jerked the gun to indicate that he should get off his knees and stand. Slowly, he did so, still pleading. She lowered the gun. Paice thought she was planning to let him live. Not so. This time she took careful aim and put a bullet, perhaps two – on the video it was impossible to be sure – into the area between his legs.

"My god, she's shot him in the balls, Nick."

Momentarily, Mwamba stood before falling to his knees. He looked down in disbelief. Then he fell backwards on to the pavement. He was on his back, writhing in pain. She stood over him, saying something to him. Then it was possible clearly to see the gun recoil four times. It was calculated. She shot him in the stomach and abdomen before turning on her heel and walking calmly away as he squirmed helplessly in a steadily expanding pool of blood.

Then she was gone, out of the shot. Paice quickly rewound and watched the entire episode again, this time checking the time code. "Forty three seconds from start to finish and every shot perfectly placed. That's what you call a real pro, Moses."

"You mean it was a contract killing by – well, I was going to say a hit man, but that was a woman. It was a woman wasn't it?"

"Yes, Moses, it was a woman, but it was no contract killing. It was revenge."

"How can you possibly know that?"

"That lady killed Mwamba's bodyguards each with a single shot. Why not Mwamba? You saw her. She took her time. She was shooting him in broad daylight in a London street. But it was no bang-bang-and-run-like-hell operation. She disabled him with the first round – it could have been fatal if she had wanted that, but, no – then she carefully fired four further shots that she knew would cause most pain and eventual – but not immediate – death."

So, revenge was certainly the motive. She shot off his sexual appendages then put four bullets in his guts. She knew that there was no way he would survive the ensuing blood loss, but she knew, too, that his going would be accompanied by excruciating and unbearable pain. She wanted him to die in agony and that is precisely what he would have done. Paice doubted that Mwamba even made it to hospital alive.

Paice rewound again and watched the woman appear on the screen and gun down the first bodyguard. Then, just as she turned to face the second bodyguard and Mwamba, he hit the pause button. At that point she was facing the camera. He knelt down close to the TV, then moved back slightly, trying to get a clearer appreciation of the killer's face.

Paice knew from the gunfight in the hospital courtyard in Kamina Bassu that Maria Bellamy was a good shot. Lady Bellamy, wife of a prominent politician, had just given a virtuoso performance that left him in no doubt that she could handle a 9mm automatic pistol every bit as well as an AK47. It was a text book assassination.

"So what do you propose to do with the disc, Moses?"

Moses walked across the room. "Whatever the motive for shooting Mwamba, it will do Kamina Bassu no good for the facts to come out." He turned the disc back and forth in his hand, then bent down and pushed it into the security shredder. The machine chewed effortlessly through it. "It never existed, Nick. And if the police ask whether our camera can provide any useful footage, the answer will be that it was out of commission at the crucial time."

There was a knock on the office door and a young woman opened it and looked in."Ambassador, a police inspector would like to speak to you. Can you see him now?"

Moses nodded. "Yes, show him into the conference room. I'll be down immediately."

By the time Paice got back to his office, the shooting was all over the broadcast news channels. As he stood by Bryce's desk watching the television, the "breaking news" caption flashed up. The tickertape message at the foot of the screen told Paice what he had fully expected to hear: "Kamina Bassu envoy dead on arrival at hospital."

Bryce turned to Paice. "You know more about this joker than most people, Nick. We'll need a piece for the front page and some background and analysis for inside. I know that you'll cover what this means for Kamina Bassu and who might have done the killing, but your personal knowledge of Mwamba will give us a beat on the other titles. By the way, who do you think did it?"

"I don't know, Bob, but that won't stop me sounding as though I do." One indisputable fact was that the name of Maria Bellamy was never going to appear in the

Mercury's coverage of the crime. There was only one person apart from her who knew what she had done and that was Paice. He hoped that she had been sufficiently careful to ensure that the police investigation did nothing to change that.

That night, as the presses rolled and the newspapers followed their nocturnal routine of distribution, Paice indulged in the best night's sleep he had enjoyed in years. A dark presence, acquired years before in the blood and slaughter of the African jungle, always, he sensed, half a pace behind him, had faded and dispersed like smoke in a breeze, only the merest scent of it lingering harmlessly in his mind.

Chapter 28

Paice woke early the next morning and sat on the side of his bed thinking through the events of the previous day. The obvious course of action was to contact Maria to talk about the killing. Long experience of asking direct questions and persisting until an answer was given had worn his diplomatic skills thin, but he was reluctant to phone her. What would he say – "How's the family? By the way, I noticed you bumped off Mwamba yesterday. Nice shooting" ?

It seemed better to defer any action on that front. Anyway, he faced the more urgent task of trying to make his Tierra del Aguila story stand up. Williamson had given him the OK to spend time on it, but that was not an open-ended commitment. He knew that if he did not soon make substantial progress on running the story to ground, he would be pulled off it and it would land on the spike. He'd had plenty of stories spiked in his time, but this wasn't going to be one of them. His nose for a good story was twitching like a dowser's stick on steroids.

He checked the time. It was just past 7am. Jake Burkins would probably be ready to leave for work. Paice rang his number. The slightly groggy voice that answered was evidence that his expectations about Jake's enthusiasm for getting to his job were somewhat overstated.

"Jake, sorry to wake you. It's Nick Paice."

"Good morning, Mr P. What's the problem? Can't sleep?"

"I thought you'd be on your way to the office, Jake. Day off?"

"No such luck, Mr P."

"Clock the clock, Jake," Paice advised. Burkins's voice suddenly acquired an element of alertness. "Blimey, Mr P, is that the time? You're right. I should be down the road by now. What can I do for you?"

"We need to talk, Jake. Are you available at lunch time today? Usual place?"

"I certainly can be, Mr P. I'll see you there at 1 if that's OK."

By the time Paice had showered and dressed, Mrs Evans had returned from taking Jessica to school. As he passed her room, she was busy with her housework. "Good morning, Mrs Evans. I hope all is well."

She came out into the hall. "Yes, everything is fine, thank you, Mr Paice. You were in late last night. I hope that you managed to eat something."

He assured her that he had. "Any news about treatment for Jessica?"

"I'm seeing a consultant today who has dealt with the clinic in Philadelphia. He is a personal friend of the surgeon there who has perfected a revolutionary technique. He's giving his services free, but he says the costs in the United States will be quite high. Fortunately, the money we received will more than cover it. I wish you would tell me more about that, Mr Paice."

He waved away the suggestion that he should say more. "Let's just say that it arrived because someone wanted to do the right thing for Jessica." He bade her farewell and left.

Outside, he stood for two or three minutes and surveyed the street in both directions. To the dispassionate observer, he was displaying an excess of caution. To someone who had been the deliberate target of a hit and run driver, it was pure common sense.

He picked up a copy of the Mercury and half a dozen of the other dailies at his local newsagent and took a seat and a cup of coffee at the corner cafe. He surveyed his story on the front page then turned to the in-depth articles he had written on pages four and five. He had waited the previous night to see the first edition. The inside pages had been left alone, but a rejig on the front page had meant a couple of paragraphs that had been cut in the first were reinstated in the final London edition.

On the whole, he was happy with how it had turned out. He had speculated, as he warned Moses that he would, but he had given no hint in what he had written of the truth behind the killings. He went through the competition, but the Mercury's coverage was streets ahead, not least because of Paice's personal knowledge. And he was the only one to get a quote from the ambassador. It was an excellent quote, too. It should have been – Paice had concocted it.

He was satisfied with his day's work. It was what made him do the job. He had gone to the office yesterday morning not knowing what the day would bring. He woke the next morning and his work was all over the front page. He had been there when it happened while the rest of the world would simply read about it. He was content.

He did not feel the same about not having spoken to Maria. Only a hardened assassin – and then not all of them – could carry on as normal, unaffected by having shot three men dead. He pictured her contending with normality, getting the children ready and doing the school run. If she could hack that, she was, indeed, a remarkable person. But, remarkable though she may be, she would be badly in need of comfort and support – what was usually called counselling – and she had no one to whom she could turn or in whom she could confide. He felt a stab of guilt that he had not spoken to her.

Paice arrived at the office and got straight on the phone to contacts in two of the biggest international aid agencies, both in Geneva. Had they had any calls for assistance in Tierra del Aguila in, say, the last 15 years? No. Had they heard of any major disasters there? No.

Frustrated, he hung around with nothing for him in the diary, reluctantly drank machine-made coffee, ribbed Olivia, was ribbed by Olivia, then headed for his meeting with Burkins. He got to the Black Lion half an hour early. Good. Time for a few drinks before Burkins arrived. Not so. Burkins had got there early, too, motivated by the same ambition.

Paice ordered him a drink. "Good to see you again, Mr Paice. What can I do for you?"

"You can come up with something more definite on this story you've been trying to sell me, Jake. I need firm information. I've tried all angles, but I can't take it any further. I know that there's a story to be written, but I need just that single, key hard fact to trigger it. If I don't get it, the story is dead on its feet and you don't get paid."

Burkins looked glum. "I've given you everything that I can. I'll keep my eyes peeled, so if anything crops up I'll make sure you get it. There's one possibility. I've been told I'm working in SR this afternoon, Mr P. I'll see what I can do, but I can't make any promises."

"What's SR?"

"Sorry – secure records. It's where they file away all the sensitive stuff. If there's anything to help you with your story, it will be in there. The problem is that we only ever work in there under strict supervision, so it's unlikely I'll get the chance to look for anything. But I'll try."

Paice was unimpressed. He had hoped that Burkins would be able to supply that missing element of the story. "What happened at the meeting with the Americans – you said that your permanent secretary was having a session with them. I know that they arrived, and I know that they left. What happened in between?"

Burkins sipped his ale. "Be reasonable, Mr P. At my pay grade I only get to fetch and carry. They don't confide in me what happens at these high level meetings. I only get the crumbs from the table, if you understand me. But any crumbs I get, I pass straight on to you. And I have to be really careful. The day after the Yanks had their meeting, the whole place was turned upside down. I heard that everyone in the Central American section was grilled by security about their movements and contacts – they even questioned the lovely Marcia. Something must have gone badly wrong for them to get that upset."

Paice said nothing to indicate that he was the something that had gone badly wrong. "Did they grill you, Jake?"

"No fear, Mr P. I just kept my head down and got on with my work. No one said anything to me."

"That's good, Jake. Well, I have to be going." He finished his beer and stood up. "If you find anything, ring me straight away."

"Trust me, Mr Paice. You'll hear from me the minute I get anything – as soon as I get out of the office, that is. I never call you from there – too risky."

Paice was not confident that he would hear from Burkins, but his phone rang just after 6pm and Jake sounded excited. "I've got you just what you need, Mr Paice. It's dynamite. Can you come to my place tonight? I have to get the paper back to the office tomorrow before they miss it, so you've got to look at it tonight."

"Do you mean you've nicked an original document, Jake? Couldn't you have photocopied it and put the original back so that no one was any the wiser?"

"You've got to be joking, Mr P. Secure records and photocopying? If they saw me photocopying something they'd be on to me straight away asking what I was doing. As long as I get the paper back in the morning, everything will be fine. There's no way they will miss it"

"I admire your confidence, Jake. How did you get it out?"

"I slipped it between the pages of the Punter's Friend and put it under my arm." Paice knew that to Jake the daily racing paper was an inseparable companion and an indispensible aid to donating a large proportion of his income to his local bookie.

"OK, Jake. Where do we meet?"

"Can you come to my place?" Paice agreed, and Burkins gave him an address in south London.

"Right, Jake. I'll be there at 7.30."

"Don't forget to bring your wallet, Mr P."

Chapter 29

Burkins lived in a stand of council flats that were probably built at about the time of the second world war, maybe just before, maybe just after. Unlike their 1960s counterparts, they rose to only four stories, not 24. Paice stood in the light drizzle that had greeted his arrival and studied the layout. There were three blocks forming an incomplete square, in the middle of which he stood, his back to the road where the taxi had dropped him off.

It was late summer. On a sunny evening, it would still have been light, and that may have offered a more pleasing prospect. The gloom of the grey overcast that had brought the rain, however, had also hastened the coming of dusk which seemed to accentuate the mood of depression that had descended on the scene. He looked into the murk. In the centre of each block was a darkened doorway harbouring shadows that betrayed no hint of what lay within.

After a quick calculation – each block had four storeys, four flats to a storey – he reckoned that number 26 was probably in the middle block. His hunch was confirmed by the peeling painted sign over that entrance.

He knew better than to expect there to be a lift. He climbed the cold concrete stairs, his footsteps echoing up and down the stairwell. The faint odour of urine and stale alcohol prompted him to avoid breathing too deeply, which ran counter to his natural desire to fill his lungs as he struggled to complete the climb to the third floor.

Once there, he was confronted by a knot of youths who stood casually obstructing his access to the landing upon which Burkins's flat was located. They stared at him in sullen silence. This was a community where they did not lay out the welcome mat for strangers. He could see little point in bidding them a good evening or asking them to stand aside, so he pushed through the group without speaking.

Council properties of this type and vintage were constructed with open landings, exposing those who ventured along them to whatever the weather chose to inflict. In Paice's case, it was still the drizzle. He found the front door of number 26 and rang the bell. A grey-haired, elderly woman answered. Paice realised that she was Jake's mother.

"You must be Mr Paice," she observed pleasantly. "Jake is waiting for you in his lock-up. He told me to tell you to go over there. He's fiddling with his motorbike, as usual. It's breaking his heart that he has got to sell it. I hope you'll give him a fair price, Mr Paice. He's advertised it enough. Him and that bike! He thinks more of that damned machine than he does of me."

She said it with a smile, meaning it as a joke, so Paice resisted the temptation to tell her that she therefore came third in Jake's prioritised affections. The gee-gees certainly came first. She pointed him to a collection of garages on the other side of the road. After once more pushing his way through the youths he walked down the stairs and across the square and crossed the road.

The garages were arranged in a courtyard in two opposing rows. The place was deserted. Graffiti decorated the up-and-over metal doors of the lock-ups, weeds thrived in the cracks in the concrete surface of the yard. The place was in a state of terminal decay. The rain had stopped, but that did nothing to improve the atmosphere. In the fading light, he could not tell in which of the lock-ups Jake was working. He called his name, but the only response was his own voice echoing back at him.

He began a systematic search. It was halfway down the second row, just as he was about to give up, that he detected a gleam of electric light through the crack where the door met the door frame. This had to be it. He banged on the door and called Jake's name again. Still no response. He reached down for the handle and pulled the door open. It swung up on its runners and Paice peered into the half-lit interior.

He was unsurprised to be assailed by the pungent smell of oil, petrol and the odours that hung around machinery. The light he had seen was coming from an old desk lamp that was standing on a workbench located at the rear of the garage. It lit the surface of the bench, but it was shaded and directional. While its output dazzled in the predominant darkness, it provided scant illumination over the remainder of the workshop. Against the glare, Paice could see nothing and he certainly could see no sign of Jake.

He held up his hand to shield his eyes. "You there, Jake?" Still no response. Paice had expected to see him poring over his racing paper planning the next day's foray into predestined penury. His eyes became accustomed to the gloom. The motorcycle was propped up on its stand. Then, sure enough, there was Jake, lying back in an old armchair. He had dozed off and was doubtless dreaming of his next big win.

"Wakey, wakey, Jake," Paice urged, and picked his way towards him through the rubbish that littered the floor. Even when Paice tripped over an empty oil can Jake did not stir. There was a very good reason. It was the neat bullet hole in his forehead and the congealing patch of blood and brain that had been blasted out of the back of his skull and spread over the fabric of the chair where what was left of his head rested. Jake had backed his last loser.

Paice stood transfixed. He had seen more than his share of killing – he'd watched three men being shot dead in the street only a day earlier – and the simple fact of violent death had long since failed to move him. And he certainly was not about to panic. But this was more personal. He had got to know Jake well, had developed a certain sympathy for him, may even have had some responsibility for him. And here Jake was, lying dead in front of him. Paice looked in disbelief at the inert figure.

There must have been a dozen questions begging to be asked, some of them demanding urgent answers. Paice was neither asking nor answering. He was momentarily immobilised not by shock, but by an overwhelming sense of sadness for a poor sod who demanded little from life and knew better than to be disappointed or surprised at its response. And when the first question finally came, it was one born of that sadness. Who would tell Jake's mother?

He looked at the body for what might have been seconds or could have been minutes. Then the real questions kicked in thick and fast. The first was who had killed Jake and why. Paice's first instinct was to guess at a gambling debt. Jake was probably in it up to his neck with a bookie or, especially in these parts, and much more worrying, a loan shark. Whoever he owed money to had sent in the heavy mob to collect payment.

Jake would not be the first to have been offered the choice of the money or your life. The sad fact was that, for Jake, there was no choice. He certainly had no money. That was still in Paice's wallet. Even so, a bullet in the head was a bit extreme. Unless, of course, it was intended as an advertisement, a warning to the other clients of what would happen if they did not pay up.

The next question was what to do now. His inclination was to leave quietly, closing the door behind him. But he dismissed the thought the instant it occurred to him. Jake's mother could identify him. The youths on the landing had seen him come and go, doubtless following his progress from their viewpoint on the third floor as he crossed to the garages. If he legged it, he

343

would be volunteering to become the principal suspect. That made the next move unavoidable, if not exactly appealing. He had to call the police.

But, in the absence of panic and emotion, his mind was working efficiently. Jake had promised him a document that he had described as dynamite. The top priority was to find it. He had planned to meet Paice at the lockup, so he would have had it with him. Paice walked over to the workbench, taking care not to disturb evidence or provide any. Using his handkerchief to avoid fingerprints, he twisted the desk lamp to illuminate the entire scene. He knew from what Jake had told him that the paper he was after had been secreted within the pages of the Punter's Friend. It was in the harsh glare of the lamp that he saw the newspaper. It had been dismembered and scattered across the floor.

He bent down to pick it up but stopped. Crouching down, he studied how the newspaper had been strewn around the garage. Jake would never have done that to such a precious resource. Was someone else looking for the document that Jake had promised to give to Paice? But how would anyone else know of its existence?

He paused and considered the coincidence of events. Was it pure chance that someone had tried to run Paice down only a few days before and now Jake had been murdered? He mentally told himself to get a grip. For one thing, he had no proof that the unsuccessful hit and run really had been an attempt on his life.

It was impossible for the two events to be linked. True, he had confronted the Americans in the hotel and they knew about him. But his association with Jake was something no one could have established. Jake would not have been on their radar. Paice always followed the accepted and inviolable practice of protecting his sources. Even his editor did not know about Jake's existence let alone that he was the source of the story. There had to be another reason for someone to murder him. It had to be a gambling debt.

He picked his way back to Jake's body and inspected it carefully, neither wanting nor daring to touch it. He was about to turn away to leave and call the police when he spotted something in Jake's right hand. He knelt and looked closely. It was a scrap of paper. His instincts were screaming at him to leave well alone and get out, but he ignored them. He gently prised Jake's grip apart and extracted the fragment.

Smoothing it out, he could see that it was no more than an inch at its widest by three inches, torn roughly along one side but with a precise cut edge on the other. It was just a plain piece of paper. Until he turned it over. What he saw next caused him to catch his breath and made his heart beat faster. The remnant was obviously the top of a sheet because it was headed notepaper and it bore the royal coat of arms, embossed in blue, and, beneath it, incomplete because of the tear, but unmistakeable, what remained of the inscription: "Foreign and Commonwealth Office". It was all that remained of the document that Jake had promised to give Paice.

In that instant, he realised he could no longer deny the obvious. He now knew for sure why Jake had been murdered. The killers wanted whatever Jake had obtained for Paice, had forced him at gunpoint – which must have terrified him – to hand it over. Then, when they had snatched it from his grip, they had put a bullet in his brain to silence him.

It was alarming that whatever Jake had uncovered was considered by someone to be so important that they would kill to keep it under wraps. And Paice had gone public that he intended to do precisely the opposite. He had shot his mouth off to the Yanks in the hotel that he would be blowing the Tierra del Aguila story wide open.

Whoever wanted the story hushed up had killed Jake. Until now, he and Jake had had only one thing in common – the Tierra del Aguila story. Now they shared something else – being the candidate for murder, one attempted, one fulfilled. Paice was standing at the front of the queue to be the next target. And he still did not know what the story was about, why it was necessary to kill to protect it.

Paice pulled the door down to close it and leaned up against the wall as he considered his next best move. He realised that by hanging around he was exposing himself to risk. The killer or killers who had finished off Jake might come back. He had to call the police, but at least Jake had had the sense to provide a cover story that did not involve passing top secret documents to the press, so he would have no difficulty explaining his presence.

Flashing blue lights and sirens were on the scene within 10 minutes. A uniformed copper told him to sit in the back of the police car and asked him a few preliminary questions, including demanding proof of identity, while they waited for the CID to arrive. That was another 10 minutes. There were two of them. They borrowed a huge torch from the back of the police car and surveyed the interior of the garage without going in. Then they turned to Paice, the older one doing the talking.

"I'm Detective Sergeant Milburn. You are?"

Paice took an instant dislike to him, but he did not let it show. "My name is Nick Paice."

"What can you tell me about what has happened here, Mr Paice?"

"I know no more than you do, mate. I arranged to meet him" – he jerked a thumb in Jake's direction – "to talk about a bike he had for sale. I went to his flat across the road, but his mother told me to come over here where he was waiting for me – with the bike."

"What did you find when you got here? Was he already dead?"

"The garage door was closed but I could see a light through the crack so, when he didn't answer I opened the door."

"Did you go in?"

"Yes, when he didn't reply...."

"Bit silly, weren't you, walking all over a crime scene?"

"I didn't know it was a crime scene. There wasn't exactly a sign on the door. It was only when I got inside that I saw him lying there. You asked whether he was dead when I got here, and he looked pretty dead to me, but I'm no doctor."

"Then, what are you, Sir?"

"I'm a bloke who's come to buy a motorbike."

"And are you in that line of business – buying and selling motorbikes?" Paice did not want to divulge his line of business, but he knew that it would have to come out. "No, I'm a reporter for the Daily Mercury."

Milburn paused and looked him up and down. "One of our friends from the press?" He turned to look at the detective constable who stood beside him and gave a sarcastic smile. "Got a press card?" Paice took it out of his top pocket and handed it over. The cop studied it by the light of his torch, then handed it back. "Weren't you the lucky one, walking in on a big story like this?" More sarcasm.

Paice had learnt that coppers were like everyone else – some you liked, some you didn't, some were OK, some weren't. He had already decided which group Milburn came from. Time to inject sarcasm of his own. "Big? Two paragraphs maximum on page 4. The big story will be if you catch whoever did it."

"Not if, Mr Paice, when."

Paice continued undeterred. "And if you get the case to court and if you get a conviction." He put emphasis on the word "if". They both knew that he was harking back to a campaign the Mercury had run a couple of months before about police clear-up rates. The theme of the campaign was that they had to improve.

"You mustn't believe everything you read in the newspapers, Sir. Perhaps you shouldn't believe everything you write. Can you account for your movements so that we know what you were doing and when?"

"Yes. I got here at 7.30..."

"Can you prove that, Sir?"

For the first time that he could recall, Paice was glad that he was required to get a receipt for the taxi. He fished into one of the pockets of his waterproof jacket and pulled it out. "That's the cab that brought me here. The driver will confirm the time. Then I went up to the bloke's flat and his mother told me he was over here waiting for me. She will confirm that. And there was a bunch of kids hanging around on the landing. It's odds on they saw me get out of the taxi and go straight up to the flat. They sure as hell watched me come over here."

"OK, that will be all for now, but we'll need you to give a statement at the police station. We'll want your fingerprints for elimination purposes – no objection, I assume? And I may have to question you again."

"No problem. Can I ask some questions? I've got a big story to write. Got any leads? Any idea who did it?"

"Fuck off – Sir." As Milburn walked away, Paice grinned and wondered for an instant whether he had been too hasty in his assessment of the man.

Chapter 30

It was a fairly routine story. A top flight City trader had made the mistake of being a woman in a world of trousers and testosterone, and had then compounded the error by getting pregnant. When the management realised that she had ceased being one of the blokes, and being anxious to get her out before she claimed maternity leave, they encouraged all the red-blooded males on the dealing floor to make her life hell. She had jumped ship and was now seeking damages for constructive dismissal. Her barrister had whispered to Paice that she could be in line for a payout well into seven figures. He was anxious that Paice should spell his name correctly.

The employment tribunal hearing had broken for lunch. Paice had found the nearest decent pub in which to sit it out. He supped his ale, surveying the noisy crowd over the rim of his glass. No sign of anyone shadowing him or about to drop poison in his drink — so far as he could see. That did not mean they weren't there. It was only a few days since Jake's murder and he would admit to himself, but to no one else, that he was worried. He was the cool, unflappable newsman who had seen it all and could cope with anything. But he was worried, nervous even.

He felt safe in busy public places. He reckoned that, with plenty of witnesses about, no one would try anything. But he was constantly ill at ease. He sensed that someone was keeping watch on him. He had taken to stopping suddenly in the street and turning unexpectedly, hoping, or perhaps fearing, that he might catch sight of a stalker.

He had moved out of his digs for the time being and was now moving from hotel to hotel. The office had booked rooms for him under assumed names. He had confided his fears in Williamson and Bryce. They were not completely convinced, but they both knew Paice well enough not simply to brush his anxiety aside. Williamson had suggested that he take a month's holiday and lie low, but he had rejected the offer. He could not just put his life on hold.

Paradoxically, his most effective insurance was not to forget about the story, but to hunt it down, and he could not do that hiding away in a cottage in the Cotswolds. Once the story was printed and the facts were out, there would be nothing to be gained from killing him, other than retribution. But he still did not have the facts. No facts, no story. No story, nowhere to run. Williamson had given him the OK to run up the expenses necessary to keep his profile low.

Maybe he was being paranoid, and he was willing to confess to that. But where his life was at stake, he was going to be whatever he bloody well chose. And, anyway, paranoia did not preclude the near certainty that someone had decided to get him. Ask anyone on a list beginning with Thomas à Becket and ending with Alexander Litvinenko whether they had been paranoid. If they could speak they would tell how many times they had been told they were worrying about nothing. And look at what had happened to them. He was certain that Jake's murder was tied up with the story, and it was odds on, therefore, that someone out there wanted him silenced, too. All he could do was keep looking over his shoulder.

The hearing adjourned for the day at 4.30. Paice had developed considerable respect for the lady in bringing the case. He grabbed a word with her, getting some good quotes, and had then decided to head back to the office to knock out the story. It had started to rain and taxis were suddenly scarce. He had decided in principle not to use the Underground. In the inevitable crush, he could not guarantee to keep safely clear of the platform edge. He could write the headline: "Man in train death mystery". It was safer to stay above ground.

He was passing a florist's shop when a magnificent display of roses caught his eye. It was a good place to stop and verify whether he was being followed. He shot a glance back the way he had come, could see nothing suspicious, and then stood staring into the shop window, using it as best he could as a giant mirror to check what was happening behind him. The traffic was passing in each direction. Nothing out of place. A bus passed, its traditional red merging with the red of the roses. The scene assumed an almost dreamlike quality, the reflected images warped, shimmering and almost hypnotic as he saw them, distorted, in the huge plate glass window.

Too late, he realised that the looming dark shadow that now filled the glass was a bad augury. It was a black van and it slid into the kerb. Shots rang out. He had been told that being hit by a bullet was like being hit by a truck. It was true. He was knocked flat. His face slapped against the wet pavement. He felt a huge weight upon him and he was incapable of movement. A puddle of blood spread slowly out before his eyes. So this was how it would end. The fleeting regrets of things he wished he had said and done that would now remain for ever unsaid and undone faded as he grew weaker. He had always hoped that, when it came, the end would be instant, a light turned off in a windowless room. He had no perception of gratitude at the granting of his wish because then there was the blessed blackness.

He was oblivious of the passage of time, but it was 15 minutes before he regained consciousness and found himself staring at the roof of the ambulance. Instinctively, he moved his fingers and ran his hands over his torso. Everything seemed in order. He tried to get up. His head hurt like hell. The paramedic put her hand on his chest and told him to lie back.

"You'll be OK, luv. You've just had a nasty knock."

Paice's head was spinning and the giddiness made him feel sick. Slowly, he was coming to. "Am I still alive? I heard shots."

"Yeah, my dear, if you're in a position to ask, it means you're alive. Not like that gentleman there." She jerked her thumb at the stretcher on the other side of the ambulance. "We did what we could for him but we couldn't save him. They shot him twice. He must have fallen on you and knocked you down. You were very lucky."

Paice struggled to sit up despite the paramedic's protests. A dressing had been applied to his head where it had smacked the pavement. He adjusted it to avoid it obscuring the sight of his right eye. He knew that the assassin had hit the wrong man. Now, some poor innocent bastard had taken the bullets intended for him. Standing unsteadily, he looked down at the covered figure. He pulled back the sheet and flinched in disbelief. In life, Refik's bodyguard had projected an intense look laden with menace. In death his eyes had lost their colour, become flat and meaningless, deflated somehow and now could offer only a lifeless, harmless, stare.

Paice could see that the bullet had entered his neck just below the jaw. It would have caused a massive, rapid and lethal loss of blood. So this was who had been following him, instructed by Refik to keep him safe. He had done precisely that, judging perfectly when the attack would come, and paying with his life to save Paice's and to obey his master's instruction.

He flicked the sheet back over the body. "I'm just going outside to get some air. That OK?"

The paramedic nodded. "Don't go far – I need to get your details and the police want to speak to you as soon as you are up to it."

Paice waved an acknowledgement and stepped out into the rain, breathing deeply in the cool air. There seemed to be plenty of cops around, controlling the onlookers, taking statements and calling for witnesses. He walked – stumbled – across to where one of the uniforms was talking to an elderly man.

"It was amazing, officer. It all 'appened so quick. This black van pulls up and I sees the side door open and this 'and pointin' a gun. Then this bloke sprints past me and pushes this other bloke to the ground just as the gun went off. I reckon 'e deserves a medal 'cos if he hadn't done that the other bloke would have copped it." The PC was making notes as the witness was speaking.

Paice realised that they knew neither that he was the intended target nor who he was – so far he had given no one his name. Best to keep it that way. He looked back at the ambulance. The paramedic was preoccupied with dealing with the dead man and the cops were all busy with the bystanders or securing the scene. No one seemed to notice him. He pulled up the collar of his waterproof jacket and slowly walked away, slipping unobtrusively into the crowd.

The police would definitely have wanted to speak to him as a witness, and he was the only one who could tell them precisely what had happened and why. But he was not about to do either. He would be saying nothing. Anyway, being around when people were getting shot was becoming a bit of a habit for him. He knew that the police would eventually realise that he was the connection between this shooting and Jake's murder.

Hanging around simply meant waiting for trouble to develop.

As he made his way along the pavement, hugging the lee of the buildings, Paice realised that something was happening that he had never experienced before – at least, not to this extent. He was feeling the surge of panic. It was only by the most remarkable sequence of events that he was not lying dead in the back of that ambulance. He realised that he had to get a grip.

The darkened entrance to a vacant office block offered sanctuary. He took it with gratitude, walking in and turning his back on passersby. He took out his phone and realised that his hands were shaking. Then he saw that they were stained with the bodyguard's blood. It had soaked into his shirt and had spread like a black cloud drenching the front of his khaki jacket. So much blood. He realised that he was still living the nightmare he thought had been exorcised by Mwamba's death.

He stared at the phone, but who would he call? He took a series of deep breaths and managed to contain the panic. If he was to get somewhere safe he had to do something about the blood. He took the jacket off and checked the black quilted lining. There was blood, but it did not show against the dark fabric. Turning the garment inside out, he pulled it on and buttoned it up to the neck, hiding the bloodstained shirt. It was the best he could do. He ripped the dressing from his head and used it to wipe the blood from his hands before stuffing it into his trouser pocket.

Now he had to get far away and hide. It was run or die. His professional side, hardened and disciplined by a million deadlines and a succession of flint-eyed news editors, asked: "What about the story?"

"Fuck the story," was his muttered response. He had never signed his contract of employment in blood and there was no way he would die for the job.

That morning he had checked out of his hotel and gone straight to the office, leaving his overnight bag there for collection later. He needed more than an overnight bag for what he now had to do. He hoped that whoever was after him would not yet have known that they had missed him and hit the wrong man. He had a temporary reprieve until they realised their mistake. That would give him time to get back to his digs, pick up his stuff and get the hell out of London.

He bought a copy of the Mercury, opened it out and held it against his chest, hiding any tell-tale bloodstains. Then, after what seemed a lifetime, he found a taxi. First, he would say goodbye to Philo and Amalia.

Chapter 31

There was a gap in the string of cars parked along the kerb. Paice told the cab driver to pull in there. It was conveniently located opposite the restaurant. He lowered the window and looked across into the brightly-lit interior. There were a few customers, certainly nothing out of the ordinary. He took out his phone and speed dialled the number. He could see Philo get up from his table to answer the call.

"Hallo, Philo, this is Nick. Can you speak to me?"

"Sure I can. What can I do for you? Where are you?"

"I am sitting in a taxi watching you from the other side of the road. I'm in trouble, Philo. I need to keep out of sight."

Philo paused to think. He lowered his voice. "Go to the newsagent's shop on the corner. I'll see you there."

He hung up, walked to his table, drank the rest of his coffee and casually called out to Amalia that he was going for the evening newspaper. Paice watched him leave the restaurant and walk towards the corner shop. He waited until Philo had almost reached it then paid the taxi, carefully looked around and got out. He crossed the road and followed the Greek.

Inside the small shop, Philo was chatting with the Asian proprietor. The place was otherwise empty. Paice walked past him and went to the back, pretending to study the tinned cat food. Philo followed.

"Nick, dear boy, you sounded very worried. It must be a serious problem."

"It is, Philo – as bad as it gets. There have been two attempts to kill me and I am having to make myself very scarce." He unbuttoned his jacket and revealed the bloodstained shirt. "Don't worry, it's not my blood."

Philo recoiled, visibly shocked. "You must have done something very bad to upset someone so much."

"Yes, I've uncovered a story that is so big that some powerful people are prepared to kill to keep it quiet. They murdered my contact and they've got the same end in mind for me. They have been trying to find me, which is why I have not been living at my digs. Until today, I was kidding myself that I might be mistaken. This afternoon, they tried to shoot me in the street. They got the wrong man, but I now know for sure that they are out to get me."

Philo scratched the stubble on his chin and nodded. "That explains something that has been worrying me. I have had a couple of men in the restaurant spending a lot of time drinking coffee and reading the papers, just killing time. I tried to talk to them, but they were very unsociable."

Paice nodded. "I reckon they knew I was a regular there and they were there to kill more than time, my friend. They were probably waiting for me to show up."

"They certainly had that smell about them, Nick."

"Smell?"

"You forget, Nick, that I am Greek. I lived through the regime of the colonels in my country. We learnt to sniff out such men. They have a look and a smell about them. Different country maybe, but the same smell. But they have left. They went not half an hour ago."

"That's because they think they have killed me. Instead they hit some other poor sod, who is now laid out in the mortuary, but it is possible that, as yet, they are unaware of their mistake. While they think it was me they bumped off they will stop looking and I have a chance to get away."

"You have somewhere to go?"

"For starters, I'll just get out of London, then think about where I go to next. I am hoping that the Mercury will find me somewhere safe, but I cannot risk going back to the office. I had better get going, Philo. Please say goodbye to Amalia for me. I'll be back as soon as this blows over, but I have no idea when that will be."

Philo placed his hand on Paice's shoulder and muttered something in Greek, which Paice interpreted from his expression to be wishing him a safe return. The two men shook hands and Paice left the shop and headed for his digs.

He could not be certain that the assassins were not still after him. They might have spotted their mistake.

They might know he was still alive. They might still be looking for him. He could not afford to take chances. It was early September and still light. He was the hunted. He had no cloak of darkness to pull around him and shroud his presence. But, by the same token, nor did the hunters. The prey survived longer when it saw the predator first.

He kept close to the buildings and kept looking in all directions. There was no obvious threat, but if these people were any good at all, obvious would not be their style. He had suffered nasty experiences with a black or dark coloured car. He kept watch for that for a start. The street where he lived was off the beaten track and traffic was light. Regulations restricted the number of vehicles that could park. In a quiet street it was easier to assess the presence of danger. As far as he could see, everything looked normal.

He took the front steps two and a time and opened the front door, taking a last look around before going in. Still no apparent threat. The place was in darkness. Mrs Evans and Jessica were away at the clinic in the States, so the property was empty. He closed the door and caught the smell of the house – funny how every house had its own smell, a coalition of smells that reflected the lifestyle and taste of the occupants. It was the unmistakeable smell that told you that you were home.

He was ripping the tainted clothes from his body as he climbed the stairs. The first thing he needed was a hot shower and a clean outfit. Then a large Scotch and time to consider his next move. A phone call to the office –

Bryce was still expecting a story on the employment tribunal, and a hole would have been left for it on page three – was high on the list of priorities. They would have to find something else to put in the hole.

He opened the door to his room. Everything was as he had left it. Apart from the muzzle of the automatic that was pointing directly at the space between his eyes. The bearer of the weapon had positioned himself in silhouette against the window. When he spoke, the voice was quiet and controlled, but with a tone that brooked no argument.

"Come in Mr Paice. You have a choice. You can live or die."

Chapter 32

The sun was dropping out of the tropical sky like a stone as Eduardo pointed the nose of the ageing Chevrolet up into the hills. Night descended rapidly in these latitudes, and they were confident of reaching undetected the secluded stretch of the lake shore that was their objective and completing the operation under cover of darkness. Scrantz had devised a schedule that he calculated would enable them to complete the mission and leave enough time to reach an ad hoc airstrip for a rendezvous timed at 6.30, when it would be light enough for their aircraft to land.

The plan was to proceed initially by a road that climbed until it hit a break in the hills where it deteriorated into a rough dirt track. That would eventually lead them down on the other side to where Eduardo had laid up a small boat to take them round the shore to the petrochemical plant.

"Kill the headlights," Bart muttered. "Don't want to advertise our presence." In the rapidly fading half light the vehicle got under way, soon swallowed by the tropical growth that covered the side of the hill. The last afterglow of the evening finally evaporated to leave them making their way slowly by the intermittent light of the moon and the pale yellow glow of their parking lights.

An hour later, progress was becoming increasingly difficult as the track became progressively worse and difficult to follow. When the front wheel of the car crashed into a hole, the sump and front suspension grounded with unequivocal finality leaving the vehicle stranded like a ship on a shoal.

"It's by foot from here," Eduardo said, "Better start getting the gear out of the trunk. We want nothing left in the car to link it with us. It's suspicious enough having to leave it. No one in this country would just dump a car like this."

"No, but with a bit of luck the first campesino to come along will be smart enough to claim it and keep his mouth shut," Scrantz suggested. Then, as an afterthought: "Leave the keys in the ignition."

They were soon on the downward slope. Eduardo examined the luminous characters on the compass and struck off into the undergrowth, heading towards the lake, which was still hidden from them by the canopy of vegetation. Suddenly it broke into view through a clearing, the reflection of the full moon poured forth a stream of molten silver a few hundred feet beneath them. They paused while Eduardo found his bearings to determine the way forward.

Cutting through heavy growth in daylight would have been an energy consuming and noisy process. At night it proved doubly frustrating, with the silence of darkness amplifying every sound, each snapping twig magnified to sound like a rifle shot, and the occasional disturbed bird rising noisily to screech about the presence of intruders.

Then the going began to ease. Eduardo had found a dirt road. But just as they were getting into their stride, he stopped in his tracks and put his hand on Scrantz's chest, barring further progress.

The trio crouched, unnecessarily but instinctively, in the darkness as Eduardo sniffed the air. "Wood smoke," he whispered. "Stay there."

He moved noiselessly off. By now they, too, could both smell the smoke, but the black cloak of night, hitherto their ally, conspired to blind them to the risks ahead. The forest uttered no sound, betrayed no sign of life in the silver fingers of moonlight that filtered down through the arching foliage. Deprived of their senses, their assessment of time moved into slow motion, and their comrade's absence began to assume an alarming duration. Bart was about to express his worst fears about Eduardo never finding them again when they heard a rustle and he was back.

"Army patrol," he said in a subdued voice. "We'll have to go back and take a detour." They retraced their steps and swept to the left in a wide arc. The diversion added almost an hour to their journey, and when, finally, they reached the road that skirted the lake shore, it was at a point a good half mile east of where they had intended. With Scrantz muttering anxiously about the time, they set off at a trot along the deserted highway.Eventually,

Eduardo located the boat, laid up among overhanging trees where the rocks dropped sharply into the water.

"I don't know about alerting the army patrol, but it's a miracle we didn't wake Cisneros in his bed, the racket we made coming through that forest," Bart said as he threw his holdall into the boat. "It's almost certain that they know we are here."

"No way. If they had seen or heard us they would have rounded us up by now and we would have been destined to push up palm trees," Scrantz asserted.

Between them they got the boat into the water. Eduardo had the outboard engine purring on tickover by the time Scrantz had thrown in his rucksack and climbed aboard. "Keep the speed as high as you can without making too much noise," he ordered. "I'm worried about the time, but the last thing we need is for someone to hear the motor and start wondering who we are."

Eduardo gently opened the throttle. The small craft moved out into the lake, gaining some 75yds off the shore before coming round to run parallel with it, into a warm, gentle breeze, for the mile or so to the refinery. In the bright moonlight they could pick out the features on the land. They glided past the occasional lakeside shanty and then the increasing density of dwellings indicating the town. Gradually, all distinct form and outline of the settlement dissolved into the darkness as they moved along the shore until only the occasional distant twinkling light remained to show that it had ever existed.

Eduardo finally turned the boat in towards the harbour where the old chemical complex stood on the water's edge, its rusting and intermittent perimeter fence representing almost an embossed invitation to intruders to enter. "All it needs is a flashing sign saying 'Way in'," said Bart as they sat in the gently rolling boat, assessing the best way to make their entrance. It was almost the last comment. From here on in each man knew his task. Words became redundant.

Scrantz pointed to a spot where the old wire fence, weaving drunkenly along the waterside, suddenly gave up and lay down. Eduardo moved the boat in gently and as it touched bottom the other two jumped out into several inches of velvet black water.

In minutes they were over the prostrate fence and marking their bearings from the old plans. The network of pipes, valves, and tanks in the chemical plant shone with an eerie luminosity in the moonlight as the two men skirted round them and headed for the storage facility in the centre of the oil refinery.

The chemical plant had been unguarded for the simple reason that there was nothing there worth guarding. The refinery was a different proposition. They had known that there would be guards, but the sudden burst of conversation coming out of the darkness cast an immediate Gorgonian spell, freezing the intruders into temporary immobility until, certain that they had not been detected, they could retreat into the blackness of an inspection pit beneath old pipework. Still not a word passed between them.

Bart raised his eyes above the edge of the pit and peered into the darkness. He could not see the guards, but their voices continued to carry on the night air. He indicated to Scrantz to stay put and crawled out of the pit on his stomach. The two men on picket had been standing not 20ft from them, one carrying a torch, the beam of which he periodically stroked across the pipes and paraphernalia of the plant as they casually strolled along the track that followed the perimeter of the main complex.

The men were clearly on their rounds, and Bart decided to sit tight until they moved on. They did so minutes later, and when they had disappeared into the darkness of the man-made metal jungle he slipped back to summon Scrantz out of hiding. He broke the silence for the first time."Bad news. We are on an access road and beyond it there's another fence - an internal perimeter. I saw it in the light of the guard's torch. It must be 15ft high."

"Jesus Christ! Now what? We can't cut through. They'll know we've been here. We gotta climb over or find some other way in. Jesus, what a cock-up! Why weren't we told?"

Crouching, they slipped silently up to the wire and followed it along for almost a hundred yards. Unlike with the old perimeter fence, this one demonstrated a serious desire for security. The American stopped abruptly and swore vigorously through clenched teeth. Bart followed his gaze skywards to where the moonlight caught a series of five white ceramic insulators, one for each strand of the barbed wire that topped the steel enclosure.

"Try going over and you'll end up sizzling like a kebab," Bart said with resignation. "There's got to be another way in."

The sound of an approaching vehicle prompted the two men to sprint the few yards back across the track and throw themselves into the darkness. A jeep sped by, but, before they could move out, a heavier truck - a troop carrier with a dozen or so soldiers in the back – hammered past choking the intruders with dust that was invisible in the darkness.

Slowly they started a systematic reconnaissance of the perimeter, but now they were working against the clock. There was another close call involving a lone guard who suddenly appeared on the other side of the fence from behind a massive piece of pipework. "We've used up one hell of a lot of luck and time, Harry. We don't have an unlimited supply of either," Bart said.

"Yeah, I know," the American replied. "Christ, the only way in is through the main gate." He cursed again. "Why weren't we told about the goddam fence?"

"I don't know that, but I do know that we are a long way from the boat and that time is against us. I think we are going to have to abort, Harry"

"No way. We are not giving up yet."

"We have to be well clear before first light. If we get picked up, that will ruin any chance of having another crack at it. And on a personal note, I don't relish the inconvenience of having to spend the next two decades talking to the cockroaches in Libertad - or worse."

Mention of the capital's notorious prison served only to heighten the American's anger and frustration. He clenched his fists and swore fiercely. "I guess you're right. Let's head for the water. I've got one last idea."

They stood by the gap in the perimeter, peering out into the darkness of the lake. The American looked at his watch. "We can still be off the water before it starts to get light, Bart. Give Ed the sign and call him in. I've got something to do."

Before Bart could stop him, Scrantz had disappeared into the darkness, uttering a final command. "Wait for me."

The Englishman flashed his torch out across the water in a pre-arranged sequence. The third attempt drew a response, and by the time Eduardo had nosed the boat onto the mud Scrantz was back. They climbed aboard and headed out on to the water and along the shore to their rendezvous with the aircraft that would take them out.

"What did you do back there for Christ's sake?" Bart demanded.

"Listen Bart, we've come too far to go home empty handed. I fixed charges on those two big chemical tanks. If there is anything in them, with luck they will go up, take the other tanks with them and blow the whole goddamed refinery into the lake."

"And if they're empty?"

"Then no one will ever know."

The boat and its occupants were absorbed into the darkness and the light mist that was beginning to rise from the lake.

Ninety minutes later muffled thumps, accompanied by a flash that for milliseconds lit up the decaying chemical plant, rumbled out across the surface of the water. There was no secondary explosion, no great convulsion of smoke and flame. Instead, the contents of the tanks – thousands of gallons – liberated through fractured metal, poured in a gathering torrent into the lake.

And the two combined in a seething reaction that provoked the waters into a boiling frenzy. There was no one to witness the marriage of the powerful agents of man and nature, no one to see the liquid tumult, no one to watch the billowing brown cloud erupt from the lake, tarnish the moon and roll like a tidal wave, building in slow motion, to engulf the sleeping town.

Chapter 33

Paice froze and stared into the barrel of the gun. His instinct was to flee, but he knew that if the intruder meant business, he would never outrun the bullets before they ripped into his back.

Should he plead for his life? It appeared to be hanging by a thread. No, his self-esteem would not allow him to utter the words. And he realised, as the first flush of fear and surprise began to diminish, that he had been offered a choice. He could live or die. He took two steps further into the room and pushed the door shut behind him.

"Given the option, I'll go for living."

"That's probably a good choice. Why don't you sit down, Mr Paice? My guess is that you could do with a drink. I'll join you if you don't object."

Paice nodded at the gun. "I'd prefer that you poured a shot rather than fired one. Why don't you park the ordnance and help yourself. Why are you here and what do you want?"

The man gently released the hammer, flicked the decocking lever to safe and laid the gun on the coffee table next to Paice's bottle of Scotch. Three glasses on a small tray had been upturned so that they did not collect dust. He flipped two of them over, unscrewed the cap and doled out liberal quantities of liquor. He pushed one towards Paice and took a sip from the other.

He leaned across and switched on the table lamp. It brought him out of the shadow. Paice saw a man who seemed to be in his early 50s, but could have been younger. Greying hair, thinning at the front, was cut military short. His face, wearied and lined, had been the target of life's heavy artillery. It was a landscape scarred by constant assault, a battlefield torn up by the violence of conflict.

The eyes were piercing blue, but tired, bloodshot and betraying unease and uncertainty. Beneath them, dark puffy smudges were the result, as Paice knew only too well, of sleepless nights. The poor light could not disguise the unhealthy pallor of his skin. Whatever his age, this was someone upon whom time, or the experiences that had occupied it, had exacted a heavy price.

"They're trying to kill you." The man gestured with his glass towards the bloodstained shirt of which Paice had been attempting to divest himself as he entered the room. "It looks as though they came pretty close. I'd guess that you had a lucky escape there. Are you hurt?"

"No, and you guess right. They missed me and got the wrong man. You say 'they', so I presume that you are not one of them and you are not here to finish the job."

"I am not. I would quite like you to remain alive, at least until you have written the story you have been pursuing. I might be able to help you in that respect."

"Help me? Then why the gun?"

"I couldn't be sure that it would be you who walked through the door, Mr Paice. In my business I have learnt that you can never be too careful."

Paice knocked back a substantial proportion of the contents of his glass and fought the inclination to choke as the raw spirit seared his dry throat. "In your business? Why don't you tell me just what your business is, who you are and what you are doing here?"

"First things first. Why don't you get out of those clothes and clean yourself up? Then we can talk."

Paice nodded and held out his glass. "I certainly want to talk, but before we do that you can pour me another while I call my office."

Bryce answered on the third ring. "Jesus Christ, Nick, where the hell have you been? I've been trying to call you. Have you had your phone switched off? You know we are up against the deadline. The back bench is going barmy." He was referring to the phalanx of top editorial faces who congregated every night to supervise the production of the paper.

"I told the conference this afternoon that you would be filing something for page 3. My balls are on the block and Ernest Russell is prowling around with a very sharp axe. Where is the fucking copy?"

Russell was the production editor, a reserved and sophisticated man who, contrary to the figure he cut, was capable of the most appalling outbursts of temper and foul language whenever his deadlines were threatened by laxity or by what he perceived to be incompetence.

Paice continued to hold the phone to his ear, but he stared into space and did not respond. The silence prompted Bryce to launch into another tirade. "Nick? Are you there? I need that bloody copy and I need it now, mate."

When Paice replied it was in a tone that was both unemotional and quietly serious. "Have you got a story about a shooting in Wellington Road, Bob?"

"Yes, Nick, but that's on the front page and I want your stuff to lead page 3."

"The bloke who was shot....it was a mistake. They were aiming for me."

"What do you mean?"

"What I mean, Bob, is that the story I have been after must be important because I have annoyed someone – pissed them off big time and now they want to kill me, and this afternoon they came bloody close to succeeding. My top priority at the moment has nothing to do with giving you a story for page 3 and everything to do with making myself so sodding scarce that whoever wants to put a bullet in me won't know where I am. As of this minute, I'm taking time off."

"Are you sure you're not overreacting, Nick? You can't walk off the job just like that. This is not like you."

Paice could not keep a slight tremor out of his voice when next he spoke. "Look, Bob, you know me well enough to know that I'm not exaggerating. I signed up to do a good job for the paper. I did not sign up to get killed for it." He hung up.

He looked across at his visitor. "Now I'm getting out of these clothes, and then you can tell me just what you know about all this."

Fifteen minutes and a hot shower later, Paice emerged from his tiny bathroom naked and crossed the room to the wardrobe where his clothes were neatly arranged. "If nudity offends you, too bad – you happen to be in my bedroom." The man shrugged. Paice continued: "You are also in my lounge, kitchen and dining room – welcome to life in a one-room bedsit."

The intruder laughed. "It's bigger than mine. And I don't have the luxury of my own bathroom, Mr Paice."

Paice pulled on a pair of jeans and a sweatshirt and slumped into a chair. "Shall we dispense with the formality and you call me Nick? What's your name?"

"Alex Bartholomew. Anyone who knows me calls me Bart."

"Well, how do you do, Bart? Now will you tell me why you are here and why you want to help me write my story? And, anyway, how the hell do you know anything at all about me and my story?"

"You would be surprised to know how many people know about you and your story, Nick. I was told all about it when they asked me to kill you."

Paice jerked upright and stared into those blue eyes. "They asked you to kill me?"

"Yes, and if I had taken the job, you would have been dead by now."

"Well, I can't tell you how pleased I am that you turned them down. Can I ask why? And who are 'they'?"

"I don't know who they are, but I know what their interest is and why they want you, and anyone else who knows anything, dead. In this business, people don't exactly arrange a meeting and swap business cards.

"Why did I turn them down? There are a couple of reasons, but for the moment I will say only that what happened – the events you want to write about – took everything I had and destroyed my life, and they didn't give a damn. I want you to write the whole stinking story and I will help you do that. It's the only way to get back at them."

Paice felt that old familiar buzz as he realised that he was at last on the verge of uncovering a major story. "If you give me the facts, Bart, I'll write the story. We've got a head start because they think I'm dead and that they killed my only source – until you came along."

"They may think for now that you are dead, but it won't take them long to realise their mistake. Then they will be coming after you again, and this flat is the first place they will look. You've got to get away from here. Do you have anywhere you can go where we can lie low?"

"We?"

"Sure. I'm sticking with you until you write that story." He stood up and looked surreptitiously around the curtain on to the street below. "Turn off the light. We don't want to advertise the fact that you are at home." He slowly drew the curtains. "You need to get out of here sooner rather than later. The street looks clear. Do you have a car?"

Paice shook his head.

"Hmmm. Nor me. We need transport. In your situation, you can hardly catch a bus."

"We could get a taxi."

Bartholomew scoffed. "Be serious. You're running for your life. You are in no position to wander the streets looking for a cab. You wouldn't last five minutes. You must have someone you can call."

Paice nodded then flipped open his phone and hit a familiar speed dial. "Hallo, Biff. It's Nick. I'm in trouble."

Stilwell chuckled at the other end. "Situation normal, then. What can I do for you?"

"No, Biff, the situation is far from normal. Some very persistent people are determined to kill me and I need transport to get me out of here. I'm in my flat."

"You sound worried, Nick."

"I am several stages past worried, mate. I am shit scared. Can you pick me up?"

"Not a hope, old friend. I'm in Yorkshire with my in-laws. It will take four hours minimum for me to get there." He paused while he thought. "I'll give Winston a call. He can be there fast if he is at home. I'll get him to call you back."

Paice sat down and finished his drink. Bart kept watch at the curtains. After less than five minutes, the phone jangled and vibrated on the coffee table. Paice snatched it up and stabbed at the key to answer. The relaxed drawl at the other end could only have been Winston.

"Hi, Ace. Biff tells me you got a problem. What do you need?"

"I need to get away from here and lie low, Winston. I don't have a car. I can't risk being seen on the street."

"What's the address?"

Paice gave him the details.

"I'll be there is about 15 minutes, longer if the traffic is heavy, though at this time it should not be too bad."

"What car are you driving, Winston?"

"It's a black BMW M5. See you in 15."

It was less than 10 minutes when Bart announced: "He's here. He drove past once and turned round to come back. He is waiting for us on the other side of the road. Let's get going."

Paice looked at the time. Winston had estimated 15 minutes without holdups. It seemed unlikely that he would have done it faster. He walked over to the window and peeped round the curtain. It was beginning to get dark. The detail of the car opposite was merging into an amorphous shape as the detail retreated into the gloom. Paice screwed up his eyes as he tried to identify the make of the car. "That's no BMW." He recognised the lithe outline of a Jaguar. He flipped open his phone, took the number from Winston's incoming call and rang it. Winston answered. From the background noise, Paice could tell that he was driving.

"Hi, Nick. Don't panic. I'm on my way. I took a wrong turn, but I should be with you in five minutes."

"Bad news, Winston. My friends have arrived and are waiting for me to come out to play. They have parked their Jag across the road and they are watching the house."

"You want me to give them something to think about other than you?"

"That depends on what you've got in mind."

"That depends on what they are doing. Are they about to kick down your front door?"

Paice explained that they were in a car and where they were parked. He watched the car as he spoke and saw the front passenger door open. Someone got out and looked across at his house.

"It looks like we are about to get a personal visit, Winston."

"OK, Ace, When I get there I'll keep them occupied. You just be ready to make a break for it when you see the moment is right. Get clear of the house and I'll pick you up when it's safe. I'll be there in a few minutes."

With increasing concern, Paice watched the man who had got out of the car. He was now crossing the road and heading straight for them. There was no way out, and now they were coming in to get him.

Chapter 34

Paice suppressed the panic that threatened to wash over him. He beckoned urgently to Bart. "We've got a problem. We've got an unwelcome caller and I'm not sure that the lock on our front door will keep him out."

Bart picked up his gun from the coffee table, checked that the safety was off and confirmed that there was a round in the chamber. "Leave him to me," he muttered. He opened the door took a step out of the room on to the landing and looked down into the hall. The front door slowly opened illuminating the entrance with a shaft of streetlight.

Paice grabbed his arm and pulled him back into the room. "Don't shoot him for Christ's sake," he whispered. "We've got enough problems without having a murder to add to the list. Anyway, the shot will only alert whoever is in the car. Then I'll never get out of here alive."

Bartholomew reluctantly complied, looking around the room and sizing up their options. "OK, but you do exactly as I say. Sit in the chair and turn on that light." He pointed the gun towards the lamp on Paice's bedside table. Paice looked in consternation first at the chair and then at the lamp.

"Are you sure about this? This is my life you're fucking with."

"Look, Nick, I want you to stay alive almost as much as you do. If you do as I say, that's what will happen and he will live, too. If you don't, I'll shoot him now. Make your mind up."

Paice thought for a moment then nodded. He flicked on the lamp. It cast a dull glow, barely illuminating anything beyond its immediate vicinity. He walked across to the chair and sat down, facing the door. Most of the room was in semi-darkness. While he was in shadow, it was nothing like enough to let him feel comfortably hidden.

A series of creaks told them that the intruder was climbing the stairs. Paice heard him moving around the landing. In addition to Paice's room, two others also opened on to it. He could be heard trying one of them before coming to Paice's. From where he sat, Paice could see the door handle slowly turn and the door open. It swung wide revealing an empty doorway. This bloke was no amateur. He was never going to present an easy target. Paice stared out through the void on to the landing, wondering who was making the muffled thumping noise. Then he realised that it was the drumbeat of his heart hammering in his ears. He must have been mad to go along with this crazy scheme.

A silhouette moved silently and swiftly through the doorway and for the second time in an hour Paice found himself looking down a gun sight from the wrong end. The man saw Paice and levelled the weapon at him. In the poor light, he paused as he attempted to identify and confirm his target. His hesitation determined the outcome. For him the mission was about to end. Out of the darkness, Bartholomew appeared like a shadow, smashing his gun into the back of the man's skull. The intruder collapsed with a grunt into an unconscious heap.

Bartholomew scooped up the man's gun and gestured to Paice to move. "Come on, let's get out of here and hope that your rescue squad is waiting for us," he snapped.

They descended the stairs into the unlit hallway. The front door was slightly ajar. Paice sidled up to it and looked around the edge of the doorframe to survey the street. He could see the Jaguar on the other side of the street. From the cover of the darkness within, he could look out without being spotted by the hit man's two accomplices whom he could just discern sitting in it.

From his viewpoint, he could see in only one direction without revealing himself and it was with anxiety that he failed to spot any sign of Winston. Then he heard the deep-throated roar of an exhaust coming from the direction that was hidden from him. The BMW suddenly flashed into view. At the speed at which it was being driven, Paice assumed it was not intending to stop. But then as it passed the parked car, the brakes were slammed on, the tyres whimpered in pain and, in a swift and accomplished manoeuvre, it was reversed into the vacant space in front of the Jaguar.

The speed at which it all happened left Paice confused, which meant that the occupants of the Jaguar were almost certainly experiencing the same emotion. Confusion turned to disbelief when a loud crunch echoed along the empty street as the rear of the BMW struck the front of the other car. Winston was a big, muscular man, and it was with an unexpected agility that he leapt from his vehicle.

He ran to the rear to survey the damage, cradling his head in his hands. He turned to the driver, his arms outstretched in an apologetic gesture, slowly shaking his head. Paice heard him say, "Look, man, I'm really sorry. I don't know what went wrong." Bartholomew thumped Paice in the back. "Come on, that's our cue. Let's get out of here while he keeps them busy."

The two men slipped as unobtrusively as they could down the steps to the pavement and began walking away from the scene. If the assailants had looked in their rear view mirror they might have seen them, but Winston was ensuring that their attention was all on him. Paice wanted to run, but his companion kept a tight grip on his arm. "Walk slowly and you won't attract attention. Let's just take it steady."

The nearest turning, and their first opportunity to get out of sight, was 150yds along the street. It seemed agonisingly distant. Meanwhile, the driver of the Jaguar was showing no inclination to get out and exchange insurance details with Winston. Winston's admission of guilt provoked only an impatient wave of the man's hand, telling him to sod off. The truth was that he had more to think about than a bit of bodywork damage. Winston had achieved precisely what the man was desperate to avoid – being distracted from the task in hand.

Winston expressed his thanks, apologising repeatedly as he got back into his car and fired up the engine. Again the tyres squealed as he did a U-turn and drove back the way he had come. As he drew alongside the fugitives to pick them up, an anguished shout announced the hit man's return to the scene. He had recovered from being smashed in the skull and had made it back down to the street, shattering Paice's hope that they would get clear before the man could.

Paice looked back to see the man, staggering and half on his knees on the pavement, shouting to his accomplices and pointing frantically at them as they opened the car doors. The engine of the Jaguar burst into life. Paice knew that he was in trouble of the worst kind.

Winston bellowed, "Move it!" and hit the accelerator while the two men were still getting in. Hitting the accelerator in the BMW meant releasing all the raw power of a 5-litre engine, putting 500 horsepower through the rear wheels, and catapulting the car away from the kerb so that the smoke and smell of burnt rubber provided the only evidence it had ever been there.

Before he had a chance to shut the door and grab the sides of the seat, Paice could see that they had covered the remaining distance to the turning and that it was too late to turn into it. Winston needed no telling. He knew what he was doing. Almost level with the turning, he slammed on the brakes and hurled the car to the left. In a manoeuvre that seemed to defy the laws of physics, they had changed direction by 90 degrees. The rear end slewed slightly wide and Paice and Bartholomew lurched to the right grappling for something to hold on to and finding nothing useful.

Winston gave the horses their heads. The massive surge of power reached the wheels, corrected the drift and set the car lunging off on its new bearing. The two passengers were immediately pinned back in their seats, their bodies contorted as they struggled to regain control of their posture.

Behind, the Jaguar was howling after them. The street was narrow with vehicles parked on both sides, reducing the carriageway so that two vehicles could pass only with care and great difficulty. Paice had barely formed in his mind the hope that nothing would be coming the other way when something did. The headlights of the approaching car dazzled him so that he could barely see its outline.

He grabbed the dashboard with both hands, wished he had had time to strap himself in and shouted: "Jesus Christ!" Winston would have to stop, which meant the Jaguar would instantly be upon them. Instead of hitting the brake, Winston hit the accelerator. Paice gritted his teeth and waited for the inevitable sound of metal smashing into metal. It did not come. Instead, the car had shot through the gap and when Paice opened his eyes he could see that they were hurtling towards a busy junction. Buses and cars were crossing it, but Winston had gained them valuable seconds as the Jaguar had slowed to pass the obstruction that had seemed to shrink to insignificance in the face of Winston's uncompromising and unerring approach.

He slowed and, to the accompaniment of blasting horns and flashing headlights, he threaded the car into the stream of vehicles, again planting his foot to the floor. But the traffic was too dense. He cursed as cars and vans pulled out to frustrate him. In his rear view mirror he could see that the Jaguar was gaining ground, taking advantage of the path he had carved through the mêlée of cars, vans and taxis.

The car ahead of him stopped to allow a bus to pull out into the flow. Winston flicked the steering wheel, poured power into the engine and aimed for the diminishing gap between the bus as it picked up speed and an oncoming lorry. Winston judged it perfectly. Almost. The mirror on Paice's door disappeared with a crack as it hit the front edge of the bus, but they were through. The Jaguar did not make it. By the time it got there, the gap had narrowed to nothing. In his mirror, Winston could see it veer as the driver braked heavily. He could not tell whether it had hit the bus or the lorry or both, but now it was out of the chase. He took the next turning off the main road, took a left and a right, followed various back streets and eventually came out on to another busy thoroughfare.

Paice spoke for the first time, breathing heavily. "Christ, Winston, where did you learn to drive?"

Winston smiled, his beautiful white teeth shining in the darkness. "A misdirected upbringing and too much time spent in amusement arcades. Never mind that, Ace. You owe me for a new mirror."

"And a set of tyres – you must have left most of them on the road back there." Bartholomew spoke from his seat in the back for the first time. "That was nice driving, Winston. By the way, I'm Bart. Nice to meet you."

"Likewise, Bart." He reached over his shoulder and shook Bartholomew's hand. "Where do you guys plan on going? I take it you have in mind a destination that is safe and out of sight."

Paice nodded. "There is only one place I can think of immediately." He gave Winston the directions and they settled back for the journey, finally assuming a speed that was both legal and lacking in adverse consequences for Paice's nerves or blood pressure.

Chapter 35

Winston pulled the car into the kerb outside the impressive residence. Paice reflected on the last time he had been here. Then, the air had reeked of sewage, the family who lived in it were beset with the stench of scandal, and its fortunes were at their lowest ebb. But that was then and this was now. Roles were reversed. Money and physical endeavour had brought the house back to life. The family had looked to Paice for help and he had used the power of print to engineer the revival of its fortunes. Now it was his turn to ask for help.

He looked up at a lighted window. Sir Oswald and Maria had retired to bed. He felt uneasy as he walked up to the huge oak door and rang the bell. He had chosen to come here when he could have disappeared from sight and lain low until his pursuers had lost interest. But that would have meant suppressing what, over decades of work and hundreds of headlines, had become an instinct – to get the story into print and tell what had happened. God knows what had happened, but if armed assassins were prepared to kill him to stop it coming out he knew that it must be worth exposing, and a prerequisite of that was that he should stay alive.

Inside the house, the hall light came on. The security intercom rasped its metallic interrogation. "Who is it?" Paice recognised Sir Oswald's voice. After the ordeal he and his family had endured, he would never open the door at night without confirming that it was safe to do so.

"It's Nick Paice, Oswald. I...well, I.....I need help." Paice's ingrained streak of self-reliance and independence required him to force the words out.

Bellamy was taking no chances. "Stand in front of the camera where I can see you." Paice looked up at the lens and positioned himself more precisely. Bartholomew stood close to him. There was a pause. "OK, Nick. I can see you. But who is the other person with you?"

"He's a friend. We both need help."

"Just a moment."

A sequence of mechanical sounds was evidence that unlocking was no quick and easy operation. The door eventually opened to reveal Bellamy in his dressing gown. "Come in, Nick. Tell me how I can help you."

Before entering, Paice turned to look back to where Winston was waiting in his car. He waved and gave a thumbs up. Winston responded with a wave, slipped the car into gear and manoeuvred it to return the way he had come.

Inside the house, they were in a spacious hallway overlooked by a galleried landing. Standing, looking down was Maria Bellamy. "Hallo, Nick. What's happened?" There was a hint of alarm in her voice.

"Hallo, Maria. I'm in a bit of trouble and I did not know who else to ask for help." He turned to Bartholomew. "This is Alex Bartholomew. He's .... a .... friend." Paice was unsure how to describe his new associate.

Bellamy held out his hand and Bartholomew shook it. "My friends call me Bart."

Bellamy smiled. "My friends – and I have discovered that they are fewer than I had thought and those can be somewhat unexpected" – he paused and smiled at Paice – "call me Oswald."

By now, Maria had descended the stairs. She gave Paice a peck on the cheek and shook Bartholomew's hand, introducing herself. "Come through and I'll make some coffee. You can tell us what this is all about."

"You get that organised, my dear, and I'll get these gentlemen something a bit stronger to be going on with. Come on in." He led the way into the drawing room. Paice let the other two go on ahead.

"I have a call to make, Oswald. I'll join you in a moment."

"Of course."

After they had gone, Paice took out his phone and studied it as he marshalled his thoughts. It was not an easy call to make. Then he searched the list of contacts for the number. Titus Refik answered with his standard form of words, tersely delivered: "Hallo, who is this calling?"

"It's Nick Paice. I'm sorry about your boy, Refik. I take it you know what happened."

At the other end, Refik was doing his best to suppress his emotion, but the obvious difficulty he was encountering in enunciating a response told Paice that he was not quite succeeding."Thank you, Mr Paice. The police have been in touch. It is very sad – upsetting. I had asked him to keep an eye on you."

There was a pause while neither of them spoke, then Paice broke the silence. "He died saving my life, Refik. Whatever his motive, that is the most that one human being can do for another. Had he worked for you for very long? Have you told his family?"

"That boy had been with me since he was six years old. He started hanging around my business premises back home and I began giving him occasional errands to run. Like me, he has no family. When I took him in, he was living on the streets. He has been with me ever since.

"As you may have come to realise, Mr Paice, I am not given to establishing relationships based on affection, which is why I have never taken a wife or had children. But that boy was the closest thing to a son to me. The grief I feel tonight only confirms to me that it is better never to become emotionally entangled with another person."

Paice nodded to himself. "There are times when many people might find it difficult to argue with that sentiment. I'm alive tonight and I have you and a dead man to thank for that. In view of what has happened, from my side the slate is wiped clean between us. I owe you a debt. If you think I can ever repay it – assuming I survive long enough to do so – you should feel free to call it in. I'll destroy the material I collected on you."

"That would be good, Mr Paice. I think you should tread carefully. These are dangerous people, and they mean to kill you. That would be a great pity."

"Goodnight, Refik." He hung up.

From the kitchen came the sounds of Maria at work getting the coffee on the go. Paice headed straight for the source of the noise. Maria looked up as he entered.

"What's going on, Nick. Are the police after you?"

"No, Maria, it's worse than that. There are people who are quite anxious to kill me, and I am even more anxious to ensure that they don't succeed."

She looked at him with astonishment. "They want to kill you? Have you reported them to the police? You can call them from here. You must have done something very serious to make someone want to kill you. What have you been up to?"

"I've been trying to put together a story that someone does not want me to write. The harder they try to make me dead, the bigger I know the story must be – when I get the facts I need to write it. That's why Bartholomew is here. I think he has some of the answers.

"Talking of killing people, did you see that Mwamba was shot dead in the street outside his embassy?"

Maria turned her head away. "I saw something about it in the newspaper." There was a pause as Paice worked out how to say the next bit. "I did not know you had such hatred for him." Maria kept her eyes averted. "The world is a better place for what you did, but you took one hell of a risk."She turned to face him. "How do you know?"

"It was all caught on the embassy's CCTV. I watched it with the ambassador. I cannot recall whether you ever met Moses Mkoko."

Maria shook her head. "You say it is on the video. Does it show much detail?"

"Enough to get you locked up for a very long time."

"Should I be handing myself in, then?"

Paice shook his head. "No need. Moses destroyed the only copy and told the cops that the system was down at the crucial time. To be frank, he was quite pleased that someone finally caught up with that rattlesnake. Mwamba had been up to no good and his death solved a tricky problem for him and, I reckon, for Kamina Bassu.

"I owe you a big thank you, too. He instigated the killing of an old friend of mine over a deal to do with illicit diamonds. There are lots of people who are relieved, if not delighted, that someone put a bullet in him."

"It was more than one bullet, actually, Nick. I had to make sure."

"Well, you did that all right. He was alive, but only just, when they put him in the ambulance, but he was dead well and truly when they took him out at the other end."

Paice looked puzzled. "I have just one question: where did you get the gun?"

She shrugged her shoulders. "That was easy. It was one that I picked up in Kamina Bassu. You know as well as I that it was a very dangerous place. After the scares that I had, I realised that I needed to be able to defend myself. Weapons were two a penny at that time. I know it is unethical, but I swapped it for a carton of painkillers, and I have kept it ever since.

"To be frank, I had almost forgotten that I had it. It had lain hidden in one of the boxes of stuff in the garage, but when those two thugs broke into our house and threatened my family I got it out and cleaned it up. I have to tell you, Nick, that if they had come back I would have shot them dead and to hell with the consequences.

"No one has the right to come into another person's house and do what they did. When you told me about Mwamba, I felt I had an obligation to all of his victims who suffered so much, whose blood was on that man's hands.

"He may have escaped the law. I could not allow him to escape justice. I'm not proud of what I did, Nick, but it had to be done and it was I who had to do it."

Paice nodded. "Perhaps it's a difficult thing to take pride in, but you should try really hard and you might succeed. I hope so. I take it Oswald knows nothing about it."

"Good God, no. And it must stay that way." By now, the coffee was ready and Paice held the door open.

"Let's join the others then I can tell you my tale of woe," he said.

They went through into the drawing room. The two men were talking, each caressing a glass of spirit. As they entered, Bellamy reached down and picked up one he had poured for Paice.

"Get this down your throat, Nick, then let's hear what this is all about."

They sat down and Maria handed out cups of coffee. Paice downed a large proportion of the contents of the glass Bellamy had given him. "I'll tell you what I know, but I am hoping that Bart will provide the missing pieces of the jigsaw. It all begins in Tierra del Aguila, which, even if you know Central America, while you have no doubt heard of it, you have probably never given it more than a passing thought." He explained how Burkins had alerted him to the possibility of a story, how he had tracked the American team to their hotel and confronted them, how Burkins had been murdered, and how, earlier that day, an attempt had been made to kill him, too.

Bellamy stared at him in disbelief. "They tried to kill you, Nick? Are you serious? That sort of thing only happens in Hollywood films."

"Am I serious? It doesn't get more serious than that a man is tonight lying dead in a mortuary as a result of being shot when they were aiming for me. Something happened in Tierra del Aguila that people – powerful people – don't want the rest of us to know about. It's my job to discover what happened and tell the world about it. As journalists we do a lot of things to sell papers that people don't like, but this is different and it is something I have to do. It's why I became a reporter. It evens up the score for all the rubbish and trivia we print, and it makes me feel worthy of my craft. "

"Even if it risks getting you killed?" Maria asked.

"If someone is prepared to kill to stop a story, that makes it even more imperative to write it. Sometimes, we have to take a risk to do something we believe to be right." He looked straight into Maria's large, brown eyes. The message he was seeking to send was received and understood. She gave a slight nod.

"I just need to find out why they want to stop me."

Bartholomew spoke for the first time. "It was an undercover operation that went badly wrong."

His words reduced the group to a moment's silence while they absorbed what he had said.

"How do you know this, Bart?" Paice asked quietly.

"Because I was one of a three-man team that was inserted into Tierra del Aguila to carry out sabotage."

Paice took the recorder from a pocket in his jacket. He held it up and looked at Bartholomew. "Do you mind?" Bartholomew shook his head. "Why the sabotage?" Paice inquired, pressing the record button.

Bartholomew leaned back in his chair and sipped his coffee. "The situation in Tierra del Aguila had been running away from the US. We've seen it often enough before in that part of the world. Rafael Cisneros had led a rebel army to victory over the then President and was firmly in control. He had a lot going for him. The old regime had been as corrupt as hell, and a fair proportion of the people thought that under Cisneros things might be different. After a couple of years, it had become obvious that they weren't, of course, and that has bred its own difficulties.

"But it wasn't his domestic activities that were causing problems. The trouble was, he was turning his back on the country's traditional ally to the north and was facing east, responding to overtures from China and North Korea, both of which were desperate to obtain a secure supply of oil, which Tierra del Aguila could provide, while at the same time enabling them to sit sunning themselves in the Americans' backyard.

"Washington's reaction to all this was best described as fury nurtured by panic. They made it clear that they would do whatever it took to prevent a hostile presence establishing itself at its back door."

"But what precisely could they have done?" Maria asked.

"Christ, you should never underestimate the Yanks. They are brought up to believe that there is no substitute for firepower. They teetered on the edge of going nuclear when the Russians tried to put missiles in Cuba. The hardliners in Washington wanted to go in with all guns blazing, but the events of 1962 and all that followed had cooled heads. Cuba to this day is hostile. The smart thinking in the White House and the Pentagon reasoned that persuasion backed by the threat of a good kick in the nuts was better than a straightforward good kick in the nuts. They wanted to come out of it with workable relations with Cisneros, not live in a constant state of military and political antagonism.

"We were led by a former colonel in the Green Berets – Harry Scrantz – and we went in with a plan to create mayhem, which would have been the signal for the

US to step in with aid and assistance to get them out of trouble – all backed with the unspoken threat of military action if those advances were spurned."

Oswald Bellamy was looking perturbed. "I am assuming that you were a member of British special forces, Bart. So why in God's name were we involved? The Americans could easily have handled the whole thing themselves. Why did we get sucked in? You said there were three of you. And who was the third man in the operation?"

"The third man was a former colonel in the old regime's air force. Eduardo was a good man and committed to bringing Cisneros down. I was ordered to go because I had spent time in the country under the old president.

"The answer to your first question, Sir Oswald, is politics. At the time, the President and the Prime Minister were very close, both politically and personally. The friendship meant that they had been particularly helpful to us when we really needed help, and this was an opportunity for us to return the favour. That's the special relationship for you. What I did was no big deal. But its symbolic significance was out of all proportion to the scale of our involvement."

"And what was it you actually did?" Paice was anxious to get to the nub of the story.

"The military objective was to disable and, if possible, destroy the huge refinery at Puerto de las Islas. It not only refined substantial quantities of crude oil, but it was also an integral part of the port from which the oil was exported. It was calculated that knocking out the refinery would cripple the port."

"But surely Cisneros would be able to work out who had done it, and he could get it repaired, however great the damage, with the help of his new mates from the East," Paice suggested.

"We had to make it look as though the whole thing was an accident, the result of incompetence. That was why we had to be so careful and not leave any evidence of our presence. And fixing it would not have been that simple. The port and refinery complex had originally been designed and installed by the Americans, and there was a complete export embargo from the US to Tierra del Aguila. That meant no spare parts, no replacement equipment, not a single nut or bolt. That was the reasoning behind the whole operation."If we did our job properly, the entire facility would have to be rebuilt by the Chinese from scratch, and that would put it out of action for months. The country's economy would be ruined, the people would, with a bit of encouragement, rise up against the new president, and the Americans would come to their rescue with support and a few billion dollars.

"The alternative was for Cisneros to come cap in hand to the Americans to help with fixing the damage. Either way, Washington reckoned it would come out on top."

"But you said it went badly wrong."

"Yes, Nick. And in a way that no one could have foreseen."

Chapter 36

Bartholomew explained how, a decade before, he had flown into Tierra del Aguila, been picked up by Eduardo and had then joined up with Scrantz. He told them of the hike over the mountains to reach the lake in the dark and finally, having taken a boat along the shoreline, how they had arrived at the refinery.

"We thought we'd be able to just walk into the place and go to work. That was the briefing, but they omitted to tell us, or just hadn't noticed, that the security was actually as tight as a nun's knickers – we wouldn't get in without a struggle. My guess in retrospect is that it must have dawned on Cisneros or his top blokes that their most valuable asset was vulnerable so they had beefed up their arrangements. We were just unlucky.

"It meant that we were up against electrified razor wire and armed patrols coming around like taxis in Piccadilly in the rush hour. We were under orders not to leave evidence of our visit, but if we were to get the job done that was never going to happen. Either we had to smash our way through the perimeter or shoot our way past the guards, or both. Whichever, they would have known we had been there–assuming that we were able to get out afterwards.

"I was all for aborting the mission and pulling back until we could find a way round the problems. But, to be realistic, that was a non-runner. We were on a tight schedule and we couldn't hang around. Harry said he wanted us 'in and out and no messing' and we had a small private plane organised from a discreet location to get us out. We had to get to it on time because it would be taking off with or without us and our orders were to be on it or die trying. Under no circumstances were we to be taken prisoner.

"Harry told me to go on ahead and join Ed in the boat. There were a couple of big storage tanks on waste ground outside the refinery. He reckoned that if he could blow them, it might just provoke a chain of explosions that would send the whole site sky high.

"It didn't work out quite as we had hoped. Cisneros had a nasty little secret and we blew it wide open – literally."

Paice leaned back in his chair. "The tanks?"

Bartholomew nodded. "Yes, the tanks. Cisneros harboured ambitions to become the major force in the region but he needed muscle to do that. He needed a bigger stick than any of the other countries, so, with the expertise of a few rogue scientists, he had secretly attempted to develop a biological agent – a chemical weapon. His megalomania blinded him to the fact that just having the oil gave him power enough.

"His new friends had more sense and were more respectful of international law. They persuaded him that it was a bad idea and he had quietly abandoned the project. But the trouble with that stuff is that once you've made it, it is not easy to get rid of it. The poison he had made had been sitting in those tanks waiting for someone to do something with it."

"And that someone turned out to be you, Bart," Paice suggested.

"Yeah. From that point on, what had been a mission turned into a nightmare. I haven't a clue what that stuff was, but I reckon it worked by reacting with the moisture in the air because when it ran out of the tank and into the lake, it went berserk.

"We didn't know what we had unleashed or even that we had unleashed it. We were in the boat and clear of the area before the disaster kicked off, but the reaction of the chemical and the water created a massive cloud of nerve agent that blew straight into the nearby town on the lake shore.

"It's been estimated that it " – he paused and surveyed the faces of those ranged around him. "I suppose I should say 'we', because it was our doing. We killed between 5,000 and 10,000 innocent people that night. But that wasn't all. Cisneros panicked. He was desperate to prevent any word of his little scientific experiment leaking out, so the next day, when the poison gas had dispersed, he sent his thugs into the town to finish off anyone who had survived. No one was left to tell the tale."

Bartholomew held out his glass and Bellamy obliged with a refill. He threw a large proportion of it down his throat then stared into the now almost empty glass and shook his head. "I said it turned into a nightmare, and for me the nightmare returns every time I close my eyes."

The group sat quietly as they considered what he had said. It was Maria who broke the silence.

"So that's the big secret. How come we never knew anything about it?"

"Simple. Cisneros was desperate to avoid the world knowing what he had been up to – that was why he wiped out the survivors. And when subsequently the facts became known to them, neither the British nor the US Governments wanted anyone to know what we had done, the suffering and death we had wreaked, at their behest, on their orders."

"Did you get to the plane OK?" Paice asked.

"Yes, we got to it but not on it. Things can happen. You can never know how things will turn out. You know how it is. You turn right instead of left, you leave on time or you do something that makes you a few minutes late, and because of that you meet someone or something happens that changes the whole course of your life and the lives of those around you.

"That night, as he was pleased to tell me subsequently, a local police chief could not sleep and, on a whim, he rose early and went walking to watch the sun rise and think over his problems. It was just by chance that he spotted our aircraft pass overhead as it came in to land. He knew there was something fishy about it, so he called out his men to investigate.

"The agency in the States had hired a pilot who was a Colombian who normally flew drugs across the Caribbean. Cisneros's police located the plane, pulled the Colombian out of the cockpit and slapped him around a bit until he told them he had been paid to pick up three men. All they had to do was lie low to wait for us to turn up and find out who we were and what we were up to.

"When we reached the rendezvous everything was as we had hoped. The Cessna was where we expected to see it, standing ready to take off with its engine on tickover. The situation seemed OK – it was meant to. But we were completely unprepared for what happened next. We walked straight into an ambush. Ed had gone on ahead and reached the plane. He shouted back that the pilot was missing – the engine running and no driver? We knew immediately that there was a problem. Then they put a few shots over our heads to pin us down and ordered us to put up our hands.

"Given our orders, we had no choice but to try to fight our way out so we started returning fire, but it was hopeless. I reckon we were outnumbered three or four to one, and they had the cover. Harry was hit in the chest by a burst of fire and he was dead before he hit the ground. Eduardo was the smart one. By now he was in the plane and moving. Against all the odds, he got it airborne while I was lying flat dodging bullets and keeping the opposition engaged. The last I saw of him was as his arse disappeared over the treetops. I assumed he wasn't hit because he kept going.

"He was dead lucky because they were flinging enough lead at him to sink a battleship. But because it was the police, not the army, they had only light calibre weapons. So, while he probably took a few rounds, they had nothing big enough to knock him out of the sky, certainly not once he had put distance behind him.

"That left me swinging defenceless in the breeze. It would be only a matter of time before I would follow Harry into oblivion. But, orders or no orders, I wasn't about to lie down and die. I just put up my hands and crossed my fingers that I would survive. What I did not know was that survival can mean many things, and in my case it meant hanging on to my life by my fingernails. At the hands of Cisneros's specialists, even they were to become a scarce commodity."

"At least you got out alive," Bellamy pointed out, trying to find the upside of a very downside situation.

Bartholomew nodded and smiled grimly. "Yeah, I got out. But alive? That's not how I remember it. When they got me to the interrogation centre, they put me through a living death. The police chief told me I had killed thousands of their people, and he wanted to know why. I told him I didn't know what he was talking about, so he took me out to the town and showed me what he said were the results of my sabotage. That was how I learnt what had happened – the disastrous consequences of what we had done for those who lived there.

"He kept asking me how we knew about the chemical tanks, how we had known to blow up those containing the nerve gas. He was convinced that we had been sent in to knock out the chemical weapons. He kept asking what I knew about them, and when I said I knew nothing, he ordered one of his men to work me over.

"As we drove around the town, I could see that they had not bothered to clear anything up. It must have been some days after the raid, but still the bodies of men, women and children – babies and tiny tots – were everywhere. They had died badly. It was terrible. And all the time, he was telling me that I was responsible. I saw people who had been shot but when I said that I had not shot anyone, he simply said that these people had to die because of what I had done, so they were on my conscience."

Maria's forehead crinkled into a frown. "But how did they keep it quiet? Surely people in Tierra del Aguila must have known something had happened. They would have had relatives in the town or may have worked there or gone to the market or whatever. You cannot just pretend that a town inhabited by thousands of people suddenly ceases to exist."

"I am sorry, Lady Bellamy, but when one man has such an iron grip on a nation – it happens in more places than we care to admit – he can make anything happen or, to take your point, not happen. Cisneros was no fool. Already as we approached the town, it had been closed off and notices warning of a cholera outbreak had been hastily erected around the perimeter. People were warned

411

that they approached the town on pain of death, and that and the fear of disease was enough to deter even the most inquisitive. And when a man like Cisneros is running things, inquisitive is something you don't want to be."

Paice had been jotting notes in his book. He looked up at Bartholomew. "So what happened next?"

"They wanted me to tell them everything, and I had been trained to tell them anything but what they wanted to know. The problem was, they knew that and when they had beaten the 'facts' out of me, they discarded all that bullshit and started all over again. The second time around, they were not nearly so gentle.

"I spent time – a long time, maybe weeks, maybe months, I just could not tell – in the pit, a stinking hole with no light and no human contact other than with my guards and tormentors. They finally broke me on a little device they called 'la tumbona'. It means the sun lounger or deck chair. It was an adjustable metal frame with electrical contacts strategically located. Sometimes, they would strap me to it on my back, sometimes on my chest, but the worst was when they forced me to sit in it so that – how can I put it without offending the lady?" – he looked at Maria, slightly embarrassed – "So that my most sensitive parts were carefully lined up with the contacts.

"I held out for as long as I could, but I could take only so much. They warned me that I would beg them to let me die, and eventually I did. That was when it was all over. I told them everything. I expected that they would finish me off once I had spilled the beans, and, frankly, I could not have cared less. Instead they moved me to a cell with a bunk and a light and left me alone with my thoughts – and my conscience. All I could see when I closed my eyes were the twisted and agonised bodies of those innocent children."

As he spoke, perspiration appeared on his forehead and he was visibly distressed. Paice could see the man was racked with anguish. The events he had endured had virtually destroyed him. "You were not responsible, Bart. You could not have known," Paice said, realising instantly that his clumsy attempt to alleviate Bartholomew's distress was ill judged. He was seeking expiation, not justification, and telling his story, sharing with others the secret that had burned within him for so long, would offer him a degree of atonement.

"Of course I could not have known, but that does not help me. I have had to live with that, but I have also had to live with my betrayal. I betrayed my comrades and I betrayed my profession and I find that a heavy burden to bear. In my business, you just do not crack under pressure and you die rather than reveal what they want to know. I failed on both counts."

Paice looked up from his scribbling, his brow furrowed. "They decided to let you live. I'm surprised. I would have expected them to kill you once they had wrung out of you all the information they needed."

"Yes, I reckoned that I was finished, but I suspect that Cisneros could see that I was a valuable asset that he might be able to use in his dealings with his adversaries."

"You mean the threat of a show trial?" Bellamy chipped in. Bartholomew shook his head. "No, given the sensitivity of the situation, I don't think it would have been anything so public. He probably had something more subtle in mind. He was not to be underrated. He was a very smart operator."

"So, why did they let you go? How did you get back home? Did the Government negotiate your release?" Paice asked, keen to discover the price they had been forced to pay.

Bartholomew snorted with disgust. "As far as my own Government were concerned, I was dead meat and, to be frank, they wanted that to be the case. I was an embarrassment and they were more than happy for me to rot in Cisneros's jail. They did nothing to get me out of there. I'll never forgive them for that. Bastards.

"My salvation came from a most unexpected direction. Gradually, my prison regime was relaxed – it was never going to be pleasant or palatable, but it got noticeably less dreadful. The food was better. I was moved to a cell with a window. They even turned the light off at night. Eventually, I was allowed time out of my cell to exercise with four or five other prisoners in my category. We were, of course heavily guarded.

"There was one thing I never told them, even at the worst of the treatment. I never divulged Eduardo's identity. I simply said that the man who had skipped off in the aeroplane was an American agent, and they had seemed content to accept that.

"Then one day in the exercise yard, there he was. I did not see that it was him at first. He looked like the other guards from behind, just a bit bigger than the others – he was a big man, and he stood out a bit.

"He was shouting at the prisoners and pushing them around, but when he turned to me he gave me a crafty wink, then ordered me to get in line. I don't know how he got the uniform or how he got into that prison, but there he was. For the first time since I had been captured, I felt a surge of hope. I nearly broke down in tears, but I managed to hold myself together. I knew that Ed must have a plan.

"When the time came to return to our cells, he produced a very formal looking document, waved it in front of the other guards and told them that I was to be taken for more interrogation. Then he marched me off. Before I realised it, I had been thrown into the back of a prison van and driven to freedom. The journey home was not an easy one, and there were some scary moments, but Ed realised that I had not given him away, and he was determined to pay me back for that."

"You were deeply in his debt, Bart," Maria pointed out. "He was taking a big risk going into that place."

"Yes, but we were comrades, and comrades take care of each other. I admit, though, that what he did took enormous courage. But that was a measure of the man. I only wish my own Government and my own top brass had displayed that sort of courage and commitment.

"When I did get home, they did not exactly put out the flags with a welcome home sign. They wanted me – expected me – to die rather than talk. They could not forgive me for that. The trouble is, I could not forgive myself for what had happened.

"Under the sort of treatment I endured, you learn what sort of a person you are. I did not like what I discovered about myself. It does no good to say that, until you experience it, you don't know what the fear and the pain will make you do." He paused and looked at the floor. "I should have kept my mouth shut, done what was expected of me. Death would have been better than what I have tried to live with."

Oswald Bellamy had been listening attentively. He leaned forward, shaking his head. "There is something I do not understand, Mr Bartholomew. Why now, years after the event? What has suddenly happened to provoke you into breaking your silence after all this time?"

"Because Cisneros is back in favour. The US and Britain can see the pendulum swinging back in their direction, now that Cisneros has changed sides again. They want to bring him back into the fold, they want to forgive and forget. And it's not just us and the Yanks. Other European countries are keen to establish good relations with him. It's all about the oil."

Bartholomew's mood had changed. Now he looked at the others with a sudden intensity, his eyes flashing with fury. "They want to overlook the fact that he is a murderous tyrant who, for too long, has been oppressing his people and running one of the most vicious dictatorships on the planet. Suddenly, all his past mistakes are to be conveniently forgotten and he is to be embraced by the so-called civilised world.

"His love affair with his oriental allies did not work out as he had hoped. He found that by joining them and isolating himself from his country's traditional friends, he was actually becoming dependent on something even more ruthless than power based on capitalism. They exercised power based on ideology. He realised that they did not care whether they made a dollar profit or a dollar loss. They just weren't talking his language. While he wanted the money, what they wanted was to control people's minds, tell them what to think, because in the naked pursuit of power that was a much more valuable resource than mere money.

"He could see that, far from an alliance that strengthened him, he was getting involved in something that was going to sap his authority. He was making himself dependent on them and, in the process, weakening himself. They were beginning to tell him what he could and could not do. He had to get rid of them before they actually took over. So he realised that he needed allies who cared about the power of money and didn't give a damn how he ran his country so long as the oil kept flowing. That was what he wanted, because then the dollars kept rolling in. So now he is back making overtures to the Western powers. And because of the oil, they are greeting him with open arms."

He sat back in his chair and finished what little remained of his drink. "Well, they may think that he is suddenly wonderful, someone they would invite to tea with the vicar, but I don't. I remember those tanks of filthy poison, I remember how his secret police went through that town and slaughtered anyone who had survived it, I remember those children lying dead in the streets. But most of all, I remember what he did to me. He destroyed my life, and I will do anything I can to return the compliment."

Paice snapped his notebook shut and clicked off the recorder. "Well, Bart, I think we have a good chance of doing that – provided I can avoid getting killed by MI5, MI6, the CIA or whoever is after me and get the story into print."

"I doubt very much, Nick, that you are being pursued by one of the state security organisations."

"Then who is doing it?"

Bartholomew smiled grimly and shook his head. "There is a huge amount at stake in this affair. There is nothing so potently evil and immoral as the ruthless pursuit of power, and oil means power, and Tierra del Aguila offers plenty of both. You have to understand just how desperate the West is to lay its hands on the oilfields. They are located within the US sphere of influence – nowhere near the powder keg that is the Middle East, with all the risks and uncertainties that exist there. There are plenty of people who would think less than nothing of killing a newspaper journalist if he was getting in the way of something so big."

"So what now, Nick?" Bellamy asked.

Paice looked at the others and then looked to the ceiling, an unspoken reference to the children upstairs. "We can't stay here, Oswald. The people who are after us will stop at nothing. I'm not putting your family at risk. You've already endured enough."

"So where will you go?" Maria asked with obvious concern.

"The paper will hide us away somewhere comfortable I expect. It will only be for a couple of days until the story hits the streets. Once we blow the whole thing wide open, there will be no point in trying to kill us. The publicity will be our greatest protection."

"And tonight?" she persisted.

Paice thought for a moment. "Would you object to us bedding down in your summer house? We'll be gone in the morning."

Chapter 37

Half an hour later, the two men were standing on the verandah that fronted the summer house. Paice had accepted Sir Oswald's offer of the remains of the bottle of Scotch. He sipped from the glass he had refilled from it, perhaps too many times. The Bellamy household had retired to bed and the house was now in darkness. The lights of the summer house cast a golden glow across the lawn.

"Do you have family, Bart?"

"Family?"

"Yes. Do you mind me intruding on personal matters? I just wondered whether you had anyone and how they coped with what happened to you."

"I did have a family – past tense. Not any more. My wife – ex-wife – couldn't put up with the absences and the uncertainties. We had a daughter – "

"Had?" Paice was beginning to regret having initiated the conversation.

"Her name was Susie. While I was away she drowned in a friend's swimming pool. My wife needed me and I wasn't there. She could not manage the guilt –

she blamed herself for what happened – and she needed someone to give her support, to tell her it wasn't her fault – it wasn't. I wasn't there to do all of that. When I got back from Tierra del Aguila she just wasn't around. How about you?"

Paice took another sip. "Yeah, I had something similar. Looking back, I can see that I had a choice between my marriage and my job. I chose the job, although I didn't realise at the time that that was what I was doing. Work came along and I did it, not considering the effect it would have on her and the children."

"Children?"

"Yes, a boy and a girl. My son Sean is working in the States. My daughter, Nicola, is married with children. "

"Do you see them much?"

"No." There was an uncomfortable silence. It was Paice who broke it. "I may have been their father in biological terms, but beyond that … well, I was always in some distant part of the world writing stories rather than being at home and reading them to my kids at bedtime. They learnt to live without me and that is how they want it to remain. Their loyalty is to their mother. In truth I cannot blame them."

"So what is your life?"

"My life, Bart?"

"Sorry, now it's my turn to apologise for intruding."

"Forget it. My life is –". He hesitated as he grappled with the truth. "The simple fact is that not a lot happens. I still have my job, but even that does not mean as much as it did."

"At least you have that much. I don't."

"Hindsight is great at stating the obvious. It tells me that I could have handled things better. But it does no good to have too many regrets."

"Or too much anger, Nick, but that is more difficult to manage."

"It seems that we are both wandering aimlessly in the same wasteland, picking our way through the wreckage of what is left."

"Just the human remains, Nick."

"Yeah, the remains of the living." He swallowed the last of his drink and they went inside to settle for the night, closing the door behind them.

Paice had slept, but he had no idea of the time, aware only of being roused as Bartholomew hissed in his ear. "Wake up, Nick. We've got problems."

He was instantly awake and functioning. "What's happening?" He sat up, aching in his joints from having lain too long within the confines of a cane armchair never designed for sleep and aching in his head from the whisky.

"There are people outside. I reckon two or three. And it's not a social visit."

"How the hell did they know we were here?"

"You join up the dots, Nick. Other than us, only three people knew we had come here and I doubt that Oswald and Maria said anything."

"Winston? I don't believe it. I'd trust him with my life."

"That's exactly what you did. Want to revise your assessment?"

"But how did they know we were here in the summer house?"

"They saw the lights earlier and worked it out. Not difficult."

"OK, Bart. This is your territory. What do we do now?"

"We should get out of here for a start. We are sitting ducks."Paice instinctively turned towards the door. "Not that way, Nick. They will have that side covered." Bartholomew carefully looked around the curtains first at one window and then at others. "This way," he commanded. He opened a window that was largely obscured from the outside by a sizeable shrub that had been allowed to grow up the side of the summer house.They slipped awkwardly out into the low, natural shelter created by the arching branches. Once out, they lay on the damp earth, listening for movement in the surrounding garden, but hearing nothing.

"Are you sure there's someone here?" Paice whispered.

"They're here all right," Bart muttered. It was then that Paice heard the metallic click of Bart's gun. His heart skipped as it dawned on him that whoever was out there was aiming to finish the whole issue here and now. He suppressed a momentary surge of panic and swallowed hard. It was difficult. His mouth was dry. He realised that his life was wholly in the hands of the man lying beside him.

"We need help, Bart." He pulled out his mobile phone.

"Who the hell are you planning to call? The AA? You can't call the police. If these boys are a covert group from MI6 or something like that, the police won't be allowed within a mile of us. So who are you going to call?"

"Well, certainly not Winston," Paice snapped back. "There's only one person I can rely on. When I called him earlier, he was in Yorkshire, so he won't be able to help personally, but he might have an idea." He pulled Biff's number out of his contact list and pressed the call button.

From somewhere behind the black curtain of the night wafted the jaunty, cheerful and wholly incongruous melody of The Archers theme tune. It was cut short by a curse uttered by some invisible but doubtless angrily contorted mouth. Paice was stunned into silence. He had heard that ringtone before

The ensuing silence was shattered by the sound of splintering wood and breaking glass as the summer house door was smashed followed by bursts of automatic fire, softened by a silencer. The sound was unmistakeable to those who had heard it before. That included Paice and Bartholomew.

Paice feared that he was about to fall apart with panic. He did not. Bart grabbed his arm and steadied him. He whispered into Paice's ear: "Get a grip, Nick." Then, coolly and with utmost care, he eased open the window from which they had come and raised his gun. He peered into the gloom, listened, picked up the sound of movement and took carefully calculated aim. He fired three quick shots. There was a cry of pain from inside the room then silence.

"Let's get out of here." Bart hissed. "We have to get back to the house. You go first. Keep low, head back across the lawn and don't hang about. It's dark, so you should be OK. If there are any problems I'll do my best to make sure no one comes after you. When I think you've made it safely I'll do the same, so wait for me there."

Paice was terrified. He realised that within the next few minutes he could be dead. He took a deep breath, crawled carefully out from within the bush and lay motionless until he had gathered sufficient resolve to move. Then, crouching and stumbling in the darkness, he made his way out of the shrubbery and towards the edge of the lawn.He could see the outline of the house against the night sky, but the intervening space was black and unknown. He took a deep breath and, bent double, ran as fast as his contorted posture would permit. He had taken no more than a dozen paces when he was flung to the ground by a massive weight that knocked the wind from his lungs.

"Keep quiet, Nick – for you own sake."

He attempted to struggle, but his endeavours were futile. He was held fast by a big man. Gasping for air, he managed a single sentence. "What the fuck are you doing, Biff?"

"I'm sorry, mate, but this has all got out of hand. I was asked to do a surveillance job on your mole, Burkins. I didn't know that he was working for you until we met in the pub that night. I needed the work, Nick. I had to show Louise that I could offer her a better life. She deserved it. I never knew it would come to this. But the Cisneros story has upset a lot of people."

"Who are you working for Biff? Are they official – MI6?"

"No Nick, these people don't have any rules. I'm sorry."

"And why Winston? What did he have to gain from all this?"

"Winston had nothing to do with it. He simply rang me afterwards and told me where he had taken you."

A voice, hard and business-like, penetrated the darkness. Paice could not see the person to whom it belonged. If he had, he would have seen a man dressed completely in black, wearing a ski mask and equipped with night vision goggles. "Out of the way, Stilwell. I've got to finish this now."

"No, it was never the deal that he should die. I am not letting you do it," Biff said, his tone halfway between begging and demanding.

The weapon was a Heckler and Koch universal self-loading pistol equipped with a silencer. It fired a .45 calibre bullet which left the barrel at a speed of 850 feet per second. It had to travel the 95mm down the barrel and the 185mm length of the suppressor. The speed of sound is more than 1,100 feet per second.

In theory, Biff could have heard the gun fire before the round entered his skull. In practice, of course, he did not. And nor did anyone else. The suppressor effectively silenced the sound of the blast from the cartridge, and the .45 bullet, travelling below the speed of sound, did not produce the secondary supersonic crack of the 9mm slug as it emerged from the muzzle. The firearms experts would maintain that such a round had nearly half the range of its 9mm counterpart. But when a bullet had to travel 30cm rather than 30 metres, the question of effective range did not arise.

A cold analysis of the effect of a bullet of that calibre was that it created a deep and substantial permanent wound channel that lowered blood pressure more rapidly than the smaller round. All that was irrelevant. It smashed its way through Stilwell's skull like a tank going through a barn. He died instantly. That brain, full of skills, memories and regrets accumulated over a lifetime, was transformed from a miracle of pulsing nerves and neurons to a lifeless mess of wrecked protein.

As the round continued its inevitable path of destruction, it delivered the merest glancing blow to Paice's temple and knocked him unconscious. It meant that he did not hear the unsilenced cracks of another weapon. In the few minutes that had passed since Paice left him, Bart had gone back into the summer house, retrieved the night vision goggles from the downed agent and emerged from the shattered doorway. He had passed out of training as a class I marksman. At a distance of 10 metres he was never going to miss.

The second agent in the two-man team, having killed Stilwell, was about to put a bullet in Paice's head, too. Instead, he took Bart's first round through his neck and the second through his back and into his chest. Paice was mercifully unaware that he was buried beneath two men, one dead and the second dying, and that, by now, he was drenched in their blood.

His nightmare of Mwamba had, yet again, materialised into reality.

Chapter 38

When the Daily Mercury hit the streets, the story about Cisneros, the chemical nerve agent, and the immorality of the oil companies was all over the front page. Paice had done again what he had achieved so often in the past by monopolising the news. Sir Gavin had called him up to the top floor to congratulate him, and Olivia had actually put her arm round him and told him she thought he was an ace reporter.

"Paice the Ace," he had muttered in reply.

"What was that, Nick?" she inquired.

"Nothing important, Ollie."

At that point, Bob Bryce wandered across the newsroom. "That's a nasty bruise on your temple, Nick. Fortunately, whoever clouted you wasn't aiming for anything vital or sensitive."

Olivia burst out laughing. "Fortunately, also, Bob, he avoided serious injury because, unlike most people, that is not where he keeps his brains." She raised her eyebrows and gestured towards Paice's nether region.

Only Bart and the Bellamys knew how he had acquired the bruise. The true events of the night would remain a secret between the four of them.

Bryce nodded in agreement at Olivia's humour. "By the way, Nick," he said, "In all the excitement you won't have heard that there was a bit of a gun battle in dear old Oswald Bellamy's garden. They found three dead blokes and the police are at a bit of a loss to know exactly what was going on. Drug dealers is my guess, though why they would pick Bellamy's property to carry out their feud is beyond me.

"Also, the Prime Minister is to make a statement to the House of Commons at 3.30 on Britain's involvement in, and relations with, Tierra del Aguila. Downing Street is briefing that he's got the US onside to take the matter to the UN. You've really kicked over the shitcan, mate. The future certainly don't look too bright for that crook Cisneros. There is talk of hauling him before the International Criminal Court. I reckon that, six months from now, someone else will be running that poor bloody country."

The phone on Paice's desk rang. He picked it up: "Nick Paice."

There was an uncertain silence at the other end."Hello? Who's there?" he asked.

"Hallo, Dad."

"Nicola?" He took 10 seconds to marshal his thoughts and come to terms with a call he never expected to receive. "Well, Nicky...it's er...well... er... how are you? It's good to hear from you." It was always difficult to talk to his children. Perhaps it was that he so rarely did it, perhaps it was the guilt, or perhaps it was just that he did not know what to say. He thought about apologising for not having been in touch, but decided against. What was the point? "How are Joe and the two girls?"

"They are fine. Ellie is about to start school and Isabel is into just about everything."

"I'd love to see them." He thought, but did not say: "They wouldn't know me from Adam."

"They would love to see you, Dad. I see you got the front page again."

"Yes, it's a good story. It's not like you to ring. Was there a particular reason?"

"Yes, it's Mum. She's not too good."

"How 'not too good'?"

She was silent for several seconds. "It's serious, Dad. The doctors say they can't do much more for her. It's a question now of just taking care of her the best we can." Paice could hear her voice breaking. He knew that she would be in tears.

"Does Sean know?"

"Not yet. He's working on a deep-sea trawler somewhere off the west coast of Canada. I've been trying to get a message to him, but, even if he gets it, he's in no position to get home any time soon."

"Is there anything I can do? I'm due some time off. I could pitch in, but would she want to see me, Nicky? We have not spoken for a long time."

"You know that there was never anyone else for her, Dad."

433

"Nor for me. But I did not treat her well."

"I think this is the time to put all that behind you. Forget the regrets of the past. Just make sure you don't have any for the future." They conversed only rarely, but when they did she always spoke sense, usually telling him what he did not want to hear.

"OK, Nicky. Will you warn her that I'll be coming to see her?"

He hung up and was deep in thought when the editor's PA touched his shoulder. "He wants to see you, Nick." Paice nodded in acknowledgment. As he walked to Williamson's office, he was concerned not with the impending meeting but with whether this was the time to be there for his wife, a small attempt to rectify past omissions.

He knocked on the door and Williamson beckoned him to enter. "Come in, Nick. Have a seat. That was a great story this morning. I understand that Sir Gavin told you how pleased he was."

Paice nodded. "Yeah, he said he was happy."

"This is just the sort of thing where we need you to run a blog for the on-line edition, Nick."

"I know, Jack, but you know my feelings about that sort of thing. It's just not something I want to get involved in."

"You are the only reporter who doesn't do it. I can't let that continue. This sort of thing is the future for this industry and particularly for this paper. I can see the time when the printed page will be consigned to history. We have to move with the times. I'll get the IT people to talk to you about setting it all up. We can have it up and running in no time."

By the time he got back to his desk, Paice had made his decision. He hammered at the computer keyboard, hit the print command, walked over to the printer and waited for the sheet to appear. When it did, he looked at it for several seconds before pulling a pen from his pocket and scribbling down his signature. He walked over to where Bryce was sitting at the news desk.

"You've always been a good mate, Bob. You should see this before I hand it in."

Bryce stared at the single paragraph Paice had typed. "You've gotta be joking, mate. You can't jack it in just like that. You're the best reporter we've got."

"All good things come to an end, Bob. This one just did." He reached across the desk for an envelope, addressed it to Williamson, sealed the letter in it and threw it in the internal mail.

He walked out into the busy street.

Chapter 39

"It was good of you to drive me all the way up here, Winston." The stark beauty of the Peak District was looking at its best under a peerless blue sky.

Winston gave him one of his brilliant smiles. "That's OK, Nick. What are mates for?"

On the journey north, Paice had explained everything that had happened that night in Bellamy's garden – how Biff had sold him out but then tried to save his life and paid for it with his own, how the Bellamys had cleaned him up and got him and Bartholomew out of the way before the police arrived, and how they had kept quiet about what had actually happened.

He also told Winston how Bart was now the Mercury's security consultant. "He's a good man, Winston. With all the terrorism in the world, he'll be kept busy. I reckon that once he gets into his stride, he will have his own occasional column."

The BMW's V8 engine was ticking over with something between a purr and snarl. "Time to go, Winston. Thanks for everything."

They shook hands and he got out of the car, grabbed his holdall from the back seat and set off down the rutted driveway that led to his wife's cottage.

Winston waved, but Paice did not see him. He was not looking back.